JAMES P CONWAY

Hibiscus & Home

www.jamespconway.com

First edition

Illustration by furhel on Fiverr
Illustration by Caitlin Storey

This book was professionally typeset on Reedsy.
Find out more at reedsy.com

For Trans Youth,
You're loved – more than you can ever imagine.

1

Everett

My head-of-year has always been a very simple woman. She smells of rich tea and *Strictly Come Dancing* reruns that I often overhear her conversations about, despite the fact that I quite literally could not care less about Anton Du Beke's grey hairs that have started coming in this season.

"Alright, Everett." Ms Branchford says with a grin that her education degree has manufactured onto her face. "I've done a bit more digging. And I *think* I've found something for you."

"Okay. Okay, yeah, what?" I ask her, allowing myself to lean forward in the seat that I look at her from.

The situation that's been plaguing my life at the moment is that this woman, in conjunction with my mum, won't stop trying to pose solutions in attempts to cheer me up.

It's not that I'm unhappy, it really isn't. It's just that recently I've been feeling more and more at a loss with myself. Probably something to do with leaving secondary school. I've liked it here - it's been almost like a safety bubble for me. But, come the end of exams, the bubble will pop; I'll go to this brand new sixth form college and have to exist as a trans

1

person in wider society.

The thought has been making me lose sleep.

I've felt okay at this school because everybody knows I'm trans. It's familiar to me. The ones that support me support me, and the ones that don't, don't. And that's been okay, because there's been no pressure on me to be perfect. You know, how everybody expects that I 'should' behave as a trans person. Because I have tried to be how society expects me to, but I've never been able to force myself to be something I'm not.

Next year I *do* have to be perfect. Or else everyone will see me as some fraud. I want to pass next year, fully, and I don't want people to just look at me and think 'that's the trans one', like they have for the past couple years of my life.

Study leave starts incredibly soon, like, next week, and then (aside from exams) that's it.

I don't know. It feels like overthinking but clearly I've been bogged down enough that Mum has noticed. She'd sent an email, and now I'm sitting in a plush blue office chair that's spinning subtly as my school shoes tap against the wheels.

"Well, your mum thinks that you've been feeling a little bit lonely as of late."

Isolated is a better word. I don't say that, but I think it. Because, nobody understands my innermost feelings. Not even Ms Branchford, who is meant to be *the* sympathiser; she's the woman in charge of the well-being of our whole year group, but even she doesn't get it. She can't.

"Yeah." I sigh, averting my eyes to the little cactus plant on her desk. "I guess so."

"I think it would be good for you to connect. With other kids like you." She suggests, and I can imagine where she's going.

"Yeah, I do go to the Pride Group. Sometimes. It's just that it's full of year sevens, and I feel really proud of them for being so confident, it can just get a bit much."

Ms Branchford laughs under her breath, as if I'm not sitting the width of a desk away from her.

"I'm not suggesting that you go to the Pride Group, although that would be great. And, anyway, this time next month you won't be at the school any more to even go to the Pride Group."

Oh yeah, of course.

"Okay, so what?"

She tilts her monitor around about a hundred and fifty degrees. The sunlight streaming in through the window leaves a glare on the screen, so I take the liberty of awkwardly shuffling the chair a few inches to fix the issue.

On the computer, she presents me with a website. It looks shitty and home-made. And I know it is, because the URL starts with the name of one of those website-making websites. A header in purple font reads 'Activities @ The Aconite Centre', and just under it is a second header, which I can't help but feel like Ms Branchford is nudging me towards. This aforementioned second header proclaims 'LGBTQ+ Young People's Club.'

I look back over at her with narrowed eyes.

"Aconites are poisonous."

"What?"

"They're a type of flower. In the buttercup family. And they're poisonous."

"Everett, come on. Work with me a little." She sighs.

"They are! I'm not saying I won't go, but I don't understand a single reason why someone would name their community centre after aconites. Out of all the flowers."

Ms Branchford looks mildly entertained for a few moments, and it's enough that maybe I can forgive her for suggesting I involve myself in some poison-club.

She spins the monitor towards herself once more and clicks on the header.

"It's just a little something I found out about. I just thought that it might be helpful to surround yourself with other kids like yourself. Outside of school. I know there aren't many like you here."

She means queer kids. Queer kids, trans kids, whatever. It's all the same to her, but she won't say it out loud. Maybe she thinks I'll get offended.

"Yeah, could do." I agree, only for the common courtesy that she's gone to all this effort for me.

"Well, I'm glad you think so. I was on the phone with Mum earlier and we signed you up to pop down after school tomorrow. Five-thirty 'til seven, but the lovely lady on the phone said you're more than welcome to just stick your head in for a little bit to suss it out."

I nod idly as she speaks. Although it might not be the most enthralling thing in the world to me, I concede that I should go. If not for Ms Branchford, then for Mum. She worries about me a lot. And I feel bad about it a lot.

"Okay." I say, before quickly adding "Thanks."

"Of course. Promise you'll come back and let me know how it goes." She asks of me, and I know I will.

If there are three things in the world that Ms Branchford likes, catching up about social events is probably number three. Right under *Strictly* and Anton Du Beke's hairline. I'm

4

not sure if she's in a relationship, or married, or anything like that. But I feel like if she is, her husband has some competition with that man. So, it being in the well-established idea that I have of her top three things, I suppose I will have to catch up with her at some point.

"Right, best you head back to your lesson then. What have you got?"

I think for a moment. It's Wednesday morning.

"Maths."

"Ah, okay. Well let me write you a note to excuse your tardiness." She offers, picking a highlighter-pink post-it-note off her stack, as expected. If there's three things that she hates, unexplained lateness is definitely in the top three.

"I've also emailed you the website link. You know, so you can have a look for yourself." She explains.

"Alright. Thanks."

And so, she sends me back to class, with a pink post-it-note and newly acquired plans for tomorrow.

"Are we going?" Mum calls from beside the door. It's time to leave, and I can tell because her coat is on. Mum putting her coat on is serious business, and it means we better get a move on. Asap.

A glance down to my watch confirms that.

"Yep, yep." I reply, digging through the mound of shoes under the stairs. I'm not sure what the dress etiquette is for this place, but I did have a reluctant snoop on the website last night, which had a range of photos from the youth club. From what I saw, it's a jeans, t-shirts, tank tops, and leggings type of club. I opt for grey, wide-leg jeans and a band t-shirt that I bought at a kilo sale without ever even hearing of the band. When I got it, I listened to a couple songs on the train home, and it's a pretty lacklustre band. I wear the t-shirt anyway because they have a beautifully designed logo.

When I yank out a singular high-topped *Converse*, I waste no time in putting it on. It's from the pride collection a few years back, and Mum had gotten the pair for me when I'd first come out, as a kind of present. At the time it had meant the world to me. It still does.

They're cream-coloured shoes with laces that were once white until I walked through a puddle about a year ago. The mud came out of the shoes, but never out of the laces as much. They're more the colour of book pages now - maybe a little darker.

The small circle that encases the *Converse* logo is decorated with the trans flag. It's subtle in the best way possible, and it feels like appropriate footwear for the occasion of the day.

Once the first of the two shoes is on, I continue to rummage through the remainder of the shoes we have, in a frantic search for the other one.

"Rhettie."

"Yeah, I know. Give me a sec." I defend myself as I continue to forage. About five seconds later, something lightly hits me in the shin. I look down, and it's the other shoe.

"It was by the door, where you left it." Mum reminds me. I roll my eyes in playful exasperation.

"Well, then why was the other one in the cupboard?" I laugh.

"Don't look at me as if I have any idea what goes on inside that head of yours."

of the tub.

"Awesome, right. And now I'm gonna give you this card, and this plastic cover. Oh, and a marker pen. It's pretty self-explanatory."

True to her word, Thalia then hands me the three items.

At this point, the trio of teenagers that I had spotted down the street walk in, and I awkwardly move off to the side as I write on the card.

"Hey guys!" Thalia smiles. "Come in, Rowan is just setting up and I'll be through in a few."

They already have lanyards on, and I try my best to ignore them out of my own anxiety and just focus on finishing up the lanyard. It ends up reading:

Name: Everett

Pronouns: He/him/his

I take the initiative to slide the completed card into the plastic holder and clip it onto the bottom of the lanyard. Once the other three kids have disappeared, Thalia looks up.

"Perfect! Didn't even have to tell you what to do." She praises, standing as I put the lanyard around my neck. "Okay. So, I imagine you're a little nervous. I think, personally, that it'd be good to introduce you to someone your age that can show you around and then help you fit in. Not that you won't, but, you know."

"Yeah."

"Cool, cool. Follow me, then." Thalia instructs, and she begins a brisk pace through a different door that the three other teens had gone through. "I think he's around here somewhere." She mutters to herself as she guides me through a corridor that feels far too narrow.

It comes out in a room larger than the last one I saw.

The walls are painted white, with oak wooden floor and a little square serving hatch that appears to lead into an industrial kitchen. On the back wall of the room is a large mural that combines trees with flowers with rivers with a sunset-covered sky. There's also a set of wide open double doors that showcase a room full of stacked silver chairs with red cushions. There's still a semi-circle with about fifteen chairs left in the centre of the room.

Thalia hums for a second, and then she smiles when a boy comes walking out of the chair room.

He's taller than I am. With, light, mousey blonde hair that's styled neatly and shaved at the sides but straight and side-parted into what could be called curtains. He has blue eyes and pale freckles that I imagine are probably a lot more prominent in the sunlight. His light blue, baggy jeans fit him well underneath his grey hoodie. Atop the hoodie is his own lanyard, in a dark green, and a pair of wired white earphones stick out of his hoodie pocket and into both ears. He doesn't appear to notice us, and absent-mindedly carries on stacking chairs.

"Kylen!" Thalia calls at him, and the boy, Kylen, falters for a moment as he glances up and blinks. He takes the earphones out of his ears, and for a good ten seconds I hear the distorted gargle of his music playing at a surely harmful volume before he manages to pull his phone out and silence it.

"Hi, Thalia." He says in a rough voice. "Sorry. Didn't notice you come in."

"Yeah, no worries! Sorry to interrupt you." She apologises

before turning back to me. "Everett, this is Kylen. Kylen, Everett. I was thinking that you could show him the ropes and everything, Ky. I think you'll get along. He's new, and you're the only other trans man here – also the same age as him. I just think it might do you both some good to talk and all, and Everett, you can hear about what we do here from someone like you." She rambles for a few moments.

Kylen raises his eyebrows and very visibly looks me up and down, but his facial expression remains indifferent.

"Um, okay. Sure." He says. "I mean, I would prefer it if you didn't just out me to every next person that walks through the door though."

"Acknowledged." Thalia says softly. "But it's not like he's going to be unsupportive."

"That's not the point." He mutters back, gesturing loosely in my direction.

"Okay. Yeah. I'm sorry. I need to go help Rowan start up, are you good to talk to him about the place and give him a tour?" Thalia asks, still in the same sweet voice as always, despite having just been told off.

"Yes, that's fine. We'll come through later."

"Awesome. Thanks, Kylen." She says before turning back around and leaving. I don't blame the guy for getting annoyed at Thalia for telling me that he's trans, because I would *not* have been able to tell. In fact, if I were to pass him in the street I wouldn't even think twice about him being anything but a cis man.

And I know I shouldn't say that. But it's true. He doesn't look trans. Which, like I said, I know is wrong to say. Because that's like the whole point.

But I can't help but feel this horrible surge of jealousy wash

HIBISCUS & HOME

over me. We're the same age. And I'm not naive, I know I don't really pass. So, I get why he got irritated. If I passed that well, I wouldn't want random strangers to know either.

The glance up and down that he gave me thirty seconds ago suddenly feels ten times more judgemental. Like he knows that he's perfect trans. And he knows that I'm not.

"You just gonna stand there, or?"

I blink back to myself and Kylen is staring at me, eyes sceptical.

"Oh. Um, no?"

"Cool. You can come help me put these chairs away. They're out from the under fourteen's group that I helped out with earlier."

"You help out with the younger kids? That's so sweet." I reply, clinging onto each semblance of conversation.

"Yeah, well, I'm trying to be an example, I guess? A lot of those kids feel like they don't have futures as... people like us. Thalia thinks that having an older role model like me helps them feel hopeful, I don't know." He explains, and I suddenly feel really small. Like one of those kids. Because I was one of those kids, still am one of those kids who feels that way. "Anyway. What's your business here?" He asks, and I reply whilst picking up a chair.

"My teacher. She told me to come, said I needed some community to feel less lonely. I probably wouldn't be here if my mum hadn't made me."

Kylen flashes me a smile that feels forced. We don't talk for the remainder of the five minutes it takes us to put the chairs away, and then when we're done, he swallows and looks up towards me.

"That's a- um, nice hair colour." He says. "What do you

14

call that? Rhubarb purple?"

"Well it was marketed as magenta. But I have brown hair, so it's kinda dark since I didn't wanna bleach it." I tell him. I think that dyeing my hair was one of the most exciting things I've done. It's done a lot for my self-confidence, because I guess I feel like I'm expressing myself more. I've had plenty of colours before this one, when I was younger, but even so, it's still special to me.

"Right." Kylen replies. "Tell me to shut the fuck up if this is an overstep, but, you know that you aren't gonna pass with coloured hair, right?"

For a long moment I can't find the words to reply.

"What?" I ask under my breath eventually.

"I just mean, like, it's a clock-able feature. How long have you been out, like six months?" He squints at me, crossing his arms over his chest.

"Two years."

"Right, close enough. It's just- it feels counterproductive."

I almost laugh at him. Is he serious? Ouch. Like, actually.

"Me having dyed hair is counterproductive?"

"I don't mean it in a rude way, I just- you know that you don't pass. Don't you?"

"Wow." I reply, astonished. There is no way another human being just said that to me. "You're a dick."

He rolls his eyes and relaxes his body position, clearly feeling nonchalant about all this. "I just mean that it kind of ruins your chances."

In that moment, hearing his words, my mind glazes over with a distinct fragility that makes my eyes start to water and my body tense. I wish we were still stacking the chairs, because I totally would have thrown one at him if I had one in my hands right now. But, instead, I dignify him with a response. Fine. If he wants to be like that, then so be it. Mind made up, I swallow down a sob and tilt my head up towards him.

"You must really hate yourself, huh?"

"Excuse me?"

"For you to be projecting your insecurities and the apparent mountain of internalised transphobia that you're hiding behind onto me. You must really hate yourself if you feel *this* threatened by a trans guy with coloured hair." I bite back, and when he meets my eyes again, he looks almost vulnerable.

"We do four groups here, weekly." He says in a change of tone, turning away from me and walking over to the room with the chairs. "Two for ten to fourteen-year-olds. And the others for fifteen to nineteen-year-olds. One of those two, the one you're at now, is on a Thursday afternoon, and is the general LGBTQ+ youth group. The other is on a Sunday. At four. That's the trans and gender exploring group. The stuff we do there is - as you might guess - more specific about trans shit."

"Oh, am I welcome at that one?"

"Well, yeah."

"Good, good. Just thought I ought to ask. You know, since you're the gatekeeper of transness."

Kylen locks the chair room up with a key on the end of his lanyard. It takes him a good ten seconds to reply, and I feel proud that I've won.

"Sorry." He then says. "I shouldn't have said anything. Not my place." He admits, and then I watch as Kylen puts his lanyard back on and turns around to me. "How about that tour, then?" He offers, hands resting on the fabric of the lanyard nervously.

"Yeah, sure." I agree. Maybe seeing the rest of the place will be helpful. I sincerely hope that not everyone here is like Kylen. That would risk not having anything productive to feed back to Mum, or to Ms Branchford for that matter. After all of this trouble, good news is the least they deserve.

2

Kylen

I feel Everett's eyes on the back of my neck for the whole time that he's walking behind me. If looks could kill, I'm pretty sure Thalia would have to call the morgue. And also a psychiatrist for all the other kids here that would've just watched my corpse get carried out of the building.

It's not like I was trying to hurt his feelings. I guess It's complicated. Or, whatever I can tell myself. His dysphoria must not be as bad as mine. That's it, easily. Either that or he's just so secure in his masculinity that he doesn't care how he's perceived.

Fuck, what I would give.

"I'm sorry." I say from the doorway of the kitchen. "Like Thalia said, um- we're the only guys like us here, in this age group. And, if you're gonna stay, I'd rather not have you hate me." I rationalise.

"Alright." He replies after a moment of clear thought. "I'll forgive you. But promise me something, Kylen." Everett walks past me into the stainless-steel coated kitchen and stands right in front of me. I've got a good three inches of height on him, but I try not to look down too much. Not sure how well he'd take that.

"Promise you what?"

"That you won't act like that again. Not towards me, and not towards anyone else. Because, quite frankly, my transness isn't any of your business and vise versa." He states, firmly. I suppose I take too long to reply, because he carries on talking after pushing his hair back a little. "I know your type. I've met a lot of your type."

"My type?"

"Yes. Your type. You're the type that has never climbed a single mountain at any point. Considering the way that you looked at me like the dirt beneath your shoes when I told you I'd been out for two years, I'm pretty sure I know your type. I bet you came out before the age of twelve. And, good for you for figuring it out so young, but I bet you never even went through female puberty. You're the type with a wholly supportive family that means you've had it easy. And, it's not a bad thing to be one of the lucky ones, Kylen. But it's more often than not your exact type that goes around shitting on the rest of us for not having the same access to resources and healthcare as you've had."

Christ, this kid knows how to rant. He also knows how to make some pretty strong assumptions based on a two-minute conversation. I don't correct anything that he says, simply because I don't think he would believe me if I tried.

"Just, promise me that whatever rhetoric you've been taught that made you act that way towards me gets unlearnt."

"Yeah." I manage to say under my breath. "Yeah. I'll, um, yeah."

"Good. Thank you." He says, and it sounds sincere. I feel

this cloud of shame hovering above me. "Are you gonna tell me about the kitchen then?"

I hadn't really meant to upset him like that. Right after I said to him that I'm meant to be the role model for the younger kids.

Everett snaps his fingers in front of my face.

"Yo, man. Didn't mean to trigger an existential crisis or anything. You okay?"

And my eyes dart back towards him as I nod as quickly as possible.

"Yup. Sorry."

"Alright. So, the kitchen?"

I blink a few times and look through the large rectangular hole that provides a window between the kitchen and the main room.

"Can we start again?" I ask.

"Yikes. Have I rocked the boat that much?" He asks, and to me, it sounds like a tease. He's just the perfect guy, isn't he? Knows exactly what to say to come across as casually charismatic and uncaring. Envy is the best word I can think of to describe the emotions that it brings up.

He sighs out, and before I can register it, he's gone. Out of the kitchen and back through the door into the hall that we met in. I waste no time in following him as well. But, he doesn't stop when he gets there, he carries on walking all the way back through the door that leads to the building's entrance.

For a moment, I stand in the middle of a room, a little shocked. Has he.. left? Just like that?

Turns out that, no, he hasn't left. Because about ten seconds later, the door flings open again, and he flashes me a wave as he approaches me.

"Hi." He says easily. "Thalia told me come to come through. She thinks that you might be able to show me around the place."

I can't help but let a smile slip onto my face. This guy is such a dork. Maybe I can entertain whatever he's going for a little.

"Um, yeah. Yeah, that's fine." I reply, playing along through my smile.

"Cool. As indicated by this little lanyard around my neck, I'm Everett. He and him pronouns."

For the first time since meeting him, I realize that he's chosen a spiderman lanyard. I feel quite jealous for a minute, because I definitely would've chosen that one if it had been in the pot when I first started coming. But I wouldn't dare swap my lanyard now, it's like, a part of my outfit. And it has all the keys that Thalia and Rowan have trusted me with on the end.

I hold my hand out in front of myself, and he takes it. "Kylen. Um, also he/him. Some people call me Kylo sometimes." I explain as we shake hands.

"Okay, Kylen. Well, let me know if we get there."

"Yeah." I say. "Yeah, I will."

Everett nods, flicking his head in the direction of the doorway that leads to the kitchen. "Shall we?" He says, and I can't help but snicker.

"Sure thing."

And I have a better feeling about it this time.

It only takes us about ten minutes to do a whizz around the building. I show him the lounge area that we run our movie nights from, and I show him Thalia and Rowan's offices. I also show him the 'over eighteen's lounge', which we're (technically) not meant to go in, because they keep alcohol in the cupboards (god forbid), but the TV is a lot better definition, and Thalia always lets me catch up with my shows in there, provided there's no actual over eighteens inside. If there is, I usually get kicked out, which, like, I get. But, our last adults recently aged out of the club, so it's been all mine as of late.

I think it's because Thalia feels bad for me a lot. She knows that this place is kind of like my home, hence why she never seems to care what I get up to within the walls. Just as long as I don't cause too much trouble. Here and school are the only places that I get to use to escape everything, and school is ending soon, so I'm pretty sure I'm on her radar even more recently.

Lastly, I show him the toilets, and then we pretty much circle back around towards the entrance.

"Okay. We'll go in now. We're about twenty minutes late, so they'll probably already be doing something. But we always start our sessions with a chair circle."

"A chair circle?" Everett smirks.

"Yes. Like the one we tidied away in hall B, from the younger kids' group. We always start and end the nights with chair circles. Every session, there's a new question we answer around the circle. Last time it was: if you were a flavour of water, what flavour would you be?"

"And what flavour would you be?"

"Mint."

Everett scrunches his nose up. "Mint flavoured water?"

22

"..Yeah."

"Ew."

"Hey." I shoot back playfully, and he laughs. "But, whatever. They'll probably be doing something crafty at this point. I'm not sure though, I didn't check the itinerary." I say honestly, but it's usually something like making bath bombs or painting on canvas using our pride flag colours. A couple years ago I got to help paint the mural in hall B, and it had been one of the most fun days I've had at the club.

"Well, I know a way to find out." Everett says, gesturing towards the entryway inside.

I take his hint and pull the door open, leading us into hall A.

Okay, well they aren't bath bomb making or painting.

"There they are!" Thalia calls, and everyone in the room diverts their gaze towards us. "Boys, come on. You're missing out."

"Right. And what exactly is going on in here?" I ask septically. At the moment, the room is divided into two. Half of everyone is on one side of the room with Thalia, and the other half is with Rowan.

"Well, firstly, you missed circle. So, introduce yourselves." She prompts.

Every time I come here, I always introduce myself to everyone as if I've never attended before. It gets more and playful each time.

"Hi, guys. I'm Kylen. Um, what was the question?" I ask, and everyone snickers a little bit.

"Right, right." Thalia says. "Preferred method of public transport?"

"Uh, gonna have to be buses." I say, and then I look over to Everett.

"Trains." He says effortlessly, just before introducing himself.

"Awesome, well, we're putting on a bit of an acting competition."

"Sorry?"

"Mhm! I've left two spaces on Rowan's team."

"Yeah! Which means you're gonna lose." One of the people on Thalia's team, Brynn (whose hair is genuinely so blue that it threatens giving me a migraine) exclaims, which results in a cheer from their whole group.

"Not on my watch. And not on yours either." I smirk, looking back to Everett briefly whilst striding over towards Rowan's group. He's a younger guy than Thalia. About twenty-five. When I first started coming to the clubs, he had been a fresh-faced volunteer, but now he works here in cahoots with Thalia. He's more of the paperwork guy, to be honest. Thalia has the charisma, and he has the actual seriousness that keeps the place logistically running. From time-to-time; you have to get to know him. I say all that, but he's a really chill guy deep down. I like being around him because he's shorter than me, and being taller than people is very affirming.

"Welcome to the team." He greets, running a hand through his dark hair. "Nice to meet you. Everett, was it?"

Everett nods. "Yeah. It was."

"Good, good."

It's explained to us pretty quickly that we're putting on a flash production of Little Red Riding Hood. A pantomime, if you will. The other team is doing Cinderella.

It seems like Everett is finding himself quite enjoying the circumstances. There's a moment where, in my role as the big bad wolf, I just kind of stand at the edge of the 'stage.' I must dissociate a bit, because I find myself just watching him.

I can't help but take what he said to me earlier to heart. The only other trans people I've really associated myself with have been ones like myself. The kind that are stealth, and don't really have any queer friends. Visibly queer friends, I should say. And even those associations never last long. It's too precarious.

Sure, I have friends here. At the club. But they aren't *friends* friends. I don't hang out with them outside of these walls. Sometimes I wish I could, but then I remember what I'd be risking. So I don't.

Sometimes it feels like I don't exist outside of this place.

I don't know what I'll do when I grow out of it. Maybe I'll be like Rowan. Stay here. But then again, I probably won't. I can't stay in this town forever. I think I'd suffocate.

Speaking of suffocation, I have a grandmother to lock in a closet.

When Everett (read: Woodcutter) hacks me to death at the end of the performance, most of Thalia's team applaud. From the side of the stage, Rowan applauds the loudest.

Amongst our five other teammates, (again, read: Little Red, Little Red's Mother, Grandma, Tree One and Tree Two) we exit the stage (which is actually some coloured tape made into a box on the ground) feeling pretty confident.

We know we've won when both of Cinderella's shoes fall off in her attempt to be rid of just one. It's hilarious, and over half of Thalia's team break down into raucous laughter, as do we. To be fair, Dallas, the young person bringing Cinderella's character to life, runs with it very well by providing an exclamation through her laughter. "Oh, no! I only have time to grab one shoe before midnight! I shall have to abandon the other!" They gasp.

In that team's defence, it was a good performance. But I didn't growl in front of the whole sixteen club members for nothing.

After the club finishes, I hang around for a further half an hour, pulling the tape off the floor and helping to wash up the dishes from when everyone got their entitled cup of lemonade in between performances.

Then, I help Rowan file away all of Everett's joining paperwork. He kicks me out of his office to make a phone call, and I end up sitting on the sofa in the over eighteen's lounge, on the fifth season of *Criminal Minds*.

At nine, Thalia flicks the light on, announcing her presence in the room. I pause the TV and look over towards her with pleading eyes.

"Time to go home. Come on." She encourages.

"Are you and Rowan leaving now?" I ask.

"Rowan left twenty minutes ago. Minors aren't even ensured to be in the building past eight, you know that."

"Yeah." I admit. And I do know that. I'm really grateful that these two even let me stay late, but I suppose since I help out with the odd jobs here and there, it makes up for it.

"Alright. So, it's time to go home." Thalia repeats, and I stand up from the sofa and turn the light off as I leave the room. "How was Everett? Do you think he'll come back?"

I think he will. No thanks to me. Well, I don't know. We seemed fine after we 'started over.' And, knowing myself, I'll act like that again. I've never really had any competition here, being the only trans guy. We've never been shy of genderqueer teens, but it's always felt like *I* was the one that all the younger

26

trans kids looked up to. But people seemed to really like Everett tonight.

You know, maybe he's the example of what a trans man should be like. He seems much more proud of it that I am. It's always only ever been something that I've been ashamed of, but I saw the little flags on his shoes. He's a better role model for the younger kids, that's for sure. It's probably for the best.

"Yeah, I reckon so."

"Good, yeah. He seems like a nice lad." She laments whilst locking up hall B. "And, I'll see you on Sunday?"

"Yep. You know you will." I reply with as much of a smile as I can muster. I know that's her nice way of telling me to fuck off now, so I do. I bid her farewell and leave the building.

It's dark outside whilst I walk home, and I end up doing two laps of the block before finally sticking my key in the door.

"Your dinner is in the microwave." My mother calls from the living room. Inside, just the lamp on the side table is on. It creates an ambience that is far too calm for my liking. Instead of hanging around to experience any more of it, I thank her and head into the kitchen. When I open the microwave, it's about a third of a meal. Spaghetti, plain. I shut the microwave door closed and add a minute to the timer, before heading into the living room, where my mother is filling a sudoku in silence.

"Is that, um, is that everything?" I ask. She sighs dramatically and puts her pen down.

"It's our leftovers, to be honest. You didn't text or anything, so I don't know how you expected us to know that you'd want dinner. It's almost ten-o-clock. We expect to be kept in the loop."

27

"I know. Sorry."

"Can you not speak like that around me?" She questions gruffly. We've spoken about it before. And she never understands. I've tried a million times over to get it through her head that this is quite literally just how my voice is (which she gets very upset when I mention). I could probably force it higher to please her, but it's not really something I'm too interested in. Instead, I just hum at her and go back into the kitchen. When I'm in there, I cancel the microwave that is still running. After deciding that I don't want to eat their leftovers, I pour myself a glass of water and just take it straight to my room.

I'm halfway up the stairs when the burning in my lungs reaches my oesophagus, making me gasp for air. I have to put my water down to take some deep breaths and half-sit on the stairs. I drop my head against the step in front of me and beg the world to make the feeling stop.

Fucking hell. I've had it bad before but I've never had it 'immobilising' bad. I don't cry because I'm not a crier, but if I was a crier, I would definitely cry.

There's a creaking above me, triggered by one distinct floorboard that I know is dodgy. "Are you okay, Ky?" Alfie asks me from the top of the stairs. I look up at him, standing there in his pyjamas with blearily tired eyes.

My heart shatters a little upon seeing him. He shouldn't be awake this late, he's got school in the morning.

"Why are you still up, teddy bear?" I whisper through my pained voice.

"Couldn't sleep knowin' you weren't home." He says meekly. And, fuck, I feel awful.

"Well, I'm home now, okay. I'm sorry I made you worry.

That wasn't very nice of me." I explain to him, holding the glass of water in one hand and standing back up, despite my body screaming at me not to. "Come on, let me tuck you in." I offer, hoisting him up into my right arm. He wraps his legs around my torso and giggles.

"Okay."

When I walk past Mum and Dad's room, I can hear dad snoring. At least somebody in the household is getting some sleep.

Alfie has these glow in the dark stars all over his ceiling that stick out against the dark paint on his walls. He might only have the small room, but he doesn't need much more. He has a little stuffed elephant - which is his favourite - alongside a mountain of other stuffed and fluffy animals. It's more than enough guests in one space.

Alfie jumps right into bed and pulls his elephant into his chest. I lay his duvet over him and lean down, planting a kiss onto his forehead.

"Alright. Sleep well, Alf. I love you."

"Nigh' night." He smiles, and when his eyes drift shut, face illuminated by his nightlight, I let myself leave the room.

The first thing I do when I get into my bedroom is head over to my chest of drawers. I drop to both knees to open the bottom drawer, feeling around at the back. I know it's unlikely that my testosterone would be gone, but I trust my parents to take it more and more each day. It's there, though. Everything's fine.

Next, I practically rip my t-shirt off. In any other circum-stance, I would keep binding for my own dysphoria's sake, but it feels like I might stop breathing at any point, so I bite the bullet and take it off in a practiced motion. I'll wear tape to bed if it still hurts when the time comes.

After that, I put my favourite dark-coloured hoodie right on and just sit on the edge of my bed.

I don't look in the mirror. I have no reason to. What I do, however, is press a careful hand to the bottom of my ribcage overtop the fabric of my hoodie.

It hurts like hell, and I can't help but thinking back to something that my mother would always say to me whenever I would get hurt as a kid. I would say something along the lines of 'It really hurts whenever I do this.'

And she would say, 'Well then, don't do that.'

So I move my hand away from my torso and just lie myself face down on my bed.

"You must really hate yourself, huh?"

I pull my phone out of my pocket and plug it in while I remember to - having it die on me and then subsequently being forced to face my own thoughts is literally the worst case scenario.

Pulling up Instagram in front of me, I see that Lilia has added him to the youth club group chat. I rub my eyes and click on the profile, *@Ever.ettEnfi3ld.* Can't fault a guy for having an alliterative name, it's quite catchy.

His profile picture is certainly himself. It's a picture that somebody else must have taken; he's on a beach and looking out towards the ocean from about two metres away from the camera.

His display name is just 'Everett', with a little rainbow flag emoji beside it, followed by a sunflower emoji, too. I can see an array of pictures, but I just switch my phone off instead of looking at them.

"You must really hate yourself if you feel this *threatened by a*

trans guy with coloured hair."

I groan into my pillow because it isn't fair. It isn't fair that someone like him gets to be so happy and I don't. When my phone pings, and I can see that people on the group chat are talking and active, planning a meet up of some kind on Saturday, I mute the chat.

Rather than participate in *whatever* that is, I open my phone app and pick a certain contact, clicking on it instantly.

Tobias answers after two rings.

"My man. Bit late, isn't it? What's up?"

"Nah, nothing. Listen, you in town tonight?" I ask him.

"Can be. Rough day?"

"Sure."

"Want me to invite the others?"

"Don't see why not."

"Cool. Text me when you get there."

"Yeah."

And I hang the phone up. I know exactly what we'll do, I can predict it to a T. We'll meet up in the town centre, then probably spend too much money on fast food, and by midnight, we'll be smoking in an alleyway or a graveyard.

Sometimes hanging out with my friends is difficult. None of them know that I'm trans, in fact, I've heard the way that they talk about the trans people in the media. And it makes me feel ill. But, not really. Because I'm not like those kinds of trans people. I know that I'm one of the good ones. They'd get that. If they ever found out, they'd get that.

Tobias lives thirty minutes from town and I only live twenty, so I'm in no rush to get there. The others, if they decide to come, will probably show up intermittently – as they do.

I put my binder back on, as much as it pains me, and keep

the hoodie, storing my phone and wallet in the main pocket.

When I climb out of my bedroom window, I'm careful to leave it slightly ajar so that I can get back in later. Mum seems to have a sixth sense for the front door opening and closing, especially when in bed, but she won't check that I'm in my room. She'd probably like as little to do with me as possible, actually.

The feeling is mutual, so it's okay.

When I meet up with the boys, it goes a lot like how I expected it to. Being stealth in a friend group of all cis boys is probably the most masculinizing experience that someone can have. It is for me, at least. There's no better feeling in my mind.

The moon watches us disapprovingly as we make a public disturbance, laughing in the streets. After a certain time in the evening, everything feels funny. Liam walks into a *Mini Cooper* and the car alarm goes off, and fuck, it's the most hilarious thing I've seen all day. Dare I say even funnier than the double-shoe incident at the club.

And, yeah. No matter how much self-confidence Everett might have, he doesn't have this. I bet he's asleep right now. When, if he played his cards differently, he could too be sitting on a swing in a playground, watching his friends start talking about rationing tobacco.

Eventually we just nominate Jack to go into the twenty-four-hour off-licence with confidence.

He doesn't get served. And it's honestly fine, because now we can make fun of him for looking young for the rest of the evening. That's entertainment enough.

I try not to think about the fact that we have school tomorrow. Mainly because it's unlikely I'll go. But I can't stomach another phone call home about not showing up, so I probably will. I'll just be tired.

When AJ very proudly exits the same off-licence with not only tobacco, but also an oversized bottle of cranberry vodka, I mentally correct myself.

I'll be tired *and* hungover.

3

Everett

On Saturday, a few of us from the club meet up. And, as much as I despise the notion that Ms Branchford was right, I do feel a lot less lonely. I've been avoiding her like the plague around school so she won't ask me about the club and I won't have to tell her that.

We've perched ourselves now in the middle of the park with a few packs of biscuits.

"Everett, are you coming to trans-plus tomorrow?" Asks Mars. They're a year younger than me, but have a good couple inches of height on me, as well as a pretty mature clothing style that makes them look older.

"What's that?" I reply, a little confused until they continue talking.

"Like the youth club, but just for trans or trans-curious people."

"Oh, yeah. Kylen told me about that. Yeah, I probably will." I reply, and there are a few snickers from the group.

"Kylen told you about it?" Lilia says with a slight smirk. I don't really understand what's so funny for a few moments.

She raises her eyebrows at Mars across the group.

"Yeah? Does he not go?"

"Oh, he goes." Mars says. "He's just- well, he's Kylen."

I can't help but laugh a little at the bluntness. "What do you mean?" I ask in as kind of a tone as possible.

"Well, you know. You've spoken to him. He just kinda thinks he's above all of it." They explain.

"Mm." Eli hums in agreement. "He's like- He's been going to the club since he was like twelve. He kinda acts like he's on a pedestal above all of us."

"Yeah, at trans-plus he always just sits on his phone. It's like, what's the point in coming?" Lilia agrees.

Once again, Mars interjects, leaning against their bag slightly. "I think he likes to pretend that he's not trans. I mean, we all know that he only comes to the club because it gives him somewhere to be. I see his Instagram stories and stuff, he's totally a road-man that's like never home in his spare time."

I snicker. It's definitely an image that I can imagine.

"If I passed as well as he did, I'd pretend I wasn't trans, too." I say. "In his defence."

"Well, yeah." Lilia replies. "We all would. But he's just such a dick about it. Sometimes I feel bad for him."

"What shit has he said to you guys?" I pry. Mars stuffs a biscuit into their mouth before replying.

"About six months ago, back when I thought I was trans - like, within the binary and shit - no offence -" They gesture to the rest of us, "I asked him for general passing tips. And he told me to cut off all my trans and visibly queer friends."

"Fuck off, really?" I say, astonished by the information.

"Yeah. He was like 'you can't hang out with people that

make you look trans.'"

"Oh my god."

"Yeah, and I was like, 'but I am trans', and he told me not to ask him for advice if I wasn't gonna take it."

Lilia sighs. "I do feel bad for him. He just has no sense of community. He doesn't really understand that we're on his side. And that us trans folk have to stick together."

"I think he's insecure." I say finally. "Obviously, I don't know him that well, but I get the sense that his masculinity is quite breakable." I tell them, and I mean it. I've thought about him quite a bit whilst I've been away from him. And, yeah, he was a total asshole to me when we first met, but I don't blame him that much. He's clearly had a lack of good role models.

I don't know, at the same time, I feel jealous of him still. He seems to know everything that you could possibly know about being trans. When the others seem to give out slight noises of agreement, I offer something else.

"Why don't we invite him out with us?" I suggest.

"He's on the group chat. He could've come." Mars argues.

"Yeah but maybe he's just a bit shy about it. Like you said, he needs a sense of community."

"Sure, but like Mars said, I don't think he'd show his face in public around us." Eli supplies.

"No harm in asking." I push again. And Lilia nods.

"Fine, yeah. I'll DM him."

After that, we kind of forget that we've messaged him and keep just chatting about random things. That is, until, about twenty minutes later, Lilia's phone pings.

"Oh." She says, eyeing her phone curiously. "*Oh.*" She repeats, in a lighter, more humoured tone this time.

"What?" I ask, and she snickers, showing me her phone screen.

She had texted him saying:

Hey dude, a few of us are at the park right now. Wondering if you wanted to tag along? We'll probably be here until 2

And, just under that, Kylen had sent a picture back. Except, it clearly wasn't Kylen who had taken the photo.

It was a different guy, with light brown hair, wearing a Nike Tech fleece with the hood up. He'd taken it from a selfie angle, flashing two fingers facing outwards at the camera.

In the remainder of the image space, he was trying to capture another boy on the floor.

It's clearly Kylen. He's unconscious, lying on a grey carpet on his side. From what I can see, there's a permanent marker dick drawn on his face, and in the background, an empty bottle of alcohol litters the ground, as well as two other boys, one of whom is on his phone, and the other still asleep too.

Underneath the photo, the text reads:

he cant make it lollll

I can't help but laugh out loud. After the phone has been passed around, I ask for it back and screenshot the picture of Kylen conked out on the floor before messaging it to myself.

"Alright, so it seems like he's busy." I chuckle. At least he's maintaining some kind of social life.

When I go to trans-plus on Sunday, I arrive at exactly two, as indicated by the shitty website.

After Thalia waves me in, I see that the circle of chairs is set up in hall A. But, most notably, Kylen is standing against one of the walls looking a little bit annoyed as he talks to Lilia.

I make my first order of business to go over there.

Just as I arrive, I hear Kylen laugh a little, which is something that I wasn't aware he was capable of.

"What's going on here, then?" I ask, and Kylen sighs over-dramatically.

"My friends think I'm chatting up fourteen-year-olds." He says.

"Are you?" I reply, mainly just to tease him.

"No! But some fourteen year old decided to message me asking to hang out while one of my mates had my phone."

"He's talking about me, by the way." Lilia smiles in utter amusement.

"Ah, I see. Well, was it a fun night?" I ask him. "See you managed to get the dick off your face."

Kylen rolls his eyes and crosses his arms. "Yeah. Totally ratted me out."

"What do you mean?"

"My parents didn't know I was out. I snuck out just fine on Thursday, and it would've been the exact same, but when I got home yesterday morning and my parents saw it, I either had to admit that I had been with my friends, or that I had drawn a penis on my own face."

I burst out laughing, and he lightly kicks my shin. "It's not funny! They were really irritated." He defends himself, but it falls silent on my ears. I keep laughing until an adult speaks from across the room.

"Alright! Circle in!" Thalia calls from the centre of the chairs. There's only about six of us here, so it doesn't take long for each of us to claim a chair. "Right." She continues. "Nice to see you all. I've got some stuff to do today, but Rowan is gonna run the session." She explains, and then minutes later, we've all introduced ourselves and are now having a discussion. Today's topic of talking is: 'How did you realize you were trans?'

Much as I had expected, Kylen pulls his phone out the minute we actually start talking about being trans. Like he's trying to distract himself. Decidedly, Rowan isn't having it. Maybe Thalia doesn't care, but it seems like he does.

I don't know Rowan that well, but he seems like a nice guy. He's kinda young but he has a mature smile that makes me want to trust him for no reason other than that.

"Kylen, put it away please." He says. Kylen swallows his pride and clicks the device off whilst Mars carries on their story about how they realized they weren't cis.

By the time the story-sharing order reaches Kylen, who is just before me, he's hunched over and looks a bit fed-up. The person with the electric blue hair finishes talking.

"Great, thanks Brynn." Rowan says. "You're up, Kylen."

He looks around, more directly looks at me, and then he sits up a little before speaking.

"I, um, you guys know. I just always knew something was wrong. I didn't know what the word for it was back then, but I came out to my parents when I was eight."

Knew it. Absolutely knew it. He is *exactly* like one of those types that I had told him he was on Thursday.

"So, um, obviously I don't remember much of it. How I figured it out. I just knew that I hated having to be a girl to

39

everyone around me because I knew I wasn't one."

Everybody kind of hums in agreement at that. I do kind of sympathise with him. Since I didn't figure it out until much later, I haven't had to live as a trans person for quite as long as he has.

"Thanks, Kylen. Alright, your turn, Everett. Whatever you're willing to share." He instructs. I then realize that I probably should have been thinking about what to say whilst everyone else was talking.

"Well, I- I always knew what trans people were growing up. It didn't occur to me that I could be one of them until I was about thirteen. I spent a lot of time trying to figure out my sexuality, and then when I was confident in that, the whole gender thing kinda hit me like a truck." I say, and it gets some laughs from the group. "So, um, I started going by Everett online, and then I properly came out to everyone shortly after I turned fourteen."

Kylen smirks a little from where he sits beside me. I can imagine what's going on in his head. He probably feels a sense of superiority. He has six years on me, after all.

Rowan doesn't get time to thank me and ask the next person to speak, because the door to hall A opens slightly.

We look over at the squeaky sound that the door causes, and Thalia hovers a little before speaking.

"Sorry to interrupt!" She apologises. "Can I just borrow Kylen for a second?"

"Yeah, of course." Rowan replies.

"Thanks. Kylen, just come through to my office when you get a second."

There's a collective "Ooh!" before Lilia speaks.

"Someone's in trouble." She teases, and Rowan sighs.

"You're not in trouble." He reassures with a smile. "Let's all take five, okay?"

When we disperse from our chairs, and most people head over to the snack table, Kylen disappears in the direction that Thalia went.

I look around briefly. Nobody seems to be watching me at all, and even though I know it's wrong, I follow Kylen. Kill a guy for being curious.

I remember where Thalia's office is from the tour that I was given when I first showed up. And, much to my relief, it's left ajar when I reach it.

I hear the conversation before I even get right up to the door frame.

"Okay, so. I'm not gonna sugar coat anything." Thalia says, and her voice sounds much more serious and professional than I'm used to.

"What's wrong?" Kylen asks in what is almost a whisper.

I approach the door cautiously and settle down in a seated position on the ground for hopes of the most covert eaves-dropping possible.

"Well, you're aware that the building got some new owners a couple weeks back."

"Yeah. The older couple. They seemed really nice." He says.

"Well, I've just been informed by them the other day, that as of the start of next month our costs to rent the community centre are almost doubling."

"What?"

"Kylen, um, I thought it was best that I told you one-on-one, because I know how much you rely on this place."

"Tell me what? Tell me what?" He repeats frantically. I know where she's going with this, and it's shit. I was really

41

enjoying it here. "We just can't afford to keep the club running any more. It *has* been going for seven years now - we've had a good run."

My heart sinks into my stomach at her words. The confirmation out loud is unlike any amount of speculation. I can tell that Kylen's heart sinks too, because he doesn't say anything.

"Look, I know it's not ideal." Thalia carries on. "But maybe this is what you need. Gives you a chance to spend more time at home, or with your friends."

I can hear his heavy breathing as it fills the room, and when he speaks, he sounds exasperated.

"What, so that's it? You're just giving up?"

"We don't have a choice."

"Fuck you. You can't- you can't do this to me, Thalia."

"Kylen, it's not my decision. We don't have the money."

"Then find the money! Fuck's sake, find the money."

Thalia audibly sighs. "Kylen." She says softly. "I called you in here because I thought we could have an adult conversation about this."

"I'm not an adult, and I don't want to have an adult conversation." He replies quickly, voice wavering. "Please, please, don't shut the club down. I can't- Thalia, you know I can't do this without it."

"I know. Which is why I'm telling you now. We have just over a month left on our lease. Maybe you can start phasing yourself out a little." She suggests softly. "Come on, you're almost seventeen. I worry about how much time you spend here. This might be good for you."

"Oh my god." Kylen mutters quietly, so quietly that I almost can't hear it. When the sound of an office chair's wheels sliding against the floor pours into my ears, I leap up off the ground as quickly as I can.

I head back into the hall with haste so as to not get caught snooping. About ten seconds after I make it into the hall, and see everyone still milling around, the door of which I came through is shoved back open.

Kylen walks in and it's like he's a new man.

He's crying. Silent tears, the kind that spill down your face and are hot, not messy. His eyes are red and puffy, and he looks terrified. Like a little mouse caught at the mercy of a ravenous cat.

The room goes completely silent at the mere state of him. He pushes past me and he practically runs towards the exit.

"Kylen!" I call after him to no avail. I don't even recognise that I've started running after him until I'm outside the building, having left all the gaping faces behind.

The cold air of the afternoon hits me suddenly, but I push past it in favour of looking for Kylen, wherever he went.

He's only walking down the street now, and at my moderate running pace, I get behind him quite quickly.

When I say his name, he ignores me.

"Kylen." I repeat, grabbing his arm to get him to turn around and look at me.

"Everett, fuck off!" He yells back, jerking his body to get me to remove my hand. His voice is strained and weak-sounding, despite the general upkeep that he's been trying to present.

"Hey, it's okay. It's just a youth club."

About half a second after the words leave my mouth, I realize that they probably weren't the right choice.

Kylen stops walking and spins around to face me. "Don't." Is all he chokes out. "It's not okay. It's not just a youth club."

And at this point, I can tell by the look in his eyes that

43

I've won. The second sign occurs when, following about five seconds of steady eye contact, he collapses onto the pavement and starts sobbing into his hoodie sleeves.

It's a confronting sight. I hadn't really planned this far ahead. He looks a lot smaller on the ground, back leaning against the bricks of someone's garden wall.

I bring myself down to the floor too, and sit next to him against the wall.

His breathing is erratic and he's gasping for air through his own tears.

"Alright, Kylen. Take my hand." I offer, holding my hand out at an appropriate distance.

"Piss off." He struggles out between breaths.

"Take my hand, and pull your head out of your knees. All you're doing is restricting your air even more." I instruct him in a firm voice that feels a little too similar to a teacher for my liking.

He brings his head up and turns to look at me almost angrily. Upon exposing his chest, I notice how strongly it rises and falls with the strength of his attempts to breathe. Once again, I gesture my hand towards him, and this time, he takes it.

"Good. Squeeze my hand every time you breathe in, and release it whenever you breathe out." I say, and once again, he looks at me like I'm stupid. "Do it." I repeat, and he does.

He tilts his head back and watches the sky, having to focus solely on his breathing. The first few attempts that he makes are completely out of time with his erratic breaths, but after a solid five minutes, he's nailed it.

It's only then that he lets go of my hand and swallows.

"I don't cry." He says, looking out onto the empty road ahead of us.

"Okay."

"I just, I want you to know that. I don't cry, I'm not a crier."

"What was that, then?"

He only dignifies me with silence.

I turn my head to look at him again. "You really care about this place, don't you?"

"That's a stupid question." He spits out bitterly.

"My business teacher always says that there aren't any stupid questions. Only stupid people." I bounce back, and Kylen smiles a little bit.

"Why don't you care?" He asks suddenly. "I know you've not been going for four years like I have, but- but you'd think to be a little bit upset."

"I don't know. I don't really form emotional attachments to things. Or people. That's why I got told to come to the club in the first place."

"Oh." He says. "Yeah."

"Yeah?"

"Yeah, I get that."

"Mhm? What about those trackie-wearing lads you were getting pissed with the other day?"

He blinks a few times. "I don't know. I don't think I really like them that much. And we get drunk way too often. Way too often."

"Alright." I reply, standing up and brushing myself off. "You need this place to stay open, right?"

"More than anything."

"Right then." I say, and I reach my hand out again, for an entirely different reason this time.

Kylen grabs onto it and hauls himself to his feet. I don't let go of his hand when he's up, instead turning back around and marching him back in the direction of the club. He makes a few noises of protest, even as I drag us through the main hall where everyone has reformed the circle and seems to be carrying on without us. We head straight through the building and right back into Thalia's office, where she's sitting at her desk.

On the walls of the office, there's multiple framed paintings and posters all over, along with stacks and stacks of paper.

She looks startled when the door opens, and I slam my hands onto the desk, leaving Kylen standing awkwardly behind me.

"Hello, Thalia."

"Um, hi boys. You okay?"

"I'm glad you asked. No, we aren't okay, as a matter of fact."

She smiles and leans back in her chair a little.

"Oh, yeah?"

"Yeah. And we won't be okay until you agree to fight for this place." I say, and this time, I raise my hand in the air, dragging Kylen's hand up with me so that we're creating an arch in the air.

He uses his other hand to rub his eyes in mild embarrassment. Thalia smirks.

"If you two can get me the money, legally, for the charity that funds us, then fine. But I don't know how you're gonna come up with it." She challenges us. Challenge accepted, then.

"How much?" Kylen asks quietly. Thalia flashes him a sceptical look.

"Well, six-hundred was-"

"We can get six hundred quid. Easily." I say.

"Yeah, six-hundred was what the rent was under the old owners. Now, it's closer to twelve-hundred."

Kylen furrows his eyebrows for a moment, deep in thought. "Wait, wait. Surely if we could afford six-hundred quid before, now all we need is another six-hundred." He rationalises, and yeah, it makes sense.

"A month." Thalia reminds. "For the rest of the foreseeable future."

"Right, right. But, including the younger group, there's like thirty of us that come here. So, ask every parent to give twenty pounds a month."

"Kylen, I can't start charging kids to come here. This is meant to be a safe space for everyone, regardless of money or stuff like that." She scolds lightly.

"You could at least ask."

"If I had charged you twenty pounds a month when you first started coming here, you wouldn't have been able to come."

"I know."

"Right, so it's not happening."

"Okay, okay." I interject. "We'll do it. Just don't do anything, okay? Don't start waving any white flags until that deadline arrives and we still have nothing."

"Alright, Everett." She confirms. "It's June next week, and this new rent doesn't come in until July. Just keep me informed about whatever you're getting up to, yeah?"

I promise her that we will, and then I take Kylen back out of the office. When we get outside, and the door is shut, he breathes out a sigh of relief.

"Thanks. For doing that." He says.

"Yeah. You're not the only person that needs this place." I remind him gently, allowing my gaze to drift back over to the doors where the remainder of the club members in attendance are.

Kylen nods in agreement, and then he falters. "Hold on. How did you know about the money stuff? I didn't even tell you why I was upset."

It takes us about ten seconds of silent company until the cogs in his brain begin to whirr.

"Oh my god! You were eavesdropping!" He accuses with a jokingly shocked expression.

"...No, I wasn't." I reply in a way that is by no means actually an attempt to defend my honour.

"Yeah, yeah. Tell it to the judge." He says again, turning and heading in the direction of hall B.

I roll my eyes and follow him.

4

Kylen

I've never liked June. Well, I suppose not *never*, but since I've had the ability to comprehend what the month even stands for, I've had issues with it.

So, when May rolls over into nothingness, I end up confronted with the sixth month of the year - yet again. And this June is even worse because of exams, even if it wasn't shitty enough before.

The youth club always likes to do things for June. It was the most extravagant as ever a couple years back. Thalia had taken charge of decoration, plastering hall A in an array of different pride flags and also taking the liberty of organising a little soiree for us.

I hadn't gone.

And it wasn't ever that I didn't want to, I've just never been the biggest fan of that kind of thing.

When I walk into the Aconite Centre on the first, I learn pretty quickly that Everett does not hate June.

He seems like he's in a good mood when he notices me, a

wide grin spread across his face as he glances in my direction whilst mid-conversation. It annoys me, just because I've had a shitty day at school (my science teacher is out to get me) and he clearly hasn't.

When he finishes what he's saying, he doesn't waste any time in approaching me.

"You look cheery today." He says whilst bouncing over, tone sarcastic as ever.

"Thanks." I reply, walking past him and towards the pre-established chair circle. His footsteps follow me from behind.

"Hey, dude." He calls, and I feel bad for ignoring him for a brief moment, so I turn around. "I know you aren't the most prideful person in the world, but you must be at least a little bit happy."

"I don't know why you're acting like it's a national holiday." I bite back smoothly. Honestly, this whole 'June' thing has got me in a bitter mood, so I don't give too much of a shit if I seem like an asshole. I'm pretty sure Everett already sees me as such either way.

"It's the first day of Pride Month, Kylen." He reminds me, as if I don't know. "And we're at a LGBTQ+ club. Lighten up a little. Anyone would think you don't wanna be here."

"I do want to be here." I insist, because it's true. I wouldn't've come here twice a week for the last four years if I didn't. "It's just that.. I don't know. It's stressful."

"It shouldn't be. It's about community and celebration, not brooding."

"I'm not brooding." I argue back. It's pissing me off. The way that he acts like he's some kind of pioneer for the queer community. Like he knows better than me or something. Because, quite frankly, I know pretty well and sometimes

I wish that I didn't. Sometimes I wish I was as naive as he is. "I just get stressed, okay. I just like to stay under the radar." I say quietly.

"Well, yeah. But nobody's forcing you to do any of this stuff. You realize that, right? You could be at home right now."

Oh, look. There's that obnoxiousness again. Typical. I make the quick decision that I'm over it. So, in an attempt to disengage, I give him a quick "Okay." back and walk away to talk to someone else.

Dallas tells me about their weekend up until circle starts. I feel kind of awkward talking to her, because she was one of the witnesses to when I stormed out the other day, but she acts like nothing has changed. I appreciate it.

Thalia telling me that the club was gonna have to shut down was difficult. I think it might have something to do with why I feel so shit and bitter about all of this 'Pride Month' crap. I don't feel like I have anything to celebrate. I feel so alone and ashamed in myself, and then the only place that kind of eradicates those feelings is gone, and everyone expects me to be smiling and jumping around for joy. It's a piss-take.

The even worse part is that Thalia asked me and Everett not to tell anyone about the circumstances. She doesn't want to cause any unnecessary upset, apparently. Which feels futile after the way she made me feel on Sunday.

I'm still not really sure what happened on the street that day. I was fine, and I was just gonna go to the park or something and recollect my thoughts. Have a smoke and forget about it. But then Everett had to get involved.

And then he made me hold hands with him to help me calm down, which, by the way, I think he was just doing to make fun of me upon reflection. Which I suppose might also be a contributing factor into my sour mood.

Either way, if Dallas has any adverse feelings towards me about the whole thing, they don't show it whilst we talk. And then, when Thalia calls us all in, we sit beside each other out of habit.

She seems far too excited about something, especially considering the circumstances.

"Alright. Super exciting stuff today, firstly, happy Pride Month!" She says, and everyone seems pretty enthused by the occasion. "So, this Saturday there's an event going on in town to celebrate. And I think it'd be great for us to go as a club." She announces, and I feel a pit of dread form in my stomach. "So, we're gonna go and do a bit of fundraising just to get a little bit of money for the club, which was Everett's idea, so thank him for that."

I look over at him and he gives me a double thumbs up. I'm not sure that I expected anything less, to be honest.

I'm glad that we're gonna make some money for the cause. Or, rather I'm glad that *they* will.

When Thalia explains that we all need to sign up to go on the sheet (and that she needs parental consent from any under sixteens, which doesn't apply to me), she passes around a clipboard with space to write our names down.

Dallas writes their name down and hands the clipboard to me, which I just pass right over my lap and to the person sitting on the other side of me.

"Are you not gonna come, Kylen?" Rowan asks from where he's standing outside the circle. He sounds genuinely concerned, so I shuffle uncomfortably in my seat with all of the eyes in the room now on me.

"Uh, no."

"That's a shame." He says, giving me a look that tells me that he wants me to go.

"Yeah, come on, dude. Don't be the only one that doesn't go." Everett says as he simultaneously writes his own name down. And I realize that he's right, literally everyone else is going.

So, now I suppose I have a point to prove. To show Everett that I'm not some kind of sulking child, I can have fun. I can get involved.

"Fine." I mutter as I beckon for the clipboard back. I'm sure to maintain firm eye contact with Everett as I write my name down, too.

It's not like I would choose to go independently, but I've never been to something like this before, and I suppose it could be a new experience. Maybe I'll even enjoy myself, but probably not. We'll see.

On Saturday morning, I leave the house early. We're supposed to be meeting in town at twelve, but I've left my bedroom desolate by ten.

A gentle ache pulses through my chest for the entire bus ride, signifying the anxiety rising steadily inside of me.

It's not that I don't want to go. In fact, I'm surprised that it's taken me so long to go to one of these events.

I've dressed as inconspicuously as possible - dark grey hoodie over slightly lighter cargo-style joggers. When I walk from the shopping centre that I've been wandering around to pass the time to the designated meeting place, I keep my hood up.

It's clearly a celebration if the world around me is anything to go by. Our city has put up banners that declare it's support for the community, but what makes it all more real is the hundreds of people that have come together for something like this. It's mainly younger kids, maybe newly out, who have their pride flags wrapped around their shoulders like capes - a bold statement of their identities. Definitely something Everett would find fun.

I quickly shush the thoughts of him in my mind, but I'm dragged right back to the place I was before when I see other people from the club all milling around the meeting point.

There's a band playing, and the music drowns out any of my negative thoughts. We're in the centre of town, in the heart of the city, in the heart of the community.

When I see everyone smiling and really in their elements, I realize slightly that I'm not going to fit in here. I'm not like them, I don't stick my hand in the air and admit that I'm not cis-het like they do.

And, fuck, I suddenly get this tightness in my chest. As cars whirr past me through the town centre, the road separating me from them. It feels like crossing the River Styx to have to go and socialise in the same way that they do.

"Yo, you alright man?" Comes a voice from behind me. I turn around slightly and notice Eli looking down at me slightly concernedly. It irritates me that he's got like two inches of height on me. I hate it when cis boys are taller than me. It makes me feel inferior, like shit. To be fair, though, my voice is deeper than his, so I win on that front.

"What? Uh, yeah." I reply as nonchalantly as I can muster.

Eli quirks an eyebrow at me. He's wearing a black shirt with some generically colourful graphic on it. Over top lies a sage green hoodie that goes nicely with his white, wide-legged jeans. A necklace with the two interlinked emblems of the male gender symbol dangles around his neck.

"You sure about that? Kinda staring off into space there."

"Yeah, yeah. Just waiting to cross the road."

"I watched you just kinda stand there when the lights went red. Are you worried about going to the event?" He asks invasively.

"No."

"Okay. So, let's go." He says, walking past me and crossing the road kind of recklessly in-between cars. I give my left and right a quick once-over before dashing across with him.

We greet everyone unnecessarily. Thalia says she's proud of me for coming. I nod and stuff my hands into my pockets. The day can't go any slower.

Or, I think that. Until Everett shows up. He hops off a bus on our side of the road, saying hello to everyone.

The actual event kicks off no less than thirty minutes later, and it's quite the display.

A march comes through, people screaming and cheering. The police come not shortly after, but they don't seem like they want to engage. There are flags waving everywhere, and it must be quite diverse identity-wise; I don't recognise about half of them.

We stand on the corner of the town square for what's realistically hours, but it feels like less.

At one point, Rowan even let me hold the money-bucket. Each clunk of a coin hitting the bottom of the pot gave me a little extra inkling of hope for the club.

"Kylen!" Everett yells over the loud noise of people enjoying themselves in the streets.

"Mhm?" I reply turning to look at him. He's grinning.

"You look happy!" He says at the same volume, gesturing outwards with his hands. I look around at all of the people here – all here in support of who I am.

"I am!" I find myself admitting.

"Yeah?"

"Yeah! I didn't know it was like this." I say, and it feels like my voice is echoing. It's true. I've never been to one of these Pride events before. I'd imagined it was like the club, just ramped up a ton. Which, it kind of is. But, unlike the club, it feels less suffocating. Less like an excuse, less like somewhere I just *have* to be. Somewhere I want to be. Full of people that care.

"Maybe next time you should trust me." He teases. I guess he's right. Maybe I have been a little close minded about this whole thing.

He walks away to do something else, and the conversation leaves a smirk imprinted onto my face. A gaggle of younger teenagers, maybe about thirteen, sprint past us, all smiling and yelling with glee. I can't help but feel jealous of them. Maybe I should do things like this more.

"This is new for you." I hear from behind me, and it's Rowan. I'm taller than he is, so Eli can suck it.

"Hm?" I hum, stepping back to be standing next to him.

"I just mean, I've never seen you like this. You've really come out of your shell."

"Thanks, um, I guess." I say, hands stuffed into my pockets. From here, I can see almost everything. Rowan and I shelter under some scaffolding as the parade begins to die down, and now people are just shuffling around and enjoying the show.

There's a couple in the middle of the street, clearly pissed out of their minds as they both spin around in each other's arms. People on the sidelines cheer and scream at them. They're probably equally as drunk. It's entertaining, and I allow myself to smile at it all.

We're still in the town centre when the sun begins to go down. The donations pot is heavy, and people have that tiredness-fuelled giggly coating on their personalities. The day has gone on for a long time, and it's signified by the golden glow shone all over the town. The light catches on some flags and the colour shines right onto the centre of the road.

All down the street, people seem happy.

Happy and celebratory. The air feels comfortable as I breathe it in, and for the fleeting moments of the rest of the day, I completely forget about everything else. I forget about my parents, and what they would say if they knew I was here. I forget about about all the pressure to look a certain way, to be a certain way.

And, very suddenly, I wish more than anything that I could forget about my friends.

"Oh, shit. Fuck, shit." The curses tumble out of my mouth as I duck behind most of our group.

Everett turns around with a slight smile on his face. "You okay there?"

"No, fuck, shut up." I push out in a whisper.

Seeing a trio of my friends swaggering through the town like the Titanic through the ice berg causes me to remember all the reasons I didn't want to fucking do this.

Thalia's eyes bare down on me for a moment before she glances to the group of boys on the other side of the street. Her face contorts to one of sympathy.

"Oh, do you know those boys?" Lilia asks easily, as if she can't see me very clearly hiding from them.

It's not the whole group. Just Tobias, Liam and AJ. I think if the whole group was hanging out without me I'd feel a little betrayed. Liam is cradling a can of Redbull in one arm, and AJ holds a football that I recognise as the one that we accidental kicked into an old man's garden a few months back. I remember how he had yelled at us for being 'reckless youth' and we had laughed at his frustration.

I ignore Lilia and go to stand next to one of the pillars that holds the canopy of the building we're beside, watching them from across the road.

My heart thrums out of my chest. My eyes lock onto them and I will them just to walk past, walk past, walk past.

Tobias spares a bitter glance at us across the street, and then he does a double take.

I don't know why they would be here. There's still people here for Pride everywhere.

Tobias hits AJ on his chest and flicks his head in our direction. I feel sick. I'm going to throw up.

They start to cross the road and I move completely behind the pillar as I release an expletive that Thalia scolds me for.

"Alright, what's all this, then?" Tobias asks in his cocky voice, arms crossed as he approaches everyone. I feel my breathing pick up from where I shelter behind the pillar.

"Uh, we, uh-" Mars starts to say, clearly intimidated by the boys.

"We're fundraising. For our youth club." Thalia supplies, stepping in front of them somewhat protectively. She speaks clearly, asserting her position as the adult in this situation.

At this point I can only hear what's going on. I can't risk so much as a glance in case one of them sees me.

"Your youth club?" He replies on a snicker. "For what? Fags?"

And I'm pretty sure my heart has stopped beating in my chest.

"Excuse me?" Thalia says, rage filtering through her voice, but she keeps herself level in the way that I know she always does.

"You heard me." He repeats. And then, Liam snickers, edging his way forward into the gaggle.

"Fuckin' weirdos." He says.

My adrenaline levels shoot through the roof at the sound of his voice so close to mine. And I have to get away, I have to get away.

"Kylen!"

I turn away from the pillar just as AJ grabs my arm and I stumble towards them. From the angle, and from the way that I had dashed a few seconds prior, I guess it appears to the boys that I had come from a different direction than with the rest of the group.

Just the sheer amount of anxiety caused by the idea that they might have seen me associated with this lot makes me realize something.

That this isn't worth it.

Getting to have this, this one day of celebration. It's not worth the years and years of effort that I've funnelled into what I have now.

I've been able to balance my life outside of and inside the club quite well, but I can't start mixing the two. It's just not worth it, and I think I've just learnt that the hard way.

"Didn't know you were in town." AJ says, arms crossed

with the same smirk that he always has etched onto his face.

I nod a few times. "Yeah, well it's Alfie's birthday next week so I need to grab him a present." I bluff, and although it *is* Alfie's birthday on Tuesday, that's not why I'm here.

My eyes flicker over to the group from the club, and Everett looks at me with his eyes narrowed as if I've just killed someone.

"Oh, right, right. His birthday? Sounds like an excuse for a party." Liam says, snickering as he pulls a packet of cigarettes from his tracksuit pocket.

"He's turning eight, man. Give it seven years and he'll be doing all that stuff." I dismiss.

"I'm sure he'll take after his brother. Nothing like a good role model." Tobias adds, slapping me on the back a few times. I smile amusedly at the comment, anxiety still spiking in my chest as I remember that the entirety of the club is watching.

Liam holds the pack of cigs out towards me. "Want a fag?" He asks. "One of these, not those ones." He clarifies, gesturing towards the members of the club.

Fucking hell. Just being associated with these guys is making me look like a major dickhead in front of all these people that know me.

I ignore his slight and take one anyway, because goodness knows I need one after this interaction. He hands me a lighter, and just after lighting it, I hear a voice from beside me.

"You shouldn't be doing that, Kylen." Everett scolds, and I look over at him with a piercing look of anger. "It's not good for you - for your lungs. Especially if you're binding, which I assume you are."

I feel all the compassion I might have had towards him drain from my body. All the happiness that I've accumulated from the events of the day. Is he fucking serious? In front of my friends that he knows very well think I'm cis? What a prick. I get that he might be annoyed at me for pretending I don't know them in public but that's not an excuse to try and out me to my friends.

I would expect him to get that, out of all people. But I guess he's never had to worry about being outed. I'm so incredibly lucky that none of my mates know any of the trans-oriented terminology that he's just thrown down.

I glare at him as Liam, AJ and Tobias look between myself and him.

"Do you.. Know this kid?" Tobias asks me whilst snickering. I take a drag from the cigarette and blink a few times.

If he has the audacity to talk about my gender like that in front of my friends, knowing I'm stealth, then screw him.

Respect is meant to go both ways.

"Nah." I say, casually. "Nah, I don't know this tranny." I spit.

And Everett looks at me as if I've told him I want him dead. It's entertaining. He's not the only one that can be a major asshole. I can do it too.

The three of my friends laugh. They think it's really funny. I can tell by the expressions of all others from the club that they don't find it funny at all. Lilia mouths a swift 'what the fuck?' at me. I don't look at Thalia or Rowan.

"Do you wanna fuck off from this freak-fest?" AJ offers, gesturing around to the decorations everywhere with the hand that he isn't holding the can in. "We were gonna go have a kick about in the park."

"Yeah. Yeah, okay." I say, and we start to walk away.

Anger seethes through my veins at the thought of Everett

trying to out me like that in front of my friends. So I don't even look back. I hear that everyone starts to talk when I get a few metres away. I think Thalia asks Everett if he's okay. And I hope he's not.

The park is uneventful. Over the course of a few hours, we play many football games that turn into most of our mates showing up.

Our games take place inside the big ball-game cage in the middle of the park, and we easily dominate the area.

At one point, a group of younger boys show up wanting to have a go, but we don't let them because we're just like that.

At about ten-o-clock, between games when everyone is just talking, I check my phone.

My inbox has been quite active.

At first, I try to actually reply rationally, and then I just end up getting irritated and not dignifying anyone with a full response.

Dallas (youth club)

What the fuck was that??
you've really upset him
fucking christ

he was a prick first
but ok don't acknowledge it

Brynn (youth club)

Not cool dude.
  Like at all

                              he tried to out me
                              that also wasn't cool

Lilia

you're making me worry
  it's not like you to act like that
  are you okay??

                        yea don't lose sleep over it

Eli (youth club)

don't bother coming back to the club
  not after whatever the fuck that was

                                        k

Mars (youth club)

dickhead

I don't even bother replying to that last one.
    "What's gotten you all kicked—puppy-looking?" Jack asks
as he kicks the ball in my direction.
    "No, nothing." I reply, switching my phone off and taking

a deep breath of the night air.

"Okay. Well, if it makes you feel any better, Tobi was thinking about inviting some girls from school down. You know, like Abbie."

And, yeah. Seeing Abbie would be nice. I've known her for a couple of months now, and we get along really well, so everyone keeps saying that we should get together. And I do want to. I really do like her, but she doesn't know that I'm trans and I think that if we go out and I have to tell her, everyone will end up finding out. I'm pretty sure she likes me too, but we've never really gotten any further than flirting. I hope that one day that'll change, but the hope becomes hard to find when I realize that I'm not like the other boys. I'm not like the perception of me that she probably has in her head.

"Yeah, alright." I reply smoothly. I kick the ball back and forget about the texts. It doesn't matter any more, what's done is done, and right now, I'm having a good time with my mates that I actually do want to be friends with.

5

Everett

It's practically impossible for me to comprehend what Kylen has just said about me; what he called me.

I known he's a bit fragile in his identity, and I known that he has some shitbag friends, but, *fuck.*

He walks away down the street with his mates as if nothing has happened and everybody's attention turns rapt onto me.

"What a fucking dick." Someone, anyone, says. People are all talking and yelling like they're pissed off, but I can't find the words in myself to speak.

I blink a few times and suddenly Thalia is in front of me, bent down slightly to make eye contact.

"Are you okay?" She asks.

I should be. It's just not fair for him to get the respect of his friends at the expense of my dignity. I feel violently exposed, like people look at me every day and the first thing that comes to their mind is that word.

Before I even know what's going on, I'm crying. Crying like a child as she hugs me. And that makes everyone stop yelling and just look over at us. After a good minute or two, I step back a little and keep my gaze downcast.

Transphobia isn't something that I can say I've had count-less experiences with. Of course, I've had weird glances in the corridors at school, and I've had other teenagers snicker and whisper things like 'Is that a boy or a girl?' in my direction, but I've always been good at brushing things like that off.

I guess I'm lucky in that regard. My mum's been really great about it, and so have my teachers at school. Never before has someone been so.. abruptly direct about their hatred towards me.

I think I would feel differently if it was just an uneducated, ignorant cis person calling me that, like my cousins used to do.

But it wasn't. It was Kylen. It was another trans person. Someone that's meant to support his trans siblings. But clearly, community means very little to him - especially when he seemed so eager to say that when the opportunity arose.

"I thought he was my friend." I say. "I was nice to him." And I meant it. I genuinely had tried my best to get through to him. If I was a lesser person, I would've cut all contact the minute he first made that comment about my hair when we met. But I didn't, and clearly I was stupid for having even an inkling of hope that he could be any different. Maybe some people just aren't capable of change.

And, yeah, maybe I was slightly out of line confronting him about smoking like that, but it was because I think he forgot that he was one of us. I wanted to remind him that he was trans, too. And we have to stick together if we want to survive.

"He's a very complicated young man." Thalia says, looking off in the distance in the direction that he went. "But that was just unacceptable."

The whole thing leaves everyone kind of shaken up. You never really realize how scary being confronted by a group of homophobic teenage boys really is until it happens to you. I'm just glad that we have the adults here with us.

Speaking of them, they've gone off in one of the corners having a hushed conversation, both looking stressed.

"I just removed him from the group chat, by the way." Eli says, arms crossed in front of him.

"Yeah. Good idea." Dallas agrees. "I can't believe he's friends with those boys."

"We said this at the park. He's basically one of them." Mars then adds. I don't contribute to the conversation, in fact, it's hard to even think over all the pounding in my head.

He called me a *tranny.*

Which is ironic, because *he* was the person who was invalidating my transness to begin with. So, I'm not trans enough for him, and then I'm trans enough that he can call me a slur in front of his friends and the whole club.

And, like I said, it's not like nobody has ever been transphobic towards me before, because they have. It's just different when it's another trans person. It feels like an attack on *me personally,* rather than on the existence of trans people.

Because I know that he's not against the existence of trans people; he literally is one. It's just to do with me, then. And that thought hurts me way more than his words did.

"Guys, it's fine." I say finally, and they all stop talking. "People that act like that usually only do it because they're insecure." I reply, preaching the rhetoric that I've been a firm believer of my whole life.

"Maybe, yeah. But even if he does it because he's depressed or insecure or whatever, that doesn't make it right." Brynn

67

says.

"Exactly. It's an explanation - not an excuse." Dallas states, and yeah, she's right.

"Okay, guys." Rowan says, breaking the circle to stand on the edge of it. "I think it's been a long day, so it's about time we head home. We'll see some of you at trans-plus tomorrow, and the rest hopefully next Thursday."

We already had made plans that we would stay out after we finish with the club, so we bid Rowan and Thalia goodbye before turning to leave and drift into town.

"Ah, Everett? Can you hang back a sec?" Thalia calls out, and I do as she asks. It's probably gonna be another 'you sure you're okay?', and I can deal with that.

"Yeah?"

"I'm just- I'm gonna ask you because you were affected. What do you want us to do about Kylen?" And, oh. I hadn't really expected to be asked that. "As in, do you want us to contact him and tell him not to come back to the club? Or are you okay for him to come again? We have a zero tolerance policy for this kind of thing, *especially* for slurs and the like. I just thought it was worth asking you."

"Um, yeah. I don't know. What do you think?"

She falters for a moment and looks over at Rowan. "I just worry-" she says, making eye contact with her colleague.

"Yeah." He replies, sympathy oozing through his voice. They're clearly silently communicating about something.

"But, to be fair," Rowan adds. "Zero tolerance is zero tolerance. It'd be wrong to start allowing loopholes because of the past."

"What do you mean?" I ask.

"Don't worry, um, yeah. Why don't we just see if he shows

up tomorrow? And if he does, I'll deal with it then." Thalia suggests, and I'm happy with that negotiation.

I think everyone can kind of tell that I don't want to talk about it, so we pretend that it never happened when we're in town. He's taken up too much of my energy already, it'd be wasteful to give him any more. I'm sure he's not even spared a second thought about his actions. So, why should I? And when I get home, I don't even tell Mum about it. I just smile and hug her before tucking myself away in my bedroom and doom-scrolling on social media for a couple hours.

I stay up because a small part of me expects that Kylen might text me. He might say 'Hey man, I'm sorry. That was out of line and I hope you can forgive me.' Or, maybe, he might even just send a quick text. One word would be enough, just 'sorry', or 'I shouldn't have said that.'

But the text doesn't come. It doesn't come by ten o'clock, it doesn't come by eleven, or twelve, and when it still hasn't come by one, I assume that he's probably passed out in another of his friends' houses without a care in the world for how he's made *me* feel.

There's nothing in my mind that makes me think he'll have the audacity to show up at trans-plus tomorrow, and if he does, I can't visualise it going well.

He does, in fact, show up on Sunday. And it's awkward.

Everybody is buzzing in conversation before circle when he walks in. And when we see him, wearing dark colours and looking particularly dishevelled, everyone goes silent. He looks tired.

For a moment, I feel slightly bad about his appearance, but if his feelings have been eating away at him so, why did he not bother to make contact with me? And, if he's just been out all night and not sleeping, why would he make the effort of showing up here knowing that he's unwanted? I got told about some of the texts that some club members sent him, and I can't say that it would make *me* feel welcome here.

He stops in his movement and looks at me before averting his gaze.

"Ah, Kylen." Rowan says from where he's stood by the wall watching over all of us. "Can you go through to Thalia's office? Like, now." He asks, and his voice doesn't leave any room for argument.

Kylen doesn't reply, but he sets off walking in that direction with a sigh. This time, when he gets called to the office, nobody makes any jokey noises or comments about it. It's a different atmosphere entirely.

"He's so fucked." Mars says after he disappears through the doors.

"Language." Rowan scolds, and we all fall into an uneasy silence.

I can only imagine what type of conversation is happening in Thalia's office, until I don't have to imagine it any longer.

She must be quite angry; we can't make out exactly what she's saying, but we can hear the muffled sounds of her yelling.

And then, about five minutes later she returns. Kylen follows her out of the office, and his eyes are red and watering. He somehow looks worse than he did before. I kind of get it, getting yelled at by Thalia, someone who's usually quite sweet and he's clearly known for a long time, must be hard. It's not like he didn't bring it upon himself, though.

"Go on." She says, voice frustrated.

He looks over at her and then starts idly walking towards where I'm standing.

"Oh, hello." I say, not being able to help fight back the smirk that works its way onto my features.

He appears to take a deep breath before he speaks.

"I'm sorry."

I raise my eyebrows at him. He's sorry? Clearly not, if Thalia had to yell at him to get him to apologise.

"Sorry for what?" I ask, narrowing my eyes in accusation.

He swallows and looks around a little. "I'm sorry that I called you a tranny." He states plainly, before dropping his voice to a much more hushed volume. "I wanted to hurt you because what you said beforehand hurt me. And, I guess I could've chosen a better word. A less hateful insult, something more accurate to your personality. Like 'ignorant douchebag' or 'obnoxious prick.'"

It might have been at a lower volume than usual, but the room was completely silent otherwise, so everyone heard it.

"Excuse you?" I ask rather loudly, and he keeps his gaze determined, although he looks like he's about to cry. There's a surge of emotion behind his pupils that I fail to recognise.

"Right, Kylen. That's enough. You need to leave." Thalia says from across the room, striding over.

Kylen doesn't really react. He just keeps his eyes locked onto mine.

When Thalia touches his arm to instruct him to leave, he flinches backwards rather violently.

"Fucking hell." He says, sniffling as his eyes dart between myself and Thalia. "You don't care, do you? About anything."

He's clearly talking to me, but I think he's having some kind of mental breakdown. Either that or he's decided to take up method acting, and he's pretty good at it.

"What do you mean?" I ask on an exhale that catches in my throat.

He tilts his head back and takes a deep breath in. "You- you just- I-" He takes his time finding his argument, or, if he has it, he struggles to get it out. "I've been coming here for years. And then you think that you can show up, act like you're better than me because you don't care how people perceive you. Dye your hair and frolic around at your pride events because you don't care. You- you made me feel all these stupid things about myself, and then you try and out me to all my mates because, what? You're jealous, or something." He keeps on rambling, and his voice gets closer and closer to breaking into sobs with each word.

"And you, then you take away the one thing that I had. The one thing that's kept me going-" He glances over at Thalia. "The one thing I had, Everett, and you don't even care whilst you do it. You don't care. You're just happy to get your way, because you always do, don't you?"

He steps back when he finishes talking, bringing a hand to his mouth and closing his eyes softly as he crouches down slightly and looks at the floor.

For a moment in which everyone is silent, I feel bad for him. But he's dug his own grave.

"Kylen," I say, in the most gentle voice that I can manage as to not push this further, "You can't act like any of this has been out of your control. You chose, I don't know if you remember, it *was a whole day ago,* but you chose between us or your friends. And you chose them."

72

He's had everything that he could have possibly needed to turn out fine, and he still gets angry and jealous towards me for all of this? It's confusing.

Kylen wipes his face with the back of his hand and shakes his head.

"You- you don't get it. Fuck, you don't get it at all." He whines, almost like a child as he turns quickly and leaves the room.

This time, I don't chase after him to make sure that he's okay.

The events linger in the air for a good minute of silence. After this duration has finished, Thalia claps her hands together in front of her.

"Alright. Uhm, let's get on with circle then." She declares, pulling a chair back and sitting on it awkwardly.

"Hold on, no." Mars quickly interrupts. Everyone's attention becomes rapt on them. "We can't brush that off."

"Yeah." Brynn adds. "We would never be able to do a normal session after that anyway."

I agree with them. We need to do something about this tense atmosphere. It won't go away if we pretend nothing has happened.

I don't really know how to feel about Kylen's outburst just then. I disagree with the idea that Kylen's behaviour is my fault, he very clearly just feels entitled to everything and throws a hissy fit when he doesn't get it.

But, then again, I'm a fundamental believer of the idea that everybody deserves a second chance.

"Okay." Rowan says softly, clearly in an attempt to diffuse the horrifically dense atmosphere. "Okay, then let's talk about it."

Thalia looks up from her chair, and in a way that I've never seen before, she looks devastated. Her eyes are watering and she looks like she might burst into tears at any moment.

"Are you okay, Thalia?" I say out of pure instinct. She blinks a few times and then shakes her head.

"It's just- It's just difficult." She says finally. "I've known Ky since he was no taller than my elbow height."

"Yeah." Rowan agrees. "He joined the club when I was just starting to volunteer here. We watched him grow up, and for him to have grown up to behave like that, it's- I don't know, it's just upsetting."

I nod in agreement, but I fail to find anything else to say. We lull in quiet for a moment.

"I think he's just going through it." Lilia adds in a whisper.

"What do you mean?" I ask, attention definitely captured.

"I just think- I don't know, he's been seeming a little off recently. Unlike himself. Has anything happened that might make him upset? More than he usually is."

My eyes go right over to Thalia. Is it a possibility that this has something to do with the club shutting down?

It seems that she thinks the same thing, as we make eye contact. Everyone seems to notice our silent communication.

"Yeah, there was something." Thalia admits. "I don't know, but it's not an excuse for him to be like that."

"People do weird things when they're in panic mode." Lilia continues.

"Sorry, why are you defending him right now?" Dallas asks, seeming annoyed.

"I'm not. I just think we're being really quick to cast someone out that we've known for years."

"Alright, well, you were the one talking shit about him at

74

the park last week."

And before I know it, everyone seems to be squabbling. Loudly and with annoyance. Lilia thinks that we need to be more lenient about it. Dallas thinks that we need to just cut him off full stop. Brynn thinks that this isn't the kind of discussion that we need to be having behind his back. Mars makes eye contact with me across the circle with widened eyes. Rowan looks absolutely mortified and powerless to stop anything. Then Thalia glances over at me, desperate, and I know what I have to do to bring us together.

"The club is shutting down." I proclaim loudly, and they all stop yelling as quickly as they started.

"What?"

"We don't have the money to stay running. Kylen and I knew, if anything's messing with his head, it's probably that. But we want to save the club, and we can't do that by bickering."

Lilia blinks a few times and casts her gaze towards the two adults in the circle. "The- what?"

"Yeah, so we need to get ourselves together instead of fighting." I practically repeat.

It's a complicated issue, yeah, but it's about time that everyone gets on the same page with all of this.

"Is that true?" Mars asks, eyes painfully aware as they look at Thalia and Rowan.

"I'm sorry." Thalia says. "It's just tricky. We're trying our best." She admits, and it's almost pitiful.

The news sinks into everyone's skin like an uncomfortable sunburn. In just a matter of weeks, the life and joy has been sucked out of the room. We're gonna need to do something to fix this mess, but for once in my life, I've run out of ideas as to how.

Nobody's fighting any more, and we're all united in our upset.

We spend the rest of the time at the club asking Thalia and Rowan questions about the specific circumstances, and also brainstorming ideas of what to do. None of them really take off, though, because it's all stuff like 'bake sale' and 'car boot', but it's not like we can do that every month with the *hopes* that we'll make twelve-hundred pounds out of thin air.

And, despite my annoyance towards him, Kylen had seemed kind of invested in getting a way out of this mess. After we spoke to Thalia before, when I had eavesdropped on him, he seemed okay. And now, without his help, I feel a little at a loss in regards to what we'll do.

But I plan to hold onto the small fragment of community spirit in the room, as if it's a life jacket, and I hope things will work themselves out.

When I get home, my mum notices that something is wrong pretty quickly. She looks right at me through her dark brown eyes and I find myself sniffling at the build up of care and emotion.

"Oh, honey." She frowns. "What happened?"

"A lot."

"Okay. Should we have a talk or would you rather we put a few episodes of *Young Royals* on and get some ice cream?"

I find myself smiling at her consideration. She always seems to have a grasp on exactly what I need to hear in every situation.

"Can we do both at the same time?" I ask, maybe somewhat pushing it, but she grins and turns towards the kitchen where I'm assuming she'll make us some bowls of ice cream. "We can go to see the flowers soon, if you want." She adds whilst sifting around the fridge.

I really love my mum. It always feels like she genuinely wants the best for me, which does make sense considering that it's just the two of us.

It's been just us ever since a couple years ago, but I think a large factor towards her compassion is her age. She was quite young when she had me (and I hear about it every single time I even mention a boy that I think is attractive), so my dad never bothered to stick around.

The two of us lived with my grandparents until I was about four, and it was that point when Mum was able to put a down payment for the flat that we live in. It's nice in most ways, because it's cosy and feels like *ours*. We don't have much, but we're grateful for what we do.

Once of those things in particular is the TV that my Auntie Kristie gave my mum as a house-warming gift. We pay for Netflix, which has led to the two of us ploughing through shows together like a bullet train through wind.

We're watching *Young Royals* right now, after Eli told me it was really good a few weeks ago. And he's right, it is a pretty well-made show.

I get the episode lined up and Mum comes back with two bowls of caramel ice cream. She sits behind me and does the long, exaggerated sigh that's typical of her before any of our 'feelings' talks.

"So, what's going on?" She asks, shovelling a spoonful of the ice cream into her mouth, effectively giving me time to speak.

I shuffle a little. May as well start from the beginning.

"Okay, so, there's this boy at the club-"

"Sorry," She interrupts. "Just for the purpose of story-telling. Is this a boy or is this *a boy*?" She teases, and I scrunch my nose up at the thought of even mildly liking Kylen like that.

"He's just a normal boy, Mum. Sorry to disappoint; I know how desperate you are to be a grandma at thirty-three."

She snorts with laughter and shakes her head. "Don't even joke about that." She says lightly, clearly not serious, but I don't miss the way that anxiety seeps into her voice. "Sorry, carry on."

"Right, yeah. So this boy, Kylen, he's a bit of a prick."

"Language."

"But it's because his friends are pretty bad influences."

"Well, remember you shouldn't excuse bad actions just 'cause of his friends." She chides.

"Yeah, yeah. I know, but it's different. So, like, he's trans and his friends don't know, so he tries really hard to impress them by acting as irritating as possible."

On the TV screen, Simon and Wilhelm are talking about something, and I know we'll have to rewatch this episode anyway, so I may as well keep talking over it.

"So, you know how we like, went to the Pride event at the weekend?"

"Mhm."

"He was quite shy about going, and then his friends showed up and noticed him, and he had to pretend like he wasn't with us."

"Did he do something bad?" Mum asks, clearly seeing

where I'm going with this.

"Yeah."

"How bad? Redeemable bad or not?"

"Pretty bad, I don't know. It's like, I kinda don't wanna forgive him, but I think it might be about something else." I admit. As a person, Kylen is confusing to me. And as a fellow trans person, he's even more confusing.

"Okay. So, this happened on Saturday?"

"Right."

"So how does it tie in to today? Did something similar happen?"

"Yeah."

And there's a moment where we're both eating ice cream that allows for some silence as I reflect on what I'll tell her next. It's difficult because I don't want her to worry. Which is why I chose not to tell her exactly what Kylen called me, because she'll get defensive and upset.

"He came back to the club like he hadn't done anything wrong, then he had some kind of freak-out when he got kicked out. I don't know. He acted like it was *my fault* that he's not welcome at the Aconite Centre any more, when he literally chose to act up, and besides - it's closing down anyway at the end of the month."

Mum blinks at that one, and I realize that I hadn't told her yet.

"Shit, really?" She asks.

"Language."

"Funny. But, really?"

"Yeah, there's like new owners of the building that want double the rent, which we don't have."

"Can't you- I don't know- ask for donations or something?"

"I don't know. It's not really viable month to month."

Mum frowns and wraps her arm around my shoulder. "I'm sorry, honey." She says, snuggling into my shoulder as her eyes focus in on the television screen. "You were really enjoying it, too."

"Yeah, I know." I murmur, pushing my body into hers as I allow myself to receive the affectionate comfort that she's giving me.

"Oh my god, I think they're about to kiss." She whispers suddenly, eyes intent on the screen. I snicker and put my empty ice cream bowl on the ground, freeing up my hands and allowing all my focus to melt into the show we're watching.

My Mum might not know the solution to this problem, if there even is one, but there's something about just being with her, knowing that she cares, that makes it all feel okay.

6

Kylen

I hadn't assumed that getting kicked out of the club would have this much of a toll on me. I don't know. You'd think that if Thalia *made* me leave, it wouldn't be as bad when the club shuts down, because I wouldn't have been welcome anyway.

It was just the look of betrayal in her eyes. And I know that she doesn't deserve it, not after everything she's done for me.

Part of me had hoped that she would have followed me out, but she didn't. Which I guess I deserved.

I didn't actually intend to go off on Everett the way that I did, but in the moment it just *hurt* so much. The smug look on his face as he knew he'd won.

Forty minutes after it all, by the grace of zoned-out-Kylen, I found myself back in the town centre. I'm glad for it, because despite the fact that I'd used it as an excuse in front of AJ, Liam, and Tobias, I do actually have to get Alfie a birthday present, and it won't magically happen before his party on Tuesday.

In all fairness, I highly doubt that he would even notice

if I didn't get him anything, considering that there'll be a stampede of seven and eight-year-olds in our garden who will likely have all gotten him gifts. But I'd also bet money on the fact that Dad will likely want us to do family presents before any of his friends arrive.

The first place that I go is the Lego store. It's all too colourful, but I would *really* like to find something for Alfie here, because Jack works here and fifteen percent off is sounding really good right now.

"Affectionately," - Speak of the devil - "you look like shit." Jack says, placing a hand on my shoulder with a smirk on his face.

"Hey." I reply. He's certainly one to tell me that *I* look like shit, he's the one wearing a stupid yellow apron.

"What's the occasion, then? Do you need anything or did you just miss me that much?" He snickers. He doesn't mean to hurt my feelings, but his tone of voice makes me feel small around him.

Then, an older woman with stress wrinkles etched into her face walks past holding about four boxes of the Lego Friends cafe set. "You're on the clock, not having a mothers meeting." She chastises to Jack as she strolls by. He rolls his eyes.

"I'm conferring with a customer!" Jack calls in her direction before returning his attention to me. "Okay, you gotta actually buy something now or else she's gonna start deducting pay."

I can't help but laugh at that.

"You're in luck. It's Alfie's birthday on Tuesday."

"Aww. Well, you came to the right place, *paying customer.*" He says, slinging a hand around my shoulders and raising his voice, probably with the hopes that his manager will hear.

"You're ridiculous." I say endearingly as he guides me over towards the area that the younger kids usually favour. I'm not hoping to get him some collectables, just the kind of thing that he'll get excited over and spend an hour or two building. Then it'll sit on a shelf in his bedroom until he moves out.

"Here, look. Get him this, he'll love it."

"Eighty quid for a fuckin' knight castle?"

"Great value for money, the kid'll love it."

"What about that?" I ask, gesturing in the direction of a much smaller, twenty pound train with two carriages. Alfie quite likes trains, and it wouldn't take up too much room if he built it.

"Is your little brother not worth eighty pounds to you?" He asks, arms crossed in a way that tells me he's clearly joking.

"Stop acting like you work on commission. You're getting minimum wage whether I bankrupt myself or not." I throw back snarkily, snatching the train up off the shelf. Jack laughs and walks beside me to the counter.

"Hey, well, I can take my lunch break now if you're gonna stay in town. We could go get some food and maybe you can talk to me about why you've been crying." He suggests in a way that seems far too casual.

"What?"

"I have a little sister, bro. And she cries like nobody else, so I can tell. Your eyes are all red and puffy around the edges. And you keep sniffling." He explains whilst ringing me up. "That's seventeen-pounds. Cash or card?"

I gape at him for a moment. "Um, card."

"Awesome." Jack says, clicking the button to set my card transaction up. "Yes to lunch or do you have to get home?"

"Yeah. Lunch sounds good."

83

"Cool. Do you need a bag for this?"

We find ourselves in some shitty little cafe in which we're the only customers. Apparently, Jack's step-mum swears by this place.

The woman running the cafe takes our orders and we find a two-person table by the window. It's a good spot for people watching, because almost everyone who wants to get from the shopping centre to the bus stop has to walk past the front of the cafe. Considering it's the weekend, the streets are mainly populated with gaggles of teenagers, that are all-too enthusiastic about spending their parents' money.

"Alright," Jack says, elbows poised on the table, still wearing his work uniform but minus the obnoxious sunshine yellow apron. "What's going on, then?"

And, I want to tell him the truth. We're friends. He's probably one of my favourites out of my mates, mainly due to the fact that he actually seems to care. I won't, though. I won't risk our friendship over something so trivial.

"Just got some stuff going on, I don't know." I end up mumbling into my hand that my chin rests on. Jack looks at me in thought for a moment.

"Is this about your parents again?"

He's referring to this one night, maybe a year ago, where I had a really bad fight with my parents. He thinks it was about my grades at school. It was actually about changing my name legally - since I'm still a minor, I need their permission to do so. I kind of brought up the concept over dinner, since my parents *know* that I'm trans, they just like to pretend I'm not.

Mum had gotten really upset, and Dad had started telling me off for making her upset.

We had ended up practically screaming at each other over our macaroni cheese and then I'd stormed out in tears.

I had ended up on Jack's doorstep, and his dad had let me stay with them for a few nights.

"I wish it was." I admit. And, I do. Because whenever I've had issues at home, I've always been able to run away and hide in the sanctity of the Aconite Centre. Sometimes I didn't even care how things were at home, because I always had the club.

"Okay, so what happened?"

For a moment, I imagine what I would say to him. *'Well, Jack, for some background context, I'm actually transgender, and I know you don't support that but just bare with for the sake of the story. I got very defensive and annoyed at this guy who got on my nerves and then I called him a transphobic slur and now I'm not welcome at the one place I've always been welcome at.'*

"Just stuff."

Jack looks at me dis-trustingly. "Do you not want to talk about it? 'Cause, like, that's fine too. We can talk shit about Madeline if you want."

(Madeline, his ex-girlfriend that he's completely still in love with).

I snicker. "I think you've said all that you want about her, mate."

"Maybe, yeah." He laughs. "I just want to- you know, I've been seeing a lot of stuff online recently."

"About?"

"About like, telling me to check in on my boys. Things on Tiktok and that." He pauses as the employee puts a portion of fries in front of each of us. "And, yeah. Maybe the universe showed me them videos because it knew that you were gonna have a shit day. And I'm the hero that's gonna come and ask if you need anything."

I laugh around a mouthful of the food. "Yeah, thanks." I say, somewhat sarcastically. In actuality, I find it quite sweet.

"Apparently it's men's mental health month, too." He says.

"Oh, yeah." I acknowledge. I'm pretty sure it's currently men's mental health month in America, not here in the UK, but I won't correct him - not when he seems so passionate about it.

"But the thing is that nobody even realises it because of all this gay shit going on." He complains.

"What, Pride month?" I ask, glancing out the window at the progress flag banners that are still up around town.

"Yeah." He confirms with an annoyed look on his face. "Guys like us, normal men, we don't get shit."

And I want to tell him that the two months can very comfortably co-exist, and that more often than not it's queer and trans men that are more likely to have bad mental health. But I don't. It's weird, because when he attacks Pride month like that it makes me feel this defensiveness, despite the fact that I'm usually the one who doesn't like it.

"It's chill, dude." I say. "Gay guys aren't hurting us, just leaving more chicks up for grabs." I laugh in a jokey manner, trying to move away from the uncomfortable topic of conversation.

I suppose it's also in my legacy to defend gay guys, despite the fact that I'm not one of them, all of the ones that I know are pretty nice people. Within reason.

"Careful there. People might start thinking you're gay when

you talk of them so highly." Jack teases me, and I know he's joking. It's a weird topic for me, I guess. I've always liked girls, since as long as I can remember. So much so that I've never even really considered if I'd like a boy. I once described the feeling to Dallas and she told me that I could be bi-curious, but honestly, it all seems like too much effort.

"Oh, fuck off." I laugh back at him, and he smiles, clearly humoured.

"Speaking of girls," Jack continues. "How's Abbie?"

"She's fine, yeah." I reply easily. "She's coming to Alfie's party to help out."

"Oh, wow." Jack snickers. "Meeting the parents already, huh? When are you proposing?"

I raise my eyebrows at him unamusedly. "Shush. We're not even like, official yet. Don't start."

"And when will you be?" He asks. I think that Jack would be a great host of Love Island with the way he's so invested in my love life.

"I'm not sure. Soon, maybe." I say, and I hope so. It's just difficult because Abbie doesn't know that I'm trans. And, I don't want to tell her until we're genuinely serious about each other.

"You should ask her at Leo's on Friday."

This Friday, this guy, Leo, is having a party to commemorate the end of the school year - for us Year Elevens, at least, because after this week we're on study leave or some shit. Leo doesn't go to our school, but Abbie and her friends are friends with his girlfriend, so all of us lads have made the cut to attend.

"Yeah, maybe." I entertain. "But, um, how are you then?"

Jack looks a little caught off guard but nods. "I'm fine, yeah.

My manager is pissing me off but I guess that's what she gets paid for." He explains. "How was the park yesterday? Tobias told me you were a little spacey."

"He did?"

"Yeah. Not in a weird way, just like, 'bet he was daydreaming about all the things him and Abbie will get up to later tonight' kinda way." He laughs. It leaves a sour taste in my mouth.

"Oh. Right. Kinda weird of him to say."

Correction: It seems that all my mates could host Love Island.

"Well, you know what he's like."

"Mm,"

Tobias is definitely a character, especially when it comes to girls. He's effectively been with at least half of the girls in our year group, and we hear about it whenever we bump into any of them in public; he always has some kind of anecdote about what they were like.

I like Abbie because she's kinda above all that, and she's never had anything even mildly flirtatious with Tobias. Not that it's the only reason, but it's a lot easier to pursue a relationship without his looming commentary. We've been on a few dates, and she made it really clear to me that she wanted to do everything slowly or not at all, which I respect, and it makes things feel easier for me, too.

Despite the fact that I'm pretty sure our whole social circles think we're already together, we aren't. Not yet, because like I've said, it's not always that easy when she doesn't know I'm trans.

The possibility of losing Abbie is one of the biggest things that makes me absolutely resent my transness. It pisses me off because I have to work so hard to even have a small chance at a relationship with a girl, but I'd bet all the money in the world that someone like Everett could just date whoever he wants, because they'd know he's trans before they even start thinking of him that way.

It's just that that makes me so jealous of him. If things between me and Abbie get serious, I'll have to tell her, and then she might freak out and I have to get back to square one.

Fuck, I just wish I could have normal relationships. Without having to worry like this.

"Didn't mean to upset you. Is everything okay with Abs?" Jack asks, interrupting my train of thought and genuinely sounding worried.

"Yeah, it's all good. Sorry, just thinking." I brush his concern off.

"Okay. But, um, you'll text me, right? If you need to talk?"

My whole body aches at the way that he seems to care. It's not something you find often, especially not in friend groups like mine. Jack is definitely a conflicting person to me.

In my mind, he's (one) a good person, because he says stuff like this, and he actually follows up with it. He's always around when I need him to be, and he's nice to hang out with.

But, he's also (two) mildly homophobic and quite strongly transphobic, and also borderline misogynistic (you should've heard the way he spoke about Madeline for the first month after she broke up with him). I just wish he could be a *good person* as well as a 'good person.'

The fact that he's the best of my friends is often worrying.

I know that they're dickheads, and by association that too makes me one, but I can't help but try and look for the nice traits in them. I try my best to attribute their malice to ignorance.

Like, Jack doesn't *hate* queer people. He's just never really met one properly and was never taught compassion properly. Right.

I dislike it even more because I was perfectly content with my friends until Everett started meddling with it all. I wouldn't have thought twice about the way I acted yesterday, and even though I didn't in the moment, I suppose it's different when it's someone you actually know.

Like constantly proven, it's super easy to insult someone you've never gotten to know. It's less easy to do it to someone who you know only means well.

"Of course." I say. "And, um, you too."

Jack nods, looking down at his watch. "Shit, that's my thirty minutes. Time flies when you're having fun." He snickers, putting a fiver on the table. "I've gotta tip that waitress. Had a great view of her curves this whole meal." He whispers with a snide smile.

I blink at him a few times and then watch as he leaves. Yeah, okay. Decidedly, he's not a good person, as much as I'd like to pretend he is.

We start setting up for Alfie's party as soon as I get home from school. Dad has picked him up from his school and taken him for ice cream to stall. His friends are coming over at four, so we've gotta put a rush on setting up. Not so much of a rush that I don't get changed out of my uniform first, and Abbie (who has come to help because, in her words, it 'sounds like a fun time') went home to change first, too.

My mum was delighted to hear she'd get another 'big kid' helper for the party (you can never have too many of those when rampaged by eight-year-olds), and even offered to pay Abbie for her trouble. I'd let her know and she'd smiled and said that she was just happy to get to spend time with me. It was a really great feeling.

"I'll get it!" I yell, hopping down the stairs three at a time when the doorbell rings. "Hey." I greet her once the door is open.

"Hi." Abbie grins. She opens her arms and pulls me in for a hug right on my doorstep.

I'm not going to use the word 'butterflies' to describe the feeling it gives me, because that's childish and stupid, but it's something akin to that.

"Thanks for coming to help. They'll be a handful." I chuckle as well pull away.

"Yeah, of course! I'm mainly just excited to meet your brother, honestly. And besides, I love little kids, they're so pint-sized and cute."

(Abbie wants to be a primary school teacher, if it wasn't glaringly obvious).

"You won't be saying that when thirty kids an hour ask you to tie their shoe laces." I chastise as she comes in and I close the door behind her. She giggles.

"You look really nice." I say, and it comes out way too awkwardly. "By the way."

And she really does. It's been super hot outside recently, so she wears a white summer dress with little red roses dotted all along it, the exact same colour as her high-topped converse. The dress has a v-shaped neckline and short sleeves, and she pairs it with a golden necklace that totally clashes with her silver-framed, rounded-rectangle glasses, but the glasses also match with a Pandora bracelet on her wrist.

"Thanks, yeah. You too."

I can't help but smile, because I know I don't look that nice. I look the same as I always do, wearing some black cargo pants and a cobalt blue t-shirt.

"Alright, don't push it." I laugh as I guide her through the house.

We're about to get to the very difficult bit of the day.

Challenge: Don't let my parents out me to Abbie.

It's putting me on severe high alert, just having her in proximity of my parents. But, like she had also said, it's worth it to spend time with the girl I like.

We make our way through the living room and find the patio doors. Outside, dad is trying his best to blow up a bouncy castle with sheer determination and willpower. Mum is scrutinising over the buffet table.

"Oh! Hello!" She calls, grinning broadly as she marches over to us.

"Mum, this is Abbie." I explain.

"Nice to meet you, Mrs Lysander."

"Oh, please. Jennie is fine. We'll want to be well acquainted so you can shout my name when the kids come running towards you."

Abbie giggles with a distinct level of graciousness that's always been typical of her when around adults.

"Um, what needs doing?" I ask, looking around at the preparations.

"You could help bring the food out from the kitchen for one." She suggests. So, we bring the food out, filling a few folding-tables with various beige coloured things that kids like.

At about five to four, they start pouring in. Alfie comes first. He practically throws himself into my arms with a delighted squeal. "Kylo!" He yells, and I hoist him up into my arms.

"Oh my god, is that Alfie?" I tease, pulling him away to do a dramatic once-over. "Can't be. My brother is way too little to be this *old* guy in front of me."

He giggles and gets quite visibly excited. "Yep, it's still me."

"No!" I cry out. "Who is this big kid and what has he done with Alfie?"

"I'm Alfie, stupid." He chastises and I put him down.

"Happy birthday, teddy bear." I finally say affectionately, bending down and kissing him on his forehead.

He turns to where Abbie watched the whole interaction. "Who's she?" He makes an attempt to whisper, but it really doesn't do much considering how close she's standing.

"That's Abbie."

"Oh. *Oh.*" Alfie repeats himself. He glances between me and her. "Do you have a crush on her?"

I blink a few times as I feel my face heat up. Damn, sussed out by an eight-year-old. Probably because he has such a child-like view of the world, where boys and girls can't be friends without liking each other. It's annoying because he's right just this once.

"Maybe a little bit, but it's a secret so you can't tell her." I say, making direct eye contact with Abbie whilst she raises her eyebrows and smiles endearingly.

"Okay. I won't tell her." He snickers.

"Alright. Now go collect your presents from your friends." I say, shooing him off in the direction of where others are coming in the garden gate. Alfie giggles and runs off.

"He's sweet." Abbie says, closing the gap between us.

"Yeah."

It's about an hour later when the party gets in full-swing. I've managed to keep Abbie and I away from my parents, which has made me able to evade the chance of getting outed quite well.

Or, that is until Alfie runs past, clearly pretending to drive the Lego train I'd bought him.

"I want a go!" One of his friends yells. "I want a train."

My dad smiles as he takes photos before speaking. "Alfie's sister got it for him. You could always ask her where it's from." He suggests. My heart practically drops into my stomach at his words.

"I didn't know you had a sister." Abbie says curiously, leaning against the garden fence with a cup of blackcurrant squash in her hand. It's fine, it wasn't an accusation or an assumption, and I've been bluffing my way out of parent-induced situations like this for as long as I can remember.

"Yeah. She's at uni."

"Oh, cool. My brother's at uni too. Computer Science."

"Sounds boring." I say teasingly.

"You're telling me. I've spent the last three years being the test subject for all his coding and whatever it is."

"Kylen, Kylen, Kylen!" Alfie chants as he suddenly runs over towards us.

"Alfie, Alfie, Alfie!" I repeat back with the same enthusiasm.

"Can you come bounce in the bouncy-castle? Your girly-friend can come too." He suggests, and then he starts to walk away, clearly anticipating us to follow.

94

"Shall we?" I ask, striding forward and turning around with my hand extended towards her.

"We shall." She giggles, taking my hand and letting me guide her towards the bouncy castle.

It's when the 'Pass the Parcel' starts that Abbie and I find ourselves with pretty much nothing to do in terms of helping out. The kids are all occupied, and my parents are doing a fine job running the games without our help.

Abbie squeezes my hand and turns back towards the house. "Do you wanna, like, go to your room?" She asks.

Fuck. Go to my room? That usually means something romantic and or sexual, right? But, I haven't even kissed Abbie yet and she's not the kind of person that would jump right into things like that. Go to my room. She might just mean so that we can chill in some peace and quiet, away from the kids.

"Okay, yeah." I agree. I guide her up the stairs and into my bedroom, immediately finding myself embarrassed about how messy it is.

"You're coming to Leo's tomorrow, right?" She asks, sitting down on my bed.

"Yeah."

"Pick me up at seven."

"Will do."

We flick some shitty Netflix show on and end up just laying down on my bed. Abbie drapes herself on top of me and rests her head on my chest, my right arm wrapped around her waist in a way that produces a certain level of sexual tension.

It's short and sweet when she finally tilts her head towards mine and closes the gap between us.

She slides her body upwards, maintaining delicate eye contact with me for a couple of seconds, and suddenly we're kissing. It's definitely been a long time coming. I bring my hand up to her chin and guide her in her movement as she practically pushes me against my headboard, sitting gracefully on her knees in between my legs.

She pulls away after a moment with a glassy look in her eyes.

"Fuck," She says, breathing out. "You have no idea how long I've waited to get to kiss you like that."

Oh. Fuck. "You can do it again if you want." I say breathlessly in my best attempt to play 'hard to get.'

"You're so stupid." She says lightly, moving herself to be more so straddling my lap as she kisses me again. I put more effort into it this time, sitting up properly and pulling her by her waist so that our hips touch. It feels like our bodies slot together perfectly.

It feels so good to finally get to have her like this, when we've been flirting for so long.

When we finish our kiss, she looks down at me and grins. The show on my TV continues playing in vain.

"Kylen." She says, hand going to my shoulder.

"Yeah?"

"We should date." Abbie lets me know, and then pauses to laugh. "Soon. Not now, we need to-" She cuts herself off, leaning down again to pull me into another kiss. "To get to know each other better. Do you wanna go on a few dates? Get dinner or something?"

I knew the question was coming, but it still catches me off

guard.

It's difficult. Because I want to be her boyfriend more than anything I've ever wanted before.

But if I'm her boyfriend, and if she's my girlfriend, I'm gonna have to tell her I'm trans.

She'll expect things from me or similar sooner or later. Things I can't give her. And I'd rather not have to have that conversation in the heat of any moment.

Abbie is the kindest girl I've ever met. I can't imagine a world where she would get really angry and storm off. But still, we've never spoken about anything to do with transness – we haven't had to.

I want to tell her. It feels wrong to not tell her, but when I go to, the words die on my lips.

"Earth to Kylen?" She teases, pecking a kiss onto my forehead. "Do you wanna take me out? Let me know in one to two business days, 'cause if you will I need to start soft launching you on my Instagram."

I smile endearingly. "Don't think you can soft launch someone that the whole year group already thinks you've been dating for months."

"Is that a yes?" She giggles, hooking a hand around my neck and looking up at me expectantly. I lean down to kiss her again.

"Yes, please."

7

Everett

I wish I could say that things have been as eventful the past few days as they were last week.

Last week, I got into a scandal that everyone at the Aconite Centre has been whispering about non-stop since, that also lead to the guy who's been going to the club the longest being kicked out.

This week, the most exciting thing I've done was upgrade my house on *Animal Crossing*.

Which is why I'm looking forward to going to the club so much. So much so, that I decide to walk down and leave my house with plenty of time to swing by the corner shop and grab myself a chocolate bar to eat beforehand.

Everything that happened with Kylen had been sending my head into a whirl of thoughts, but since Kylen stormed out of the club in tears on Sunday, nothing else has gone on. I haven't heard from him - not that I particularly expected to, but you know.

At the club, we end up having a 'bake off' using the kitchen that extends out of Hall B. The theme is that you pair up with someone and make some cupcakes to decorate with icing that creates your pride flag(s).

There's a lot more of us in attendance because it's a regular club session, and I end up pairing off with Eli as we rush to spread some icing on our cupcakes since we decided to leave them to cool for way too long.

"Hey, um," He says, leaning against the counter whilst mixing the food colouring into his icing. "I don't know if it's your scene, but there's a little thing going on this Friday, tomorrow."

"A little thing?" I ask, a little unclear on the context of this situation.

"It's a party, is what it is. To celebrate school being over, hallelujah." Eli clarifies. "My mate was gonna come with me, but he's got the flu and doesn't think he'll make a recovery." He explains, picking up his piping bag of icing.

"Oh, so am I your back up plus-one?" I ask, feigning shock, but actually, I'm quite excited. Being invited to do something one-on-one is the first stage of a genuine friendship forming. Well, I suppose a party isn't really one-on-one, but he could have asked anyone from the club to come to this party with him.

"Fuck, I did the purple at the top." He says, cursing the way he messed up his depiction of the gay male flag. "But, yeah."

I roll my eyes at him and spin the tray so that the purple is at the bottom. "Who's party is this?"

"Oh." He says, and I laugh at the look on his face. "It's this kid from my school, Leo."

"And how do you know him?" It's like I'm doing some kind of background check, despite the fact that I'll likely go either way.

99

"We're kind of in the same friend group. It's weird, I don't really speak to him much, but his girlfriend is my friend."

"And he's okay with that?"

"Psh, yeah. She calls herself my 'fag-hag', likes the 'gay best friend' aesthetic, despite the fact that I'm in no way her best friend. I like some of her other friends more." He says, which leaves a bit of a grimace on my face.

"Well, I suppose if it's got you invited to his party."

"Yeah."

"Wait, what do you even mean '*end of school party?*' I swear to god you're in sixth form. Your school year doesn't end until, like, July."

Eli smirks at me as a little burst of laughter slips from him. "Yeah. But, Leo's in Year Eleven. And I go to the sixth form that's attached to my school, so loads of my Year Twelve friends are also mates with the Year Elevens." Eli explains.

"Right, okay. So, you're mooching off *our* celebration?" I tease.

"Pretty much." He agrees smoothly.

When he's done doing all of the purple icing he hands me the piping bag so that I can start doing the middle stripe of my bisexual flag cupcakes.

"You'll come, then?" He says.

"Sure, sure I'll come."

"Cool. Might wanna bring your own shit, just because I'm not even sure if I trust those boys to mix drinks properly."

I snicker a little. "Alright. What time?"

"Um, starts at half seven but we wanna be fashionably late. Text me your address and I'll swing by when it starts. We can walk if it isn't too far. See look, perfect." He states, stepping away from his tray of cupcakes. They are *not* perfect by any means, but Thalia comes over and thinks it's funny that the icing kind of melted together.

"Right." Mum says, sitting down on the sofa. She eyes me awkwardly. "Be safe. Don't drink anything more than four-percent, I mean it."

"Mhm," I hum, slouching back on the sofa as I receive the lecture. She's bought be a case of cider under the pretence that 'I was young once, too, Everett.' Clearly not young enough, though, because I know for a fact she was much more wild at sixteen.

"Text me when you get there. And be home before midnight, 'cause I have work tomorrow and I won't sleep until I know you're home safe. And I shouldn't have to say this, but don't be reckless. Don't get in a car if the person driving is drunk, and if it gets to it, remember to use protection."

"Ew."

"Needs to be said."

"No, it doesn't."

"Ach, I know what teenagers are like. I was-"

"*Young once too!*" I finish for her, making little jazz hands as I lean forward with a tone of voice that mocks her.

"Just use your common sense. That's my advice, I'm done now." She states finally, hands in the air as if I've accused her of something as she walks into the kitchen. I roll my eyes playfully and stand up off the sofa, using the long mirror in the living room to double-check my outfit.

About two hours ago, I made Eli send me a picture of what he's wearing so that I don't accidentally over or underdress.

He said that he's just wearing a black shirt and blue jeans.

I personally consider myself a little more adventurous, so I choose to wear a light grey t-shirt and black jeans, but I stick a sage green hoodie over the top. It's the same colour as the selected Converse of the day.

I finish clasping my necklace together just in time for my phone to buzz.

eli!!

im outside

omw

"Bye!" I yell, slinging my backpack over my shoulder and treading down the hall. The cans of cider clink together as I walk.

"Have fun, love you!" Mum calls out. I pull the door open and turn around to reply.

"Love you too."

I don't want to keep Eli waiting for too long, so I make quick work of trampling down our building's staircase. When I get to the lobby area, I see that there's some new posters on the noticeboard, and I almost go to look until I see Eli lingering in the car park and feel a little bad.

Once I've left the building (and am careful to shut the door behind me properly), Eli and I drift into a lull of conversation as he leads the way down the road towards the house we're going to.

It feels weird to be attending a party at the house of someone I'd never even heard of, but Eli assures me that there's gonna be so many people there that nobody will even question it.

The moment we get in proximity, it's unbelievably clear to me which house we're heading towards. I'll be surprised if the police don't show up at all tonight, because the music blares from at least ten houses down. And, besides, I feel great. School's over, and as long as nobody mentions exams, everything's awesome.

"You'll do great, don't even worry." Eli assures me, stopping on the pavement to unzip his backpack. I watch as he pulls out a half-bottle of vodka. "Hold this," he says, handing me the lid.

"Thought you were meant to drink when you get inside the building." I say sarcastically. He shakes his head and tips his head back to take a quick swig of the alcohol, straight. He hisses as it burns down his throat. It's impressive.

"Confidence." Eli replies, taking the lid back from me. "Did you want any?"

"Not before I decide whether or not it's safe in there." I laugh, making a slightly comical comment out of the fact that I'm a little scared. Visibly trans and going into a party full of boys that are probably just like Kylen and his friends.

We reach the front of the house, where there are some steps up, and see that the door is wide open.

"They're harmless really. They'll act all tough, but I promise you they aren't." Eli says, starting to make his way up the steps as I follow him like a lost puppy.

The music is even louder inside.

Teenagers mill around everywhere, most holding drinks and chatting. There's a main corridor that's easy to navigate. All of the lights in the house are off, but of course LEDs and lamps are on for the atmosphere.

"We gotta go see Leo first, hold on." Eli says, but as we move down the corridor he's quickly ambushed by a girl with dyed red hair and crystal blue eyes wearing a body-con pink dress.

"Elliot Turner!" She screams, practically jumping into his arms.

"Hi, Shea." He greets on a laugh.

"You're late." She says, grinning. "Madeline brought another gay boy over, was thinkin' you could get together with him. He's fit."

"Wow!" Eli exclaims over the blaring of the music. "You're pretty drunk."

"Hey, 's not the drink, you deserve to get laid, man. Live a little! School's over for the year." She says, hitting him on the arm as she slurs her next words. "Jus' check it out. Say hi and then invite me to the wedding."

"Shea, just because we're both gay-" He began, but Shea was gone, run off into another room.

"Was that your 'fag-hag?'" I ask, catching up to him and snickering.

"She means well." He dismisses, and then he leads me out of the corridor and into the largest room of all.

It's an open-plan living room, kitchen and dining room with white walls and a kitchen island in the left corner. It's clearly where the main event is going on.

"Alright." Eli says, surveying the room. "Dickheads at two-o-clock. Most of their girlfriends at twelve."

Firstly, my eyes wander to the 'dickheads.' My heart nearly stops at the sight of the two boys that dragged Kylen away from us on Saturday, standing cockily with their drinks. They're with a few other boys too, and most notably, *Kylen himself.*

Despite everything, he looks okay. Much better than he did on Sunday when he was in such a state. Tonight, he looks much more alive - white shirt with a blue 'Adidas' logo and light coloured jeans that are far too baggy. He laughs at the words of one of his friends.

"Sorry." Eli apologises. "Didn't know he was gonna be here. I mean, I could've guessed that the assholes he calls his mates would be here, but honestly I assumed he wouldn't show face."

I nod a few times absent-mindedly. He has much more of a right to be here than I do. Seeing the big group of boys makes a pit form in my stomach, mainly dread and upset. If there's one thing that manages to always get to me, it's seeing groups of boys just be boys. Just talk and kick footballs about and all that stereotypical shit. It upsets me because it's the one thing that I've always missed out on. I dismiss the thought quickly and move on to look at the next part of the room.

The group of girls to their left outnumber the boys quite massively, so I find it hard to believe the notion that they're 'most of their girlfriends.' They all seem equally as engrossed in the party and laughing as they chatter about and take selfies that will undoubtedly end up on Instagram. The two groups mingle in the middle.

Kylen takes a sip of his drink and then his eyes drift over to Eli and I. He looks away faster than I can fathom it, falling back into the conversation with his friends. It irritates me just how easily we get dismissed in his mind.

"It's chill." I tell Eli. "Won't be an issue after you share that vodka with me."

❀

The night moves on fast after the first few drinks. I talk to quite a few people, none of whom I can remember their names. There's one point where I get approached by a guy with dark hair that flows down to his jawline. He's much taller than me, and has a long-sleeved mesh shirt with many necklaces all layered together. He stands with his hands on his hips, leaning on one leg as he talks.

I'm really not one to stereotype, but I would bet at least a hundred quid that this is probably the guy that Shea was pushing Eli towards.

"Don't even know why I'm here, to be fair." He says. "Place is full of road-men, really not my scene."

"Why'd you come, then?"

"Dunno. Thought maybe I'd meet someone or something. It's good to socialise."

The music hazes my mind as this boy, whose name I don't even know, speaks to me. My thoughts flashback to the girl- the girl with the pink dress from earlier.

"Have you met Eli?" I ask, realising that I'm totally playing into stereotypes, but whatever.

The boy laughs. "That twink? Not my type." My expression sours as it feels like this boy is making fun of my friend. "*You* could be."

Is he flirting with me? In the blur of thoughts racing around my head, I know it's wrong, but it makes me swell with pride.

He's gay. He's a gay guy, and he's flirting with me. It's the most euphoric experience I've had in a while.

From across the house, I hear a horrifically loud bang. It's clearly a door slamming of some kind.

"Drama. Come along." The boy gasps, grabbing my hand and tugging me in the direction of the door slam.

He pulls me out into the corridor. Others are flocking in the direction too, and I spill pretty much half of my drink on the floor as we make our way into the main room.

There's a crowd forming around something going on in the centre of the room.

"No, fuck you!" A girl yells. She wears glasses and has light brown hair that falls nicely down to her elbows. The boy I'm with drags me to the front of the crowd with no shame and I get a full look on what's going on.

Oh. *Oh, this will be good.*

"Abbie." Kylen pleads, shutting a door that's on the side of the room behind him.

"No, you're a little bitch." She accuses, clearly fuelled by high amounts of alcohol in her system. Kylen doesn't seem much better off as he walks up to follow her quickly, stumbling in his wake.

"Abs, don't do this."

"I bet you get off on this, huh?"

"On what?" Kylen asks, eyes desperate as if he's willing her to stop talking.

"On this!" She yells. "You- you, fuck- talking to girls for ages, making them like you. Making me think you're gonna sleep with me- and then you won't!"

All of Kylen's friends in one area of the room release a set of 'oohs' and he death-glares them.

I'm a little confused about the context of the situation, but from what I can pick up, this girl, Abbie, is Kylen's girlfriend? Or, they've at least been flirting. Something tells me they won't be after tonight. I feel a spike of jealousy that he gets to be in a relationship when anything like that feels a million times harder for me as a trans person.

"You don't mean this, Abs, you're drunk." He tells her, but his words are slurred in a way that completely ruins his point.

"Sober enough to know you've been leading me on. You're all over me like I'm the best thing in the word, but you're yet to show me that you actually mean it." She raises her voice, spinning around to face him angrily. "Bitch-ass little boy."

A few people snicker and I'm not really ashamed to say that I'm one of them. The boy that I came in with laughs heartily.

"God, I love it when straight people fight." He muses, sipping his drink.

Kylen looks around anxiously at the large crowd. "It's not like that. You know it's not." He pleads. Abbie doesn't look convinced; she crosses her arms.

"Stop it! If you didn't wanna be with me you could have said that. But you had to make me feel like you want *things* when you don't."

"That's what this is about? Sex?"

"It's more than sex, Kylen! It's that you clearly don't love me enough."

As everyone listening screams out of excitement and shock, I suddenly feel a lot worse for him. I'm not really a detective, but from my perspective, it's pretty clear that she doesn't know he's trans. He won't sleep with her because she doesn't know, and she thinks it's because he doesn't like her enough.

It's a complicated issue, but it makes me feel horrible for Kylen because it's not his fault. He steps back as if he's been pushed, eyes raking over Abbie's face for any sign of clarity that he can get from her, but the defeated look that he hones tells me that he finds none in her drunken state.

"Abbie, come on-" He tries, taking her hand. She takes a few seconds to glance down at where they've connected before stepping away with a shake of her head.

"No! Am I not good enough for you?" Abbie asks, tears pooling in her eyes as she looks up at him. Kylen's face softens as he tries to get through to her.

"Of course you are."

"Then why won't you prove it? We've liked each other for months, just man the fuck up. Or, if you don't have the decency to show me that you like me, at least have the guts to ask me out."

"You're drunk, and you know I love you. It's not that."

"Oh, right! What, then?"

"You don't understand- you can't-" Kylen breaks his gaze from Abbie and looks right over at me for a split second. "You can't understand."

"I understand perfectly fine!"

"No, you don't."

Abbie looks around at the crowd as if thinking. A lot of people are filming.

"Just so you can remember what you've just lost." She says with annoyance and then Abbie reaches forward and grabs Kylen's shirt collar, pulling his upper body downwards and pressing her lips against his in an obviously drunk kiss. Before Kylen even has time to react to it, she shoves him away and slaps him right across the face.

His body jerks with the force of it, and the whole crowd of drunk teenagers basically screams in exhilaration at the scene.

Kylen is totally stunned into silence, but it appears that his maybe-girlfriend is not.

"We're fucking done, bitch-boy." She spits, tears flowing freely down her face. Her voice is laced with her sobs, but she doesn't act like she's at all upset as she quickly throws her drink all over him. It was pretty much a full cup of fruit-flavoured whatever, and she threw it right at his chest so that it splashes around and gets on his jeans and face, too.

And within five seconds, Abbie is gone - having pushed through the crowd and left the house. Kylen is left standing in the centre of the room with pretty much the whole party watching on, a little stunned and clearly close to tears.

There's a silence in the room for what feels like forever until another boy, obviously one of Kylen's mates - one who was there at the Pride event on Saturday - steps out and slings an arm around his shoulder.

"She's not worth it, eh, bitch-boy?"

Kylen blinks a few times. "Don't let that stick."

"Too late. She's clearly crazy, you dodged a bullet." He chuckles, absent-mindedly handing Kylen a glass bottle of straight vodka. "Forget about her."

I watch, a little worried as he nods and takes a large swig from the bottle and gets pulled back into the crowd with his mates.

The music is turned up and everyone forgets about the incident as soon as it happened.

The night carries on, and with each new song that plays on the cheap speakers, and with each refil of my clear plastic cup, I'm having more and more fun. I haven't got the faintest of ideas where Eli is, but I'm just wandering around the house and enjoying myself.

That's my favourite thing about drunk people. Everyone is always a million times kinder when they're drunk. In most cases.

Nobody has been a dick to me tonight, about anything. For a moment, whilst the lights are low and the music is deafening, I feel like a cis boy with nothing to worry about other than whether or not my team will win the Premier League.

I'm on my own, and have been since the boy from earlier got mixed back up in the crowd, and so I stumble up the stairs towards where I'm hoping I'll find a bathroom.

At the top of the stairs, one of the doors is ajar and I can see some tiles that indicate *bathroom*. The lights are off, and I push the door open then tug on the chord that turns the light on.

Whilst I expected the bathroom to be completely empty, I quickly see that it isn't.

I curse myself for getting involved when the boy sitting on the floor with his back against the bath looks up at me with tears streaming down his face.

"Fuck, hi." Kylen says, voice wavering, and I can't tell if it's the sadness or the alcohol. Probably the latter, because he has a half-empty bottle of beer in his right hand. He wipes his face with the back of his hand. I don't know how long he's been here, but it's been about two hours since the scene with his girlfriend. Or, ex-girlfriend.

"Thought you weren't a crier."

"Piss off." He whines, trying to stand by leaning against the bath, but he struggles tremendously and then just resigns to dropping back onto the floor. His breath smells like too much booze. His clothes aren't soggy any more, but there's a

111

clear stain on his white shirt that's pretty sticky.

Considering how vulnerable and *alone* Kylen looks, mixed with the fact that there's something very sobering about stepping into a bathroom during a party, I feel like it's now my responsibility to deal with him.

The music is ten times quieter, and it feels like an isolated world away from the rest of the commotion.

"Is this about.. The girl? Abbie?"

Kylen drops his head back into his arms and continues to cry. I watch, feeling a little awkward until he looks up. "She doesn't understand and I can't tell her." He sniffles, taking a swig of the drink.

"Alright, alright." I say, moving over and taking the bottle out of his hand. He chases it but gives up when I set it on the counter out of his reach. I then turn and shut the bathroom door.

"Next time you wanna come and cry in the dark, you should lock the door. Would've been pretty emasculating if literally anybody else had come in here." I say, slightly snarkily.

Kylen frowns and wipes his eyes. "Oh, god. You're mad at me, aren't you?" He wails. "Everyone's mad at me, it sucks."

I can imagine that his drunken state is probably making everything seem like much more of a big deal than it really is.

"Maybe you should be less of a dick then." I say, probably due to the buzz that the alcohol has given me. He gazes up at me and blinks a few times, and then he continues to cry in earnest.

"You have no idea how hard my life is." He speaks, sloshing his words together. "I've lost everything."

I push his words away. He's not coherent enough to be thinking properly, so there's no point in trying to rationalise his statements - especially considering that he likely won't remember this tomorrow.

"I think you should be getting home, dude." I'm a little concerned as to how he's gonna get to his house safely like this.

"I'm staying over at Tobias' place, can't leave 'til he does."

"Who's Tobias?"

"My friend."

I roll my eyes and step away from him a little. It certainly feels like my responsibility at this point. "Stay here." I command, unlocking the door and leaving Kylen alone in the bathroom. I head down the stairs and start walking around in search of this elusive 'Tobias.'

"Everett!" A voice calls, and I recognise it as Eli's. My head spins in his direction and I recognise that he's with the boy that was mildly flirting with me earlier. You know, the *'That twink? Not my type'* guy.

"This was so fun, I'm goin'- goin' home, I'll see you at the club, yeah?"

Eli clings to his arm and the boy has the other arm around his waist protectively. The boy chuckles drunkenly, and much more sober than before I found Kylen all upset, I worry for a moment that Eli will regret this - especially after the way that the boy seemed to be like earlier.

"Are you sure you wanna go home with him, Eli?"

"Yeah, yeah." He slurs. "It's a problem for tomorrow morning, not right now."

I very strongly contemplate not letting him leave, but I decide I will. He's older than me, he's responsible. I have bigger things to worry about.

"Have you seen a 'Tobias' around?" I ask both of them as

they stumble towards the door.

The boy shakes his head. "Nah, but, he's the lad that pushed all those drinks onto the boy that got broken up with."

Okay, that definitely puts a face to the name, if Tobias was the boy that first approached Kylen after his public fight with Abbie. One of the boys from Saturday.

"He is, yeah." Eli confirms. "Ask all those boys wearing the trackies. He'll be around."

I don't even get time to thank them for their input before the boy leads Eli down the steps of the house and into the distance.

I shake off the interaction and turn around, beelining down the hallway to the main room.

The fact that I'm pretty drunk gives me a lot of confidence when I'm approaching the boys. None are the one that I recognise as the one speaking to Kylen earlier.

"Hey. Hey!" I call out at them. "Have you guys seen Tobias?"

They all tell me no.

"Nah, he went home with a bird like an hour ago."

"Seriously?"

"Yeah."

I look around at them all, exasperated. "Your mate Kylen is upstairs, he's pretty upset about that fight. Maybe one of you could take him home." I suggest. They look at me all confused for a good few moments.

"He's a great guy, but I'm not his babysitter." One of the boys says, and the others laugh.

"Yeah, he's a big boy, he can handle himself."

Fuck. What shitheads. Their friend is going through it and they'd rather be downstairs drinking?

I turn around without another word and head back upstairs. This time, I can hear Kylen crying before I even get into the bathroom.

"Everett." He whines. "I thought you weren't coming back."

"Sorry. Look, um, Tobias went home earlier." I say, and he looks at me desperately.

"I can't go home." He says. "My parents will kill me if they knew I'm this drunk. They'll hang me out to dry on the washing line."

Oh, speaking of parents, I look down at my phone as I remember that I do have a curfew.

It's already eleven-thirty. I need to leave, but I can't have it on my conscience if I leave Kylen sitting on the floor of this bathroom crying his eyes out and clearly completely unaware of his surroundings.

He's gonna have to come home with me, I realize. Anything could happen if I leave him here.

"Alright, up we go." I say, hooking my arms under his and attempting to pull him up. He stands on his feet for a few moments before his legs practically collapse underneath him.

"Sorry." He slurs, clearly his head is spinning and he's not really aware of what's going on.

"That's okay. Let's try again."

It takes us about twenty-five minutes to get home. I know it was unsafe of me to drag him home when he's clearly drunk out of his mind, and I'm visibly quite small and unable to defend myself.

But it's fine, and we make it home fine. I unlock the front door to our building and decide that there is no way I'm braving the stairs with Kylen. Never before have I been so grateful for the elevator.

"Where are we going?" Kylen asks when we get out on our flat's floor.

"To my house, don't worry."

"Oh, Everett, you shouldn't have to have taken me home, I'm sorry." He apologises, but it doesn't make it to my ears because I know that either way he won't remember this. When we get to the door, I ring the doorbell because I can't be bothered to trawl through my pockets for my keys, and I know that Mum is still awake. She opens the door in about twenty seconds, wearing her pyjamas.

When she sees that I'm not alone, her jaw drops.

"Oh, hello."

"Hi, Mum."

"Hi, Miss Everett's mum." Kylen grins, and then he lowers his voice to a whisper. "You didn't tell me your mum was fit."

Mum raises her eyebrows. "Who's this?" She asks, hands on her hips and voice a lot sterner.

"Um, this is Kylen. Remember?" I feel slightly nervous now that he has not made a good first impression, meaning that Mum is a lot less likely to approve him staying over.

"Have you told her about me?" Kylen asks, sounding worried. "I bet you were mean about me to your mum, weren't you?"

Mum takes a step backwards and crosses her arms. "Rhett, I know I said I was okay with you doing things now that you're sixteen, but, um, I didn't mean you could just start bringing boys home from parties."

116

I scrunch my nose up and Kylen laughs obnoxiously. His drunken mood is flipping like a gymnast. "Ew, oh my god, no." I say, grabbing his arm as Kylen starts to wander off down the corridor. He pulls me back a few steps but I get his attention to the door again. "It's not like that, like at all. Um, he's just really drunk and he can't go to his house and I couldn't in good conscience leave him at the party like this."

"Oh." Mum says. "Okay. That's good of you." She steps aside and lets me in, then she pulls me in for a hug. I can tell that she was probably anxious about me being out and drinking. "Where's he gonna sleep?"

"Bedroom floor probably." I suggest, and then I realize that I need to get Kylen to bed before he falls asleep standing up. "I should take him there. Night, love you."

"Be safe." She says softly, pressing a kiss to my temple.

I drag him into my bedroom and let him sit on the edge of the bed, swaying softly.

"I feel sick." He says.

"Oh, don't you dare throw up on my rug."

"It's a nice rug."

"Mhm."

From then, he watches in silence as I fumble around. "Do you want to borrow some clothes to sleep in?" I ask. "Just 'cause yours are covered in that sticky drink that Abbie threw on you."

"Um, okay. Yeah."

I find one of my oversized t-shirts that would fit him and also a pair of joggers that I never wear because the legs are too long. Then, I throw them at him.

I grab my own pyjamas and leave the room to go and change in the bathroom whilst he changes in my room, sincerely

117

hoping that he can put the clothes on without managing to get himself into too much trouble.

When we've both changed, I head back into my room and pick his old clothes up off the floor.

I look over at him and he still looks really uncomfortable.

"You okay?"

"Yeah, just my binder's all fucked up, like, with the drink. Can't take it off though, 'cause I gotta sleep in it so I wake up flat and don't hate myself." He says, dropping down onto my bed.

I grimace at his words. "Do you- do you sleep in it every night?"

He nods absent-mindedly. "Unless it really hurts before bed. Sometimes- um- well, I have tape, too. But it's so fuck'n tedious to like cut it into the strips and-" He trails off into my pillow as he drops his head to the bed.

I try my best to think of something to help him, but he's drunk already and it would be worse to upset him more.

"Well, um, it's all sticky. So, obviously do what you want but I would take it off." I suggest.

He hums and then nods. "Yeah, sure."

I nod and take my clothes towards the laundry basket, back in the living room.

When I get back to my room, Kylen is lying face down on my bed, mumbling to himself in his haze. On the floor, he's left his binder on top of the rest of his clothes.

I don't have the most awareness about my person right now, but I have the common sense to put all of his clothes in the washing machine successfully, too.

When I've made my way back to my bedroom, a little giddy on my feet still, I see that Kylen has now totally conked out on my bed. It's not so good that I've surrendered my sleeping space to him, because I'm still drunk, but not drunk enough to pass out on the floor.

I just sigh and decide I need to just sleep. It's been a long day, and at this point, the sofa is calling my name.

8

Kylen

When I wake up, my head hurts like nothing ever before.

Fuck, I need to stop drinking so much.

Hold on, where the fuck am I?

I know it's not my bed, because my bed is *not* this comfortable. There's a window right to the left of the bed with sunlight streaming in, and I guess that's what woke me.

It's an awfully saturated bedroom. The wall behind the bed is a mid-green, and there's a light blue rug on the floor, the same tone as the bedsheets that I'm lying atop of.

There's an array of posters all on the wall that the bed faces, as well as a large full-body mirror.

Other than the pounding of my head, I notice that my chest feels *a lot* lighter. I'm mostly just confused when I realise I'm not wearing my binder, because I almost *always* go to sleep with my binder on, or if not, then with tape.

But I'm not even in my own house and I suddenly feel really vulnerable. I'm not even wearing my own clothes.

The feeling is washed away as I get a horrible surge of nausea, and before I know it, I'm on my feet and leaving the room to find somewhere, preferably a bathroom, before I throw up on whoever's carpet this is.

I don't think about how clean the hallway is because I'm so desperately glad to see a bathroom. The nausea rises in my throat until pretty much everything that I ate yesterday is hurled up into the toilet.

The taste of stomach acid and alcohol burns in my throat. I don't know how long I'm throwing up for until I'm just left on my knees in front of the toilet, coughing. When I'm pretty sure that I'm done, I pull the lid down and flush it, dropping into a seated position as the bathroom door opens slowly.

"Good morning, sunshine." Everett says, voice rough from just having woken up.

Oh, for fuck's sake.

It had to be him, didn't it? Out of all people, it was always gonna be him. The universe could've given me a little bit of mercy and let it at least have been one of my mates whose house I woke up in.

He glares down at me on the floor with the smuggest, shit-eating grin I've ever seen.

"Shitting Christ." I mutter. "You dragged me home with you?"

Everett raises his eyebrows. "Gee, Everett, I'm awfully thankful that you let me come home with you and sleep in your bed, meaning that you had to sleep on the sofa, all because I got broken up with and decided to drink way more than my body could handle and then my shithead friends left me to cry in a bathroom." He says, clearly quite irritated with me.

But, I'm not focusing on his mood. His words bring back a flood of memories from last night.

Abbie. Fuck, I need to call her.

My blood runs cold and he seems to notice it.

Sighing, Everett shuts the bathroom door and sits down cross-legged on the floor in front of me. He looks different today, somehow more human. His hair is rustled from sleep, wearing a black t-shirt and blue, plaid pyjama bottoms as he hunches his body over slightly, probably out of dysphoria.

I feel even more sick to my stomach when the presence of another person looking at me kickstarts my own anxiety.

It's been at least two years since I've been in front of anyone other than my parents whilst not binding. I know that out of all people, Everett is probably the last that would judge me. But, despite that, all of a sudden I'm thirteen again, sitting on the sofa at home as my mum makes me watch her cutting my binder that she'd found up with fabric scissors.

My dysphoria hits me like a truck, and all of the walls I've been hiding behind crumble.

Within two seconds, I'm on my feet and yanking the bathroom door open.

"Ow!" Everett exclaims as the door hits him. "I thought we could have a conversation."

The bedroom door is right next to the bathroom. The obnoxious blues and greens of Everett's room are ten times brighter as I start frantically searching through his clothes on the floor, but I can't find mine.

"Um, you okay?" He asks, hovering in the doorway.

"Where's my binder?" I snap at him, not really meaning the aggression.

He seems to fumble for a second, looking a little guilty.

"Um, I washed it. So it's like, still wet." He admits. What the fuck? What a prick. He, fuck, fuck. I catch a glimpse of myself in the full-body mirror and I don't see myself.

I see a girl, a scared little girl.

"It was covered in that drink that Abbie threw on you."

I see that my shoulders are too narrow. A boy's would be way wider.

"Hey, it's fine. It'll be dry soon."

My arms are too skinny. I should work out more.

"Hey?"

My hips are too wide. My jawline isn't sharp enough. My nose is too small. My hair is too long.

"Hey, it's fine." Everett says, reaching out and touching my arm.

"It's not fine, fuck off."

"Okay. Okay, it's not. What's wrong?"

"Everything."

He turns around and pulls one of his drawers open, starting to dig through it, and then he throws something at me.

"What's this?"

"A binder. Um, I have three. 'Cause my mum always makes sure I wash them regularly. That one is technically for swimming, but it works just as well. It'll probably fit you, but let me know if it doesn't, 'cause I have old ones that are different sizes."

I look down at it and swallow harshly. He has three? I barely manage to pay for and hide one, and he has three? And old ones? His mum buys them for him like they're t-shirts?

"Thanks." Is all I get out.

"Yeah. I'll make some breakfast and we can talk." He says, leaving the room and shutting the door behind him. Before I even think about getting changed, I pick my phone up and switch it on. I'm pretty low on battery, so I hope that Everett has the same kind of charger as me.

My notifications are a mess.

Instagram
Deanster34_ tagged you in a post
Tobias11shaw and 12 others commented on a post
that you're tagged in
Jack_Aston2006: U ok? Kinda just disappeared
Sheabutterfly._: you're in deep shit

WhatsApp
You have 9 unread messages
You have 2 missed calls

Snapchat
Maddyxox sent a chat
Tobias.shaw sent a snap
Tobias.shaw sent a chat

None of the notifications are from Abbie. I'm not exactly clear on the situation, but I desperately need to be.

I don't even realize that my I'm phoning her until it goes to voicemail. And then for the second time, and then for the third.

I'm screwed. Like, royally.

I fumble my phone into my pocket and turn away from the mirror, taking my shirt off and putting the binder on before replacing the shirt.

I feel ten times better instantly. And then I feel a little bit worse that I've kept Everett waiting for so long, so I leave the room and manage to locate where he's fumbling around in the kitchen. He acknowledges my presence with a nod.

"Made you a coffee. There's sugar in the pantry if you want it. Oh, and toast, which you should eat, 'cause you just vomited up what sounded like your last week's worth of food."

His kitchen is small and homely. It's it's own room, which leads onto the living room. His house is sweet, just like the gesture of making me breakfast.

"Why are you doing this?" I ask, the question a little foreign to me. He doesn't reply instantly, so I clarify. "Like, letting me stay here. Making me breakfast."

He takes a sip of his coffee. "You were really upset last night."

That's embarrassing.

"I was really upset on Sunday and you didn't care half as much then."

"It's different. You couldn't even stand up you were so drunk. None of your friends wanted to take you home, and you practically begged me not to take you to *your* house."

The thing that's even more humiliating is that I don't even remember what he's describing. I remember arriving at the party with Abbie. I remember our fight. I remember Tobias letting me finish his vodka.

"Yeah, but, you could have just gone home."

"I know you seem to think so, but I'm not an asshole. Anything could've happened to you."

"I don't need protecting."

"I know. But even the strongest of guys get too drunk sometimes."

I reach onto the counter and take a swig of the coffee that he made me. It's good, much better than the stuff that we have at my house. It reminds me that he didn't have to do any of this, but he did. I don't really get why, but he did.

"Thanks." I say, swallowing my pride. "Actually, why were you even there? I didn't think you were the type to know any of those people."

"Oh, Eli asked me to come with him." He says, and then he hums as if remembering something before placing his coffee onto the kitchen counter. "Eli, right."

"What?"

"Just a sec." He says, scrolling through his phone contacts, and calling someone who I assume is Eli. It rings about seven times before anyone answers.

"Hello?" Eli says through the phone, voice raspy.

"Hi."

"Everett, hi." He yawns.

"Hey. I just wanted to check that you're okay. After last night."

"Mhm. Yeah, I'm all good. Why?"

"I was just a bit worried. I know you went home with that guy and I wanted to check that you hadn't been kidnapped or anything."

Eli laughs. *"You're really sweet."* He says, and then another voice comes through.

"Who's really sweet?" The other person says. This guy has a deeper voice than Eli, sounding more humoured than genuinely curious.

"My friend, Everett. He was at Leo's, too."

"Oh, the little guy? Purple hair?"

"Yeah, did you meet him?"

"Mhm, yeah. Just before Abbie and Kylen started fighting."

Hearing this random boy say my name makes me feel like

I should know who he is. Someone that was at the party last night who likes boys. Or, if I'm interpreting the context of Eli seeming to have woken up next to him correctly, he does.

"I'm gonna fall out of this bed in a second, move up."

"I'm as close to the wall as I can get!" The other boy snickers back. I squint, trying to listen to his voice.

"I don't believe you. Let me go on the inside." Eli commands, and then there's some shuffling on the line. *"What kind of eighteen-year-old has a single bed?"*

"I do." The other boy says. *"Wasn't a problem for you last night."*

"Yeah, well I had other priorities last night."

The shuffling ends and Everett raises his eyebrows at the phone, clearly unimpressed.

"Okay, well you seem fine."

"Yeah, thanks for calling though. Hey, did you see the video of Kylen getting dumped? Dean Holden posted it."

Oh, great. Fucking perfect. Dean Holden? He's an asshole, and now he's much more of an asshole for putting it on social media.

"No, not yet."

"I feel kinda bad for him. She could've at least done it in private. Hope he's okay." Eli muses.

"He is." I interject, a little bitter. Eli reacts instantly.

"Oh, shit! Is that him? Did you take him home?"

"Yes, and yes." Everett says, sounding a little dejected. "I'll call you back later and we can catch up, okay?"

"Okay. Bye, both of you."

"Bye, little guy and bitch-boy." The other boy says, and then the phone hangs up. The snide remark is said in such a teasing tone that it reminds me exactly who this boy is, his name is

Will - he's in Year Thirteen.

Considering that he just called me 'bitch-boy', I can't say I'm his biggest fan. I had forgotten about the nickname. Knowing my friends, that'll definitely stick.

The worst part is that everyone seems to think I've been with Abbie for months, but I literally never even got to ask her out. I would've, at some point. But I never did.

"Okay. He seems fine." Everett says. I take a few moments to process the phone call - mainly the fact that people are undoubtedly talking about last night.

"I think you care too much." I say to Everett. "About others."

"Well, I think you don't care enough." He replies with no hesitation.

There's silence for a lot longer than is comfortable.

"So, are you gonna tell me about what happened last night?" Everett asks. It feels invasive.

"Do I have to?"

"No. Just think it might be good to talk about it."

There's the sound of a door opening down the hall. The floorboards creak and I look up to see a woman leaving one of the other rooms. She looks young, almost too young to be Everett's mum, but I don't really know who else she could be. She's wearing a short-sleeved shirt and leggings, with a lanyard around her neck, partially obscured by her long brown hair.

She sees the two of us and smirks a little.

"Good morning, boys." She says, walking past us and going to the sink to pour a glass of water.

"Morning." Everett says. My eyes dart between them.

"What's that look for?" I ask, whispering to Everett. He

pauses before replying.

"Probably to do with me dragging you in the door wasted last night."

My face heats up, embarrassed. "I feel bad enough. I don't need any more shaming." I muse.

"Okay, yeah. So, tell me what went on. No shaming here, I promise."

"Are you sure we should talk about this with your mum right there?"

"Yeah, it's fine. She's chill." He replies. I'm not that convinced, but she just continues to potter around with the fridge.

"I'm a cool mum." She interjects, closing the fridge door and looking at us with a carton of orange juice in her hand.

"Oh my god." Everett groans. It makes me a little angry. He clearly has a very good living situation in terms of support, and he's acting like it's the worst thing ever. "But, seriously, dude, what actually happened last night?"

I try to think about my words before I say them.

"Abbie had been, like, flirting with me on the way to the party. After a few drinks we went off to some place, I think it was Leo's parents' room." I start saying, face in my cup of coffee. I will admit that it does feel a certain degree of good to talk about it.

"And then, like, we started to kiss and stuff. And she clearly wanted more, and so did I, but I couldn't- we just- I kind of snapped at her and told her to drop it. And she took it as 'I'm not attracted to you enough', and, um, well, you saw the fight."

There's a strong sense of tension in the room, but not on me. I feel way better, even after that short confession. And then, Everett's mum clears her throat whilst pouring juice into a glass.

"Maybe it isn't my place." She says. "But if she doesn't like you in your whole, she's not worth it."

"Yeah. I guess. It's not her fault that she doesn't know, though. Sorry."

His mum blinks a few times. "Hey. You're perfect how you are. You can't change yourself for some *girl*. Just be unapologetically yourself, and the rest will work itself out." She advises, placing a hand on my shoulder. Suddenly, I want to cry. It's not fair. It's not fucking fair that Everett gets a mum like this. And I don't.

"She's right, you know. I've been telling you this since we first met." Everett says.

"Yeah. I remember." I reply, sounding annoyed.

"Just stop living how others want you to. Whilst we're on the subject, especially stop living for cis people, trying to get their approval like I know you do. You probably won't get it either way, and it'll make you hate yourself."

"That's a pessimistic view." I mutter.

There's more silence. "Are you two gonna be okay when I head off to work in a couple minutes?" Everett's mum says.

"Yeah." Her son replies. "Kylen needs to get started on damage control from his fight with his girlfriend last night."

"Oh. Well, good luck." She smiles. "Love you, Rhett."

"Love you too." He replies, and then it's just us in the kitchen again.

We finish our toast in what is practically silence. It gives me a lot of time to mull over the scenario that I've put myself in.

When I first met this kid, I thought he was annoying. And

130

he still is. One of those trans people that makes the whole community look bad because he puts no effort in. But, I only put so much effort in because I feel like I have something to prove. I have to prove to my parents that I'm a boy, despite the fact that they're yet to believe me. I have to prove to my friends that I'm a boy, and to Abbie, and to my teachers at school, and to everyone.

But it seems to me like Everett doesn't really have to prove anything to anyone. He seems much more happy and relaxed because of it.

I mean, with a mum like that, he could probably completely grow his hair out and start wearing dresses, and he'd still be supported.

Fuck.

"I'm sorry about you and Abbie, by the way." He says sincerely. "I didn't even know you had a girlfriend."

"I feel like there's a lot you don't know about me." I reply easily. I don't tell him that we never got together, because that would make me seem pretty pathetic. "But thank you."

Considering his kindness today and last night, I feel a little guilty for everything.

"For what it's worth," I begin, putting my mug of coffee down on the counter. "I'm sorry, too. For the way I treated you."

He looks like he's thinking for a moment. "I'm worried about the youth club shutting down." He finally says. It seems like a weird response to give.

"You worry about a lot of things."

"Valid things."

"Maybe."

Again, for about the tenth time, we remain in silence. Or,

that is, until Everett lets out a dramatic sigh.

"I think we need to join forces. You're confident and assertive, you can really help."

"Think you forgot the part where I'm not welcome at the Aconite Centre any more."

"Yeah. But that's your own fault. And you can fix it, probably. If you play a role in keeping things afloat."

"You're saying that you think us finding the money to save the club will make Thalia and Rowan let me back in?"

"I'm saying it might help. And I know that you care about the club a lot, even if you like to present as if you're all nonchalant and don't give two shits about anything."

I blink a few times. "I don't know where you're getting this idea from." I say honestly. "You know, you're one of the only people outside my family that I've frequently cried in front of, on purpose or not. Surely that makes me a little more human to you. Emotionally."

"It does, yeah. But I think you'll want to help the club either way. Whether you pretend you want to or not." He thinks out loud, turning towards me and pointing an accusatory finger in my direction. "Somewhere deep inside of you, there's someone that cares."

"Right. So why are you bringing this up?" I ask, in an attempt to get his rambling back on track.

"We aren't really the kind of people that would get along. I know that Thalia seemed to think that we'd be great friends because we're both trans guys, but that's not actually how anything works."

"Well, yeah."

"Right. We're from very different worlds, I feel." He comments, eyes unfocused.

"Clearly."

"So, I think we need to try and relate to each other more. So that we can work together effectively."

"You're sounding awfully business-y. It's worrying."

"Well, I'm just asking you. If I proposed that we work together, despite our *differences*, what would you say?"

I think about it for a long while. He's difficult to be around. He comes across very entitled in my eyes. He's pretty confrontational, but that's probably just to do with me. Still, I can't help but feel intrigued by him. There's something about it, something that he's figured out that I haven't.

"Fine. Sure." I accept. "Not for you. For the club. Because it does a lot for those kids."

He laughs. "Yeah, go on. Say that as if you aren't one of those kids." He teases. Then, Everett reaches his hand out towards mine and I look at it for a moment. "Shake it, dude, shake my hand." He says, a little exasperated.

"Oh." I say. "Now you're *acting* awfully business-y." I tease, but I shake his hand nonetheless.

I'm not too sure what his intentions are in regards to any of this, but it seems like he's quite desperate to make friends with me. It's almost flattering. And, sure, I can concede a little of my pride to try and relate to him, granted he'll put the effort in to do the same.

9

Everett

"Oh my god." Kylen groans, phone in one hand and the other propping his head up as he replays the video of his and Abbie's fight last night. "This is so bad."

The comments are even worse, he decides, handing me his phone so that I can read them and save him the embarrassing trouble of having to declare them aloud to me.

It's almost pitiful.

> **Tobias11shaw** *free up my man he aint do nothing*
> **Alexanderthegr34t** *Get these two on Love Island asap*
> **Sheabutterfly_.** *you're a dick for posting this*
> **Deanster34** *giving the people what they want isnt a crime*
> **Sheabutterfly_.** *it is when it's personal*
> **Deanster34** *if they wanna fight in public i have every right*
> **Madel1ne.Cambel1** *Take this down*

Deanster34 *lol u wish*
Beastedliam *What a scene*
Freddyovel *wish i was there to see this*
Lilyluvsxox *holy fuckk*
Lilyluvsxox *that was BRUTAL*

I grimace at the phone and the stressed young man on the sofa snatches it back from me, defensive. He tries calling her again to no avail. Kylen worries his lip between his front teeth.

"She's probably with her friends." I supply, and he looks a little lost. "I lived as a girl for much longer than you did, and if I know anything, it's that they stick together when one of them is upset. Try calling one of her friends."

He mumbles something unintelligible and nods, nails coming to his mouth so that he can bite them anxiously as the phone rings.

I recognise the voice of the girl that answers. It's the same girl that practically jumped on Eli when we first got to the party. Shea, I think.

"You've got some audacity calling me." She says, skipping any kind of greeting.

"Please, Shea, are you with Abbie?"

"Even if I was, she doesn't want to talk to you. I would've thought not answering all your calls had made that clear." Shea speaks with a cold indifference that is nothing like how I heard her act last night.

"Can you pass on a message, at least?"

There's a little bit of movement through the phone, and then Shea's voice returns.

"She's listening. You have ten seconds."

Kylen's eyes widen a little and he spends a good two seconds figuring out what to say.

"Abs, you have to know, it's not you."

"He's giving you an 'It's not you, it's me' speech, holy fuck." Another girl murmurs.

"Yeah, because it *is* me. You have to let me talk to you, I can't lose you over one drunken fight, 'cause I love you."

When I look over at Kylen, he looks close to tears and I feel a little bad for the guy.

"Give us a moment." Shea says, and then the line goes completely silent as if they've muted their microphone. He looks over at me as if asking what the hell he should do, but I don't really have experience with drama like this, so I just shrug.

He mutes his own microphone.

"I hate this. How long do they need?" He complains, fidgeting with the hem of his shirt. He's wearing his own clothes again now, because they'd finished drying and he now looks a lot more himself. A lot more like the guy I remember.

The ambiance of the room that the girls are in returns through the phone.

"Right." Shea says. *"We've come up with a deal. If you can get Dean Holden to take that video from last night down, she'll talk to you."*

Kylen looks at the phone, bewildered. "Like fifty people will have screen recorded it already, there'd be no point."

"It's not about that, it's about the effort you're willing to put in for her."

He rolls his eyes, but the annoyed tone doesn't even come through in his voice when he speaks.

"And if I do this, she'll talk to me? Properly, in person."

136

Then, finally, there's another girl's voice. A voice that says, *"Yeah."*

I can tell just by Kylen's reaction that it's Abbie. It's like a switch flips in his head.

"Abbie, Abbie, call me back, or text me, please." He tries, but the phone hangs up half way through his pleas. "Fuck." He says. "Fuck, fucking asshole."

Kylen stands off the sofa and kicks my coffee table rather angrily.

"Hey, alright. Don't go punching any walls." I say, reaching out towards him and placing my hands on his shoulders. "We'll get the video taken down."

"No, we won't." Kylen argues. "It's Dean Holden, that guy's a major prick. He doesn't like me, that's probably why he posted it."

"That's fine, that's fine." I try to reassure him. I'm not entirely sure that it's fine, but if I can convince Kylen that it is, then maybe our confidence will make it true. "This is just another quest. Save the youth club, and save your almost-relationship. You scratch my back, I'll scratch yours."

Kylen looks a little annoyed by my positivity. "Fine." He grits. "You're in charge, then. How are we doing this?" He asks, flopping back down onto the sofa unceremoniously.

It's a good question. How are we doing this?

"Your wardrobe is shit." Kylen says, sifting through all my clothes like it's nothing. There's now an agreement in place.

We've come to the realisation that maybe we just aren't compatible. As people. We're far too different. But then,

Kylen suggested that maybe it's because I 'just don't get what it's like.'

Which I disagree with a little. I can pretty easily imagine what his life is like.

But he doesn't believe me.

And so I fired back with the statement that he doesn't get what my life is like, either. Because he lives differently.

Which is how he ended up trawling through my clothes.

"Better than yours."

"Not for what we're doing." He retorts quickly, pulling one of my hoodies off of the clothes hanger and lobbing it in my direction. Kylen clicks his tongue inside his mouth as he starts to examine all of my jeans. "This'll do." He proclaims, pulling out a pair of my denim jeans. I don't wear them often because they're way too baggy to be socially acceptable.

"This is my Leavers' hoodie." I say, a little dumbfounded.

"It's your only one that's not a ludicrous colour." Kylen says in an insulting tone. "And besides, having the fact that you finished secondary school this year on the back will be helpful. Otherwise they might mistake your five-foot-five ass for a thirteen year old."

"Ouch."

Kylen just shrugs. And it pisses me off, how he gets to insult me like that. I don't voice my annoyance.

"Just, just change into this and we'll go from there." He smirks. My eyes follow him playfully as he leaves the room.

I do, because I had agreed to, and when I step out of the room, he claps his hands slowly.

"You'll fit right in." He says. "But what are we gonna do about your hair?"

I pause and cross my arms. "What about my hair?"

"Everett." He says, eyebrows arched. "It's purple."

"You promised that we wouldn't have issues like this."

"It's not about that. If you were a cis boy with purple hair it still wouldn't work if you're gonna try out my life for a day."

"What, because you don't have purple hair?"

"Because the kind of people I hang out with don't have purple hair."

"Are we actually talking about purple hair here?"

"I don't know. Are we?" He retorts, arms crossed as he stands before me in my hallway. "You asked to do this." He adds, probably sensing my irritation with him.

"Okay, well I don't know what you want me to do about my hair." I fire back, because, literally what does he want me to do about my hair? It's not like I'm gonna dye it back to it's natural colour.

"Fine. Leave the hair. You'll just have to compensate."

Despite my mild annoyance, I can't help but laugh at the implications.

"Not like that." He snickers, shoving his hands into his pockets. "Look, come outside with me." He instructs, flicking his hand in the direction of the door.

After he spends the whole two minutes of us going down the stairs complaining about the stairs, Kylen takes me outside of my building and onto the street.

"Right." He says, out of breath. "Holy fuck, those stairs, man. How did you get me up them last night?" He asks, and I know that I'm going to have to be the bearer of bad news.

"Oh, we took the lift up last night."

He gapes at me. "Lift?!" The boy exclaims, clearly exasperated.

"Yeah. But, like, how else are you gonna get gains if you

always take the lift? Also, I think you might need to evaluate how safely you've been binding if you're out of breath going down the stairs." I tease, although I do mean it, hands in my pockets as I walk down the street and he follows me.

"Alright- well, firstly, your body language is off." He calls to me, and I spin around to entertain his words.

"Go on."

"You walk on one line." He supplies. "Like, you feet go inwards with your steps." Kylen explains, demonstrating what can only be described as a catwalk in which he places his feet on one of the lines that the pavement tiles connect on. "Boys walk on two lines. Like train tracks. Um," He cuts himself off to think, and then holds both of his arms out in front of him. "Imagine a narrow gauge railway, like, all along the pavement, and walk on the sides."

He then demonstrates doing just that, stopping when he sees someone walking along the pavement in our direction.

"See, okay. Watch and learn." He smirks, turning to look at me, where I stand against a garden wall. The man walking along the pavement approaches and Kylen reverts back to his usual gait, passing the man with a downwards nod that is reciprocated.

Then, he spins around and holds his arms out as if to proclaim victory.

He looks at me as if expecting something, so I start to slow clap sarcastically.

"He nodded at me." Kylen says. "As in, he recognised me as a dude. That's what we're going for with you."

I roll my eyes a little at his antics. "You know, passing isn't everything. Especially when you're only sixteen."

"It is to me. And you agreed to walk in my shoes for today,

so, yes, passing *is everything.*"

Kylen makes me practice walking on 'two lines' for about five minutes, until he's happy with the way that I walk.

I end up sat on the red brick wall of a nearby house, hands in my lap as my eyes follow Kylen. He's found some manky, deflated football on the side of the road and has started kicking it about in the empty street because 'you gotta keep your game up.' I had just laughed and sat back so that he could entertain himself, but now I'm starting to regret it.

The way he moves is so fluid, so confident. He practically bounces from foot to foot, smiling when he manages to keep the ball in the air against his foot, then his knee, then his other foot.

"Oh my god, I'm literally goated." He says, still doing his keepy-uppies. I get this horrible gut-wrenching feeling, and when the ball hits the floor, Kylen looks over at me after groaning.

"You okay there?" He asks, in that rough, scratchy, masculine tone of voice.

He stands in front of me, hands in his pockets, shoulders squared back, wearing his baggy jeans and baggy t-shirt.

And I know that he's ten times more a man than I will ever be.

"Can you give me some more passing tips?" I ask abruptly, because as much as I dislike the idea, I know that he can help me stop feeling so dysphoric at just the sight of him.

He looks at me for a moment, confused. "I thought you didn't want my unsolicited advice."

"It's not unsolicited if I asked you, dumbass." I reply, feeling a little shameful at even having to ask him.

"Seriously?"

"Seriously. Not too harsh though. Only things I can *actually* change – none of this, 'you're too short' bullshit."

He pauses for a moment, looking deep in thought, seemingly contemplating his next words.

"Well, actually... Something I've noticed," He starts, clearing his throat. "Is that, you *do* make yourself look a lot shorter than you really are by slouching."

I glance down at myself and realize that I am pretty hunched over. But, there's a reason for that.

"Yeah, but if I don't slouch then it's more obvious that I don't have a completely flat chest." I retort, because that's what I've always seen and assumed.

Kylen tilts his head to the side and pats his pockets down. "Alright. I've got my phone and wallet. Walk with me." He instructs, guiding me to stand up with his hands. I do so and we settle into a rhythm walking side by side down the road.

We don't say anything for a while. Five minutes passes, then ten.

"Where are we going?" I ask him, and he looks back at me with a smirk.

"To the corner shop."

"We've passed like two corner shops already." I reply, turning around where I can literally see the last one in the distance.

"Okay." He concedes. "To *my* corner shop. The one I go to."

I decide to just let him do whatever and continue to follow him. It's just five minutes later when we get outside a little convenience store. Kylen doesn't hesitate to push the door open, and the door makes a commercial beeping noise, then it does again as I follow him inside. It's stocked up pretty high, full of food and drinks. There's a broad, bearded man behind the counter, wearing a polo shirt and a flat cap.

"Alright, little man." The clerk says, bowing his head.

"Hi, Kev." He replies, not even hesitating to grab two Redbulls off the shelf.

"Let me guess," The guy, 'Kev', begins. "You want a pack of reds?"

"Well, you've got a lot on that shelf. I'll take the extra stock off your hands. For how much today?"

"For you? Ten."

"You're the man."

"I know." Kev finishes, turning around and pulling the packet of cigarettes from the shelf. It dawns on me then that Kylen has dragged me along with him to make illegal purchases. "Who's your friend?" He asks, and Kylen turns towards me.

"Oh, this is Everett. He's chill."

"Not the type I usually see you 'round here with." Kev comments, starting to ring Kylen up for the cigarettes and drinks.

"I'm expanding my social circle."

"Is he okay with this? Looks a little nervy."

Kylen takes a peek back at me and then nods whilst tapping his card on the machine.

"He's fine, it's just that he's about to lose his nicotine virginity."

"He is?" I ask, crossing my arms in front of my chest as Kev laughs.

"Alright. Don't have too much fun."

"We won't." Kylen smirks, spinning around after pocketing his wallet and the cigs. He hands me one of the Redbulls and walks past me to get to the door. I sigh and follow him out.

We step out onto the daylight of the street, the door making a noise as we leave, and I have to jog a little to catch up with Kylen in his stride.

"What the hell?" I ask.

"What?"

"You just made me an accessory."

He snorts in his laughter. "I promise you, Kev is the only person who could get in trouble for that interaction."

"Does he know you're underage?"

"Do you know how much money there is in the market of teenage smokers?"

"I can take a guess." I reply bitterly. Again, I stop talking after that and we continue to walk down the road in a newly uncomfortable silence. Another five minutes down the road, and I find myself growing impatient.

"So, why exactly did you need to buy cigs to give me advice?"

"Because, young Everett, we're gonna have a heart-to-heart in about ten minutes' time." He declares proudly. Oh, really? Are we?

"Yeah, 'cause you're the kind of guy that likes to get emotional with his mates." I tease him lightly. He just scoffs. "Where are we even going?"

"To the place that I always go to stew in my feelings."

"This is a playground." I say sceptically, arms crossed at the sight of the rusty space before us. It's a series of damaged slides, monkey bars, ping-pong tables, and even a zip line.

Not that any of it looks functional, but it's a playground in the back corner of a larger park. I've been to this exact park many times before, but I've never even known that this playground existed.

"Correction: It's an abandoned playground." Kylen says, striding up to the gate that is barely hanging on by its hinges. "An actual child hasn't set foot here since they built that new one on the other side of the park."

The gate squeaks deafeningly as he opens it. For a disused area, it's pretty big. Which, I guess makes sense, because the whole park is like a twenty minute walk from one end to the other. It's not like they're shy of space for it.

There's also a circle of trees around the confines of the playground. It seems to disconnect us from the outside word as I begrudgingly follow him into the area.

"You come here often, then?"

"When I need to think, I do."

"Do your friends come here, too?"

He kicks the dust on the ground under the swing set before planting himself on one of the two swings.

"You're actually the first person I've brought here." He says. "So don't fuck it up and start bringing your friends."

I copy his notion of dragging my feet against the dirt when I sit down on the swing next to him. Now that we're well into the afternoon, the sun has moved behind the clouds and it feels a lot more genuine to be sitting in an old playground.

"Oh, you don't have to worry about that, I promise." I assure him, trying to make myself sound humoured. Instead, he just slowly turns his head towards me and raises his eyebrows.

"What, you don't have any friends or you just don't like

145

taking them places?" He asks.

I guess he did warn me.

"I just don't keep friends that easily." I admit. I don't want to or plan to get into specifics with him. I lost a lot of friends when I came out as trans, for one. It was never that they were massively transphobic or anything, but we just drifted after I came out and I could always tell that it was the reason behind everything.

And making friends is hard. It's even harder as a queer, trans person.

By the time we made it to Year Eleven, everybody already had their established friend groups. I couldn't manage to infiltrate any of those at that point, too focused on exams and stuff.

"Woo, okay." Kylen nods, pulling a lighter out of his wallet. "Any reason?"

I shrug and push myself back on the swing. "It's just weird, I guess. Girls don't really wanna be friends with me, and boys *definitely* don't."

"Yeah."

"What, you've had similar experiences?"

"I've been out a long time. It's not always been how it is now." He murmurs absent-mindedly, lighting his cigarette whilst it's hanging out of his mouth.

"How long have you been living this... stereotypical teen boy lifestyle for, then?" I giggle, and he looks at me slightly annoyed before exhaling the smoke from his cigarette with his head tilted back.

"To be honest," He begins, pushing himself into a swinging motion just as I'm doing. "It's quite a recent thing. After I moved schools at the start of Year Ten. Ach, shit." The wind created from his swinging causes his cigarette to go out and he plants his feet in the dirt to stop the momentum.

"Alright. So, are we gonna dip into that wealth of knowledge that you were gonna give me?"

"Oh, yeah. Yeah." He says, sliding off the swing after relighting his cigarette. "Right, so, in my experience, there's only one element of passing effectively."

"Go on."

"Confidence is perceived as the most god damn manly trait you can have." He proclaims, standing in front of me. "That's what you were kind of alluding to. I told you that you slouch too much and you said that it's because binding doesn't make you one-hundred-percent flat." He says, and he's literally just repeating what I had told him earlier, so I don't really get the relevance.

"But, I'll let you in on a little secret. Two secrets. Men aren't usually completely flat. And *you* walking like *this*," He pauses his speech and starts strolling in front of me. But, it's an overexaggerated caricature of myself in which he hunches his shoulders massively and stares at the floor, taking tiny steps and pretending to look around worriedly the whole time. "Doesn't help you look more masculine."

I frown at the impression. It's a little bit hurtful, but I can kind of see where he's coming from.

"Stand up." He says, beckoning me off the swings. "And c'mere."

I reluctantly do so, walking over to him. "Hold this." He says, passing his still-lit cigarette towards me. I do take it despite my disagreement with his lifestyle, and he immediately plants both his hands on my shoulders and spins me around to be facing away from him.

147

"Ah, relax." He says, and then he pulls my shoulders backwards to righten my posture. I make a somewhat startled noise, but he doesn't say anything. "See that birds' nest?" He asks, hand outstretched towards where one sits in a tree directly in my eyeline.

"Yeah."

"Look at it with your head, not just your eyes." He instructs. "You're still looking at it with your eyes. Look up." I try my best, and he steps away from me. "Now walk, but keep your eyes on the prize."

I take one step forward and suddenly his hands are back on my shoulders, pulling them back to be upright. "Keep your posture straight. Try again."

I huff a little but this time put effort into maintaining the position. "Remember the train tracks!" He calls when I get a little further away.

"That good enough for you?" I ask when I reach the edge of the playground, turning around. He grins at me.

"Confidence in your gait is worth ten times more than the appearance of a flat chest, I promise."

"Okay." I nod, getting back to him. "Thanks."

"Yeah. Anything else you wanted help with?"

We're still in the playground when darkness starts to infiltrate the treeline.

Kylen made me go through some quite honestly ridiculous voice training exercises, only at the discretion of 'there's not a person in sight.'

We sit side by side on one of the many ping-pong tables as

our conversation lulls into some more personal territory.

"Did you want one?" Kylen asks rather abruptly.

"Want what?"

"A fag. I realize I've had like four but I never actually asked you if you wanted one."

"Oh, I don't smoke." I reply easily.

"Well, yeah. I just assumed you'd definitely want one by now."

"Your friends are bad influences."

"Maybe." He concedes, lying down backwards on the table and staring up at the sky.

"Why do you even smoke?" I ask, turning to look at him.

"I used to just do it socially. And I hang out socially a lot. Feels like once you start.." He trails off, swallowing. He doesn't need to finish the sentence.

"Yeah. That's why I'm not all that interested. My mum hates it, always says that my dad being a smoker was one of his most unattractive traits."

Kylen laughs. And, yeah, it is a little funny. She doesn't talk about him all that much, except for when we're in the street together and we walk past anybody who could be remotely close to my age smoking. Then she just *loves* to yap about how much of a turn-off from my dad it was. I've never really been put off by smokers, it's just really not something that *I* want to do.

"Um," I begin, copying him in lying on the table. Now that we're being somewhat friendly with each other, I can't help but want to scratch an itch in my mind. "Speaking of calling things with other names slurs,"

"What?" He snickers, taking a drag from his cigarette and tilting his head to look at me.

"You called the cigarettes fags." I confirm. "So, I'm using it as a segue."

He squints for a moment and then his face falls. "Oh. *Oh.* You, um, you want to talk about the pride event."

"Less about the event. More about why you called me that."

"Everett-"

"I'm not trying to start an argument, I'm just confused. In a week, you went from calling me a transphobic slur to giving me tips on how to pass better. The only conclusion I can draw is that your friends make you a shitbag, but I think that's evident even without the name-calling."

I feel like a weight is lifted off my shoulders after I confront him with that statement. He seems a little taken aback until he eventually speaks.

"You're right. My friends do make me act like a prick."

"Oh, joy." I smirk. "Say that again."

He sits up and rolls his eyes. "You're right. And I'm sorry. I wouldn't- I don't actually think of you that way." He admits, and it is a bit of a relief. "I think I felt threatened by you."

"Threatened?"

"You're just so, so unapologetically trans."

At that, I sit up. He looks at me and can pretty clearly tell that I'm gonna need more than that. He sighs and slides himself off the table. "Walk with me. The words'll come out easier." He instructs, heading for the exit of the playground.

"Walking." I let him know. "What did you mean by that?"

He exhales some smoke and taps the cigarette to shake the ash off the end.

"I think that there's a lot of shame in being trans." Kylen says quietly. "Like, trans people feel a lot of shame about it. Most things to do with it are taboo. Dysphoria, hormones, surgeries, deadnaming. It all feels pretty shameful."

I nod along absent-mindedly as we leave the playground and rejoin the path around the park.

"But I don't see that in you." Kylen carries on. "You walk around with your coloured hair and your pride flags on your shoes. Everything about you screams 'I'm trans and I'm not ashamed about it' and I guess I just.."

"You're jealous." I finish for him, realising quite easily after his rant. Abruptly, I feel pretty stupid for not realising it before. He's a prick to me because he's jealous that I don't tear myself apart from the inside out like he does. That I live for myself and not for others.

"I'm not jealous." He denies. "I just wish that it was different sometimes. That I could have the confidence to do all that." He continues, going a little quiet at the end of his sentence.

He's spent the better part of the day teaching me how to be confident, but in actuality, *he's jealous of my confidence.*

I think for a moment, letting my eyes wander around the trees we're walking through.

"So, that's why you called me that?"

"I just wanted you out of my life. The club is shutting down, so it was like- like I could push everything away. It gave me a chance to fuck off from the club on my own terms, I'm just.. Sorry that it was you who took the impact of it."

I feel pretty bad for him all of a sudden. "Hold on," I laugh a little. "You made me be like you today. Walk like you, talk like you. But, actually, you want to be more like me?"

He swallows anxiously. "I don't know." Kylen whispers, shrugging with the hand not holding his cigarette in his pocket. "I had to work all of this out for myself. Watching trans YouTubers at three AM with earphones in under my duvet. I don't want you to have to do the same. Because, obviously someone has to show you the ropes and shit, but it doesn't mean I'm perfect." Then, I get an idea.

"What are you doing tomorrow?"

"Um, nothing planned. Most of my hang-outs are quite spur of the moment." He admits.

"You're coming to mine. Today, you gave me some advice. And tomorrow, I'll give some to you." I say as joyfully as I can as to put his mind at ease.

"Okay." He nods. "Yeah, okay."

There's a gaggle of teenage boys in the distance as we continue to walk. We get a little bit closer to them and Kylen stops walking all of a sudden.

"Oh, shit. I know those boys." He says, grabbing my wrist and spinning me around so that we're both facing away from them. "Do you wanna put what we've gone through today into practice?"

"You want us to go talk to them?"

"It'll be good for you." He assures me. "Just follow my lead, I believe in you." He jokes with the last part, and then within a second he's striding towards the group of boys.

"Shit," I mutter, hopelessly following him too.

The group notices us when we're about two metres away. One of them does a double take and then a grin spreads across his face.

"Kylen Lysander." The boy grins, holding his arm out. Kylen connects hands with him and they perform a bro-hug. "What the fuck are you doing 'round here?" He asks playfully.

"Oh, you know," Kylen begins. "Just out for a smoke. This is my mate, Everett."

They all look in my direction. "Alright, mate." The same boy that spoke to Kylen says.

"Yeah." I reply in the deepest tone possible.

"Haven't seen him with you before. How'd you two know each other?"

Kylen takes a drag absent-mindedly. "From a youth club. But, hey, we can't stick around. Gotta get back to the mumsie before she gets all pissy about us being out."

The boys laugh. "Alright, well, see you around, yeah?"

"'Course."

When we get a good distance away, Kylen looks at me with a grin. "You passed." He declares.

"Guess so, yeah." I realize. It was fucking intimidating, but it was less scary knowing that I wasn't the only trans person there. If Kylen can be so good at fitting in, surely I can't be that far off.

Satisfied with how my day has gone, I walk beside him through the rest of the park giggling under the soon-to-be night sky.

10

Kylen

I leave as early as possible on Sunday. Not because I'm excited to see Everett, because I feel like it.

When he walked me home last night, and I went inside, neither of my parents batted an eye to the fact that I hadn't come home for twenty-four hours, and to be honest, it's not like I expected them to.

It did feel really good to shower and put some clothes on that weren't tainted by the memories of Abbie and I's public show on Friday, though.

She still hasn't called me or anything, so I guess she's serious about this whole 'get Dean Holden to take the video down or else' ultimatum.

I'm not sure what else I expected.

Despite everything, I woke up this morning feeling okay. Well, in comparison to yesterday morning - waking up in a random bed and then promptly throwing up - it was okay.

Now that I actually know where he lives (and, no, I certainly didn't have to get him to text me his address again) the walk is quite pleasant.

Everett had offered for me to stay over, but honestly, I couldn't do that to his mum. I can only imagine how stressful it would be to have a guest in your house for days at a time. And, besides, Everett's house really isn't that big. I get the feeling it wouldn't take that much prolonged proximity for us to get royally sick of each other.

I get to his building at ten, and am painstakingly embarrassed to have to buzz on the intercom at his flat number and then stand there awkwardly whilst I wait for him to let me in.

"Sorry, I don't want a quote for you to clean my windows." He says teasingly through the speaker.

"Asshole, just buzz me in." I reply somewhat bitterly. I hear him laugh through the intercom and then the electronic door makes a noise to tell me that it's unlocked now.

The lift is at the back of the lobby area, which is probably why I didn't see it yesterday morning. Right now, I make a beeline for it.

He doesn't have a doorbell, so I just knock.

"Oh! Hello Kylen." Miss Enfield says after answering the door. "Rhett didn't tell me you were coming over."

"I don't have to announce it to you whenever someone comes over, Mum." He drawls, walking out of his bedroom with his hands in his pockets. He's dressed much more like himself today, wearing an oversized grandpa sweater and grey jeans. He isn't in shoes and his socks have little crocodiles on them.

"You do if it's in *my* house, young man." She scolds. Everett having a mum that doesn't even hesitate to gender him correctly like that makes my heart ache.

"Okay." He says, clearly not actually conceding. "Can he come in yet, or?"

"Goodness gracious. Do you talk to your mother this way, Kylen?"

"Uh,"

"Don't answer that." He laughs. Clearly they're both joking, and are able to poke fun at things like this. "Just come in."

I do come in, feeling a little bit of an outsider to their dynamic.

"Alright. I'll be playing candy crush on the sofa if you need me. Don't get into too much trouble." She instructs, disappearing off into the living room.

"Sorry about her." Everett says. I don't really think he should be apologising for having a great relationship with his mum.

"She seems nice." I say, trying not to seem too weird about the fact that I would kill to have a mum like her.

"Yeah." He agrees easily. "Right - first order of business is your outfit."

"What about my outfit?" I frown, looking down at what I'm wearing.

"It's nice. But it's not good enough to get you called a trans-trender on the internet. So, you're clearly not doing my lifestyle right."

Yikes.

"Okay." I say. "Just a heads-up, though. I dress this way mostly because it's all that my dysphoria will allow. So, um, you might have to be a bit patient with me." It's quite the vulnerable admission, and I feel a little exposed.

"Yeah, of course." Everett answers quickly. "I'll give you some options that you can pick from."

He takes me to his bedroom and makes me stand in front of his full-body mirror.

"What would your parents have called you? If you were born male." He asks while he sifts through his clothes.

It's a good question. One that I can answer very easily.

"Oscar. Um, it's my middle name."

"Wow. Kylen Oscar Lysander? What a name."

I raise my eyebrows at him, unimpressed.. "Well, I did it because I thought it would make my parents feel better about the whole thing."

"Why not use it as your first name?" He asks.

"I don't like it enough for it to be my *first* name. I wanted to choose that on my own terms."

"Oh, well, it's what I did." Everett says, returning to me with about five different jumpers in his arms. "Everett is what my mum would've called me." He shrugs. "When I first realized I was a boy, after I came out to her, I, like, sat down with her told her she could pick my name."

"Oh. So we both had that kind of idea." I comment, and he smiles.

"Right. Pick your poison." He declares, shoving all the jumpers into my chest. They're an itchy woollen texture, mostly brown. Having said that, there is one that jumps out to me. It's a jagged mixture of dark blue, light blue, and green. The same kind of obnoxious tones as Everett's bedroom, but it works quite well on a jumper.

"Alright. What about jeans?"

"Well, which jumper are you wearing?"

"The blue one."

"Right. Then, you can't wear blue jeans. I think I have some black ones that I got from a charity shop. Never wore 'em 'cause the legs were too long, but you're tall enough." He explains distractedly as he finds the jeans in question. Once he gives them to me, he leaves so that I can get changed.

The outfit itself isn't bad. It just looks *wrong* on me. The sleeves are too long, they go over my hands. The jeans hug my hips, but I keep the jumper untucked and draping over my waist so that only my legs stick out. I will admit I'm glad that he jeans are straight leg, which is the kind that I usually wear in rotation with 'unbelievably baggy.'

I must stare at myself for too long, because he knocks on the door.

"You done having a crisis, yet?"

"Um, yeah. Sorry."

He comes in and grins at the sight of me. "You have never looked better."

"I look like a gay boy." I say.

"Is that a bad thing?" He asks, feigning offence.

"It is when I'm not a gay boy." I complain, crossing my arms.

"*Kylen* isn't gay."

"Why are you talking about me in the third person?"

"Because, last night I had a realisation. This is gonna be hard on you and your toxic masculinity. So, you need an alter ego."

"Seriously?"

"Seriously. Today, you aren't whoever this 'Kylen' guy is. You're Oscar."

"Oh, is that what that was about?"

"Yeah."

"And here was me thinking you were genuinely interested."

He laughs. "I was a little. But I can't say there were no ulterior motives. Now, is Oscar the kind of guy that would paint his nails?"

❀

I don't think I have ever pushed myself further out of my comfort zone than I am right now.

For the second time in two days, I find myself sat on Everett's sofa. This time, though, he's performing a critical analysis of my psychological state. After I had refused to let him put eyeliner on my waterline, we sat down to just talk about a few things, like we did on the ping-pong table yesterday.

"Being trans," He begins, talking in a slow voice. "Isn't a bad thing."

"Yeah, I know."

"Do you?"

"I mean, actually- it kind of *is* a bad thing."

Everett looks a little bewildered before recollecting his thoughts. "It's a shitty situation to be in. Doesn't make it a bad thing to be trans. And, Kylen-"

"I thought I was Oscar."

"You're still trans whether you hate yourself for it or not." He says, a little loudly for the fact that I'm sitting across from him. "One of the hardest things that I had to come to terms with is that I'm not just gonna wake up one day and be cis. This shit is for life, and you can't do it miserably forever."

His voice is so stern and commanding when he says it, that I'm scrambling for a response.

"I'm not miserable."

"I think you're forcing yourself to be something you're not." He keeps trying. "For the sake of, what? Fitting in?"

I lean all the way back on his sofa and exhale. "Well, yesterday you told me that you *don't* fit in and have zero friends as a result."

"Ouch."

"Sorry." I apologise, feeling a little bad about the outburst. "But, you must get what I mean. It's so unbelievably shit trying to fit in anywhere when you're trans. If any of my friends found out, I'd probably get jumped."

"Good friends you've got there." He comments sarcastically.

"Yeah, I know they're shitty. But they're all I've got. Especially after Abbie decided to fuck off."

He nods slowly. "I just- I feel like you're living for other people."

The statement lingers in the atmosphere for a long while. It weighs heavy on my chest and very quickly Everett's wool jumper is too scratchy. "You need to live for yourself." He finishes.

"Yeah." I breathe out, and that's all I manage to say. I start biting my nails and Everett looks towards the hallway, then back to me.

"Right. Today, then, you're gonna do one thing for yourself." He decides, shuffling to sit cross-legged on the sofa. "Is there anything that you've always wanted to do, that your ultra-stealth-road-man-cis-boy-lifestyle has held you back from?"

I raise my eyebrows at him, unimpressed. He's never been the type of person to beat around the bush. I think for a moment about all of the things that I gave up.

"Um, I don't know."

"Oh, come on." Everett drawls. "I refuse to believe that you were always like this."

He's right. I wasn't. So, I dignify him with thinking a little harder. My mind wanders into one memory and I find myself snickering a little.

"What?" He asks, mirroring the humour evident in the room.

"No, just thinking about a thing." I say.

"What thing?" He pries, and I realize that he probably won't drop this until I show him.

"Fine, fine. I'll find a photo. Give me a sec." I excuse myself, pulling out my phone and going into my gallery folder with all of my childhood photos. To be honest, I deleted most of them out of resentment during a rough day a few years ago, but some that I still quite like survived the purge.

This particular picture is certainly a gem.

It's of me, when I was about ten. I'm grinning broadly, wearing knee-length jorts that were certainly a fashion choice, with a green nature-themed t-shirt.

The part of the photo that I'm deigning to show Everett, however, is the fact that when I was this age, for about six months, I had highlighter pink hair.

I actually had it because I kept insisting to my parents that I hated my long hair, and they said that I could change it however I wanted *without* cutting it. Tell that to a ten year old, and suddenly you've got pink hair.

"Don't laugh." I say, holding the phone against my chest.

"You just laughed thinking about it!" He argues, reaching towards me to try and grab my phone.

"Okay, okay! Just, be considerate, okay?"

He snickers, and I slowly turn the phone towards where he sits watching me with eager anticipation.

His eyes widen and he bursts into a fit of laughter.

"Oh my god!" He exclaims, completely snatching the phone

from my hand. He starts tapping around, and by the time I get my phone back, I see that he's on Instagram, and he's sent the picture to himself. "Sorry!" He says through his laughter. "Couldn't help it."

"You're the worst."

"So- so, hold on. You - Mr 'your-coloured-hair-sucks,-dye-it-back-to-normal' - are actually a veteran of unnatural hair colour?"

"Okay, well I was like ten." I defend myself to no avail.

"What's so funny?" Miss Enfield asks, hovering in the doorway of the living room with a mug of what I presume is tea in her hands. Right, thin walls.

Everett keeps snickering as he pulls his own phone out, and I realize that all of my dignity has been thrown out of the window.

I feel pretty anxious at the sight of his mum, or really anyone, seeing a picture of me pre-transition. I burnt pretty much all of them for a reason. But, to my surprise, she doesn't even comment on the fact that I look like a girl in the picture.

"Aww." She grins, clearly holding back laughter. Then, she lightly hits her son on the back. "He looks just like you."

This time, it's my turn to laugh. Everett is less impressed by the comment. His mum and I both laugh at the comparison for a little bit, until she smiles and kisses the top of his head. "I'm sorry, love. I'm only joking."

He pouts. "This isn't fair. I'm being ganged up upon by people with normal hair colours." He complains, and then he gasps as if remembering something. He leaps up like a frog and suddenly he's gone from the room. Miss Enfield raises her eyebrows and looks in the direction of the bathroom. We can both hear his footsteps plodding along the hallway, and he appears back in the doorway in record time.

"I've made an executive decision." He announces, clearly holding something behind his back.

"Oh god." I mumble.

"*We* are going to reignite your childhood."

This cannot be good. I know for certain that it isn't when he slowly reveals what's behind his back.

It's a box of hair dye. A light blue colour. Everett shakes it in his hand with a devious grin.

"I bought this a few months ago, before I decided that I would rather do a darker colour like the one I have now."

"No way." I say without any hesitation. "I have a social life. You know that, right?"

"Yes." He nods. "But, personally, I think it'd be great for your confidence."

I'm fully ready to not budge at all, until his mum chimes in.

"Why don't you two compromise?" She suggests, taking a sip of her tea. "Like, do a little bit or something. Like Anna from Frozen and her silver streak."

Everett grins from ear-to-ear. "Oh my god! We can do the underside of your hair."

"Excuse me?"

"Your hair's layered, right?"

"Yeah?"

"So, let me dye the underside of your hair. Like, not the top layer that people can see. The bit underneath. Nobody would notice unless you push your hair back. It's like a little bit of reclaiming your youthful joy."

And, fuck. I can't believe I'm considering it. Everett hands me the box and I look at it. It's only semi-permanent, to be fair. And the colour is subtle. Icy blue is a good term to describe it. It'd probably be even lighter against my blonde hair.

"You're thinking about it, aren't you?" He grins, giggling.

I sigh. "Oscar's thinking about it."

He has never looked so hopeful. "Well, it's only twelve. I've got to leave here at like three-thirty for trans-plus. We've got time." He says, voice wavering in suggestion.

"You don't think it'd stop me from passing?" I ask out of genuine worry. The only reason I even said that to Everett in the first place is because I believe it, or I have believed it for so long.

"Nobody will see it unless you want them to." Everett confirms for me.

It only takes ten minutes before I'm sitting on the lid of his toilet as he reads the instructions on the box out loud.

"Smile!" Everett calls. I look up from where I'm scrolling on Tiktok just in time to hear the fake shutter sound of his phone camera going off.

"Hey!" I protest, reaching out towards his phone, but he steps away. He giggles, turning the phone around so that I can see the picture.

There's a white towel around my neck that is absolutely ruined with dye, and the shirt that I am wearing has also fallen victim to it. (He made me take off his jumper before he even opened the box of hair dye).

He also used a claw clip to separate the top layer of my hair from the part that he was dying, which looks positively stupid when combined with the cling film around the parts of my hair that *has* been dyed.

"Delete that right now." I say jokingly.

"Already sent it to Eli, sorry."

"You're insufferable." I reply. "I can never show my face in public again."

Everett chuckles at his device. "Hah. He said 'who is that and what has he done with Kylen?' Oh my god, he forwarded it to the Pride club group chat." He rambles. "They're freaking out."

I groan and dive back into my phone to hide from it all.

"They want a video." Everett says.

Without missing a beat or looking up from my phone, I reply. "Don't push your luck."

He giggles in a way that tells me that he was filming that interaction. "Captures your angsty personality perfectly."

Just then, his phone starts blaring and vibrating in his hand. "Ach! That's time. We need to rinse."

Begrudgingly, I agree to cooperate. After absolutely assaulting my hair with the shower head, he drags me into the hallway to plug the hairdryer in.

"This is the most fun I've ever had." He declares. I can barely hear him over the sound of the hairdryer blowing heat into my hair and subsequent face.

"I'm sure it is."

Before I know it, he's turned the hairdryer off. "You're all good." He announces, standing up and encouraging me to do the same. "Come see."

We get into his bedroom and he pushes me towards the mirror.

And, to give him some credit, Everett was right.

You can't even see the colour at a first glance. My hair has fluffed up considerably from the use of the hairdryer, but behind that, it looks pretty normal.

Or, it does, until he tells me to push my hair back. I do, and it reveals the blue colour hidden underneath the first layer of my hair. The colour has turned out really nice. Very light blue, almost silver-like blue, and it matches my eyes perfectly.

"Oh." I exhale, pushing it back further and further to see more of the colour.

"Do you.. Like it?" Everett asks slowly.

Just for now, I allow myself not to think about the social repercussions of this. I've been throwing myself into a box for so long that this is liberating. In reality, I don't think I'd dye my hair like this again, but it's like I'm allowing myself to take a step out of a darkness that I've been hidden in for so long.

"Yeah." I affirm in an airy voice, turning to look at where Everett looks at me curiously. "Yeah, I do." I repeat, feeling the overwhelming surge of emotion start to get to me.

He studies my face for a moment before clearing his throat. "Are you about to cry?"

"No." I deny, but my voice breaking a little gives me away. After that, he's quick to wrap me in a hug. It's not overly weird, and it's not at all romantic. The bond that we share in this moment is one that I've never felt before.

There's a bit of a spring in my step when I leave Everett's house. He had offered that I come to the club with him and we can talk to Thalia and Rowan, but I said that I wasn't quite ready yet.

Turns out that the decision to free up my evening was a good one, because I'm only about half way home when my phone buzzes. And I don't think I've ever replied to a text quicker.

Tobias

You still trying to get on Dean's good side?

Yh
What's up??

He's invited me to a meetup tnite
Said I can bring some of my mates

Oh shit yes please

Cool. Come round mine in ab an hour
We can walk to town

I get home and change into a shirt that isn't covered in hair dye as quickly as possible. It's just about half four when I get to Tobias', and he answers the door with the same cocky grin that he always has.

"Hey." He says, stepping out of his house and shutting the door.

"You alright?"

"*I'm* great." Tobias says easily, striding out onto the pavement as I follow him. "The real question is: how is *Abigail?*"

"Still hasn't spoken to me." I say, shoving my hands in my pockets.

"Well, mate, it is the perfect night to forget about girls."

He smiles, handing me a cigarette.

"Amen."

We walk into town at a leisurely pace, eventually finding the group that we're meeting up with. It's a gaggle of about ten lads, a mixture of from my school and another. I spot Dean in the group, but decide that I'll stay away from him until the opportunity is right. Other than that, it's pretty easy for us to gel in with the group, and not long later we're causing a moderate amount of mayhem in the city centre.

Whilst loads of others are walking ahead of us, I notice that Dean starts to hang back until he's eventually walking alongside me.

"So," He says. "What's your motive for this?"

"Sorry?" I ask, a little caught off guard.

"Level with me, Ky. You did not agree to come hang out here because you just felt like it. Especially not after the thing with Abbie. I assume that you want something from me."

I really don't like the way that he calls me 'Ky', especially considering that I wouldn't even consider myself acquainted with him. But I suppose he's right.

"Fine." I concede. "I need you to take the video down."

Dean laughs. "I'm sure you'd like that, yeah. But, do you know how many likes that got me?"

"Can't you just, like, not be a dick?"

"That's not a very nice way to talk to the guy that you want something from." He says snarkily, turning to flash an irritating smile at me before jogging a little to catch up with the rest of his friends up ahead.

Fuck, I should have known that this would be much harder than I thought. But, like, how do you even get through to a guy like that? He's like a forcefield of sarcasm.

I let the evening drag on nonetheless. I have about half a can of beer, but it's nothing in comparison to what some of the other boys that I'm hanging out with do.

And, maybe it's just the fact that we're young, or maybe it's the alcohol, but it doesn't take long for the mild anti-social behaviour to turn into vandalism.

A couple of them pull out some cans of spray paint and start drunkenly marking random walls with vibrant colours. I have a couple more drinks. We all find it funny, and there's even a point when someone hands me the can and I scrawl a messy 'Kylen was here' in an alleyway.

Tobias calls my name and I turn around to look at where he's put 'K + A' inside a heart shape on the opposite wall. Loads of the other boys see it and laugh. I laugh too, because after a certain amount of drinks, it is pretty funny.

When I hand the spray paint can to the next person, it leaves a neon orange residue on my skin that I carelessly wipe off onto my jeans.

Dean holds one of the cans, on his sixth drink of the night as he clambers onto the hood of a car and draws a big cross over the wind shield.

Everything feels a little blurry at this point, but I know I'm having fun.

11

Everett

The club seems pretty interested in me when I walk in. I arrive a little bit behind schedule because, despite her leniency, Mum made me clean the evidence of Kylen and I's hair dye fiasco out of the shower before I could leave.

Everybody is sat around in the chair circle, just having casual conversations that all die down the second I walk in. It's just Lilia, Brynn, and Mars. Then of course, Thalia. I'm not sure where Rowan is, but my best guess is the office.

"He's here." Lilia says, loudly enough that it's obvious I heard.

"Give us the details, then." Mars immediately adds as soon I get in proximity.

"What details?" I ask, a little humoured.

They all start talking at once, but it's Mars that gets the most clear word in. "About Kylen. Obviously. How the fuck did you get him to dye his hair? His head is usually so far up his own cis-bootlicker ass that he would never even consider that."

"Language." Thalia scolds, crossing her arms before turning her attention to me. "Nice to see you, Everett. Seems like you have a Q & A to run."

I take a seat in one of the empty chairs.

"Sure, okay." I shrug. "As long as it doesn't get in the way of what we have planned."

"No worries. We don't need the whole evening for today's activity, and I have to admit that I am a little curious about this."

"There's not much to say, really. We were just hanging out and I offered it up. Well, actually, he showed me a picture of him when he was like ten, with pink hair. And then it gave me ideas."

Brynn leans forward in their chair with a sceptical expression. "Hold on." They say abruptly. "This is not fair. I mean, this kid has been a brick wall of emotional numbness for *years*, and he goes round to your house one time and suddenly he's showing you childhood pictures? Literally what kind of magical powers do you have?"

I laugh a little at their question and then shrug. "I don't know. We had a little bit of a heart-to-heart yesterday. And then kind of also today. That might be why."

"I think it's just been a long time since anybody has put as much effort into him as you have." Thalia inputs. When nobody really reacts to what she's said, she carries on her point. "You know, most people would have given up on him the second he stepped a little bit out of line. But you didn't. I think that's why he trusts you so much."

"You think he trusts me?" I know that we talked a little bit about our feelings and stuff, but he's just so closed-off that I don't think it's possible for him to trust anyone.

"I mean, from what these lot have been gossiping about, yeah." She agrees casually.

"Okay. Well, it isn't *our* fault that he was a dick to all of us, so we didn't wanna pursue a friendship." Mars says somewhat argumentatively.

"I didn't say it was." Thalia replies in a calm tone that undermines their annoyance. "There's nothing wrong with not wanting to be friends with someone, I'm just saying that considering everything he's been through, it was never gonna be easy to get through to him."

There's some lingering silence in the air until Lilia speaks.

"Okay. So, what are we doing today?" She asks, clearly eager to move the conversation away from Kylen and his antics.

"Right." Thalia says. "I bought you guys some tote bags to paint. I have some fabric paint, and I was thinking we could stick a film on the projector. Now, we have a few options, so we can vote on them."

About half an hour into 'The Rocky Horror Picture Show', and when I'm about a third of the way done trying to paint some tulips on a beige tote bag, Mars scoots over to me on the floor.

"Hey," They say in a whisper.

"Hi."

"So, bit of gossip for you. Have you met Eli's new boyfriend?"

Boyfriend? That escalated quickly.

"If it's the same guy that he hooked up with on Friday night, then, yeah. I've met him."

Mars nods, and then turns to me with a smirk. "Alright. So, what do you think of him?"

"You're looking at me like you want me to say something bad."

"Maybe."

"I didn't know they got together."

"Don't sweat it. It won't last long. None of Eli's relationships do." They murmur that last part casually. "But, that doesn't answer my question. Do you like the guy?"

"You know, he flirted with me before Eli."

"Oh? So you're saying he's a player?"

"I'm saying that maybe he went to that party with the intention of taking a boy home, and it just happened to be Eli."

Mars laughs as quietly as possible. "So, you're saying that Will doesn't actually like Eli?"

Will? Well, at least I've solved the mystery of the guy's name.

"Maybe, I don't know. But Eli's seventeen. He can handle himself."

"Oh, I know. But it's fun to speculate."

I will admit, hearing that Eli is now *dating* this boy does make me a little anxious for him. As his friend, is it my duty to tell him that I think Will is just using him? Or, if he's happy, is it my duty not to say anything?

The thoughts swirl around my head as the film continues to play. By the time it's over, the four of us are all pretty tired, and our tote bags are on the side of a table, drying.

We go back to our chair circle to end the night at about ten minutes to six. There's an array of discussion about the film. The chatter is excited, but it's cut through by my phone ringing abruptly from my pocket.

"Sorry." I apologise, pulling the phone out of my pocket and seeing who's calling me. Probably my mum at the supermarket wondering what I want for tea.

I'm surprised to see that the call is coming from a 'Private Number.'

"Are you gonna answer that?" Brynn asks, sounding amused. I glance over to Thalia and she gives me a nod saying that it's fine.

After I answer the phone, I put it up to my ear.

"Hello?"

"Everett, I fucked up really bad." Comes a voice that I recognise instantly. The phone line is clearly quite poor, because his voice is crackly, but not overly upset. He sounds more stressed than sad, speaking in hisses that are riddled with regret.

"Kylen? Are you okay?"

"No. No, I got in some trouble. And- And I really need you to-"

"Slow down. What happened?" I cut off his rambling.

"I can't say anything on the phone, they're listening, and the guy said that if I say anything about it then they might take it as an admission of guilt, and-"

"Hold on. Where are you?"

"Um. You have to promise not to be mad."

"I promise. Unless you're about to say what I think you're about to say."

"I'm at the police station." He finally admits. At this point, everyone in the room seems curious about the nature of my phone call, so they're all eyeing me up warily.

"Yeah. That's what I thought you were gonna say."

"I didn't mean to get caught."

"Stop talking. That sounds like an admission." I warn him. I've seen a few cop shows, and I'm pretty sure if he did get arrested for something serious, he shouldn't say a word without a lawyer.

"Right. Um, can you come here? You're my only phone call, so-so if you can't, can you get someone who can?"

"Why didn't you use your call to call your parents?"

"'Cause they're gonna be really mad."

"They're gonna find out either way, you know that, right?"

"Please." He begs. *"Please can you just come?"*

"Which station is it?" I ask. As much as I'd rather not get too involved with his criminal activity, he's my friend. And he chose me as the only person that he's allowed to call. I'd be a dick to just not show up for him.

"The one near the town centre."

"Okay. Um, give me like half an hour. Hang in there."

"Thank you. I owe you one."

The line goes dead. My phone goes back in my pocket and they're all looking at me.

"What was that about?" Lilia asks.

"Um, sorry. I gotta duck out a little early." I excuse.

"Did something happen?" Comes Thalia's voice. She sounds full of concern. "To Kylen?"

"I don't know if he wants me to tell you."

"I promise you, if something happened, he'd want me there. I've known him for a long time." She says, and I nod.

"Fine, yeah." I give in. "He got arrested."

And, fuck, I've never seen Thalia look so worried. Whilst the other members of the club start chattering, she's up from her chair and on her way out of the hall.

"He got arrested?" Mars exclaims. "For what?"

175

"Slippery slope, I guess." Brynn adds.

"I don't know what he did, I guess I'll find out." I grumble, lacing up my shoes whilst I wait for Thalia to return from wherever she scampered off to.

Not thirty seconds later, she's back, and Rowan is following her, looking equally as worried.

"Okay. Rowan is gonna finish the club for you guys." She says.

"Oh, are you coming?" I ask. "To the station."

Thalia nods very easily. "I'm one of very few adults that cares about him. No offence, but they won't listen to you over someone like one of his parents, and those two won't say nice things about him if they get questioned."

She's right. If his parents are upset at him, angry at him because he's been arrested, they probably won't be too kind about him to the police officers. It's for the best that she comes.

"Also," She continues. "You can't drive, and we should get there as soon as possible."

"Right." I agree. I was planning to just call my mum and get her to drive me, but we'd get there in half the time if we set off now.

Mars wishes us good luck as we leave, but I don't even turn around. Kylen and I had a really good day today, and I can't help but feel responsible. I had to kick him out of my house so that I could get ready to come to the club, but, if I hadn't, he could've stayed at my place longer. He probably wouldn't have gotten in trouble.

"He's gonna be fine." Thalia says, drumming her hands on the wheel.

"You telling me or yourself?"

176

"Both of us." She exhales. We dip into silence for the twenty minutes that the traffic allows us to take to get to the police station. The building itself is very intimidating, and I feel suddenly really glad that Thalia has come with me; I don't think I'd have the courage to go in without her.

It's institutional in the way that the walls are all white, and the floor is a corporate grey. It reeks of stress and anxiety in here, but those emotions seem to only be felt by myself and Thalia, because the people working here seem so incredibly chill that it sends a shiver down my spine.

I've actually never been in a police station before, so I'm not too sure what the procedure is.

But, there's a desk in front of us, which Thalia strides right up to keenly.

She barely manages to get out a "Hi." before being interrupted.

"Thalia!" Kylen's voice calls out, sounding panicked. We both look over, and he's on the other side of the room, being held by a police officer by his hands that are clearly cuffed behind his back. She was obviously taking him somewhere and happened to cross our path.

The officer shushes him before addressing us. "Please tell me you're his mother." She says, exasperated.

Thalia shakes her head. "Youth club leader. What did he do?"

The officer beckons Thalia over and I follow her as closely as possible. Kylen looks a mess: eyes puffy, hair ruffled so that the blue is visible. His jaw is bruised pretty badly and he's clearly anxious beyond words. He also has some kind of orange paint splattered on his hands, with traces of it on the front of his jeans, too.

"I need you to ID him before we can tell you anything." The officer says. "He won't tell us his name and there was no identification on him. We can't contact his parents because we don't know his name, and because he insists that he's a minor, he needs them or a trusted adult in the room before we can question him."

Why won't Kylen tell the officers his name? I mean, I guess that it would prevent his parents from finding out, but they're going to find out either way, like I told him. I feel a little bit annoyed at him for making this harder than it has to be.

He looks into my eyes and shakes his head subtly.

"Dude, just tell them." I berate him, trying to reason here. "Lying to them won't make anything easier."

"Sorry, can I get your name?" The officer, whose name tag reads 'Ignis', asks Thalia. She answers instantly, and then asks if Thalia can act as a trusted adult to be in the room whilst they speak to Kylen. Of course, she agrees.

"We need his name, and preferably his address if you know it. Are you the person that he called?" Officer Ignis asks Thalia, who shakes her head.

"No, it's this one that he called." She supplies, patting my shoulder.

"Oh, good. You called him 'Kylen' on the phone, right?"

I nod, a little intimidated by her.

"Well, I tried running that name through the system. In all the variations of spelling, but none of them were a positive ID for him. So, either that's not his name, or it's a nickname."

And suddenly I realize why Kylen won't tell them his name. He looks back at me helplessly as he gets shoved through a door into another room.

"Can I talk to him?" I ask quickly. "Please."

"I shouldn't let you." Officer Ignis says, inside the questioning room.

"I can get him to tell you who he is, please."

"Or I can just ask you. And you'd have a legal obligation not to withhold information from me."

"Please."

The officer looks at me for a moment. "Two minutes." She says, letting me into the room.

She's handcuffed Kylen to the table on a metal chair. There's no chair on the other side, so I lean over the table to whisper to him.

"What the *fuck*, Kylen?"

He doesn't say anything.

"What did you do?" I ask.

"Drunk and disorderly." He says, before hesitating. "And, um, technically criminal damage? Vandalism? I'm iffy on the specifics. But, I- um, it was Dean." He whispers, looking at the door to check that they aren't listening.

"What was Dean?"

"He- he fucking pushed me. We were running from the police, and he pushed me to the ground so that they would get me. He knows I want the video taken down, and he told me that if I take the fall for this, you know, don't snake him out to the Feds, that he'll take it down." He admits.

"Kylen. Getting charged with criminal damage is not worth getting Abbie to talk to you."

"I love her, Everett."

"You don't love her *this* much." I tell him, desperate for him to just fucking listen to me.

"I can't-"

"You can't get her back if you're in juvie, Kylen."

Then, the police officer comes back into the room. She strides right up to the table and says a name out loud, sounding accusatory towards Kylen. It's a girl's first name, followed by his surname.

It's not Kylen's name, but he reacts with a strangled sound of upset anyway. His eyes go right to Thalia with a betrayed gaze, and she frowns apologetically.

"I'm sorry. I had to tell her, it's only going to get worse if you don't work with them." She says softly from the door frame. "And you can watch through the glass, Everett, but you can't be in here any more." She then tells me.

"Your parents have been contacted, Miss Lysander. They're on the way."

Kylen shakes his head. "Don't do that." He spits. "I'll talk to you, but only if you can have some basic fucking respect."

"Excuse me?"

"I know that Thalia told you, because she wouldn't just tell you my deadname otherwise. So, whilst I'm in your custody, you'll call me the name that I want you to call me, and I will not hear the words 'Miss Lysander' come out of your mouth. Okay?" His voice is stern and he's high on emotion from the whole ordeal.

"Okay." The officer says after a moment. "Well, we need to ask you some questions, Miss, um-"

"Mr Lysander." Kylen supplies in a bitter tone. The officer nods with a raise of her eyebrows.

"We need to ask you some questions. Do you want to start now with your youth club leader here, or should we wait for you parents?"

"We can start now." He says, nodding with his eyes cast onto the table. Just then, a different officer grabs my arm and

180

explains that he'll take me to the other side of the one-way window.

"Kylen. Do not throw your life away for Abbie, I'm begging you." I try, but I only get a glimpse of his upset-looking face before I'm out in the hallway and the officer shuts the door to the interrogation room.

12

Kylen

"Who's Abbie?" The officer asks.

"Swear I'm meant to get a lawyer."

"You swear wrong." She mutters back.

I groan and lean as far back in the chair as the handcuffs will allow me. They dig into my wrists painfully. This is so shit, and I'm still a little fuzzy around the edges because of the alcohol. I also know that I need to act as sober as possible to avoid getting charged with being drunk both underage and in public.

I feel like utter garbage sitting in front of this officer. Detective? I don't know.

What I do know is that if I stick this out, Dean will take the video town. It doesn't matter what Everett says.

I look back behind me at Thalia, who hones a disappointed stare. I would much rather she was angry, like she was when I came back to the club after the Pride event. But she doesn't look angry at all. She just looks upset and disappointed, like she expected better of me.

"I'm sorry, Thalia." I say. "I tried really hard to stay out of trouble."

"I know." She says softly. "Not hard enough, though. And all hell is going to break loose when your parents get here, so just keep cooperating, okay?"

"With all due respect, Mr Lysander," Officer Ignis says sternly, and I'm honestly just glad that she's back to treating me as a boy. You know, how she did *before* she even found out that I'm trans. "You're here to talk to me. Not to Mrs Ranger-Hyland. So, I'll ask again. Who's Abbie and why was your friend there so concerned about her?"

"She's my- um, this girl I like." I say after some hesitation. I'm a little caught off guard by Thalia being referred to by her surname, which is something I literally never hear, so it takes me a little longer to find my bearings.

The officer laughs under her breath. "Right. Listen, kid. I know that you're not the only person involved in what happened earlier. We counted at least eleven boys, maybe more."

I'm a little irritated that *I'm* the only one that got caught, especially when they know that there were so many of us.

"Twelve."

"Twelve what?"

"There were twelve of us." I tell her.

"Can you give me names?"

I look up to the one-way glass, to where I know Everett is standing. For a moment, I imagine him banging on the window and begging me to snake on everyone.

"No."

The officer sighs. "You know this can ruin your life." She says, as if it's supposed to be a threat. "If you get convicted, you're looking at a five-thousand pound fine. Or, you could get forced to attend classes about the dangers of underage drinking. If the owner of the car that you smashed the wind shield of wants to press charges, you're looking at a young offenders institution at best. Do you want a criminal record?"

"I didn't smash any car wind shield." I argue. Dean was the one with the baseball bat.

"Maybe not. But without any of your accomplices, a court case can pin all of the damages on you alone."

"Don't you have, like, CCTV?"

She shakes her head. "Not in alleyways. Maybe we can ask civilians for dash cam footage, but I wouldn't rely on it."

Thalia clears her throat behind me. "If, hypothetically, he tells you who he was with, what would that mean for him?"

The officer paces for a moment. Then, she leaves the room abruptly after telling us to give her a minute. I push the chair back with my legs and rest my head on the table, breathing out heavily.

"Kylen, you have to tell them." Thalia says, walking to stand next to me in the corner of my eye.

When I speak back, it comes out as more of a murmur into my arms. "You don't understand what'll happen if I do."

I can imagine *exactly* what will happen if I snake on those boys. I can basically kiss my social life goodbye.

"And I don't think you understand what will happen if you don't." She replies without missing a beat.

Ignis comes back in with a piece of paper in her hands. "Right. I understand that this is your first offence. So, I've spoken to a few people, and we're willing to make you an offer."

I pick my head up off the table and look at her.

"This isn't the first time we've been called out for something like this. We don't genuinely believe it was you that did all of the damage to those cars. But I think that *you* do know who it was. So, you give us a name, or names, and we'll reduce your bail to two-hundred."

"Remind me what it's at right now?"

"A thousand."

"What if I tell you, and then you just let me go?"

The door to the interrogation room opens suddenly, and the receptionist stands in the doorway. My stomach drops when she very smoothly says that my parents are here. Oh, fuck.

"Yeah, send them in.   Maybe they can scare this kid straight." Ignis says with a sigh.

I don't think that it can get any worse than it's about to until I see my mother appear in the doorway, holding Alfie's hand and looking very upset with me.

Alfie breaks into a run when he sees me. He wraps his arms around my waist with a sigh, clinging onto me as if I'll disappear if he lets go. "I was worried 'bout you." He says sadly.

"I'm sorry, teddy bear. I'm okay." I reply in a whisper.

"I'll give you guys some privacy." Thalia says, walking past my mother to leave the room.

Mum's voice cuts through the air with a rather loud exclamation of my deadname, followed by a stern: "What the hell do you think you're playing at?"

She walks right over to me, towering over where I'm helpless before her. I see my dad emerge in the doorway and watch from a distance.

"We can't leave you alone for five minutes! Can we?" She exclaims.

"Sorry."

"Sorry doesn't fix this! What on earth are the neighbours going to say? And what the fuck have you done to your hair?"

There's also a massive bruise on the right side of my jaw from when Dean shoved me onto the pavement, but clearly she has very little concern for my well being.

"Can you maybe take Alfie out of the room if you're gonna talk to me like that?"

"No. No, because he needs to see what's going on here so that he knows not to end up like you." She spits. "I can't fucking believe you. You know- we played into your delusions because it's what your psychologist told us to do. Because he said it would result in you living a better, happier life. But- but I just can't fucking fathom how *this* is the life that he was talking about." She raises her voice and is practically spitting in my face at this point. "Your dad told me to just let you do your thing, and you'll grow out of it by the time you're an adult. Clearly he was wrong, and this whole 'living-as-a-man' thing has gone too fucking far."

There's a million words that come to my mind. A million things that I want to scream at her, but none of the words come out. Through the tears in my eyes, my response sounds weak and vulnerable.

"I didn't mean to."

"Didn't mean to? Oh, like those jeans that we bought for you with our hard-earned money just got occidentally covered in spray paint?"

"Mama, please-"

"No. No, I just hope that you're proud of yourself. Because *you* did this. Not us. God, The things that you will do for attention."

186

I shake my head at her, desperate for her to just stop talking.

"It's okay, Kylen. I'm not upset at you." Alfie whispers.

"Alfie, don't call her that." Dad finally speaks up, walking over to him. "You know it upsets your mother."

"How the fuck do you think I feel?" I say, maybe a little louder than was necessary, but it gets both of my parents' attentions. "It's never about how I feel, is it?"

"You don't get to have your *feelings* prioritised when you're running around getting arrested, not coming home for days at a time, spending all your money on alcohol, and probably drugs, too!" Mum yells. I suddenly remember how much I hate being yelled at.

"Can you get them to leave? Please?" I beg, turning my attention back to the police officer in the room.

"No, not until I'm done talking to you." My mum replies.

"Technically, ma'am, your child does have the right to choose which trusted adult stays in the room during questioning."

"You're not questioning her, we're having a conversation." Dad replies for my mum, argumentativeness in his voice.

"Hold on." Mum says. "So, what's going to happen to her now?"

The officer refers to the paper that's in her hand as she responds. "Well, Miss- Mr Lysander, um, your child - we'll say, has been charged with vandalism and underage drinking. Other charges are yet to be processed because the evidence is circumstantial. We've set a court date for the end of the month. June twenty-eighth."

"Court?" I question meekly. That's fucking terrifying. I have to go to court? Oh god, I'm like a proper criminal. My life is over.

"It's not as scary as it sounds. It's juvenile, and for petty crime. All you have to do is look presentable and sit in front of a judge, who will read your charges to you and then decide what consequences you'll face."

"And what could that be?" Mum asks.

"Depending on the charges, it could be a fine in the low thousands, maybe even a youth offenders prison, but, considering the circumstances, I doubt it'll be anything that extreme. It's more likely to be community service or mandatory alcohol safety education."

"Right." Mum says, crossing her arms. "What about until then?"

"Until then, we keep your child in custody unless the bail is paid. At that point, we would negotiate the circumstances."

I take a deep breath in and then look up at my mum. "You're- you're gonna pay, right?" I ask.

"The bail?"

"Yeah."

"Why would I do that? You got yourself into this situation because you think you're so tough and independent. So, get yourself out of it."

"What?"

"You heard me. A few weeks here will probably do you some good." She decides, and it feels like my world is closing in on me. They're meant to be my parents, and they're just gonna leave me to rot in here for nineteen days?

"Dad, come on." I try, turning my attention to him.

"No, actually, I agree with your mum. You shouldn't have done this if you weren't prepared to face the consequences." He replies, and I'm not sure that I expected anything better.

"I didn't do anything wrong! Not compared to the others!"

"Right. So give them up to us, or else you'll never get justice." The officer says.

"Can I have Thalia back? Please?"

Ignis nods, ushering my parents and Alfie out of the room when she sees how clearly distressed I am. Within thirty seconds, Thalia is back, and kneeling in front of me.

"Did you see?" I whisper to her.

"Yeah, yeah. I watched." She confirms, turning her speech to the officer. "Um, can you give me a second? I need to call one of my colleagues."

"Of course. We'll pause questioning for a few minutes."

Then, Ignis leaves the room too.

Being alone with my thoughts is not something that I'm too fond of right now. I didn't mean for this to happen. But now I'm gonna be in police custody for over two weeks, until the court date. I can't believe I have to go to fucking court. Over some mild vandalism?

I'm so mad at myself for letting myself get arrested. But it wasn't even my fault. The police showed up, and we all started running, and then fucking Dean Holden forced me to take the fall for him.

It'll all be worth it if this results in Abbie actually speaking to me, though. If Dean takes the video down. He better, after all of this. The handcuffs dig into my wrists as I pull them towards myself.

The door suddenly clicks open quietly, and I look up to see Everett hovering in the doorway. He looks really upset as he closes the door behind him.

"I don't think I'm meant to be here. But I just-" He sighs to cut himself off, walking over and swallowing. "I'm sorry."

"For what?"

"I didn't know that your parents were like that."

"It's not your fault."

"I know. I just- I assumed that they were- I don't know. I can see if my mum would pay your bail?"

I let myself laugh a little at the ridiculousness of the suggestion. "Everett, your mum is a nurse. And a single parent. She needs the money, and I could never ask that of you. I'll live."

He nods kind of solemnly. "Oh come on." I say, purposefully lightening the tone of my voice. "Keep your head up. You're not the one in handcuffs."

He smiles. "Yeah."

"And, for what it's worth, I'm sorry that you had to watch me fight with my parents like that."

"No, don't worry. I think it made Officer Ignis feel bad for you. More likely to treat you better that way."

"Silver lining, I guess." I laugh, but my joy doesn't last long in these circumstances. "Thanks for coming." I say, locking eyes with him.

"Of course."

"Right." Thalia says, pushing the door open. "I've just got off the phone with Rowan- Oh, hi, Everett."

"Hi."

"Basically, we have about two-hundred-and-fifty pounds in the fundraising pot. From the Pride event."

I blink a few times to process her words. "Thalia, I can't let you do that-"

"You're not letting me. I'm telling you what's going to happen." She interrupts. "You're gonna pluck up the courage to tell them who was doing the criminal damage. They'll lower your bail to two-hundred pounds as a result. I will pay for it, out of the fundraising money, and in return, you'll come back to the club and help us make it back."

"I can come back to the club?"

"Yes. I'll see you on Thursday." She says, making it clear that the conversation is over. I feel really guilty about the fundraising money getting used for my bail. I didn't even do anything to help earn it.

Ignis comes back and quickly shoos Everett out of the room. She sighs. "Right, then. Is there anything else you want to say before we get you set up in holding?"

"Um," I begin. Fuck, this is the end of my social life as I know it. I will literally never be able to leave the house again. "If I tell you the name of the boy that was kind of in charge of it all, who was smashing the car wind shields-"

"If you tell us, your bail is dropped to two-hundred, and it'll also get taken into consideration during trial."

I nod. It's only five words really, but those words may as well be 'never speak to Abbie again', or 'develop 'snake' as a nickname.' But, considering that most people have recently taken to calling me 'bitch-boy' (thanks, Abbie), it probably can't get much worse.

"Fine." I say, jaw clenched. "But, but you can't tell him that I told you."

"I can't promise you that he won't figure it out." Ignis replies.

If I don't do this, then I literally have to stay in a holding cell for weeks. That's not a good look. And, Thalia was pretty stern when she told me what I need to do. I've let her down enough as of late. When they're the only words at the forefront of my mind, the only ones that I can think about, I know they'll be the hardest five words of my life. When they do come out, my voice is tired and whiny. I would be embarrassed if I wasn't so exhausted.

"His name is Dean Holden."

"I'm really sorry." I say for about the tenth time after leaving the police station.

"I know." Thalia says. "I don't think you'll do something like this again."

My parents are nowhere to be seen, assumedly having gone home with Alfie. It's past his bedtime, to be fair.

The air outside of the police station is crisp and cold from the sun setting. The colours of the sky have melted into an orange that feels so much more beautiful than it did before today.

Just as I've made peace with the fact that I'm pretty sure I have to walk home into a household of people that are very much not happy with me, a car door to my right slams shut.

"Kylen." Everett's mum says softly, her son standing behind her. She's clearly come to pick him up. "Everett told me about everything. And, I just want you to know that you're always welcome at our house." She offers, and I kind of hate how she's looking at me like I'm a charity case. But I guess it's charity that I need, so I can't really say that much.

I blink a few times. "Really?"

"Really. I mean it, you can come and sleep 'round any time you want. Tonight, even, if you don't want to go home."

"You wouldn't mind?"

"Of course not."

I turn to my left for approval from the adult that I owe my

192

whole freedom to, and Thalia nudges me. "Go with them."
She says. "I'll see you on Thursday."

"Oh! You must be Thalia." Miss Enfield says. "It's so good
to meet you. You know, the work that you do for these kids is
just incredible-"

I tune her out and end up making eye contact with Everett,
who rolls his eyes at the chatter. He beckons me over and I
lean against his car with him.

"We're gonna be here for a while." He says. "Once she
starts talking to someone her age, it can go on for hours." He
laughs.

"I'm sure you have a pack of cards on you. You're the kind
of person that would carry one everywhere."

He scoffs playfully. "I am not. And besides, they're in the
glovebox." He grins, walking to the passenger side of the car
and retrieving the deck of cards.

We end up deciding to sit in the back seat of the car to play,
because it's warmer than outside and we have the legacy of
cushion in the car.

"What's the situation with the bail, then? Like what do you
have to do?"

I shrug, because there's really not that much to say. "Just
not allowed to leave the country. Which won't be a problem.
And then she got all serious about if I don't show up to court."

"You will, though. Right?"

"Yeah. Of course I will. I might be stupid and reckless but
I'm not *that* stupid and reckless." I say, and he seems to find
it funny as he shuffles the deck. "Wait, do I need to buy a
suit?" I wonder out loud.

"For court? Yeah. If you wanna show the judge that you're
an upstanding citizen."

"I've never bought a suit before."

"What, you've never been to weddings or anything?"

"Not really. My family isn't that big."

He hums in acknowledgement and starts dealing the cards out between us. He wins the first game, and then I win the second, and we're about half way through the third when Everett's mum gets back.

The car keys jangle around in her hand as she clambers into the drivers' seat and shuts the door behind her. "Sorry, boys. Got a bit carried away." She excuses with a laugh. "Kylen, do we need to swing by your place at all?"

All I have on my person is my phone. I didn't take anything else to hang out with everyone, because whenever I take my wallet to things like that, it always results in me paying for drinks or something. It's a lot easier to just be able to say that you left your wallet at home. I suppose it was convenient today, because it meant that I didn't have any ID on me when I got arrested.

"Yes please. Um, thanks."

I put the address into Miss Enfield's phone and try not to focus on the feeling of dread at the idea that I'm gonna have to make a celebrity appearance in my household to get some stuff to stay over at Everett's with.

"Do you think they'll send me my mugshot?" I think out loud. "It'd be kinda funny."

Everett giggles concernedly as he scrolls on his phone. "Maybe. You could ask, I'd love to see it."

We arrive at my house within half an hour, and Everett's mum parks at the top of the road to give me space to walk down and get my stuff. I don't have my wallet, and therefore I don't have my house key, so it's a little bit awkward when I have to knock on the front door of my own house when they're not even expecting me home for another two and a bit weeks.

Dad answers the door and looks startled to see me.

"Oh. That was a quick nineteen days." He says, clearly trying to be funny, but I don't care for it.

"Yep." I reply, pushing past him and heading straight up the stairs. My bedroom is a mess. I have to throw some of my clothes around to find my wallet on the floor, and then I also find my school bag that I still haven't emptied out.

After successfully making my bedroom even messier, I've managed to wrangle a couple t-shirts and joggers into my bag.

"Where are you going?" Comes Alfie's voice from the doorway of my bedroom. He looks worried, and a little sad.

"Just going to stay somewhere else tonight, little man. You'll be okay, won't you?"

"Yeah." He sighs. "I wish you could stay."

"I'm sorry. But, if they stay here, they're gonna be mean to me again."

"I know. I'm sorry they're mean to you."

"Not your fault, teddy, don't apologise."

Alfie nods and walks further into my room, sitting down on my bed. "You'll come back, won't you? I get scared when you don't come home."

My heart breaks at his words. I abandon my backpack on the floor and sit next to him on the bed, wrapping my arm around his waist and prompting him to sit on my lap.

"Have you ever had a bad day, Alfie? And then you come home and Mama has the slow cooker on?" I ask, whispering because of the proximity.

"Beef stew, yuck." He giggles. "But, um, yeah. When I

195

tripped over on the playground."

"Right. Well, it's like, my life is a little bit like a playground right now. But the playground has a lot of rocks everywhere. Loads of things that make me trip over a lot."

Alfie nods. "Sounds scary."

"Yeah. And, when you tripped over on the playground, I guess you just wanted to come home and watch Thomas and have some ice cream, right?"

He smiles. "Yeah. Would've been good."

"But Mama was making beef stew, and there was nothing you could do to change her mind."

"Mhm."

"It's like, like when I stay here I can only have the slow-cooker food. But, if I go somewhere *else*, they have ice cream *and* Thomas on the TV."

"You don't get to feel better about falling on the playground when you're here." He summarises. God, he's such an intelligent kid.

"Yeah. Sometimes it makes my ouchies worse when I'm here."

"Because you used to be a girl? And Mama and Daddy don't like that you're not any more."

"You're a really smart kid, Alfie." I say, ruffling his hair. "You have to promise me you're gonna stay in line."

"Only if you promise the same." He murmurs. I press a slow kiss to the top of his head.

"I promise, teddy bear. We can keep each other in line."

He laughs as he looks up at me. "Okay, Ky. Where are you going, though?"

"To my friend's house. Um, how about, little one, I give you his address? So that way, you know where I am."

Alfie nods and wraps his arms around my neck, as he usually does when he wants to be picked up. "Alright." I say, amused by his playfulness. "Let's go downstairs and you can see me to the door." I tell him, standing up and letting him hook his legs around my waist as I told him on my hip. I use my spare hand to pick up my backpack off the floor and swing it onto my back.

At the bottom of the stairs, I set Alfie onto the floor. "You're off to disappear for three days at a time again, then?" Mum says from the end of the hallway.

"That's the plan." I reply easily.

"Who bailed you out? Assuming you didn't escape, that is."

"It's not your business who bailed me out. I'll see you whenever."

Alfie tugs on the hem of my shirt and I smile down at him. "What's up?"

"Be safe." He says.

"I'll be super safe." I assure him. "I love you, Alfie."

"Love you, too." He says.

The interaction is heavy on my chest as I walk back up the street towards Everett's car.

"Sorry." I say when I get in. "Had to give my little brother a pep talk."

"The kid from the police station?" Everett asks whilst I buckle my seatbelt back up.

"Yeah."

"How old?"

"Eight. Newly so."

"That's such a good age." Miss Enfield says. "Before they get all grown up and angsty." She jokes. Everett rolls his eyes, but chuckles nonetheless.

"You're taking the sofa tonight, by the way." Everett says. "Revenge for the neck pain it gave me when you hijacked my bed on Friday."

"Yeah. Fair enough." I reply. "Thanks."

"Don't sweat it." He replies. If I didn't owe this kid one before, I do now. In fact, I owe him a million different things. And I owe the Pride club two-hundred pounds. There's a pretty crushing weight on my shoulders, especially with having to go to court next week. And also the things that Dean will do to me when he gets word that I snitched on him. And my relationship with Abbie, if that's ever going to happen again.

But I promised Alfie that I would get back on track. So I will. Even if I have to rely on a purple-haired boy and his mum to do it.

13

Everett

Having Kylen around in my house has really not been as bad as I thought it would be. He stayed over on Sunday night, then Monday night, too. He disappeared back to his house on Tuesday, but was back on our doorstep pretty promptly on Wednesday evening, teary-eyed and with alcohol on his breath.

He didn't speak to us much that night, but he was very apologetic the whole time from when he stumbled through the door and crashed asleep on the sofa.

The truth is that I think his court date is really getting to him.

On Monday night (or, technically Tuesday morning), I woke up at like three AM to get some water and he was sitting on the sofa, duvet around his shoulders as he hunched over his phone that was playing a video. It was titled 'Top Five Angry Judge Moments In Court', and so I made the executive decision to confiscate his phone and stay up with him so that he wouldn't be alone on an island in a sea of swirling thoughts.

He's still asleep when I wander into the living room on

Thursday morning, so I'm as quiet as possible while passing through to get the laundry off the balcony. Clearly not silent enough, though, and maybe it was the sliding door clicking shut, because he's awake when I get back into the room.

"Morning." I say, smiling at him behind the mound of clothes that I'm holding.

He smiles at me weakly. "How'd you sleep?" I ask him, and he brings his legs towards him to sit cross-legged.

"Honestly? Not well. I- rough night, I guess."

"Just couldn't sleep, or did you have a nightmare?"

He almost scowls at me like he's implying that he had a nightmare is a threat to his masculinity.

"No. Just was thinking a lot. Didn't make it easy to fall asleep."

"Amen. Thinking about court?"

He shrugs. "A little. And going back to the club today. I know what those lot are like, I'd bet my life savings they've been talking."

I don't tell him that I know they definitely have.

"Can I ask you for some advice?" He says suddenly. "Um, about a thing."

"Go for it." I say, dropping the clothes down on the floor in the corner of the room. He shuffles as close to the end of the sofa as possible so that I can sit down on it too, grabbing a cushion and hugging it to my chest as we talk.

"I don't mean this in an offensive way at all, but I just know that you've dealt with it more than I have, so-"

"Say what you gotta say, man."

"I'm.. really worried that I'm gonna get misgendered and deadnamed throughout the whole of my trial on Monday. 'Cause they obviously have my deadname legally, and I'm not too confident that I can ask 'pretty please don't call me that' when it's a legal situation."

"Is that what's been worrying you?"

"Yeah. Or, or like- what if the judge is a massive trans-phobe? And gives me the maximum possible punishment out of prejudicial spite."

"I think there's laws to prevent that."

"And, everything that happens in a courtroom is public record, right? So, what if someone from my school researches the case and see that they're calling me a girl, and then suddenly the whole school knows my deadname and I have to fucking move again." He stresses, flopping backwards on the sofa.

"Hey, it's okay. Is that why you had to move schools last time?"

He shakes his head slowly. "No, it was something else. But I just can't help but think of the worst possible outcome."

It's definitely a difficult situation. "Well, I've never really had that much deadname trouble. Other than from people that knew me before I transitioned."

"How come?"

"Well, we- my mum helped me change it legally a few years back."

"Oh."

"But, I can at least sympathise with the misgendering."

"I'm just worried I'll say something that I'll regret." He sighs, rubbing his face. "If they spend the whole time misgendering and deadnaming me, I'm probably gonna react. You know what I'm like."

"Right. And if you snap at the judge.."

"It probably won't end well." He finishes, wringing his

hands anxiously. "How do you get past it? Being misgendered."

I think about it for a long while. I used to think of my deadname as an alias that I was using when doing undercover work. But, that was when I was fourteen, and I think that if I suggest that to him, Kylen would punch me for patronising him.

"I think you just have to get over it."

"Oh." He says, frowning. "That's not really what I wanted to hear."

"The thing that I had to make peace with pretty quickly is that people will *always* do that to you. You could be the best-passing person in the world and there'd still be people that would misgender you, just because they know you're trans. It's kind of inevitable. I spent a long time trying to get over it with my therapist a few years ago."

"And what did your therapist say?"

"If you're confident enough in yourself, it won't bother you."

"But that's the thing. It does bother me. A lot." He says, reaching across to the coffee table and picking up a glass of water.

"It's because I think you've got this idea in your head that the whole world will cave in on you the second you get misgendered. But, I promise it won't. I think once you learn that - and actually believe it - things will get easier."

He puts the water back down and takes a really deep breath in. "You're probably right. I just hate the idea that I'm gonna sit in a room of people who are all looking at me and just thinking 'girl.'"

"I don't have an actual solution for that, unfortunately. But, we do have a place to be later on today that nobody would ever consider you a girl at."

"Right, the club. We should- we should get ready." He says, sparing a glance at his watch. "Shit. Didn't realize how late it was."

I check my phone and see that it's about ten minutes to twelve. Considering it's a weekday, that is pretty late. We don't have to be at the club until the afternoon, though, but Kylen wants us to go down a little early to help them pack up from the younger group before, and also so that we don't have to make an entrance in front of everyone.

"I'll get started on some brunch." I say, standing up off the sofa and leaving Kylen alone.

Kylen doesn't have his lanyard when we arrive at the club, because it's back at his house and he didn't think to bring it. So, I encourage him to choose a light blue coloured one, the same tone as the underneath of his hair. Although you can't really see the hair dye with the way he's styled his hair, I think it's a nice touch. He worries to me for a moment about not having the keys to loads of the cupboards from his usual lanyard, but he also knows that Thalia has many copies, so the world won't cave in.

"Very glad to see you two." Rowan smiles as he comes to say hi. "Are you alright, Kylen?"

He nods quickly. "Yeah. I'm fine, I don't need a pity party." He says lightly. "Thanks, by the way. For paying the bail and everything."

"Don't worry about it." Rowan replies smoothly. "But

you've got to make use of it. Don't get into any more trouble, okay?"

"Yeah. I won't."

We go through into Hall A and Rowan tells us that we're doing a karaoke night. They've got two of those microphones hooked up to speakers that are also wired into what I recognise as Thalia's laptop. The projector is unrolled and they've even got some coloured lights around, although they're turned off.

He says that they still need to finish off the under fifteens group, and asked if we can bring the snacks and everything in from the boot of his car. Of course, we agree, and he trusts Kylen with the keys.

"That's a lot of squash." I say, noting the four bottles of it.

"I think there'll be a big turnout tonight. I mean, at least, the two of them are expecting it with all these fairy cakes."

We take the bags inside and lock Rowan's car, heading back into Hall A to set up all of the food and everything, just barely getting in when Kylen's phone starts ringing.

He puts the bag down carefully and takes his phone out, eyes widening.

"Oh, shit. It's Abbie." He says.

"Answer it!" I exclaim. "Answer it, I'll put the food out."

"Okay." He says, answering the phone and deciding to put it on speaker. "Hello?"

"Hi. Um, sorry. I'm under strict girl-code instruction not to talk to you, but I just wanted to check you're okay." She says, sounding a little worried.

"I'm fine, yeah. How are you?"

"It's just 'cause, I heard you got nicked." She continues, ignoring his question.

"Oh. Right. Like five days ago, yeah."

"*But, you're okay? Not in prison just yet?*" Abbie jokes, and Kylen smiles in a way that I haven't seen before.

"Yeah. I mean, I've got a court hearing come the end of the month. But other than that."

"*What did you even do?*"

"I was hanging out with Dean. Trying to get on his good side, 'cause like, yeah. But it escalated a little bit, I guess. Bit of vandalism."

"*I heard that they got Dean, too.*"

"They did?"

"*Well, that's what Madeline said.*"

"Okay. That might be my fault. So, if they did nick Dean, then there is not a chance in hell he's gonna take the video of us down."

"*What? Did you tell them he was involved?*"

"It's complicated. Dropped my bail to a fifth of what it was by telling them."

"*You're gonna be in shit with his lot.*"

"I know. But, they were threatening to charge *me* with everything he did if I didn't tell them."

"*Just stay safe. Don't go out at night alone or anything. Unless you want his mates to jump you.*" Abbie laughs. "*I'll let you know if I hear anything.*"

"Thanks, Abs. It means a lot."

"*Yeah. Um, okay. Bye.*" Abbie says before hanging up the phone.

"Well," Kylen says, shoving his phone back in his pocket. "It's nice to know that she cares."

"Of course she cares. But I feel that this might be a setback in you winning her back."

Kylen blinks at me a few times before smiling as he feigns

irritation. "You were the one that told me to grass on Dean!"

"I know, I know. I'm just saying that this significantly decreases the chance of the video getting taken down."

"No shit, Sherlock."

"Sheesh, okay. I'll stop talking." I say, holding my hands up in surrender.

After his phone call, Kylen helps me finish getting all of the food onto the tables and everything, and once we hear the excited chatter and hubbub of the younger kids clearly being picked up by parents and such, it doesn't take long for Thalia to appear.

"Hi guys." She says. "Thanks for doing that."

"No worries." I tell her with a smile.

After that, it only takes five minutes for people from the club to start trickling in. We do what we always do before we start a session, by just milling around and chatting before the circle will start in about five minutes' time. Kylen keeps quiet for most of it, just listening to other people's conversations - which I can't really fault him for, considering everything that has happened.

By the time that we all sit down in our chairs, there's about ten of us. It's myself, Kylen, Mars, Brynn, Dallas, Lilia, and a few of the quieter club members, as well as Thalia and Rowan.

There's palpable tension in the room, probably because it feels like everyone is desperate to ask Kylen a hundred questions about getting arrested (to be fair, it is quite a good anecdote if he wants to be interesting at parties), but nobody will dare attempt to ask him out of fear that he'll get upset.

Despite everything, we settle into a normal rhythm for the club. We each answer today's question (which is 'if you were a dog, which breed would you be?', and I'd be a beagle. And

Kylen would be a Dalmatian). After that, Thalia dims the lights and turns on the smaller ones so that we can start wishing the night away over musical theatre tunes.

Eli arrives about half an hour late. He giggles the whole way through the door, and as I had begun to expect, drags his new boyfriend, Will, behind him.

Will looks a lot more casual today than he did at the party. His hair is tied behind him in a messy man bun, and he's wearing solely a red t-shirt with an amount of rips that has to be intentional, and some grey cargo trousers.

From behind his cup of orange squash, Kylen chokes on a cough and takes a step backwards so that he hits the wall.

"Uh, you all good?" Lilia asks whilst squinting at him.

"Fuck," He mutters, pulling his t-shirt forward to a baggier position.

"Didn't answer the question." I tell him, glancing between himself and Will.

Kylen sucks in a deep, harsh breath before answering. "Um, he goes to my school. Went, I guess."

"Oh, that's not that bad. Just might be a bit awkward." I say with a shrug. Honestly, Kylen can be so dramatic sometimes, it's jarring.

"No, Everett. He *goes to my school.*" He repeats, bringing his hand to his mouth to start biting his nails. It's only at that point that I realize what he means.

"*Oh.*" I fumble for a moment. "He knows you as a dickhead cis-het guy."

"And, fuck, Eli knows that he knows me like that. What a prick."

"Alright," Lilia chimes in, clearly trying to mediate. "Well, Eli's boyfriend has just as much of a right to be here as you do."

Kylen looks at me with pleading eyes as if he wants me to argue with her. Instead, I just offer him a bit of an impartial shrug that says 'she's kinda right.'

Whilst Dallas and Brynn have a really good attempt at 'Love Is An Open Door', I watch as Eli introduces Will to Thalia and Rowan, before the two start coming over to where we're lingering by the buffet table.

I hear Will gasp loudly and Kylen's eyes widen. "Oh Jesus, fuck." He mutters. "Make sure I don't hit him, Rhett." He mutters. I don't comment on him calling me a nickname that only my mum ever calls me, because he seems like he might be going into fight or flight. And, besides, even if I *did* want to comment, I wouldn't have time.

"Guys," Eli says with a grin. "This is Will. Will, Lilia. And, um, Everett – you met Will at Leo's, right?"

"Sure did." I reply, raising my eyebrows at him. He gives me a slightly worried look before nodding.

"Yeah."

"And, you know Kylen. From school."

Will does a bit of a double take, blinking. It's dark, so it's no wonder that it takes him a second to process what he can see.

"Oh, shit." Will says, smirk adorned. "You're gay?"

"No." Kylen replies, almost too quickly.

"What are you.. doing here, then?"

Kylen shoots Eli what I can only describe as a death glare, accompanied with a hateful scowl.

"You know, I kind of see it." Will continues, and I really do not like where he is going. "Now that I look, you do have quite a feminine face. And figure. In the way that gay boys do."

"Will." Eli whispers, but not loud enough. "Cut it out."

"Oh my god!" Will carries on, not listening to his boyfriend in the slightest. "Oh my god, that's why you wouldn't have sex with Abbie Hutchinson. You're gay. Does she know?"

"Will."

"Dude, your friends eat queer people *alive*. I have to text someone about this, hold on." He rants, taking his phone out and typing in his passcode.

It feels like I barely blink before Kylen has whacked the phone out of Will's hand and then instantly disappeared. Gone from the room - the only evidence that he was ever here being his abandoned cup of squash, and the door that leads to the hallway still swinging on its hinges from how quickly he went through it.

Eli downright scoffs at his boyfriend, who looks very bewildered at having his phone tossed to the ground, before turning to follow with a shout of "Kylen!", clearly feeling responsible for Will's actions.

Will looks off in the direction of Eli and then back to me. "Sensitive." He mutters, bending down and retrieving his phone. Then, he swallows as if thinking. "Give us a minute, will you?" He asks Lilia, and she glances at me before nodding and taking leave to catch the end of the current song.

He looks around anxiously before shoving his hands in his pockets. "Look, dude. I just want to make sure that there's no hard feelings."

"What would there be hard feelings about?" I ask, so obviously putting it on - and the look on his face is worth it. Will lowers his voice to a whisper, despite the fact that there's nobody near us and music is blasting.

"You won't tell him, right?"

"Tell him what?" I feign innocence again, crossing my arms.

"You know. The things I said about him not being my type." He grits, again eyeing the door that Eli followed Kylen through.

"You called him a twink."

Will laughs. "Well, yeah. If the shoe fits. I didn't say it was a bad thing."

"The way you said it made it sound like it was a bad thing. Derogatory, even."

"Alright, just- just don't tell him. We have a good thing going on."

I eye him up suspiciously, but there's not time for anything else because Eli comes back out of the hallway and into the main hall. He stalks up to us slowly and Will grins.

"Hello." Will says with a smirk, wrapping his arm around Eli's shoulder.

"Um, can you come and speak to Kylen? He's upset and I think he wants to kill me, so-"

"Are you asking me, or the little guy?" The taller man asks with a quirked eyebrow.

"Both of you, ideally. I think he ought to speak to you, Will. And, I get the feeling it might get a bit violent if you don't mediate." Eli explains, gesticulating with his hands towards his boyfriend and then me.

Will rolls his eyes. "Fine. But you better not ask me to apologise, he's the one hiding stuff." He says, and then he starts walking off. Eli gives me an apologetic glance before following Will.

We find Kylen sitting on the floor inside the hallway, not

dissimilar to how I found him at Leo's party. But, this time, he isn't crying or drunk - he just looks irritated and bitter.

"Fuck off, Will." He spits.

"You always have been a ray of sunshine." The boy replies sardonically.

I kneel down next to Kylen so that we're in pretty close proximity before whispering to him.

"How are you handing this?" I ask. "Are you coming out to him or are you risking him telling people that you're gay?"

He looks at me with this desperate, pleading expressing before dropping his head back so that it touches the wall and he looks up at the other two.

"*You.*" He says, clenching his jaw. "Don't you dare repeat a fucking thing I'm about to say to you."

Will quirks an eyebrow. "Okay. I'm pretty intrigued to hear how you're gonna worm your way out of this." He states cockily, and Kylen swallows harshly. He reaches his hand out towards mine, at which point I just look at him a little confusedly. He rolls his eyes. "Hold my hand." He says, as quietly as possible. "I'm gonna squeeze the hell out of it."

I try not to laugh as I take his hand. He shakes his head a few times, and the pressure that Kylen puts on my hand is immense.

"I'm trans." He says, looking away from Will and towards the floor. It's clear that the guy didn't hear the admission, because he sequins and goes: "What?"

Kylen sighs dramatically. He squeezes my hand again.

"I'm trans." He repeats, louder this time so that it's very distinguishable.

Will pauses and looks to Eli before turning his attention to Kylen once more. "...gender?"

"No, former." Kylen spits, clearly annoyed beyond belief about having to out himself to this random guy. "Yes, fucking obviously, dipshit."

"Okay, there's no need for that." Will replies. "So, hold on. You're- you were a girl? You've got, *like-*"

"Finish that fucking sentence, Will." Kylen says, leaping up to his feet defensively and letting go of my hand in the process.

Will swallows and steps closer to Eli. "I wouldn't have known. You don't look it."

"That's kind of the point."

"Not for all of you." Will replies, sparing a glance at me. I get this heavy feeling in my chest that makes me feel kind of nauseous.

"You don't get to say things like that." Eli says, confronting his boyfriend, who snickers.

"I'm just a little annoyed that you *knew* he was trans this whole time, and you didn't tell me! Do you know how many friends I could get knowing something massive like that?" Will asks.

"Why the hell would I have told you?"

"Because you're my boyfriend."

"That has nothing to do with Kylen."

Will scoffs and then he looks up to Kylen before speaking. "Right. That's why you wouldn't sleep with Abbie." He deduces.

"No shit." Kylen fires back easily. "And like I said, you won't tell a soul."

"You'd better hope I don't. Your mates literally crucify trans people. Honestly, I'm a little impressed that you've managed to sneak around them so long."

It's just then that the door into the hallway opens, and Thalia leans against it, looking a little bewildered at the sight of us.

"Are you boys okay?" She asks slowly.

"Yeah. We're just perfect." Kylen answers for all of us angrily, seething whilst filtering past Thalia and back into Hall A.

Kylen is decidedly not in a good mood when the club ends. I know that because I can't find him anywhere. I've done a few laps of the building and it feels like he's vanished into thin air. He doesn't answer his phone when I call him, and by the time that everyone else has left the building, I end up bumping into Thalia in the hallway.

"Oh! Everett. What're you still doing here?" She asks, hauling one of her speakers towards a cupboard.

"Um, sorry, yeah. You haven't seen Kylen, have you?"

"I didn't know you were waiting for him. He's in the over-eighteen's lounge." She answers simply. "Just down the hall to the right."

I didn't consider that he could even be in there, because it's called an 'over-eighteen's lounge' for a reason. Also because the lights are all off, and I know he's a bit angsty, but I didn't really peg him as the kind of kid to sit in the dark all alone.

"Kylen?" I ask, the door creaking as I open it. There's little hesitation before I flick the lights on, and am greeted with the sight of Kylen sitting cross-legged on the sofa, eyes glued to the TV as some drawl plays. He startles as the sudden influx of light, and then flinches away from the door.

213

"Fuck, what are you still doing here?" He asks, rubbing his eyes up at me.

"Looking for you. Are you.. not coming back to my place?" I ask, kind of leaning against the door handle.

"Oh. Um, no. Sorry." Kylen replies. "I'm gonna end up moving in if I keep leeching off you. And, besides, I got a text from my dad that," He pauses, pulling his phone out and flicking it on to read off the screen. "'Alfie is worried sick' with me gone, so."

"Right." I say, not acknowledging that if he was so eager to get home, he probably wouldn't be sitting in here. "Um, you hang out in here often?"

"Thalia lets me. I'm watching a show." He explains, gesturing to the paused TV screen.

"In the dark?"

"Yeah."

I sigh and sit beside him. "How long does Thalia let you stay here?"

"Until she kicks me out." He shrugs. He has this vacant look in his eyes that makes me worry a little.

"Does this thing have cable?" I ask, pointing at the TV that sits opposite the sofa. Kylen shrugs and sags his body backwards. There's a new air about him at the moment, and I can take an educated guess as to why. Between my attempts at fiddling with the remote controller, I take a moment to gauge how he feels.

"Will isn't gonna tell anyone, you know that, don't you?"

He shuffles a little bit before replying. "I give him forty-eight hours." Kylen sighs, seeming unaffected by me completely switching his show off the television. "I'm a dead man walking."

I guess I did drink on Wednesday - in the abandoned playground. But I was alone then, and it was only because I didn't want to be at home and I felt so incredibly bad about crashing on Everett's couch for multiple nights in a row.

I know that he doesn't mind. His mum is literally the sweetest person I've ever met, too, but it isn't about how they feel. It's about how I feel, and I feel like garbage having to rely on other people so much.

I shouldn't be drinking, especially not in public in a group. I've been fine. Everett's mum has been letting me smoke on the balcony because she 'understands that it isn't so easy as to just stop because you aren't in your own house.' It's fine. I'm coping, I swear.

Having said that, things are not fine when more and more people start merging in with our group later on in the day. Namely, Dean turns up.

His very presence makes my skin crawl, and my stomach churn. I don't know if it's anxiety or anger, but probably a healthy mix of both considering what he did to me on Sunday.

Dean spends about twenty minutes not even looking in my direction as we walk in circles around the edge of the park, just talking about whatever has been going on in our social circles as of late.

On our third lap, and my second cigarette, my mind begins to wander as I absent-mindedly listen to Jack and Liam rate the girls in our year out of ten.

Or, that is, until there's a cold hand on my shoulder.

"Hey, Kylen." Dean laughs, voice strained with his fake happiness. Oh, fuck. "I just wanted to let you know that you're fucking dead." He says, grinning whilst he does so, probably so that none of my friends notice his suppressed aggression.

My blood runs cold, but I knew this would happen. I have to just play it cool. You know, either that or get curb stomped.

"Excuse me?" I ask, mirroring his energy as I turn my head to look at him.

"The police showed up at my house on Monday." He grits, although he speaks whilst walking alongside me as if it's a perfectly normal conversation.

"Oh, you got found out?" I ask with a faux naive tone.

"You fucking know I did. You snitched."

"No, I didn't." I reply with as much confidence as possible. I taught Everett that confidence is key, and I'd be a hypocrite not to practice what I preach. "Look, man, I don't know how they found you, but maybe you should just grow up a bit and face the consequences of your actions."

Dean huffs and takes a drag of his cigarette. "Well, I hope you know that the video isn't going down any time soon. And I still think you're a snake."

"You can think whatever you want, doesn't make it true."

"I have to go to fucking court." Dean complains, exasperated. There's a worry at the back of my mind that maybe we'll be in the same timeslot. That would be the easiest way to out myself to everyone I've ever met, even if Will doesn't get there first.

"No shit, me too!" I reply with as much obviously fake excitement as I can muster up at this time in the day. "Maybe I'll see you there."

Dean shoves me easily and moves to catch up with his friends. "Whatever you say, bitch-boy." He mutters. Ouch. Yeah, if there's one person who will guarantee that people continue to call me that following Abbie coming up with it, it's Dean. At least I can brush it off coming from him, because I already know that he doesn't like me, and if he hadn't called me that, he would have just come up with some other nasty nickname.

After that interaction, I feel a bit too dejected to play into the usual banter of our group. Especially when most of them are getting to that point where they're all bouncing off each other's drunkenness, and I'm no longer enjoying myself.

"Hey, um, I'm gonna head home, I think." I tell Tobias, who raises his eyebrows at me drunkenly.

"Okay. Bye." He states bluntly, wandering off to berate AJ for finishing the beer can that they were sharing.

Well, that was a lot more simple than I thought it would be. I'd be lying if I said that it doesn't hurt that he cares so little about me leaving, but he's really out of it anyway.

He's more affectionate sober, I swear.

After declaring my leave, I kind of just wander off aimlessly. From further back, my gaggle of friends looks a lot more intimidating hoarding down the road. None of them noticed me leave, which leaves a bit of a hollow of upset in my chest.

It doesn't matter. It's fine. I pull my earphones out of my pocket and have to stop myself from audibly groaning when they tell me that they're out of battery. Fucking perfect, I guess I'm walking home in silence.

I get home just before eight, feeling more emotionally detached than I have in a long time.

Is hanging out with my friends always so shitty without drinks?

The window is still left slightly open from when I left, and so I climb up the side of the house a bit precariously. The edge of the window digs into the middle of my torso pretty excruciatingly, and I'm unpleasantly reminded that my rib pain hasn't been getting any better.

When I get into my bedroom, I half-expect to find both my parents waiting for me to get home. Ready to yell at me for sneaking out.

But I don't.

It's just dead silence as I idly re-enter the room and find it to be in the exact same state that I left it in. It's desolate. Nobody even noticed that I was gone. And my friends didn't even notice me leave. Fuck. It provokes a certain feeling that I haven't felt in a while.

My phone is ringing in my hand before I even have time to register it.

"*Kylen.*" The man on the other end says, sounding a little surprised to hear from me. It makes sense, I haven't spoken to him in months. "*How are you?*"

"Um, hi, Dr Hassan." I say, kicking my shoes off.

"*Are you okay?*" He asks, with the same clinical compassion that he's always had.

"Yeah."

"*Okay.*" He says, and I hear some shuffling of papers on his desk. "*What made you call, then? Just wanted to say 'hello?'*"

"I don't know."

"*You don't know?*"

"I just picked up the phone and then I was just suddenly calling you. Sorry."

"*That's okay.*" He reassures me softly. "*You know, my office is always open if you want to pop down. Within my hours, obviously.*"

It feels almost redundant at this point to even consider the idea. "Can't. Grounded." I tell him bluntly. I probably could just sneak out if I wanted to, in fact, I know I could. Nobody would give two shits, but I'd really prefer to pretend that they would care. If I don't leave again, I'll never know if anyone would care or not.

"Ah. Okay." Dr Hassan replies easily. *"Did you want to talk about anything? Whilst we're on the phone."*

"You're probably, like, busy." I mumble into the phone.

"Don't worry about any of that. I'm your psychologist for a reason." Ex-psychologist, I mentally correct him. *"What's wrong?"* He goes on to ask. I sigh and lean backwards onto my bed and investigate the ceiling as I spill my guts to him.

"I'm starting to feel like maybe my life isn't as great as I thought it was."

"Kylen, just remind me when you've ever said that your life was great." He laughs a little, and I find it funny too. The fact that he's right.

"Okay. Fine. But, like, I got everything I wanted. And I guess I just realized that I'm still not.." I trail off, thumb hovering over the button that would hang up the call. "I guess I'm just greedy. You know, I got it all and.. What if I've been doing everything wrong?"

"Can you elaborate about that?" Dr Hassan asks, actually sounding interested. It makes me more inclined to be honest.

"Like, if I've always been doing shit a certain way. Because it was the only way I knew how, and the only way that ever worked. But then, someone manages to convince me that the way I've been doing it is bad for me."

"Well, your life is different to other people's. What works for you might not work for someone else, and vise versa."

"Maybe." I say, realising how incredibly stupid I sound. I guess I've just always thought it *had* to be this way. If I want to fit in, and be happy, I have to make personal sacrifices.

"So, why don't we run through the pros and cons of not doing things this 'certain way?'"

"Okay." I say, thinking it through. "Cons are that I could lose the girl I like. And most likely all my friends that I like a bit less. Pros are that it might change things. Be more true to myself, I guess. Stop living like I'm having an alcoholic mid-life crisis at sixteen."

"Hm. Well, who says that you have to give your friends and this girl up to be true to yourself?" He asks, and the question lingers for a moment of silence. I don't say anything, so he asks another question. *"Is this about your gender identity? You're thinking about conforming a bit less?"*

"Damn, you're good." I say. I guess it kind of is his job to psychoanalyse me.

"Allow me to make a bit of an observation, Kylen." Dr Hassan says, a little more serious then before. *"I think you seem to have this idea that your options are extreme. You think that being trans means you have to do everything in a meticulously perfect way, or else it'll all fall apart. But, the truth is that you know who you are. You're still a boy no matter how you act, and you don't have to behave a certain way to justify that."*

He leaves me with those words and some harsh silence.

"You sound like Everett." Is all I say.

"Is that a bad thing?" He asks, a mixture of fake offence and curiosity in his words.

"No. And I hate that it isn't. I hate that he's probably right."

Sometimes I find myself wishing that Everett had never entered my life at all. It was all a lot more simple when I was just blindly behaving the only way I knew how.

"I like that you're indirectly admitting that I'm right."

"Ha, ha. Sure."

"I need to close up for the evening. You called at a good time. Are you gonna be okay? I can send you an email with the online support and crisis services if you want me to."

"God, no. I'm fine. I just needed to, to get out of the spiral I was falling down. And the guy that I would usually talk to has been taking care of me a little too much for my liking."

It's irritating because I know that Everett doesn't mind me imposing on him. I wish he would mind, or he would just tell me to fuck off and that could be it. But he just has to be all kind about everything.

"Well, I promise you that anyone who cares about you wouldn't mind a little conversation."

"Yeah."

"Okay. Call me again if you need anything."

"Will do." I say, nodding even though Dr Hassan can't hear it.

"Goodbye, Kylen. Take care of yourself."

"Bye."

I keep lying on my bed for about ten minutes after the call is over. I don't even touch my phone in this time, just sitting alone with my thoughts. I can't help but feel weak after that. I spent so long convincing myself that speaking to a psychologist was the last thing I needed, and now, here I am calling him out of my own accord? It's almost pathetic.

I realize that I'm falling asleep quicker than I can register it with enough energy to stop myself.

I feel like utter dog-shit when I wake up. It's dark outside, and my room is unbelievably cold because I managed to forget to shut the window. Behind the fog of confusion in my post-slumber haze, I figure out that I need to get changed. Falling asleep in the clothes you wore during the day is never ideal, and after the day I had, it's just the cherry on top.

I stumble towards the light switch and flick it on, being blinded by the brightness that only helps to exasperate my headache. After lazily kicking my basketball shorts off and replacing them with a pair of my pyjama bottoms, I'm ready to just collapse into sleep again.

My dysphoria has been so bad recently that I don't even consider taking my binder off before lulling back into sleep after chugging my bedside-table water.

When I wake up again, I feel at least a little bit better. It's light outside now, so there's that.

I feel hungover as hell, and I didn't even drink last night. Fuck.

For a moment I imagine that one of my mates will have messaged me to ask if I got home safe, but when I open by phone and see zero messages, I'm not surprised.

It's still quite early though. Nobody else in my household will be awake yet, so I take the opportunity to drag myself out of bed and into the shower. By eight am, I'm leaning against the kitchen counter, hands hugging a cup of coffee that's still far too hot to drink.

The stairs creak with the weight of someone's footsteps, and I can tell by the sound that it's my dad.

"Morning." He grumbles, brushing past me to get to the kettle.

"Hi." I greet him, watching intently as he starts making a decaf tea. "Um, am I still grounded?"

round is if they knew I was trans already, that way I wouldn't be risking anything.

When I get upstairs to my room with my coffee and sit down on my bed, it dawns on me that if I want any company today, there's only one option.

Everett replies to my text pretty quickly. All he asks for is clarification of my address before telling me that he's on his way. I guess I could have invited someone else from the club, but I don't think any of them like me all that much these days. And, I could have also just not invited anyone at all, but I want my parents to think that I'm putting effort in.

He rings the doorbell and my mum gets to the door before I do.

"Oh. Hello." She says, glancing between him and me. "I'm assuming this is your friend."

"Sure is." I say, getting down the last few steps. "Um, Mum, this is Everett."

"Have we met before?" She says, practically ignoring my words in favour of staring him down.

"Maybe. I was at the police station on Sunday, um, yeah."

"Oh. You're the one that the phone call went to."

"Yep." I exclaim, trying to cut through the conversation. "We'll be upstairs."

"Mhm." Mum hums, walking back off towards the kitchen. Everett shuts the door behind him in silence and neither of us say a word until we get up into my bedroom.

"Wow. Okay." He snickers, looking around my bedroom like it's a museum. "You really like Star Wars, huh?"

"I have two *Funko Pops* and a poster, dude." I defend myself, sitting down on my bed and watching as he explores the terrain. I got the Star Wars poster from the cinema, because going to see the new film was the first time I ever hung out in a group of cis boys that thought I was cis, too. The film wasn't even that great to be honest, but I guess it means a lot to me. And, I have the Funko Pops because my parents took notice of the poster and put them on my birthday list.

After that, it takes him ten seconds to find one of my footballs. He kicks it across the room to me with pretty bad technique.

"So, um, why'd you invite me over? Not that I don't want to be here, but it feels out of character for you." He says, as blunt about his thoughts as always.

"Can I not have a friend over?" I ask, deflecting the way that he's clearly trying to hack into my emotions right now.

"Well, yeah. But you have a big friend group of boys that you'd much rather be hanging out with."

He has a point, I guess.

"Grounded." I say, crossing my arms and focusing intently on the football that Everett continues to toss around the room absent-mindedly.

"When has that ever stopped you?"

"I dunno. What if I wanna turn my life around?"

Everett laughs quietly as he glances towards me in a way that feels critical. "Fine. Well, what have you been up to whilst grounded?"

"Not much." I answer honestly. "Snuck out and had a shit time being the only sober one at a meet up."

I shock even myself with the honesty that I give him. But he did ask. I guess it just felt shit to know that I can't seem to enjoy myself unless I'm pissed out of my mind. Everett just raises his eyebrows and picks the ball up, deciding to sit down on my carpet as he clearly feels in the mood for a genuine conversation, eugh. Just when I was hoping to not have to think too hard today.

15

Everett

I'm surprised when Kylen tells me that he hasn't been drinking. It's not that I don't think he can, it's just that it always seemed so ingrained in him that that's what he does. He does things that make him upset and then instead of talking about them, he gets drunk to forget.

"I just-" He begins, demeanour nervous. "I kind of need to stay out of trouble. I couldn't risk it."

Ah, yeah, okay. And here was me thinking that he was actually making an effort on his own accord. My bad.

"Right." I say, my disappointment towards him evident in my voice. He looks a little hurt by it and stammers as he scrambles to find something to say that would make me less let down.

"I, um, I called my psychologist earlier." He admits quietly, as if it's a secret. "Ex-psychologist, whatever."

I will admit that it does surprise me. He's not the kind of person to see any kind of mental health professionals, but I guess I learn new things about this boy every day. The

– wanted us to feel bad."

"No, I didn't."

"Oh, come on. That's all this has ever been. For attention."

"I didn't even want you to find out. Because I knew you'd fucking act like this!" He yells at her, close to tears, and I don't miss the way that his hands are shaking. "Can we have this conversation when Everett isn't here?"

"You were going to have this conversation with them, anyway."

"I wasn't gonna tell him about the hospital." He murmurs. "I wasn't."

"Oh, come off it. Anything that'll get you attention, you'll do." She says calmly. "Oh, and, Dr Hassan sent me a message this morning, asking me to keep an eye on you. Do you now anything about that?"

"No." He answers, breathing heavily. "Can you go away, now?"

"Okay." His mum agrees, finally. "But just remember that all I have to make is a phone call."

When the door shuts behind her, I look over at Kylen, who bites his lip and shakes his head at me. "Don't say anything." He whispers. "Can you just, just look at that wall for a second." He pleads, and I nod silently, turning my head to study his wall of posters.

Once I look away, it only takes five seconds before I start to hear his sobs. They're slightly muffled, so he's probably crying into something. It gives me time for reflection. Hell, I feel like crying just witnessing that. I had kind of just thought that his life was perfect, because he passed well and he has a big friend group.

I feel horrible for the things that I assumed about him.

237

"Okay." He says, voice wavering as he sniffles. I take that as my queue to turn back around, and he's sat on his bed, arms wrapped around a pillow as he makes futile attempts to wipe the tears off his cheeks. "Sorry." He says.

I decide that I don't need any words for this next part. I just stand up and close the distance between us, staying in front of his bed. He looks up at me with a guilty expression, and I just open my arms at him. He sits still for a few seconds, and so I gesture with my hands, telling him to just accept what I'm offering. After that, he stands up quickly, and faster than I realize he's doing it, he's wrapped his arms around my shoulders, sniffling, and then crying again.

I let him weep into my t-shirt for as long as he needs.

"I'm sorry." He apologies, pulling away from me after a couple minutes. His voice is hoarse and I don't think I've ever seen him look more upset.

"Don't be." I say quietly. "Do you want me to go?"

"No. No, I can't just let you leave after that." He says, sitting back down on his bed. "I need to explain better than she did."

"Alright. I'm listening." I speak in the most caring voice possible, sitting down next to him on the bed. He sighs.

"I didn't do it to guilt trip my parents into letting me go on testosterone. That was just something that I said would make me happier when I spoke to Dr Hassan. I didn't even want them to find out about the hospital thing. It was meant to be easy."

"Surely they were always gonna find out." I tell him.

"Well, yeah. I was just hoping I'd already be dead when they did."

"Oh." I reply, not having anything else to say. That's

heavy as fuck. I feel bad for encouraging him to dig into these memories. "How did they, then?"

"Um, Thalia called them." He admits. Thalia? My eyes widen as I realize what he's implying.

"You did it at the club? That's fucked up, Kylen."

"I know it was shitty of me to put that onto her." He defends quickly. "I do. But- but, I wanted to be somewhere that I actually liked. And, it was after the club. After Rowan went home too, it was just us."

"You wanted her to find you?"

"It wasn't planned that meticulously. I just didn't want to give either of my parents the satisfaction. And, I couldn't have done it at home, 'cause I have a little brother. Would've given him PTSD or some shit."

"Fucking hell."

"Sorry. I haven't really ever spoken about it with anyone. I know it makes me a shitty person."

"Maybe you weren't a shitty person, Kylen. Maybe you were just struggling."

"Well, I can be struggling and also a shitty person."

"Fine. But, you're okay now, right?"

"Better than I was before."

"Why'd you do it?" I ask suddenly. Kylen kind of shrugs and leans back on his bed, dropping his voice to a whisper.

"Being trans is hard." He says. "Even harder when my whole family resents me for it. I don't know, all of these wait-lists and news articles, and... sometimes it feels like being trans has stolen my future. I don't think I'll ever get married, and I'll never get to have biological kids. I can't do the job that I wanted. My whole family will stop talking to me the second I move out. I can't go fucking swimming with my friends because they'll want to know why I'm wearing a t-shirt in the fucking ocean." He laughs a little concernedly at that last one. "It just feels like there's so much I can never do, so what's the fucking point?"

"You swear a lot when you're upset." I observe, noting the way that his chest rises and falls rapidly with the weight of his stress.

"Thanks."

"But, um, yeah. Trans existentialism is pretty horrible. I think we've all wished we weren't trans at one point or another. But it's all in the mindset."

"A good mindset is easier said than done."

"True. But, um, what about Alfie? Alfie loves you." I try, because from what I've seen, he totally does.

Kylen nods with a dejected look on his face. "Alfie's a funny story, actually." He begins. "He was a planned kid, unlike me. I, um, I told my parents that I thought I was a boy when I was eight, in March. I know because I have a diary entry about how nervous I was to tell them. They said that it's fun to play pretend, but I kept insisting I was a boy, pretty much every day of March." I nod along as he speaks. "And they made the decision that they were gonna try for another kid in April."

My heart sinks at his words as I process them properly. "You don't think-"

"Yeah, I do. My dad told me, when he was drunk. About two months before my attempt, he told me that it was fine that I was failing all my classes at school, because they had Alfie for that exact reason. So that when they knew I wasn't gonna turn out right, they could have at least one kid that they like."

"Shitting hell, Kylen."

"It's whatever. I'm sorry, I didn't mean to turn this into a vent session."

"No, it's not whatever. Have you seen a therapist about all this?"

He smiles at me for a moment, almost finding humour in my question. "Well, after I was in the hospital I was entitled to six sessions with that psychologist. And because I was stubborn as fuck and honestly just bitter that I lived, I didn't say shit to him. I only started opening up in our last session, but at that point it's like, futile. 'Cause we'd run out of time. Got told I could request more sessions, but it'd be up to a six month wait 'cause I was 'low priority' at that point."

"God, our country's mental health system is broken." I remark. I know it doesn't fix how he feels, but it might help to offer some sympathy.

"Tell me something I don't know." He laughs brokenly.

I realize then just how many things add up with this story. "So, that's why Thalia cares about you so much?"

"I mean, I guess, yeah. I literally owe my life to her. And, I mean, I'm glad that I'm still here. 'Cause I realized that I didn't want to die, not really. I just wanted things to be different."

"Mhm."

"You know, I admire your mum so much." He tells me sincerely. "Parents like that are genuinely the difference between a dead kid and a living one."

"Yeah. She's amazing." I say, and I mean it. I'm couldn't be more lucky to have a mum like her. "Speaking of mums, what did yours mean about making a phone call?" I ask, and it's the last thing that I don't quite understand.

"Oh." Kylen says, smirking in slight amusement. "When I was discharged from the hospital, they told her that if she got worried about my mental state again, she could phone them, and they'd bring me back in to think about what's 'best for me.' And, she totally took that as them saying they'd section me or something if she asked them to. I'm pretty sure that's not how it works, but she's been using 'I'll just have you put in a psych ward' as a threat ever since."

"Yikes."

"Well, nobody's perfect." He jokes, and then he blinks a few times as if thinking. "Um, thanks. For letting me tell you about all this. It's actually, like, a big weight off my chest."

"Yeah, of course." I reply, and I mean it. "Thanks for being honest with me about it."

Kylen stands up off his bed and walks over to his desk, which he spins around to lean against. "I don't know what it is about you, Everett. You're the only person I've ever opened up to like this."

"I guess I just have that effect on people." I tease in a light-hearted manner.

"You're also the only person I've ever cried around. You know, that's not my parents. Or Thalia." He then says. "Which is weird, because, I know I've told you a million times before, but I'm not a crier."

"There's nothing wrong with being a crier, dude."

"Now that I think about it, I don't think I've ever seen you cry." He accuses me. I consider it for a moment, and he's right. I guess I've never really shown Kylen a vulnerable side of myself before. And he's shown me a very vulnerable side of himself.

"Fine, um, well, I do cry." I admit. "I cried when I got back from the Aconite Centre, the first night I went."

"You did?"

"Mhm. Because you were the first other trans man that I met. And I thought you were so perfect. Like, literally everything I could never be. Tall, and flat, and deep-voiced, and all your clothes fit you perfectly."

"You were jealous of me?"

"Yeah. And then you looked me in the eyes and effectively told me that you were ten times the man I was. And as much as I was defensive and rude back to you, I believed what you said." I admit, and it feels good to tell him how I felt. He nods to himself. "And then I cried again to my mum, after the club on the Sunday after Pride. Which was weird, because I've had cis people be shit to me before, and it never bothered me. But it's different when it's another trans person. Because it was like you were asserting the fact that you knew you were a better trans person than me."

He continues to nod to himself as I speak, waiting about thirty seconds after I've finished before he says anything.

"I'm really sorry." He says. "I only said those things to you because I was scared."

"Kylen Lysander? Scared?" I mock, and he rolls his eyes playfully before continuing to lament.

"You were right." He states plainly.

"How so?"

"When you said that I was threatened by you." He says, fumbling with his hands. "I was. It upset me that you were trans, and proud, and happy. Because I'm only one of those three adjectives."

It saddens me to hear. But, it feels like since getting arrested, he's been going through a bit of a rough patch.

"You're not happy?" I ask.

He shrugs and looks down at his hands. "I'm a lot happier

than I was this time last year. But, I don't know. I feel like when I'm genuinely content with my day-to-day life, I'll be confident about that fact."

"I think you should get a therapist." I say. "Sorry if it's not my place, but, like, an actual one that you see regularly."

He blinks at me over and over again before turning his attention to his football and bringing it under his foot. "Yeah. But I don't trust easy, and I also don't have the money for that."

"Your parents could pay."

"They wouldn't."

"I don't know, tell them it's for conversion therapy." I suggest jokingly, and much to my relief, he actually laughs, like, genuinely laughs.

"Let's get out of here." He suggests. "This room smells like teenage angst, and it's dragging me down."

"Okay." I laugh at the sudden change in his attitude.

"You ever climbed out of a window before, Rhett?" He asks, slipping his feet into his Air Jordan's.

My mum worries about me a lot. One of her biggest rules is that I don't sneak out. She doesn't care if I want to go somewhere, because I'm sixteen and she trusts me. But, the rule is that she has to know where I'm going. And I respect my mum a lot. No sneaking out of our house means no sneaking out of our house.

But, to be fair, this isn't our house. It's Kylen's.

16

Kylo

"What a rush." Everett laughs when we get half way down the street. "I've never jumped out of a window before."

"Okay, you didn't exactly jump, dude. It was an anxious shuffle along the windowsill if anything, and I had to stand under the window and promise I'd catch you if you fell." I chide, and he brushes me off with a 'psh' before picking up his pace to more of a skip.

In all honesty, I'm surprised that he didn't recoil away from me when he found out about everything. Most people do, because they don't want to have to deal with the burden of someone like me.

In fact, if anything, he seems more inclined to be my friend now. And, now that it feels like we've aired out all of our dirty laundry, I feel good about the future of our friendship. Feeling good about a friendship is new to me. Which is why I take all of my energy to not be sceptical when he grins at his phone and then back at me.

"Oh, god. What are you up to?" I ask, jogging a little to catch up with him.

"Nothing. Just texted a few people. We're gonna socialise."

Well, if there's one thing that he loves, it's to socialise. As far as I'm aware, though, Everett doesn't exactly have a rich social circle outside of where we met, which gives me a hunch about who we're meeting up with. "These are people from the club, aren't they?"

"You know it." He says. "I asked a handful of people, but so far, I've got confirmation from Eli, Dallas, and Lilia."

I really don't want to rain on his parade, but the scars from having to out myself to Will are still fresh.

"I'm still pissed at Eli." I tell him with a bit of a scoff.

"Well, it's good to rebuild bridges." He suggests lightly. "And, he didn't *really* do anything wrong."

"Debatable." I say, and Everett gives me a certain look that tells me I'm being obnoxious. "Fine. Just as long as you promise me he's not bringing his boy-toy."

"His boyfriend." Everett corrects me.

"Tomato, tomato. I just don't like the guy." I defend, holding my hands up in the air in surrender.

"Yeah, that we can agree on." He says, slowing his pace and shoving his hands in his pockets. My interest is definitely piqued.

"Go on."

"Okay. It's just that- at Leo's party, I didn't like the way he spoke about Eli."

"What did he say?"

"Nothing that bad. He said Eli wasn't his type, then he was taking him home to hook up like two hours later. Rubbed me the wrong way."

"Ah." I breathe out. "Well, Eli's gonna be an adult later this year."

"I know."

"And he doesn't like getting lectured about his relationships."

"Talking from experience?"

"Yep." I confirm, slipping into my anecdote like it's nothing. "Last year, Eli brought a different boyfriend to the club. And Thalia asked me to go and grab some spare chairs, so I did. And said boyfriend followed me to the chair-stack-room, closed the door behind us-"

"Oh my god." Everett says.

"And he tried to kiss me. Like, properly backed me into the wall and everything."

"Jesus."

"Yeah, and I shoved him away and had to have the 'I'm straight' talk with him. Because, he probably assumed I was a slightly feminine gay guy, like Will did." I explain. I used to get that a lot, before I started voice training and taking testosterone and such. "So, being the good guy that I am, I pulled Eli aside and was like 'hey man, just a heads up, your boyfriend just tried to kiss me', and he got all annoyed at me."

"How so?" Everett asks, clearly engaged with the story.

"He was like 'I'm sorry you're not in a relationship, but you don't have to sabotage mine.'"

"Jesus."

"Yeah, and I told him that I wasn't trying to do that, and he told me that even if the boy did try to kiss me, I should let him deal with his own relationship and mind my business."

Everett gasps dramatically. "Yikes, okay. I guess I won't tell him."

"I mean, do what you want. I think he gets insecure about his relationships, that's all. Not like I can talk, but it's just an observation."

"Mm." Everett hums. "Speaking of relationships, have you heard from Abbie?"

'No', is the simple answer. And there's no way in hell that Dean is taking that video down now, so I might have blown it. The idea makes me upset, but I've done enough of sharing my feelings with Everett today.

"Not yet. I'm giving her space."

"Mm."

"How about you?" I ask, trying to diverge the subject. "Are you in the market?"

I think that if Everett had a significant other, I definitely would have heard of them by now. I mean, he's never mentioned anyone in a romantic context, but maybe that's just me not really noticing that he's been pining after someone.

"Eh. I'm not really after a partner right now." He says.

"Any reason? Or are you just not that bothered?" I ask, and I'm genuinely not trying to be weird about it. I get how jarring romance is when you're trans, and I can get why he might want to stay out of it and wait for it to come to him.

"Oh, I'm aro." He says. "It's not really my scene."

"Oh." I say, a little confused. "I thought you were bi?" I ask him. I only say so because I'm pretty sure I remember seeing a picture of him on the youth club's Facebook page. Everyone had made cookies, and his were iced in the bisexual flag colours.

"Yep, that too." He replies cheerily. I stop whilst walking down the pavement, mostly for dramatics. He's confusing me quite a bit more now, and he stops with an expression that calls me stupid in like five different ways.

"Dude, a-*romantic*" He says. "Lack of romantic attraction

to any gender, basically."

"Yeah, I get that."

"Right. Bi-*sexual*. So, I'm not gonna like, fall in love with anyone, but I still want other kinds of relationships."

"Oh. Like, you don't feel romantic attraction, but you still feel sexual attraction towards people."

"Bingo." He confirms, doing some little finger-guns at me. "Have you never met an aromantic person before?"

"I mean, I've met aro-ace people. And, I've met asexual people. I didn't really know you could just be aro."

"Yeah. I mean, I might feel differently when I'm older, I don't really know. Honestly, it's a bit of a relief to not want anything like that. Trans dating is hard, I mean, just look at you and Abbie."

"Gee, thanks."

"No, but, you get what I mean. You wouldn't be in this mud with her if you were cis."

"Yeah." I agree. I'll admit that that has been the most shit part of the whole thing. The fact that we'd probably be together if I was cis. "Um, where are we even going?"

"The park. Obviously." He says, checking his phone before grinning. "Lilia's bringing a blanket."

"Oh, joy."

We're not the first to arrive at the park, which is a surprise to me considering that I'm ninety-nine percent sure that Everett sent these texts out like fifteen minutes ago. Either way, the girls are already here, both sat down on a purple and white picnic blanket between two trees. It's a rather idyllic scene, but I can't help but feel awkward.

Everett strides up to the two of them and grins, greeting them easily as I walk behind him with a distinct level of shame.

"Hi, guys." Lilia says, leaning back in her cross-legged position to look at me as she waves. "You alright?"

"Yeah." Everett answers for us, taking a seat on the blanket, opposite Dallas.

"You okay, too, Kylo?" She asks again. The other two look over towards me at that. I guess I still look a little rough from breaking down into tears like half an hour ago.

"Um, yep. Long day." I tell her. I've had a fight with both of my parents on separate occasions today, and also thrown a massive chunk of my past out in the open for Everett to poke around. It's like two-o-clock and I'm ready to collapse into sleep again. "Tired." I add, using it as an excuse to rub my face in an attempt to get rid of the evidence of my emotion.

"Amen." Dallas laughs. "It's been so hot, too, it's exhausting."

"Tank-top season could never exhaust me." Lilia says with dramatic persuasion, looking up at the sky, where she's undoubtedly getting blinded by the sun. Her comment is reflected by her outfit, which makes us all laugh.

"What's so funny over here?" Eli asks, striding up behind us. He's wearing a pair of sunglasses that he's pushed up onto the top of his head. I'm so unbelievably relieved to see that Will isn't with him.

"Eli!" Dallas grins, standing up to hug him.

"Hiya." He says, sitting down once they pull apart. "How are you guys?"

"We've already done this." Lilia snickers. "I'm fine, Dallas is fine, Everett's fine, and Kylen's tired."

"Efficient." He remarks. "I'm tired, too, to be fair."

"Too much time with Will?" Dallas teases.

"Ha, ha. Kind of. He's just quite clingy, I had to ask Shea and Maddie to invite him out to do something so I could have the day to myself." He admits a little sheepishly. I almost feel bad for him, but it's his boyfriend.

"Oh, you didn't have to come out here if you're having a day to yourself." Everett tells him apologetically, and Eli shakes his head.

"No, I wanted to. I like hanging out with you guys, and I wasn't gonna bring Will either way. Not after the way he treated you on Thursday, Kylen."

"Oh. Um, it wasn't that big of a deal."

Everett gives me the same look that he gave me on the way here.

"It was. I had a proper conversation about it with him when we got home. And, he won't tell anyone." Eli says, looking at me like he genuinely means it.

"How'd you pull that off?" I ask. Will isn't the kind of guy to shy away from a secret like that. To be honest, I've been waking up in the morning thinking that I'm gonna check my phone and he will have told the whole of England that I'm trans.

"I told him that if he told anyone, we were done." The boy shrugs, pulling a bottle of sparkling water out of his bag and taking a swig.

"You didn't have to do that for me." I say. "Jeopardise your relationship."

"Eh," He hums indifferently. "I wouldn't be much of the trans ally that I claim to be if I let him out you to people."

"I'm confused." Dallas says, and I forget that not everyone

knows about the thing with Will. We spend about thirty seconds catching her up on it, and then after that, we slip into a comfortable lull of conversation.

It's nice to hang out with people that I don't have to worry about how I act around. There's a moment where Eli says something funny that makes us all laugh, and it was the kind of laughter that leaves us breathless. Everett falls back against the grass beyond the picnic blanket, his hair contrasting against the grass nicely. I take my phone out and start taking pictures of him without really thinking. When the moment of laughter has passed, I show him the photos and he makes me send them to him.

"Do you guys mind if I smoke?" I ask, already pulling the pack out of my jacket pocket. As much as I have some level of self control, I think I'll destruct if I don't smoke at least one a day. I know that Everett doesn't care about me smoking around him, but I have no idea about the other three.

"I'd rather you didn't." Dallas says, sounding guilty as she says it. "Sorry, asthma and stuff."

"Oh, yeah. No worries." I say, taking one out of the pack and lighting it behind my hand to avoid the wind. "I'll be a five minutes." I let them know, standing and walking away from them. I wait until I'm about ten metres away before I start smoking.

From the distance, I watch as their conversation continues, feeling a bit sad about the fact that I'm missing out on the discussion. They look like they're having fun, so I turn around and start idly walking in the other direction so that I can put my mind somewhere else.

If you had told me six months ago that I was choosing to hang out with people from the club, I don't think I would have believed you. It still feels a little uncomfortable, because I know that, despite what things I've made up for, everyone sitting on that picnic blanket has seriously disliked me at one point or another.

But they don't right now. That's all that matters. They're all okay with me now - as far as I'm aware. For a moment, my mind wanders to the idea that they might all be talking about me right now, whilst I'm gone. The thought makes me turn around and glance back at them, but I'm too far away now that they just look like little model people.

I get back to everyone within a couple minutes of finishing the cigarette, and they all seem pretty engaged when I get there.

"Kylo!" Everett yells, beckoning me over. "Side with me here."

"About what?" I ask, re-finding my place on the blanket. I'm a little caught off guard by his use of the nickname, but I decide easily that I like the sound of it more out of his mouth than out of Tobias.'

"Would you rather be a dog, or a cat?"

"Cat, obviously." I say without even considering it.

"What?" Everett groans. "That's ridiculous."

"Being a cat would be better. They just do what they want all the time. If I was a dog, I'd have to follow someone around all day."

"There's nothing worse than company, is there?" Everett teases me, doing a pouty face that gives mock sympathy.

"No, I agree with Kylen." Lilia says. "Different reason, though. Cats are just cooler."

"Okay, then my argument is that dogs are just cooler. We've achieved nothing." Everett says.

"I'll propose the question to Thalia for the next circle." Eli says. "We can do a democratic vote."

"As opposed to a non-democratic vote?" Dallas chimes in, amused.

"Oh, that's a good idea, actually. Ballots, but we only put 'cat' on them." Lilia grins.

"Feline tyranny. Great." I mutter, smirk adorned. The look on Everett's face makes it all worth it. He groans loudly and hides his face in his knees.

"You guys suck." He complains. Just like before, we slip into a conversation that I'm genuinely entertained by.

A couple minutes of talking turns into a couple hours, and before we know it, Lilia's mum phones her and tells her that to come home for dinner. She takes the blanket with her and forces us to migrate to a bench. After that, Dallas has to head home, too.

"Um, heads up. Will's gonna swing by to pick me up in like five minutes." Eli says, making a hand gesture that's reminiscent of someone using a steering wheel.

"To pick you up?" Everett asks, eyebrows arched in amusement.

"Yeah. He has a car, 'cause he's eighteen and got his licence. It's cool. He can probably give you guys lifts home if you want." He offers.

"We're fine, it's not a long walk. Thanks, though." I answer for both of us, which might be a little dickhead-y but if there's one thing I'm not doing, it's getting in a car with Will.

"Mhm. I just wanted to warn you in case you wanna leave before he gets here."

"It's okay, I'm a big boy, I can deal." I tell him - even though I probably can't deal.

Everett gasps. "Hey! That's what your friends said about you at Leo's."

"What?"

"Like, when I went to ask them if any of them wanted to come look after you when you were in a state, one of them said you were a big boy and could handle yourself."

"Oh."

"Yikes." Eli grimaces. "You have some good friends." He laughs, sarcasm dripping from his voice. I know I shouldn't, but the tone irritates me, so I fire back.

"Yeah, and you have a good boyfriend."

Everett chuckles behind his hand. "Damn, okay. I deserved that." Eli concedes, swinging his legs on the edge of the bench. Behind us, there's the honk of a car's horn that interrupts our conversation. We all look in the direction of it, and in the exact same way that I expected, a blue Hyundai Sonata has pulled up onto the pavement. Will leans out of the window.

"Get in, bitch, we're going shopping!" He yells in our direction.

"You're hilarious." Eli deadpans, loud enough that Will can hear whilst standing up and checking that has all his things in his pockets.

"You love me for it." Will grins, beckoning impatiently with his hands.

"Yeah, don't lose your shit, I'm coming."

Eli's boyfriend laughs, following Eli with his eyes as we walk him towards the car.

"Thanks for hanging out, guys, I had fun." He says, turning away from Will to speak to us.

"Yeah, of course. We'll see you at the club on Thursday?" Everett asks, and he nods.

"Yep. Okay, bye guys."

"Bye." We both say. Eli spins around and walks in front of the car to his side. Will honks the horn again whilst Eli is right by it, and makes him jump a little before giggling about it as his boyfriend opens the passenger door and gets in with a disgruntled expression. Before driving off, Will glances at me and Everett before offering what I can only describe as a sarcastic wave.

Once the couple have disappeared down the road, I realise quite uncomfortably that it's likely the next place we're going is home. This time, I think my parents will definitely have realised that I'm gone, because Alfie will have come to say hi when he woke up, and then probably freaked out about my disappearance.

I feel like I put that kid through too much.

"So, where are we headed next?" Everett asks, eyes not moving away from the road that Eli and Will disappeared down. It makes me realise that maybe there's an option other than home.

"Um, can we stay out for a little longer?" I ask hopefully.

"Yeah, of course. Let me just give my mum a text and let her know I'm okay, or else she'll worry."

When all the business is dealt with, we kind of set off in an amble through town the streets, in the direction of town. The sun is close to setting at this point, but since it's summer, darkness won't consume us for at least another three hours at minimum.

This isn't exactly how I thought my day would go, but it's not like I'm complaining. It's been a good day. Well, despite the whole thing with my mum earlier, it's been a good day. Everett was a great friend today, which is something that I think I've been taking for granted as of late.

"Thanks, by the way." I say, awkwardness creeping up my spine as I speak. "For organising that. I had a good time."

If I was being entirely honest with him, I would tell him that I think it was the most fun I've had without being under the influence of anything in a long time.

Everett nods as if I've said something genuinely insightful. "Yeah, of course. I'm glad."

We walk in silence for a little longer, making it a good half way towards the town centre until I'm very abruptly caught off guard by the sight of a gaggle of boys in the distance.

My first thought when I see any boys my age is that I probably know them, or they probably know me. I got myself very acquainted with the melting pot of teenage boys in this town a few years ago, just after I met Tobias. Because, when you meet one person from that kind of scene, you get introduced to another, and then another, and then suddenly you're going to parties with hundreds of people. At least in this city, you are.

I can't deny that dread spikes in my body at the thought of them seeing me. It's horrible to think, but hanging out with someone like Everett wouldn't be good for me socially.

To be fair, getting yelled at by my almost-girlfriend in front of a whole party of people wasn't good for me socially, either.

I don't say anything about it to Everett, because it would only stress me out more. Instead, I opt to keep my eyes downcast and hope that we can just walk past this group without further hassle. Or, that is, until the boy that I'm with stops walking entirely. I turn back towards him to see what the kerfuffle is, and his eyes dance between myself and the group.

257

It makes me look over to them also, and I'm ten times more distraught to see that–

"Aren't those your friends?"

"Yeah." I say breathlessly, my upset more than evident in my voice. They're all there. Tobias, Jack, Liam, and AJ - all stood in a makeshift circle out side the entrance of one of those local supermarkets. Tobias is smoking a pretty badly rolled cigarette as he laughs at something or other.

I pull my phone out of my pocket and check our group chat. None of them said anything at all about us hanging out tonight.

After shoving my phone back in my pocket, I leave Everett where he's standing and stride right over to them, maybe a bit recklessly, but I'm blinded by the idea that they're doing stuff without me.

"Hey, guys."

Tobias turns to look at me the quickest, and he cringes visibly, even having the audacity to look a little guilty about it. "Oh, um, hi Kylen." He says quietly.

It provides me with a little bit of satisfaction that Liam and AJ give each other a downright mortified look.

"I didn't know we were meeting up today." I say confidently, crossing my arms in front of me. Tobias frowns like a little kid that's been caught in a lie.

"Yeah, um, well, *we* are."

"Am I not?"

"Hey," Jack interrupts, putting his arm in front of Tobias. "I got this." He declares, looking back at the others and then to me. "It's not personal, you know that. But, you were a fuckin' downer when we hung out yesterday."

He's taking the piss. Like, genuinely.

"I just didn't really feel like getting drunk."

"Yeah, exactly."

"What, we can't hang out sober any more?"

"Well, we can." Tobias interjects. "It's just a bit shit."

The look on my face must tell my friends that I'm really not happy with that answer. Tobias sucks in a deep breath and looks at the others before he speaks. "It's just that there's no point inviting you if you don't wanna actually have fun."

"Well, last time I tried to have 'fun' with you, Tobias, I got a fucking criminal record. So, forgive me for being a little hesitant." I exclaim, no longer worried about raising my voice or making a scene.

"Jesus." Liam mutters.

"Look, dude, we're sorry, but like–"

"No! No, you're not sorry. Fucking hang out without me, but don't lie to my face about it." I tell them, exasperated and fucking fed up of their attitudes.

"Are you okay, Kylo? Like, actually." Liam asks on a laugh, clearly in a way that's meant to mock the vocal expression of my feelings towards them.

"I think he's having some kind of mental breakdown." AJ snickers, and it's the final straw.

"No, shut up." I say, taking a step backwards. "I'm not having a mental breakdown, and if I was, it's not like you would give a shit."

"It was a joke, dude." AJ pushes, but I don't care for it.

"No, no, I'm doing the talking, shut up." I snap at him. His eyes go a little wide and he looks over at Tobias for reassurance. "Because, jackass, I did have a mental breakdown in November. You know, when I didn't show up at school for a month straight?"

They all stare at me in stunned silence that I plough through effortlessly.

"And, guess fucking what?" I ask. "I didn't get even as much as a *text message* from any of you." I spit. "None of you cared then, and you sure as hell don't care now."

I breathe out and in heavily when I'm finished speaking. They all look at me like I'm some kind of psychopath, but I don't miss the glint of guilt behind Tobias' eyes. Maybe I'm going too far by yelling at them all, but it really hurt me at the time. Genuinely, I didn't hear from one of them, and they were meant to be my friends. The only person that actually cared that wasn't an adult that was morally obligated to care was Abbie. And by that, I mean she sent me a couple texts. But I don't blame her for that, because we weren't as close then and she had no way of knowing. My friends did, though. And they should have.

"Kylen." Comes a softer voice from behind me. I tilt my head back and Everett has approached, looking worried in a way that makes me feel patronised. "Breathe." He says.

A couple of my friends seem amused by Everett's presence. It manages to break the tension effortlessly. I feel myself calming down.

"Christ, man." Tobias snickers. "I know getting rejected was hard but you have higher standards than her." He teases.

"No, dude, you can't assume its gender." Jack replies, smirking.

"You guys are assholes." I say. Never before would I have jumped to the defence of another trans person over my friends, but a lot has changed recently.

"I mean, we'd heard some rumours that you were a bit of a fag, but we didn't believe them." Liam tells me, squinting a little in my direction. "When did you dye your hair?"

Tobias snaps his head to look at me, taking a step forward as if to get a better look. All I can think about is that someone must have been spreading a rumour that I'm gay. I don't really care who it is, I just feel like utter shit. Here I've been, putting all the effort into the world to pass as a cis-het boy. And it feels like it's been for nothing.

"Just don't get all weird on us. Don't start thinking you can show up here wearing makeup and heels, it's a slippery slope."

"Don't listen to them." Everett says, words strong, and a couple of them have the audacity to laugh.

"You're not, like, friends with that tranny, are you?" Liam asks, sounding actually concerned. I was being premature when I said that AJ was the final straw. It's this, this is it.

"You know what, yeah. I am." I declare, speaking loud enough that some people on the street start to look at us. "Because he has been more of a friend to me in the last few weeks than all of you combined have in the last *two years*!" I yell, and the boys all look double the amount of shocked as they did before. "So, you can think whatever you want about me. And I hope you enjoy your lives, but maybe you should do some fucking self reflection."

"What?" Tobias asks, sounding a little upset. "You're gonna throw our whole friendship away over this?"

"Yeah." I reply, without a beat of hesitation. "I should have a long time ago, you guys are terrible for me. Fuck you," I begin, starting from AJ, who is stood on the left. "Fuck you, too, for giving me a speech about mental health that you clearly don't believe in," I repeat at Jack, and then Liam, "Fuck you." For the third time, and then I take a step towards the boy that's meant to be my closest friend. "And also fuck you, Tobias." I whisper to him.

"Okay, fine, fuck you too." He replies, shoving me by hitting my chest and making me stumble a few steps backwards. "Good luck trying to make friends at college without us."

"Thanks." I say whilst nodding, and then I turn around and walk away from them without so much as a glance backwards. They don't say anything at all as I leave, so I know that I've made at least some kind of impact on them. I don't hear Everett's footsteps behind me until he catches up once we're around a corner.

"Dude, slow down." He says, breathless from trying to keep up with me. "You didn't have to do that for me, I'm used to that kind of thing."

"Yeah, but you shouldn't have to be. And I've realised that I don't like the kind of person I'd be if I just stood there." I tell him, and I actually mean it. I guess I'd always thought that it never impacted anyone that deeply, but the things that were said earlier made me realise that even Eli is a better trans ally than I am. It doesn't feel great knowing that I'm harming the people that go through the exact same struggles that I do.

Maybe I shouldn't have lashed out at all of them like that, but it was a long time coming.

When we get a couple minutes away, I turn around to where Everett has been trailing behind me, barking reassurances. He stops walking when I do, and we just make eye contact for a while. And then I open my arms and let him hug me. His jumper is soft against my bare arms, and this hug feels more genuine than the one earlier. This morning, he had hugged me because I was in tears and it's what friends should do. But, right now, I indirectly asked him to hug me because it's what

I need. It doesn't change the circumstances, but it does make me feel fractionally better about them, especially after this roller coaster of a day.

17

Rhett

I take Kylen back to my house after that. He told me that it was fine, and that he could go home, but he's had a hard day. As much as I used to assume his life was perfect, I'm no longer ignorant to the fact that maybe going home isn't what he needs after a shitty day.

I text my mum to ask her if it's okay after I've already insisted that he's coming over, so I'm pretty relieved when she says it's fine, followed by a *'Maybe we should buy him a toothbrush to keep here.'*

Mum makes pasta that we all eat on the sofa whilst carrying on the season of *Young Royals*. Kylen's never watched it before, so I have to give him a thirty-second catch up on the plot and everything for him to follow along effectively.

"Mum?" I speak up at the end of one of the episodes.

"Mhm?"

"You're not working tomorrow, are you?"

She looks at me with amusement in her gaze. "Do you want to go somewhere in the car?" She asks.

"Well, it's been a while since we've gone to the Pestler's." I

264

suggest, lightening my tone at the end of the sentence to sweeten the deal. Kylen looks up from his phone with a confused glance.

"Don't you have the youth club tomorrow?"

"Yeah, in the afternoon. It's not like it's hours away." I persuade.

"Okay, sure. But we'll have to leave early." She says. "Kylen, did you wanna come?"

"Uh," He says, clearly unclear on the situation. "What's the Pestler's?"

A smile spreads across my face at the announcement that he's never been before. That way it can at least be as special in his eyes as his beloved playground makes me smile. "Well, you know how you took me to that abandoned playground the other day?" I ask, and he nods. "Tomorrow, I'm gonna take you to *my* happy place, that I go when *I* need a moment." I declare, and he raises his eyebrows at me.

"We have to drive there?"

"Yep. It's worth it, I promise." I grin. I'm pretty excited to show him. It's a little nerve wracking, because like his with me, I've never brought anyone there before. But, we clearly have that level of trust established at this point, and it feels like spreading the joy that the place gives me to him.

"It's nine o' clock, and I'm the only one with shoes on." Mum says, her tone light and humorous as she stands by the door, car keys in hand.

"I want you to know, it's not my fault, Miss Enfield." Kylen says monotonously as he sits on the armrest of the sofa and watches me struggle to lace my shoes up.

Then, Mum's footsteps come down the hallway and she stands in the living room doorway and crosses her arms. "I had suspected as much." She laughs. "The rabbit goes around the tree, honey."

"Yeah, I know!" I exclaim. "I can't do it if you're both staring at me."

After the shoelace incident has been resolved, we head outside and Kylen and I clamber into the backseat. He keeps staring down at his phone, and when I make an attempt to engage him in a conversation, he'll look away every thirty seconds as if checking for something. It's clearly consuming him, so I take matters into my own hands.

"Okay, I'll just look after that." I say in a voice that reminds me too much of my science teacher for my liking, whilst yanking his phone out of his hand.

"Hey!" He yelps, reaching across to get it back, but his seatbelt locks in place from the sudden movement and he can't reach. "Come on, Rhett. Give it back."

I giggle and hold the phone towards the roof of the car, which is a lot less impactful when he's multiple inches taller than me and we're both sitting down. "What's so stressful on here?" I ask.

"Give it to me." He says.

"Not until you tell me what you're so engrossed in." I argue back, and he reaches across the seats to grab it from me, but I move my hand away.

"I'm so lucky you don't have any siblings." Mum mutters.

"Just give it here." Kylen pleads, annoyance seeping into his voice. It's only then that the text message notification sound chimes, and his eyes widen. "Everett, give it."

266

Maybe it's an invasion of his privacy, I look down at the phone, where the screen has lit up.

It's a text message, from an **'Abs<3**.' He's definitely the kind of guy that puts a heart next to the name of the girl he likes in his phone. "Abs" sent a text saying 'yeah, but he's always been like that loll.' I read it out loud, and Kylen reaches for the phone back again.

"Since when are you talking to Abbie again?"

"Since last night, now give it to me, I need to reply."

"Alright, calm down, she won't lose interest after ten sections of radio silence." I tell him, finally handing the phone back, which his hands stick to like mice to a glue trap. He taps out a text message, and then the phone pings again, and he laughs at the notification before covering his mouth with his hand. Mum eyes him in the rear-view mirror between the seats, and then converts her gaze into the driver's side mirror and raises her eyebrows at me. I snicker back, but Kylen fails to notice.

"Can I get your full attention when we get there, at least?" I ask, and he nods without even looking at me. "Kylen."

He switches his phone off at that, putting it down on the smaller seat in between us. "Sorry. Yeah, she's gone for breakfast now anyway." He lets me know.

"So, what's the sitch' with you two then?"

"You want me to tell you after you just stole my phone from me?"

"Pretty please?" I try, and Mum giggles.

Kylen does not look too impressed by my attempt at smoothing things over, giving me a sideways glance before rolling his eyes. "Well, I texted her when we were watching that show last night."

"That show? It has a name."

"Do you want to know, or?"

"Yeah."

"Okay. Well, I texted her to let her know that I'd severely pissed off my group of friends, so if any of them tried to say anything about me to her, um, not to listen to them."

"You think they'd do that?"

"Without a doubt. When Jack's girlfriend broke up with him, and then started dating this new guy, and then Jack started a rumour that the new guy had chlamydia."

"Yikes."

"Yeah, and then everyone started making fun of Madeline, saying that she had it too, and Jack felt a bit bad and told people he was joking, but the damage was already done, and they broke up, and everyone called her '*Chla-Maddie-a*' for like a week." He explains. "They probably wouldn't tell people I have an STI, but I wouldn't put something in the same alley past them."

And, Jesus am I glad I've never fraternised with people like that. Mum exhales and taps her fingers against the steering wheel. "God, I miss secondary school."

Kylen smirks. "What, did anyone make up that you had chlamydia?" He asks.

"Thankfully not." Mum replies. "It's just funny, 'cause, at the time all of this drama, the same kind that you're dealing with, felt so massive. But it didn't really matter, not if we just took a step back."

"Should I be offended by that?" I ask her. Mum laughs loudly, tipping her head back a little in amusement.

"No, darling, you matter. All the drama with your dad just didn't."

Kylen furrows his eyebrows in confusedness for a second, and then breathes in sharply. "Oh my god, are you a high school sweetheart baby?" He asks me, jaw a little slack.

"Alright, that's enough. We're nearly there." She halts the conversation. Despite that, Kylen and I carry on talking in a bit of a whisper for the following five minutes that it takes us to arrive at the Pestler's.

It's off road, and I'm surprised that Kylen is yet to ask me what it actually is that we're doing. The place itself doesn't look like much when we arrive - only presenting itself as the main building of a garden centre.

"Okay. How long do you boys want?" Mum asks as she parks.

"Well, um, I've got my phone. If you give me a call when you get bored of waiting around, we'll come back to the car." I let her know, and she nods.

"Alright. I'm gonna do a few laps looking for some of that fancy soil."

"Which fancy soil?"

"The kind that your grandmother will love get as a birthday present, because she keeps buying all those exotic plants." She says, opening her car door and clambering out in the little space between our car and the one next to it.

"Your happy place is a garden centre?" Kylen asks, almost mockingly.

"Oh, please, yours is a children's playground." I slight, half-slamming the car door and following Mum to the entrance. When we get just outside the shop, she turns around and tells me (and Kylen, who is following me a little confusedly) to have fun.

"Thanks, see you." I say, beckoning Kylen to follow me off

269

to the right of the building, not even using the front door at all.

"Dude, where are we going?" He finally asks.

"Come on, you'll see." I reply, setting us off on a dirt path that follows the edge of the nearby treeline. After about two minutes of walking, the path starts to curve around. The feeling of happiness that being here swells up inside of me before I even see the colours.

"Oh, wow." Kylen says, taken aback by the sight.

To put it simply, we've arrived at the Pestler's flower field.

But, it's not just a flower field, not to me. It's like the best place in the world.

Across about five hundred by two hundred metres of field, there's just an array of as many flowers as I could imagine. It's not organised by species, or in rows. Just loads of seeds that have created floral beauty out of this usually mediocre stretch of grass.

The tallest flower makes it all the way up to my waist, but some are so low to the ground that I wouldn't even notice them below the spikes of grass if I wasn't looking. In the the back left of the field is a large ash tree with a rope swing hanging from it.

A wave of tranquillity washes over me and I wish I could stay here forever.

"Do you have a favourite flower?" I ask, looking back at him. Kylen visibly swallows as his eyes scan over the array of options.

"Um, I've never really.. thought about it." He says.

"Well you must know the names of some of them. What's your favourite colour?"

"Blue." He tells me.

I start to scan over the plants, having to step into the field itself to reach the one I want. It's hard to see distinctly amongst the other flowers, but I crouch down on my tip-toes to get a better look. When I glance up, Kylen is still stood watching me.

"C'mere." I say, gesturing towards myself. "But, try not to step on any of them, you can weave your way around."

"Yeah." Kylen mutters. "Learnt that from *Animal Crossing*."

"*Animal Crossing* has some good flowers in it." I say, mainly for myself.

He makes it to the flower with minimal perennial casualties, blinking down at it. "It's blue. I see what you did there." He comments, humoured.

"It's a cornflower." I tell him. "An archaeophyte."

"A what-o-phyte?"

"Archaeophyte. It was brought here in the iron age, um, an archaeophyte is a plant that was brought to somewhere new by people. We brought it here from other parts of Europe."

"Oh. That's cool."

"Yeah. It's amazing, actually. So much history in a little blue thing like this."

"I think they have these in *Minecraft*. And *Animal Crossing* too, actually."

I look up at him with an unimpressed stare. "They were in the real world first." I say, and he grins.

"Well, yeah. It's just cool."

"Definitely." I agree, feeling for a second that I'm being a little bit too blunt with him, but he seems to be enjoying himself either way, so it's fine. "We'll leave him alone, he's not finished growing yet."

"How do you know it's a boy plant?" He asks, entertained grin adorned. I almost laugh.

"I don't, it's just fun to make them seem more human. I could probably tell if it's a male or female flower if I actually looked at it, but it feels like a violation. Gender isn't real anyway."

Kylen laughs and speaks to me as I take him along the safest path possible to show him my favourite flower.

"To be fair, I don't think that plants have genders in the same way that we do, just sexes. Pretty sure it's just which part of reproduction they handle." He remarks.

"Yeah, you're right. But it's fun to pretend." I concede, continuing to tread through the field. All the while, my eyes scan the ground whilst I move until I manage to spot one of the flowers I'm after.

"Ah! Look." I exclaim, hopping over a few flowers to kneel down beside it. "It's not even bloomed yet."

"Why not?"

"These little guys don't usually come out of the bud until July. End of this month if we're lucky – I'll come back next weekend to check on this one." I explain, taking my phone out of my pocket and photographing the plant from about four different angles.

"Why did you kinda jump to this one out of all of them?" He asks me. He has a lot of questions today, it seems.

"It's hibiscus – my favourite. Malaysia's national flower, since nineteen-sixty. Also the flower that Lilo wears in her hair. You know, in Lilo and Stitch." I say, eyes running over the ridges of the bud. I'll admit that it looks a little lacklustre before it's bloomed, so I can kind of get why Kylen doesn't seem too invested. "I'll show you a picture of one when it's fully grown, and you'll get why I love it so much."

"Hibiscus? Is that not a *Penelope Scott* song?"

"Do you remember what I said about these flowers being in *Minecraft*?"

"Right, yeah. It was a flower before it was a song." He sums up.

"Exactly, and the song is named after the tea. Which is pretty good, actually. But it makes me feel guilty, like, 'which hibiscus flower had to die for me to drink this?'"

"God, you can't even be vegan in good conscience." He jokes. "So, do you come here a lot?"

"Yeah. Although, not as much recently. When my mum's at work I can usually get the bus to a stop about ten minutes walk away. I just feel so much more at peace here, you know?"

"Yeah. It's nice." He confirms, hands in his pockets. "Do you take any home?"

"Not from here. I don't like picking flowers, I feel bad. And, besides, supermarkets do enough of that anyway. They sell flowers at the garden centre right there."

Kylen chuckles and looks back over how far we've walked into the field. The sound makes me remember that I'm in the company of an actual person that isn't made to listen to me spewing flower facts twenty-four-seven.

"Sorry." I say. "I just really like flora and stuff."

"No, it's fine. You seem really in your element." He observes. "Um, is that a rope swing?"

"Yeah. Let's go over there. Sorry, I probably should have asked if you have hay fever before we got here. Do you have hay-fever?"

"I think if I did, you would have noticed by now." He giggles. "Come on, I wanna get on the swing."

"Careful you don't trample them!" I yell after him and his clumsy footing. Because I'm extra careful when on the way to the tree, I take longer than Kylen does, so that when I get there, he's already hopped up onto the wooden seat that hangs from the tree.

"Oh, this is cool!"

"Cooler than the flowers?" I ask, crossing my arms up at him.

"No offence." He says, and I can tell that he's only joking.

"None taken. I mean, if you start swinging and close your eyes, you're basically in your rusty playground."

He scoffs with a roll of his eyes, but he swings his legs to gain momentum anyway. "I can see why you like this place." He comments offhandedly. I nod, eyeing up the array of flowers. Kylen's phone pings whilst he's in the air, and I get an idea.

"You should totally get her flowers." I suggest. He digs his trainers into the dirt on the ground to stop himself swinging.

"What?" He asks, caught off guard by the question.

"There's a ton of flowers in the garden centre, and I'm pretty confident that I know the meanings of all of them. Let me help you pick some out for her." I offer.

"That's a bit much." He says, but it's not in a judgemental tone, more a little worried if anything.

"Well, you're talking again, right?"

"I mean, yeah. But it's not like, 'showing up at her door with flowers' level of talking."

"You won't know if you never try." I shrug. He starts to swing again, and I take a seat on the dirt, just by the edge of where the flowers start to repopulate the area. Some people might find the mess of wildflowers of all tones kind of overwhelming, but I genuinely don't think that there's anything more precious. "If I wasn't so hesitant about pulling up flowers, we could play 'she-loves-me, she-loves-me not' with some daisy petals."

"You're a great guy, Rhett, but the day I take relationship advice from an aromantic person is the day I should give up trying to date." He jokes, looking down at me from the swing.

"Just 'cause I don't do it myself doesn't mean I don't have an opinion on it." I raise my voice back at him to make sure that he can hear me from where he's swinging.

"Fine. If I ever want to get her flowers, you're the man I'll go to." He surrenders.

"Good, you better." I laugh, eyes tracing his motion on the swing as my hands skim over some orange hawkweed flowers. With any luck, we've got at least another twenty minutes here before Mum finds the soil.

Because I feel bad for making her drive us to the Pestler's, Kylen and I are ready for the club early so that we can walk down in good time. His conversation with Abbie died down on the way home from the flower field, and a few nasty texts from his ex-friends have left him feeling less than great.

I feel so much closer to him after showing Kylen my world of flowers. It's kind of vulnerable, taking someone to the place you love the most.

I'll admit that he does look much more at home in the urban environment of the city. He strides along the pavement with a distinct confidence that seemed stripped of him in the rural area. I kind of feel the opposite.

In the countryside, there's no expectations. No social

pressures or anything – just me and whichever tree I feel like climbing today.

Kylen is the kind of person that thrives in the city. Everything he's ever done, and everything he's ever learnt about passing as a boy is rooted in other city people, and popularity, and tracksuits, and football, and, yeah. None of the stuff that you find in the countryside.

I think that I'll look at Kylen and Thalia's relationship a lot differently now that I know about the history – the fact that she saved his life. It would have been why she was so hesitant to ban him from the club until he *really* messed up.

As we walk, I replay the words that he said to me in his bedroom yesterday through my head. It makes me upset to look at him as he walks, knowing all the things that go on and have gone on in his head.

"Um, Kylen?"

"Mhm."

"Yesterday, when you said that you couldn't do the job you wanted because you're trans," I vocalise one of my thoughts. "What was that? If you don't mind."

Kylen clicks his tongue inside his mouth. "It's dumb." He says.

"Oh, come on. I made you listen to me tell you about wildflowers earlier, that was dumb."

"Fine, I– um, I used to want to play football. Be a footballer." He starts, refusing to give me his eyes in favour of the pavement. "And I know that literally every little boy wants to be a footballer, but, I actually did, and I was really good at it."

"So, why'd you stop?"

"I got onto the under thirteen's team. For our city, when I was twelve. Like, the team that gets to train with the *actual players* and stuff." He says. "And I was really excited about it."

"Of course."

"And, I don't know why, but in my head, it was a boy's team. Where I got to play like a real boy would."

"But it wasn't?"

He shakes his head. "No, it was a girls' team. And they were all lovely, but it made me hate myself having to play with them because I felt so out of place. I mean, we did get to watch the boy's team play for a bit, and that only made me more upset because I wasn't allowed to play with them."

"So you quit?"

"So I cried every night before I had to go to football training." He corrects. "Because everyone there saw me as nothing more than a tomboy, and it upset me. But, my parents said that I was being ungrateful, which, maybe I was, and took my tears for telling them I didn't wanna play football any more."

"Right. But, if they took you out of it, couldn't you have carried on in your own time?"

"I did, and I still do, recreationally. But it made me kind of hate the sport, and I'm not as good at it any more as I could have been. I follow some of the people from the academy on Instagram, and most of them are like, on track to play professionally. And it kills me that I can't even get the chance. I can't play for the men's," He rants, "because they think I'm too frail and breakable, and also, not a man. And I can't play for the women's, because being perceived as a woman makes me more upset than anything, and also, I take testosterone, which gives me a 'biological advantage' anyway."

He's clearly very passionate about it. Kylen seems to have lost out on a lot because of his gender, and it makes my body ache with a level of sympathy that's hard to imagine.

"Even if I happened to get accepted into a supportive team," He carries on, much quieter this time. "All these bills and legislation being passed mean that it would probably be illegal for me to step foot on a pitch with another man." He murmurs, kicking a stone as if it's the government.

"I'm sorry, that's shit." I try to comfort him. "So, what do you want to do for a job now?"

He pauses for a second before shrugging. "I didn't really think I'd get this far, to be honest. Not in a depressing way, just never thought it through."

"I'm not sure you can say that in a non-depressing way." I reply, making a bit of a joke out of his words. "What A-Levels are you doing, at least?"

"Criminology, economics, and sports BTEC." He says. "Don't know where it'll take me, but they were the ones that seemed the most interesting. How 'bout you?"

"Nah, your options sounds pretty solid." I reassure him before answering his question. "Um, sociology, psychology, and film studies."

"I probably could have guessed that." Kylen replies with a smirk. "You're not straight, of course you're doing film studies."

"What's that supposed to mean?" I reply with a jokey tone.

"Whatever you want it to." He answers smoothly, and we continue to talk about what we're doing in September (school-wise), up until we get to the Aconite Centre.

We arrive just on time, but it seems like it wouldn't matter anyway, because Rowan is running circle, and when we get in, he beckons us over to him.

"Thalia wants to speak to you two, in her office. You're

not in trouble." He says, but everyone sitting around the circle reacts like we are. It's Rowan's job to make us feel comfortable, and considering all of the previous endings to going into Thalia's office, I can't say that I'm too optimistic.

18

Kylo

Thalia's office is a place that I've found myself in for more bad reasons than good. She has an LED lightbulb that can be controlled with a multicoloured remote at will, but I've only ever seen it on the yellow or light blue settings. Today, the lightbulb is off, and all she has on are her fairy lights that wrap around the walls.

"Hi, boys." She says, "Come sit down."

In a worried silence, we both take seats on the small teal-coloured sofa that Thalia has in the corner, and Everett sends me a worried glance.

"Don't look so stressed." Thalia tries to break some of the tension. "I won't keep you long."

"Um, what's up?" I ask her, acutely aware of the fact that the last two times I've been in her office, I've left in tears.

"Well, it's the eighteenth." She states a little hesitantly.

"Time flies when you're having fun." Everett mutters, and I can't tell if he's being sarcastic or not.

"We've got thirteen days left on our lease for this building, unless we can fork up the money. And, obviously, it's not your responsibility, but I know you were quite keen to help out when I first told you. How do you feel about that now?"

"Oh, shit." I say. "Sorry, for um, language. I kinda forgot about that." I think out loud. There's been so much going on recently that it slipped my mind entirely. Between Abbie, and Dean, and court, and Everett, and my mates, I've not had much time to stop and think about things.

"I know you've got a lot going on." Thalia replies softly. "Which is why I don't expect you to help. But, having said that, I suppose this can serve as a heads up that you've got three club sessions left." She explains. That's, what? Thursday, Sunday, and another Thursday? Shit.

"No, no. We'll help, we'll sort something out." Everett interjects, as enthusiastic as ever.

"Okay, well whatever you think, just let me know, okay? Um, but, don't get your hopes up." She says, sounding a little upset. "You okay, Kylen? Looking a little lost over there."

I snap my head up to look at her and nod. "Yeah, sorry. Thinking."

Thalia doesn't look like she believes me, but I don't really need her to. She glances to her laptop and then back to us.

"I'm gonna be away for a few days, from tomorrow until Friday. So, anything you come up with will have to wait."

"Where are you going?" Everett asks her, and she can't help but smile.

"Majorca." She replies. "Wednesday is my wedding anniversary, so my wife and I are going away for a bit."

"You're married?" Everett interrogates, sounding a bit surprised to hear it.

"No, I just wear a wedding ring for fun." She replies with an amused tone, clicking on her laptop. I turn towards Everett and drop my voice for a whisper.

"I've known Thalia longer than her wife has, and they didn't even invite me to their wedding." I complain. I don't actually mean it, obviously, but it's a bit of an inside joke that I have with Thalia.

"Firstly, it was a child-free wedding, and you were fourteen, and secondly, that would've been weird and violated a lot of safeguarding rules."

"Next thing I know, you'll be saying I'm not invited to Majorca."

Thalia laughs to herself before continuing. "Just, if this is it for the club, I need to know that you're okay with it." She changes her tone. "It's just, with everything-" She cuts herself off, glancing at Everett, and I realise why she stopped talking.

"Oh, he knows." I tell her absent-mindedly. "About all of it."

"Oh." Thalia says, clearly not expecting that. "You two are closer than I thought."

"It is what it is." I reply with a shrug. Thalia smiles a little before continuing to make her point.

"I just worry that without the support network here at the Aconite Centre, it might get difficult for you again. And I know that you don't like it when we express concern about you, but, I won't be there to drive you to the hospital any more." She says hesitantly, using a real life scenario as a metaphor for the club's support, which I find a little bit amusing. I don't really want to reply to her, because, like she pointed out, I really don't like it when adults try and tell me that I need their help, or that they know what's best for me.

"I'm still sorry about the speeding ticket." Is what I do

say, because it's funny, and deflects enough whilst still acknowledging her words that she might drop it.

"Kylen, I mean it." Thalia says instead of doing what I had hoped she'd do. "Everett, you can head back into the group, I just need a word with him for a sec."

"It's fine, I don't care that he's here." I say, and he looks a little mortified that I'm talking about him. "Just tell me off for not accepting your worry like gospel, promise that I can talk to you if I need anything, and then send me on my merry way." I kind of snap at her. I don't really mean to, but Thalia and I have this exact conversation at least once a month.

"I know that it's not my job to care." She says, sounding like she's choosing her words very carefully. "You're here four hours a week at a minimum. Maybe you could spend the new free time you'll have doing something else that helps your mental health."

"What, like arts and crafts?" I make fun of her suggestion.

"Like therapy, or, I don't know, gratitude journaling."

"Actually, I said the exact same thing to him the other day." Everett interjects with a proud expression. It takes all of my self-control not to growl at him.

"Look, I appreciate your worry, but I don't need whatever intervention you're trying to give me. I lived for twelve years before I even came here, and I can live without it."

Thalia makes eye contact with Everett and flicks her head towards the door. It's not unkind, or like demanding that he leaves, but it's a gesture that has Everett nodding and leaving the room.

I slump back against the sofa, ready to get lectured for god knows how long.

"I know how you operate." Thalia sighs. "You're starting

to believe that you're genuinely going to lose access to the club, so you're being defensive and rude as a way of putting walls up."

"I didn't know *you* were the therapist."

"I mean it." Thalia says. "You do this all the time. You're trying to push any care you get away because you hate being seen as vulnerable. You did it to the club in general at the start of the month, you're doing it to me now, and you'll undoubtedly do it to Everett next."

Her words weigh heavy on me. I don't know what to say to her after that. Of course, she's right, and I think I know that deep down. I would never admit it, but she's right.

"I left all my friends." I tell her. "I freaked out at them and told them all to fuck off and never speak to me again. You can, um, you can add that to the list."

She actually seems surprised to hear that, furrowing her eyebrows at me.

"In the spirit of Everett," I begin, standing up to signify that this conversation is over. "We'll figure this out. I can't let the club go, because it's pretty much all I have right now. Don't have too much fun on your Ranger-Hyland Majorca trip without me, and when you get back, we'll have it sorted out." I say, and it's a promise. Not one that I'm one hundred percent certain that I can keep, but every second that I spend in this room I feel more and more claustrophobic and at this point I want to just get out.

"Okay." Thalia says softly. "We'll have this chat again in the last session at the club."

"Okay." I reply, nodding. I get where she's coming from, and the least I can do is assure her that I kind of believe in her rhetoric.

"Look after yourself, Kylen."

"Will do."

When Everett drags me to a coffee shop after the club, I deduce that he must be on some kind of mission to spend as little time as possible at home today.

But it isn't just me that he drags there. It's Mars, and Lilia, and Brynn, too. He texts to ask Dallas and Eli to come down, as well. The former agrees, and says that she's on her way, but all we get from Eli's end is a selfie that it appears Will has taken on his phone, with the caption 'he's busy soz'

Everett grumbles something about Will taking it into his own hands to reply to a text not even meant for him as we walk into the coffee shop.

It's lucky that there's a table big enough to host the six of us, but, to be honest it's probably even luckier that we're all free for this (barring Eli, but I imagine he's probably locked in Will's basement or something). I tell that joke to Everett in a whisper and he doesn't seem that amused by it, which makes me snicker and then hide my smile by taking a sip of my coffee.

We settle in the more desolate, upstairs section of the coffee shop, just chatting idly until all of the discussion starts to die down.

"So, you may be wondering why I've gathered you all here today." Everett announces as if he's the head of some kind of top secret agency (that only meets in independent coffee places).

"I can take a wild guess." Mars replies with raised eyebrows.

"Is this about ...the fundraising?"

"There was a farmer, had a dog and bingo was his name-o." Everett speaks with a miniscule grin. It's endearing. "But, yeah. Thalia seems to think that all hope it lost, and we have a week whilst she's away on hols to come up with something."

"We get more money?" Brynn suggests, obviously sarcastically, but Everett ploughs through the conversation as if it was genuine.

"Yeah, exactly." He says. "But, 'how?' is the real question."

"How much money do we need?" Dallas asks, and Everett looks at me as if I'm meant to know. He's lucky that I do.

"A thousand and two hundred pounds. Technically only six-hundred really, 'cause we usually pay six hundred anyway." I tell the group.

"Oh, have you guys seen *The Next Step*?" Lilia grins, tapping her hands on the table in excitement.

"I used to love that show!" Brynn replies with an equally as excited smile.

"Uh, what?" I can't help but ask, and Everett turns to me with a gasp.

"You never watched *The Next Step*?"

"No?"

Mars shakes their iced coffee around so that the ice makes a bit of a noise, probably for their own entertainment as they start to explain this concept like it's general knowledge. "It's like a show about teens that dance."

"Okay, um, why are we talking about it?"

"'Cause!" Lilia exclaims, maybe a little too loudly for a publicly shared space. "There's an episode where they need to make money at the beach, and, like, they start dancebusking."

"You want us to *dance-busk*?" Dallas asks, not entertaining the idea at all.

Lilia shrugs with a dejected frown. "I dunno, at least I'm contributing."

"Wait, hold on." Brynn interrupts. "What about the money we raised at Pride? That was, like, quite a bit, right?" They ask, and everyone in the circle starts murmuring a little. Everett looks to me for the second time in this makeshift mother's meeting. I'm pretty certain that they're all about to hate me quite a bit.

"Uh, no." I cut through the words of the group, and they all go silent to stare me down.

"What?" Mars asks concernedly.

"Um, she spent it. Most of it."

"She spent it?" Brynn laughs, as if it's too unserious to be true.

"Yeah, um, when I got arrested." I tell them, voice deliberately slow to gauge their reactions. "On my bail."

There's a good ten seconds of stunned silence. "The money we earned?" Mars continues to interrogate, and I nod guiltily. "That wasn't her money to spend, that was the club's money." They chastise.

"Yeah, I know- but, I'll pay her back- pay the club back. ...Eventually."

"But we need the money now, Kylen. Not whenever you can be asked to take responsibility for your actions." They tell me harshly, making direct eye contact that leaves no room for me to think of a response.

"Hey, that's unfair." Lilia jumps to my defence. "Being mean to him about it doesn't get us anywhere."

"Yeah, I'm sure he feels bad enough." Everett says softly. Mars doesn't reply, but they give me a look that tells me that I'm not off the hook. "But, we still have to figure this out. Any ideas?"

His words are lost on me, and so are the words of everyone else talking as they suggest stupid things that all of us know will never actually work, despite nodding along and humming affirmatively. I feel like I stick out like a sore thumb here. The fact that Mars jumped to attack me at the first chance they got, and the fact that nobody has said a word to me directly apart from that this whole time just confirms it.

I don't belong here.

It's a gut-wrenching realisation. Especially after losing all of the friends I've had for the last year and a bit. Sure, it was sometimes a bit depressing to be friends with them, but at least it was easy. Laughing at people we don't like, hanging out with girls we do like, and drinking too much for teenagers was easy. Actually having to work on myself isn't.

Everyone here contributes to the conversation so effort-lessly. It feels like the only things I can contribute are just to ask what the hell is going on. This table would sound no different if I wasn't here. The club would be no different if I wasn't there. Hell, the club would be better off if I wasn't there - two-hundred pounds richer, at least.

I turn and look towards Everett, sitting beside me. His eyes are nowhere near mine, and he leans forward in his chair, smiling at something that someone else said. It's like I'm not even here. Maybe I'm not.

"I'm gonna go to the bathroom." I mumble in Everett's general direction. He turns his head towards me for a split second and kind of does a half-smile-half-nod of acknowledgement before filtering back into the conversation. Nobody else notices when I leave.

True to my word, I actually do go to the bathroom. As I walk there, I think about just leaving the shop and ghosting them all. But, it would be too much like myself to do that, and I haven't been feeling much like the myself that I thought I was, recently.

The bathroom is empty apart from me. I don't actually need to go to the bathroom, obviously, I just needed to get out of that room with all those people that click together so effortlessly without me.

The mirror in front of the sink I stand before is dirty. I expect nothing less from a bathroom mirror, but the grime distorts my face and makes it hard for me to recognise myself.

I could be anywhere in the world in this bathroom. For all I know, I'm at home, I'm at school, and it's just me and my reflection in this disgusting mirror.

Five-hundred-and-fifty pounds in, what? Twelve days? People have probably made more money in less time. We can do this month by month. This month, we'll just focus on that money, and next month, we'll focus on it again.

It's just such a shit situation to be in. Surely if the old owners of the building were content with what we were paying before, it wouldn't make that much difference to keep paying it.

And it's the fact that we have enough money for the old rent. The youth club is a registered charity, because it provides help and community for young queer and trans people, so we do make the money that we need from donations and such. Just not over a thousand pounds a month, Jesus.

I mean, we could just try and beg for more donations. We

don't exactly live in a small town, and there'd be loads of people willing to help, surely.

There'd be loads of people willing to help. Loads of people.

The world around seems to slow down a second as more thoughts push themselves to the forefront of my mind.

We don't exactly live in a small town.

Shit.

I wash my hands before leaving the bathroom out of habit, and also because I can't imagine what kind of germs are on the edge of that sink I've been gripping onto.

"Guys." I say as soon as I get back to the table, cutting through the conversation that they were having before in lieu of my epiphany. "We're so obsessed with getting the money to stay at the Aconite Centre, right?"

"Well, yeah." Mars replies in a bit of a snarky tone. Clearly, they're sill annoyed at me, got it.

"Yeah. But, the club isn't the building. It's us, right? It's a youth club and we're the youth." I tell them, and Everett looks at me curiously for a moment before his eyes widen.

"Oh!" He says. "We're so stupid, how did we not think of that?"

"You're so welcome." I tell him, sitting back down at the table.

"I'm confused." Lilia comments.

"We don't have to keep doing the club at the Aconite Centre." I inform her. "We can do it at any community centre, church, sports centre, anywhere."

"*Oh.*" She acknowledges with a growing smile. "Somewhere with rent more similar to how it used to be at the Aconite Centre."

"Exactly, yeah." Everett confirms, pulling his phone out.

"I'll look for some places on google."

"Okay, yeah. Same." Dallas agrees, and pretty soon we're all looking down at screens, assessing potential options of places in our area. To any outsiders, we would look like the most anti-social group of teenagers you could possibly think of, but we're all working together to try and do something amazing.

The thing that I notice is that all of these places (if they do have any online pages) don't provide anything like that helps us decipher their costs to rent the place for two days a week.

Everett lets out a loud gasp from beside me, unable to keep the smile off his face at something on his mobile device.

"What?" I ask, and he seems to have captured everyone's attention with his exclamation of what could either be shock or extreme excitement. Maybe both.

"Stop it, oh my god." He grins.

"What?" I repeat, laughing this time at the way he's so enamoured by whatever he's come across.

"There's a place, like, twenty minutes walk from the Aconite centre." He says. "A sports centre, turned, like, wedding-party-event venue place." He explains.

"Alright. Those places are usually not that cheap." I tell him, a little reluctantly, 'cause it's, like, the kind of place that you'd get married at.

"Valid." He says, pointing a finger at me. "But, you haven't heard the best bit yet."

"Okay."

"See, I know that this is meant to be, because guess what the place is called."

"I have a feeling you're gonna tell us whether we guess or not." Mars replies, amused by the enthusiasm just as I am.

"So, like, this place has a few buildings scattered around the county." He carries on, gesticulating with his hands as he speaks. "And this specific building is on their 'Althea site.'"

He looks at us like he's just told us the winning lottery numbers, but we don't really have much to give him back.

"Okay, um-" I start, planning to ask him for a little bit of clarification about how this is meant to be the kind of revelation that he's acting like it is.

"Althea officinialis is a little white flower, the marshmallow flower, if you will." He says with an undeniable aura of joy. That makes sense, but it doesn't quite explain his level of excitement.

"You must know a lot about flowers, 'cause I've never heard of that." Brynn tells the group, and Everett nods.

"Well, I only know a little about this one because it looks remarkably similar to my favourite flower."

"Hibiscus?" I clarify.

"Yeah. I was showing it to Kylen this morning." He tells the group. "They're both bell-shaped with a darker colour that pushes outwards on their petals, from the centre."

"So, you think this is a good place to hold the club?" I ask him hesitantly.

"It's a sign, Kylen Lysander! It's named after a metaphorical cousin of my favourite flower! And this one isn't poisonous!" He raises his voice louder with each sentence, also moving his body forward until he's almost pushing me against the wall.

"Okay, okay." I laugh.

"Poisonous?" Lilia asks, and Everett nods.

"Yeah, Aconite flowers are poisonous, which is why I've always thought it was a weird thing to call your community

292

centre. But, Althea is certainly not poisonous and therefore this place is bound to be better."

"Right." Dallas nods. "Okay, well I suppose confidence is key. Do they have a phone number?"

"It's already half-way into my keypad." Everett brags, tapping in the last few numbers. It genuinely amazes me how little he hesitates when he calls these people.

It rings for a good ten seconds before someone picks up on the other end, on speaker phone.

"*Hello, you've reached Jane from the Althea Block event hall.*" An older sounding voice comes through.

"Hi, Jane." Everett replies, clearly excited by the prospect of holding the youth club at this place. "Hypothetically, if we wanted to rent your building for two days a week, how much would that cost us?"

The woman on the other end of the line laughs a little. "*How old are you?*" She asks.

"Sixteen, but, like, technically I'm calling on behalf of a thirty-something year old."

Jane chuckles a bit more obviously this time. "*Okay.*" She says. "*We usually do pricing consultations in person. I can have you come in for an appointment? Preferably with a parent or carer.*"

"Yeah, but my parent or carer isn't gonna be the one renting the place."

"*Okay, but if we're going to talk about real adult money,*" She says, and Everett rolls his eyes. "*Having an adult would be preferable.*"

"Fine, okay, yeah." He replies. "When can we speak to you?"

"*Assuming that you want to come in as soon as possible, I can see you at nine-o-clock tomorrow.*"

Everett blinks in thought for a few seconds. "Hold on, give me a second to confirm that with my assistant." He says, muting the phone.

"What assistant?" I ask him in a humoured tone.

"I'm texting my mum to ask her if she can come with us. I've just always wanted to say that." He explains, opening his messaging app. He's lucky that his mum must have been quite close to her phone, because she replies quickly and he un-mutes the microphone.

"Hi, Jane. Me again." Everett greets her. "Can you do the afternoon tomorrow at all? The responsible adult doesn't get off work until two."

Much like before, Jane laughs (we're clearly serving as all the entertainment that she needs for the day), and then there's some typing on a computer before she speaks. "*I can do three-o-clock.*"

"That's perfect, thank you so much."

"*Great. Can I get a name for the appointment?*"

"My name or my responsible adult's name?" He asks, getting to the point where he's starting to come across as irritating with all of the questions. Jane doesn't seem to care, probably because the conversation is coming to an end.

"*Either, honey.*" She says with patience.

"Oh, okay. Well, my name's Everett Enfield. Spelled Echo, Victor, Echo, Romeo, Echo, Tango-"

"*Okay. Our address is on our website, I'll see you then.*" She cuts him off, and a few of us laugh at the words, and the way that Everett frowns at being cut off.

"Oh, okay. Bye, Jane." He says. Jane bids him farewell one last time before the phone hangs up. He appears to double

294

check that the call is actually over before putting his phone back in his pocket.

"Okay, so, what's our budget?" He asks. "Like, what's the amount of money that she will tell us for us to say no?"

"Anything more than what the new owners want." Mars says, and we all seem to agree with that. Less money to pay is always better, even if we still need to scavenge for some.

"Yeah, and make sure you take videos of the place, we wanna see." Lilia tells him.

"Send them to the group chat." Dallas says. The group chat that I'm not on, by the way. I would ask to be added back to it, but I think at this point them adding me to it would be awkward, even if I did just come up with the idea that might save the club.

"Yeah, will do." He says. We stay in the coffee shop for a good fifteen minutes, just talking. I don't do much of it, but I do a lot of listening and nodding along, which is something. Eventually, we do leave, because they have to close, but Everett is buzzing the whole walk home.

"This is so exciting, I hope they have an Althea garden." He tells me with a grin as he bounces down the road. It's just us now, everyone else having filtered off. I don't know if we're going back to his house or mine, 'cause it's the same direction from town until one turn off.

"I'm sure if you hope they will hard enough, there'll be one." I tell him, clearly poking jest at his enthusiasm. He laughs.

"Are you gonna come?" Everett asks, turning towards me as he starts walking backwards for our conversation to continue.

"I didn't know I was invited." I reply honestly. I know

I've been spending a lot of time with Everett as of late, but that's been because I'm too scared to go home, not because he actually wants me there.

"Of course you are. I had assume you were staying over at mine tonight, so it would make sense." He explains very casually. I have to admit that I feel a little shitty just always staying with him. It's not that I don't want to, in fact, I really enjoy staying with him. But I feel like I'm overstaying my welcome, and I'm definitely burdening their finances with all the extra water, electricity, and food I use and eat. I know that Miss Enfield doesn't care, but I do.

"I can't tonight." I lie. Everett furrows his eyebrows.

"Oh, okay." He accepts. "Be safe, whatever you're doing." He tells me.

"No promises." I tease, trying to deflect his words by joking. The truth is that I *can't* promise him anything. Knowing myself, I'll wake up hungover in a field. There's no way that I'm going home, even if the idea of Alfie worrying does weigh heavily on me. After Everett turns off to head home, I keep walking in a direction that I usually don't.

I'll see where the night takes me.

19

Rhett

I'll admit, it did worry me that Kylen didn't stay over at ours last night. Not that I don't think that he can handle himself, obviously he can, but it's that the way he said it made me feel that he didn't have any intentions of going home. And he hadn't mentioned before that he had anywhere to be.

I spent the whole of last night telling myself that he probably went to stay with Abbie or someone and didn't want me to ask a bunch of questions, which is fair. Despite reassuring myself, though, I call him first thing in the morning. It's the exact same thing that I did with Eli when I was worried about him.

Kylen seems to understand the reason for my call.

"*I'm fine. Take it easy, Inspector Gadget.*" He drawls almost the second he picks up the phone. He sounds exhausted, but I refrain from commenting.

"Okay. I just wanted to make sure." I tell him. "Did you wanna come to see the Althea place later today?"

It takes a while for him to reply. "*Okay.*" He says. "*If that's okay, I will. Can I meet you there?*"

"Sure, yeah."

"*Okay. Thanks, Rhett. I'll see you later.*" He says before promptly hanging the phone up. It worries me how quickly the phone call went, but he sounded fine other than the tiredness.

I have the whole morning to myself because Mum left for work before the sun had even woken up. It's not often that I get to sit on the sofa in my pyjamas and watch TV for a whole morning, so I do.

I decide to shower and get dressed at five-to-two, so that by the time she gets home, it'll look like I've had quite the productive day thus far.

Despite the fact that she has a key, Mum always has a habit of knocking on the door for me to let her in. It's actually because when she used to have to go off to work when I was younger, my auntie Kristie would watch me, and I would spend half the day waiting for her knock on the door.

Then, when she did knock, I would leap up off the sofa and race to answer the door and leap into her arms.

Nowadays, I settle for a hug.

"Hey, darling." Mum says, wrapping her arms around me, which I reciprocate.

"How was work?" I ask her.

"Same as everyday, love, it was fine. Let me get changed and then we can head off to this building that you're so excited about."

"Althea building."

"Althea building, yes." She repeats with a nod, closing the door behind us.

We leave with fifteen minutes to get there, and because it's only a ten minute drive, we'll be in good time.

In fact, the traffic is so light that we get there seven minutes early. I tell Mum that we're meeting Kylen here, and so we wait by the entrance to the building.

Upon first look, it's quite big. Clearly the kind of place that weddings happen. The building is made of yellow bricks, with pillars of wood on each corner. Having said that it's big, it's also clearly on the more budget side of things. That's good for us, because we're on a budget.

I start getting anxious when it's two minutes to three and there's no sign of Kylen. I shoot him a quick text and he tells me that he's *'omw.'*

He gets here at one minute past three, but not exactly how I expect him to. He's wearing the same pair of jeans as yesterday, albeit a different hoodie on. His hair is ruffled and slightly over his eyes in a way that I'm not used to seeing. He hunches his body over as if he's trying to hide something, even though I doubt he is. Overall, he just has an aura of zero confidence. It's weird to witness. His hands are stuffed in his pockets and dare I say he looks a little stressed.

But not all of those things combined could catch my attention in comparison to what really does.

His right eye is completely bruised up, all purple and fresh-looking. The hair over his face hides it a little, but not nearly enough. His lip is slightly swollen as well as having a cut across it. To put it lightly, he looks like he's been in the middle of a boxing ring with no defences.

"Don't say anything, Everett." He whispers, voice rough and hoarse.

What the fuck? What happened to him? I swear, if his so-called 'friends' of his did this, I'm gonna be pissed.

"I won't." I reply, turning my head towards where my mum is watching in genuine shock.

"Kylen!" She exclaims, marching towards us. "What the fuck?"

Nice to know that I get it from somewhere.

Mum goes right up to him and puts her hand under his chin gently, pushing his head back to look at his injuries. "Who did this to you?" She asks. I don't think I've ever heard her sound so stressed and serious at the same time. "Did one of your parents do this to you?"

"No, Jesus Christ. Nobody did anything." He grumbles, taking a step backwards to avoid everything. "It's fine. Can we go for this meeting?"

"How long ago did this happen?" Mum keeps asking.

"Look, I appreciate the concern, Miss Enfield, but-"

"How long ago, Kylen?"

The boy in question sighs and averts his gaze to the pavement. "Last night." He replies under his breath. "It's not a big deal."

Cars drive by on the road next to us as this conversation happens. I make the decision to stand back and let Mum interrogate him, because she's much more likely to get answers than I am.

"Yes it is. Who did this?" She keeps questioning him, and he swallows. It looks like it hurts. "I'm not gonna go to the police or anything, but I'm a nurse, and above that, I'm a mother. You're a second son to me at this point, and so I need to know who did this to you." She demands. It's like something behind Kylen's eyes breaks.

"Can we, um, can we talk about it later?" He pleads. "I would really hate for us to miss this meeting because of me."

Mum sighs, and she pulls Kylen's body into hers for a hug. He drops his head onto her shoulder for the few seconds that

'responsible adult.'

"We can call it two-thousand-four-hundred."

"Pounds?" Kylen gasps, turning to me and mouthing 'that's double' with a look that does nothing to hide his shock.

"I rent this place out for four-hundred a day, on the low end." She says apologetically. "I'd be loosing a lot of my income to budge any more."

I can't help but show my disappointment. Obviously we're not gonna make an attempt to pay that much when we currently can't even get half of it. We're back to square one.

"I'm sorry." She says, and then she sighs deeply. "Okay. How about, you three tell me what you want from a building, and I can see if any of our other locations might be suitable." Jane offers.

"Yes, that'd be lovely." Mum says, voice strained as she looks at me as if telling me to suck it up and be nice to the woman. "Do you want to tell her?"

"Yeah, sorry."I mutter. "We just need like, a hall. Doesn't have to be that big, there's not too many of us. And, preferably a kitchen?"

"And at least one office, 'cause Thalia likes her personal space." Kylen adds. Jane pauses in thought for a moment.

"Oh, okay." She says. "So, you don't need that much?"

Kylen and I send a glance over at each other, before I slowly nod at Jane.

"Right, well- we have another place on this site, mind you it might need a bit of fixing up. What's your price range?"

"Um, preferably around six-hundred a month." I try, despite how low it sounds compared to what she's just given us. Jane actually seems to smile.

"That works. The building I'm talking about used to be a

community cafe, back when this place was a sports centre. We opened it for a few months, but it didn't make any kind of profit." She explains. "It's got a kitchen, and then a larger area for seating. I think there might be a spare room that was meant to be the employee break room, but could turn into an office. I've actually never tried to use it, because we didn't need to, so it hasn't been touched in a few years."

It actually sounds.. *perfect.* I find it hard to articulate my words as a result, but I don't have to worry about that too much, because Kylen does it for me.

"Our own space? Like, we'd be the only ones using it?"

"If you can be bothered to fix it up, yeah." She says, having long discarded her notebook. "I can show you, if I can dig the key out."

"And you'd do this for six-hundred a month?" I ask her.

"Like I said, it's not been used for ages, so I'm not getting any money from it right now. Anything else would be beneficial. Even, I'll do it for five-hundred."

If I was a less composed person, I would leap up from my seat and give Jane a big hug.

"You're the best." I say instead. "Can we see it?"

"I'll show you now, yeah." Jane nods, standing to move over to her desk to sift through her drawers for the building's key. Whilst she does so, Mum wraps her arm around my shoulders and pulls me into her body for a sideways-hug.

I rest my head on her chest and bask in the sound of her heartbeat. She starts running her hands through my hair maternally. Mum's love language has always been physical touch - she likes to hug a lot, which is why I think she's so protective of me.

When Jane seems to find the key, I pull away from Mum,

just in time to catch Kylen swiftly averting his gaze to make it seem like he wasn't looking at us.

Jane leads us a way we haven't gone yet, towards a set of double doors labelled 'fire exit' that I doubt is actually used as a fire exit.

The path outside is just concrete tiles on the ground. It leads to a set of stairs made out of the same material, and the grass beside the concrete is nicely trimmed.

Jane leads us around to a smaller area behind the main hall. It's secluded, and not all all visible from the road, which I know for a fact would make people at the club ten times more comfortable.

There's a few wooden tables outside the cafe building itself, and the wood is rotting from disuse and rain.

But, the building itself is what is most impressive. It's homely, and smaller than the Aconite Centre is, but not necessarily in a bad way. Like the main building, it's made of yellow bricks, with a flat roof.

There's a sign above the main entrance that obviously used to indicate that it was a cafe, but the words have faded so that all I can make out is an 's' at the end.

Jane must see me looking at the sign, because she answers my prayers.

"Oh, yes. We used to call it 'Cafe Hibiscus', to keep in with the flower pattern."

My jaw drops as I gape at the sign. From where they're both stood in front of me, I see my mum and Kylen look at each other before both turning to me with expectant looks in their eyes.

"I love that flower." I say lightly, looking over to Jane as a wide grin grows on my face.

"Oh, me too." Jane agrees. "I got to name all the buildings on this location, and I wanted to call them all trombone-shaped flower names. You know, althea, hibiscus, hollyhock, and so on."

Holy fucking shit. I think this woman is literally my senior soulmate. I turn back to my mum and she gives me an approving nod as if to say 'that's great honey', before I turn back to where Jane is studying me curiously. I clap my hands in front of myself and smile up at her.

"Jane, I think you and I are going to be great friends."

I let Kylen and my mum go into the building whilst I interrogate Jane about pretty much everything she's even mentioned in passing to do with flowers. I had thought it was a fun, quirky little bit, not that she actually likes the things.

I find out from her that she used to be a florist. But, after her husband passed, she struggled to keep the shop open, and used the money that she inherited to buy this building with the support of her friends.

I'd love to be a florist. Spending all day just getting to be around and tell people about flowers. I think the main thing holding me back from that is that the idea makes me really dysphoric. Considering how much of a female-dominated industry selling flowers is, it makes me feel like people will only take it as a reason to disbelieve my gender identity.

I don't know, maybe it's stupid.

Either way, Jane reassures me that I can ask her anything I want about getting into the industry. She even gives me her business card with her phone number on it, and she seems

under the hand dryer, which gives him no response.

"Hey, this doesn't work." He says, turning back to me. But, the second he does, it seems to spring to life, roaring loudly. Kylen half-screams and jumps backwards from it.

It's the funniest thing I've seen in a long time.

I break out into a fit of guffaw-ish laughter that he's not impressed by.

"Hey!" I exclaim through my laughter. "This doesn't work!"

"Oh, fuck off." He says. "You would've screamed louder."

"Yeah, but I didn't." I argue back. Once the moment has died down a bit, I get an actual opportunity to look around. "Are all men's bathrooms this dirty?"

Kylen looks like he's debating it for a moment before he nods. "Yeah." He sighs, and then he laughs a little. "Just thinking about public bathrooms makes me need to wash my hands." He mutters, turning the tap on and doing just that. "But, um, I think this place is really good."

Kylen's right when he says that. It's not as big of a place as the Aconite Centre, but it's arguably more cosy here. It's secluded, and the woman that owns the building is absolutely lovely. And we're getting money off.

"It is, yeah." I reply. "Have you taken a video for the group chat?"

"I'm not on the group chat, but I did take a video. I'll text it to you and you can send it." He says.

"You're not on the group chat?"

"No?" He confirms, as if I'm meant to know. He's been at the club way longer than me, why would he not be on the group chat?

"Why not?"

"Um, I got removed. After Pride, remember?" For a second, he goes towards the hand dryer after he's done washing his hands, but he changes his mind and just wipes his hands on his jeans.

"Oh. And nobody added you back?"

"Literally who would have added me back?"

"I dunno. Lilia?"

Kylen just shrugs at me. "It's cool. Send the videos and we'll see what everyone thinks, then hopefully we can get the go-ahead from Thalia." He says, and it's not upset or malicious, which kind of makes me feel worse.

He then walks out of the bathroom, and I wash my hands before following him. Whilst it's fresh in my mind, I take my phone out and add him back to the group chat. It's not fair that nobody added him back, but they probably felt awkward that he got removed for being a dick to me, so they felt like I had to be the one to add Kylen again. But it's fine, because that's what I've just done.

I see that the video has come through from Kylen to the group chat, and switch my phone off whilst I wait for responses. Overall, I'm pretty happy. I mean, of course, we might have to invest in some decent chairs and the like, but we're no longer at square one. In fact, I'm pretty excited for the future of the club.

20

Kylo

Everett's mum, Ashley, insists that I have to come home with them after we see this new building. I'm at least in a much better mood than I was before I showed up, simply because I'm no longer terrified that the club is gonna fall from underneath my feet. Sure, nothing is confirmed, but I can't think of a single reason that Thalia would say no.

We get into their flat just in time to catch the first few minutes of some mindless game show, which plays on the TV for about half an hour. It's clear the whole time that there's an elephant in the room that's tainting our interactions.

"Everett, honey?" Ashley speaks softly during one of the advert breaks.

"Yeah?" He replies, looking up from his phone.

"Do you think you could pop to the corner shop? We've run out of bread." She says, and Everett nods. Then, he looks at me, and back to his mum, and nods once more.

"Of course. Um, have fun." He says, patting me on the shoulder as he grabs his wallet from the table.

"Do you want me to come with you?" I ask him. It feels

313

weird for me to just stay in his house without him. Everett's eyes go back to his mum for a split second.

"It's fine, I'll be like five, ten minutes at best." He announces before hugging his mum goodbye, and then he leaves. The door shuts, and almost instantly, Ashley gets up and disappears off into the kitchen.

"It'll hurt for at least a week." She says, coming back into the room and handing me a bag of frozen peas. She then pauses the TV, and sits down next to me with a slight sigh. "Right, I don't expect you to tell me anything that you don't want to, but I need to know a few things."

"Okay." I agree. It's the least I can do.

"Was this one of your parents?" She asks. Her tone leaves no room for me to hesitate or lie.

"No." I say easily. She nods at me with relief in her eyes.

"Okay, then. The person, or people, who hurt you like this-" She pauses her speech to push the bag of peas against the right side of my face. "Did they do it because of your gender identity?"

I feel worse for worrying her than I do for my injuries.

"No." I promise. "It wasn't because of that."

"Okay." She nods. "Has anyone looked over you? Like, checked that you're okay?"

There's something about Ashley that makes me want to tell her everything. She makes me want to tell her how Dean and his friends followed me for blocks before they actually approached me. About how they left me afterwards and I passed out on the street because it was too embarrassing for me to call anyone.

Instead, I just shake my head. She doesn't sound judgemental at all, she just nods. "Do you mind if I do? You're allowed to say no, I just want to make sure it's nothing bad."

"Yeah, okay." I accept, purely out of the fact that I feel bad for taking up her afternoon like this. Firstly, she does a few things to make sure I'm not concussed or anything (which she assures me, I'm not) and then she gets me to take my jumper off.

The bruise that stretches across my shoulder is visible from the edges of my t-shirt, and Ashley makes it very clear to me that she's seen it by the way that she gasps.

"Kylen, this is- you need quite a bit of force to produce a bruise this big." She says softly. Then, without any warning, Ashley presses her hand down on it gently, but it hurts like shit.

"Ow, fuck off!" I exclaim with a hiss of pain, flinching away from her.

"Sorry." She says. I go to apologise for swearing at her, but she cuts me off the second my mouth opens. "It's okay." She says with compassion. "It hurts, I get it."

"I knew this was gonna happen." I tell her quietly, still refusing to look in her direction. "I should've been more ready."

"Don't blame yourself, blame the people that did this."

I nod absent-mindedly at her words. She deserves to know the truth about everything, just because of how unnecessarily kind she's being to me.

"Everett knows who it was." I state, and she nods. "He'll tell you the second I'm gone if I don't tell you, I see you close you two are."

Ashley hums at that, pulling away from my injuries. "I mean, I am his mother. It doesn't mean that he tells me everything, though."

Okay, fuck it. She's been nothing but amazing to me, she deserves to know. "Have you heard of Dean?" I ask, and the grimace on her face suggests that she has.

"The guy that your almost-girlfriend needs you to get on the good side of so that he'll take that video from the party down?"

"He doesn't tell you everything, huh?" I bite back, and she laughs a bit.

"Okay, fair. He keeps me up to date with the gossip, sure. But I keep him up to date with the drama from my work too, so it's like a trade." She explains. "You're saying that Dean did this to you?"

"Yeah." I admit. It feels good to talk to her. Talking to a maternal figure like Ashley is far more therapeutic than talking to countless actual therapists ever was.

"Do you know why?"

"It's 'cause I snaked on him to the police."

"Ah. Yeah, teenagers will give you a beat down for that kind of thing."

"Talking from experience?"

"Not entirely. Raising a teenager has given me some insight."

"Into what? Isn't Everett kind of a social outcast?" I ask her, and it comes across a little more rude than I intended, but Ashley just smiles warmly.

"You don't have to be Kylen-level popular to have experience with modern teenage culture." She just replies before urging me to put the frozen peas back against my face.

"What, has he been, um, targeted before?"

"Just because he tells me everything doesn't mean I'm allowed to tell it to you. Ask him yourself." She says, pulling out a small bottle from a first aid kit that's spawned out of nowhere. "You didn't clean these cuts, did you?"

I shake my head and she sighs. "Okay. This is gonna sting. Hold my hand if you want." She suggests, pouring the liquid onto a ball of cotton wool.

"I'm okay." I tell her. When she actually connects the liquid with my cuts, though, it's a different story. "Ow, shit." I exclaim, moving away from her. She pulls her hand away and then holds the unoccupied one out towards me.

"Offer's still open." She says, somewhat cockily. I give her a certain look that indicates how I feel. "Alright. But, I made Everett pop out for a bit because I've observed that you prefer not to be seen as vulnerable." She says softly. "Getting medical care is kind of vulnerable, especially from a parent. I know that you don't want babying, and I'm not trying to do that, but I'm not gonna judge you for anything."

The eye contact that we make this time is different. I reach forward and take her hand without thinking. Ashley doesn't say anything about it, and then she reapplies the cotton wool, and this time, when I hiss in pain, she squeezes my hand.

"I know, honey, I'm almost done." She whispers delicately. "You're doing really well." If she were any other person, I probably would have snapped at her for being so patronising. But, coming from this woman, the words only make me feel overly emotional.

Then, she pulls back for the final time, rubbing a gentle hand against my unbruised shoulder whilst packing her supplies away. It leaves a hollow feeling in my chest to no longer have that care.

"You're a really great mum." I find myself saying. I probably won't get another moment alone with her for a while, and I have to let her know. "I don't know if Everett tells you that often, but you are."

She looks at me in a way that I can't quite decipher for a few moments before responding. "Thanks, Kylen. I try my best."

"Can I ask you a bit of a personal question?"

"You can ask it, sure. No promises I'll answer."

"What did you think- or, how did you feel, when Everett told you he was trans?"

Ashley genuinely looks like she's thinking about it for a while, and then she leans back on the sofa and speaks. "I've always supported gay and trans people, I was raised that way. But, it's different when it's one of your own." She says in a way that's uniquely vulnerable of her. "To be honest, I was worried at first. I'd read all of these articles and headlines about how trans people don't really live the best lives. You know, extreme things, like hate crime, and suicide rates."

"Yeah."

"Of course, as a parent, all I want is for my kid to be happy. I was worried that being trans would stop him from being happy. But, then I realised that he's still gonna be trans whether I support him or not. I was doing research, and I saw something about how trans kids in unsupportive households are some ridiculously high percent more likely to make attempts on their lives." She keeps talking, and her words get more and more fragile as she does.

"I have to let him be who he is, because what kind of mother would I be if I didn't? I mean, it's just been us for a while. His dad's not in the picture, and in all honesty, his grandparents were eager for us to move out. Because it's just us, we *have* to be there for each other. I have to be there for him, and I realised that that means unconditional love. No matter what.

My job as a parent is to support him, and when I realised that, I never looked back." She finishes.

I get that horrible sensation of misty eyes when she finishes speaking. This feels like the perfect household, the place that I would have been okay in. It's not fair. Why is it fair that Everett gets such a great parent and I don't? Why is it fair that he gets to be happy with his childhood, and I don't?

"Oh, sweetie. I didn't mean to upset you." Comes Ashley's voice. She places a careful hand on my wrist, and her speech is laced with honey.

"No," I stutter out. "No, you didn't upset me, I just-"

"Hey, it's okay." She reassures, looking at me with genuine concern. It's like she really cares.

My voice breaks when I go back to reply. "I just wish I had parents like you." I say, and I'm crying by the last word of the sentence. This was a bad idea. Instinctively, I put my hand over my mouth to hide my ugly crying. Ashley looks at me like her heart has just broken, and then her arm is around my shoulders, pulling me into her chest.

And that motherly action just makes me cry harder.

"It's okay, lovely, you're okay." She whispers.

"I'm sorry." I croak out behind my sobs.

"That's okay, don't worry. It's been a hard couple of days."

"Yeah." I whisper between hiccups.

"Yeah." Ashley repeats, starting to run a hand through my hair comfortingly. "Do you wanna talk about it some more?"

And I think about exactly what I would say to her if I had the courage.

Well, Ashley, I got fucking beat up by a group of like five boys last night. And then, they left me lying on the pavement, and I thought about going to my almost-girlfriend's house, but I couldn't deal with her seeing me this weak and fragile when I'm meant to her almost-boyfriend.

And then I thought about showing up at *your* doorstep, Ashley, but it was really late and I wanted to prove a point that I didn't have to rely on your household. But it turns out that I do, because I'm fucking crying in your arms.

So I just fell asleep in the local park and woke up this morning feeling like shit. And then, I didn't want your son to think that I hadn't gone anywhere, so I bought a new hoodie from a charity shop to make it look like I'd gone home and changed.

And then my almost-girlfriend's best friend texted me to tell me to stop talking to her when I hadn't fulfilled my end of the deal. So now I feel like I'm never gonna get her back, because my end of the deal has recently become completely unattainable.

But telling her all of that wouldn't solve any problems.

"I miss Abbie." I whine pretty pathetically. It's embarrassing. She says something to me that I don't register before getting up and coming back into the room with a glass of water.

"I think," Ashley says, taking the water from my hand once I've had a sip. "That you should go and have a shower, put some comfier clothes on, and when Rhett gets home, we can pick *Criminal Minds* up where you left off."

"No, it's okay. We can watch *Young Royals*, I'm kinda invested." I tell her, and she smiles.

"Okay. I'll grab you some clothes to wear, let me just text Everett and make sure he's okay with you borrowing his clothes. Um, when he gets back, do you want to pretend that showering is all that's happened whilst he's been away?"

Everett is the least likely person in the world to judge me for crying to his mum. Maybe, apart from the woman herself.

"You can tell him. About all of it, I'm sure he'll be eager to propose a solution to everything. He has a knack for that." I mumble that last past, and Ashley scoffs playfully.

"He gets it from me." She says, walking towards the exit of the room to presumably get me some clothes to change into after I shower.

"Ashley?" I call after her, and she turns around slightly to look at me. I take a deep breath in to calm myself as I address her. "Thank you."

Much like I had anticipated, Everett is eager to fix everything.

"No way she said that to you!" He exclaims, staring down at my phone. "Back the hell off from Abs, I've blocked you on her phone. She'll talk to you when the video is down like we said." He reads the text from Shea out loud for the second time, with more shock in his voice this time.

"It's fine, dude." I say softly. We're sitting on his bedroom floor, after two episodes of *Young Royals* and his mum deciding to go to bed for the night.

"It's not fine, that's so shitty of her. Hold on." He says, taking back his own phone and opening an app that I can't see between the distance. Suddenly, his phone is ringing.

"Hey." Eli's voice comes through. *"What's up?"*

"Eli, you're friends with Shea, right?"

"..Yeah."

"Is there any chance you can get her to call me?" He asks hesitantly.

"*Probably. Any reason, or just for funsies?*"

"So that I can use her to talk to Abbie. But, don't tell her that. Just say that a friend of yours wants to talk to her. Girl stuff."

"*Girl stuff?*" Eli laughs. "*What are you planning?*"

"Not planning anything, do you think you can get her to give me a ring, asap?"

"*Hold on. Can you not just call Abbie yourself?*"

"She doesn't answer calls from numbers that she doesn't recognise." I pipe up.

"*Oh. Hi Kylen. He's roped you into this too?*"

"Unfortunately."

"*Can you not just text her?*"

"This is a dire situation, Elliot." Everett says with mock seriousness.

"*Ew, never call me Elliot ever again.*"

"*Babe!*" Comes another voice from the phone. It's definitely Will, which makes me roll my eyes at the phone. Eli is heard heading down a staircase before he must enter the same room as Will. "*I love you.*"

"*You had to call me downstairs to tell me that?*"

"*Yeah. And, since you're already on your feet, some of that pizza from last night microwaved would be great.*" Will says, and Eli sighs before more footsteps are heard.

"*Sorry, gotta go. The King needs attending to.*" He spits in a way that is half bitterly sarcastic and half playful.

"Do you guys, like, live together?"

"*My parents are out of town for the week, I'm staying at his.*" Eli replies smoothly, and the sounds coming through the phone tell me that he's opening the fridge. "*But, yes, sorry. I'll text Shea your number, um what did you want me to say?*"

"Tell her that one of your friends needs to have a chat with her." Everett says smoothly.

Eli laughs. *"Okay. Good luck with this, then."*

"Thanks, Eli." Everett says, and then he hangs the phone up. "She'll call me within the hour, I promise."

"I still don't get what you're gonna do." I mumble into nothingness.

"You don't have to get it, just let me work my magic." He says. We spend a couple minutes waiting with eyes on his phone as if it'll start trilling any second now, but it doesn't.

The later we stay up waiting, the more tired I get, and just when I think I'm gonna fall asleep leaning against Everett's bookshelf as he sketches something, his phone buzzes.

The number isn't saved in his phone, and he practically throws his sketchbook across the room to answer it.

He fixes his posture the second that he answers, raising his voice up in pitch very intentionally. "Hey." He says, grinning. He speaks in a way that he's definitely learnt from being socialised as a girl, and it makes him sound a lot more feminine. "Is this Shea?"

"Yeah?" She replies, and I could recognise her voice instantly. It makes me irrationally angry in a way that I'm kind of ashamed to acknowledge.

"Shea, hi. Listen, my name's Evelyn," He says cheerily, and then he tells her that he, or his character, 'Evelyn' goes to one of the schools on the outskirts of town. "You're friends with Abbie Hutchinson, right?"

I don't have any idea how he found out her last name, but I'm not gonna question it.

"Yeah, I am. Why, what's up?" She asks.

"Okay. Sorry, I tried calling her on Instagram but she didn't

323

pick up, so I had to ask Eli for your number 'cause she posts you on her story a lot." He explains, and he's pretty good at bluffing.

"*Right. What about her?*"

"Well, I heard that she's got a thing going on with Kylen, um, Lysen?" I roll my eyes as he purposefully fucks up my surname when he could be asked to find Abbie's perfectly.

"*Ugh, Kylen Lysander? Unfortunately, yeah.*"

"Right, yeah. I just- there's a thing that about him that I need to tell Abbie."

"*A good thing or a bad thing?*"

"Oh, girl, trust me, it's bad." Everett tells her, looking down at his nails. He's proper getting into character.

"*Please tell me he's been getting with other girls, maybe if he has, Abs will finally realise that she's too good for him.*"

"We can only hope." Everett laments, making direct eye contact with me as he shakes his head hopelessly.

"*Shit, yeah, okay. I'll tell her to call you.*"

"Thanks so much. I just can't stand to know about it and not tell her."

"*Yeah, totally. Thank fuck she'll finally have a reason.*"

"Mhm, okay, bye, Shea, thank you." He hangs the phone up and tosses it on the ground. "Voila."

"I really don't like that girl." I mumble.

"She's out to get you. Have you done anything to her?" Everett asks me. I can think of a few instances where my group as a whole might have pissed her off, but I don't think that I have personally.

"My friends have, I think I'm a prick by association." I shrug. "Do you bust out this 'Evelyn' character much?"

Everett laughs. "Only when necessary. She's my alter ego,

since it's the closest girls' name to my actual name."

"What would that make my alter ego?"

"You'd be Kylie, dude." He laughs.

"Right. Well, I don't think that Abbie will call us tonight. She doesn't go on her phone for an hour before bed, and she goes to bed at ten-thirty." I let him know, and he nods. We decide to turn in for the evening after that, and I end up falling asleep on Everett's sofa feeling a hundred times better than I did when I woke up this morning.

"Kylen!" Everett whispers, shaking my shoulders and pulling me out of my slumber. "Kylen, wake up!"

"Piss off." I mumble, rolling over to bury my head in the sofa.

"Kylen, get your ass up. You're meeting Abbie in an hour."

His words shock me into sitting up, thoughts frantic. What the hell is he on about?

"Huh?" Is what actually comes out of my mouth.

"Yeah, she called. I spoke to her, she's meeting you at eleven." He tells me.

"What? What did you say to her?"

He stands from where where he was kneeling beside the sofa, chucking a t-shirt and pair of jeans at me. "Mum washed your clothes, here. Uh, yeah. I just told her that there was no way in hell you were gonna get that video taken down, and it doesn't mean she has to ice you out."

"I've told her that before." I mumble. I don't know why it's different when Everett does it.

"Yeah. Well, I told her that it's just a quick chat, and if you fuck it up, she doesn't have to speak to you again. I also said that you're going through a bit of a rough patch. You know, practically living with me, talking to your psychologist again, and it would really help if you knew that she doesn't hate you."

"Dude!" I exclaim, standing up. "That's not cool."

Abbie and I don't talk about that kind of thing. I've never shown her that side of myself and I had never planned to. She doesn't know about any of that. Or, she didn't.

"Cool or not, she's agreed to talk to you."

"I don't care, it wasn't your place to tell her about everything." I half-yell at him, pretty pissed off about the whole situation, because I didn't give him permission to tell Abbie about any of that. I had assumed that it would come up eventually, but when the time was right.

"I just helped you." He says, instead of apologising. "You're meeting her at the park."

"There's nothing helpful about that, man. You told her stuff that I didn't want you to tell her!"

"You wouldn't be talking to her today if it wasn't for me, don't yell at me."

"Well, maybe I don't need you and your saviour complex!"

"Saviour complex?"

"Yeah, you think you're gonna fucking rehabilitate me, make me all sober and happy, and shit. But you're not." I tell him.

Everett breathes out heavily and starts to pace around the room. "I didn't have to help you, you know that, right? I did it because I was raised to believe that if you're nice to horrible people, it'll help them be better." He explains, and ouch.

"You think I'm a horrible person?"

326

"I didn't mean it like that." He whispers.

"Yes, you did, it's fine. It's whatever, you're not the first and you won't be the last." I say, silencing our conversation as I leave the room and head towards the bathroom.

What an asshole. Now Abbie definitely thinks I'm some kind of weak little thing, and she won't like me any more, and fuck.

I don't really mean to slam the bathroom door as loudly as I do, but Everett doesn't say anything about it. I half expect him to knock on the door and apologise, but he doesn't.

When I'm done changing, I head straight for the door, and I'm gone in seconds, without even looking back to see if he notices me leave.

21

Rhett

Our front door slams and I think about the complaints that we'll get from our neighbours.

I want to give Kylen the benefit of the doubt, that he's probably having a shitty day and an even shittier week. But I don't get why he's so pissed off; I did him a favour. He's gonna speak to Abbie, and he's annoyed at me for getting that for him?

"Is he okay?" Mum asks slowly, leaving her bedroom. "That was a door-slam and a half."

"I think I upset him." I mumble. She comes over and gives me a hug that I appreciate.

"How so?"

"I told Abbie that he's having a hard time to get her to talk to him, and he yelled at me that he didn't want her to know." I whisper. "But he wants to get together with her, and if they were in a relationship they would tell each other anyway." I justify my words, raising my voice and looking up at my mum.

"Well, maybe he wanted to bring up his mental health on his own accord."

"Yeah. But I was just trying to help." I say honestly, and Mum seems to melt a little.

"He'll be back, remember. He's left half of his stuff here for one, and you two are too good of friends to stop talking over something like this."

I suppose we are good friends. We've definitely been spending enough time together to count as such. But, it's weird, because he's not the kind of person that I'm usually friends with. He's the kind of person that I usually hate.

"Yeah, I guess."

"It's alright. We'll just leave him to his day, and he can leave us to ours."

It's kind of embarrassing to admit that I have nothing to do when Kylen's not here. Mum left for work shortly after Kylen went to meet Abbie, which left me with an empty house and not much to do.

After a few too many moments of being left alone with my own thoughts, I make the executive decision that I can't just sit here waiting for Kylen to come back, if he decides to.

Since I'm the only one home, I don't bother putting my big headphones on, just blasting my summer playlist from the armrest of the sofa whilst I curl up, hunching over my sketchbook with my laptop open and resting on my right knee. It displays a picture of a singular cornflower. When I woke up early this morning waiting for Abbie to call me, I ended up doing a little more research in to them because they're the flowers that I picked out for Kylen.

And of course, since I've done the research, I need to do a

sketch of it so that I can write the facts about it around the picture. Then I think I'll tear the page out of my sketchbook and give it to Kylen so as to make up for him being upset at me earlier.

Although, the information that I learnt tells me that, maybe not, because it turns out that men used to wear cornflowers on their jackets to show that they were single. I'm pretty sure that encapsulates everything that Kylen is not trying to gain out of today, so maybe I'll only give it to him if things with Abbie went well.

On my fourteenth song, and when I'm just about to start going over the facts I've written in a fine liner, my phone buzzes and interrupts the music. I absent-mindedly reach over and grab it, only to see that it's a text.

eli!!

which number is ur flat

I click on the notification and sit up a little. Without really thinking about it, I abandon my sketchbook and laptop and head towards the front door.

Grabbing my key off the shelf, I leave in my socks (the rest of the building is carpeted, so it's fine) and start padding down the stairs towards the lobby area. It's only been a minute since he sent that text, so I'm hoping that if I interpreted it correctly, I won't have missed him.

When I get down the final flight of stairs and to the equally as carpeted lobby of the building, my suspicions are con-firmed.

He's standing in the corner of the space, one hand fidgeting with one of the rips on his jeans, and the other hand is holding the phone that he's gazing down at.

"Eli!" I call out from the bottom of the stairs. His eyes look up to meet mine, and his shoulders sag with relief. He looks tired and maybe not put together in the nicest way possible.

"Hey. I'm sorry. I didn't know where else to go." He says softly as he approaches the stairs.

"There's a lift if you'd rather take that up to mine." I suggest, and he nods.

"Thank you."

"Yeah, of course. Did something.. happen?"

He tells me that he'd rather wait until we're at my place to talk about it, which is fair enough. "I find that taking the stairs down is quicker 'cause of the momentum, but the stairs are never faster on the way up." I explain quietly due to the enclosed space, and he hums in agreement.

Then, we go into my flat silently, and he takes his shoes off as I guide him towards the sofa. "You know, you're not the first upset teenage boy I've had come here for refuge."

Eli laughs. "I still can't believe you managed to get through to him. Actually, where is he?"

"He has a life other than staying here, you know." I say jokingly.

"Okay, okay, fine." He concedes, and then his eyes start to wander as if he's trying to find something to say to disperse the tension.

"Nobody else is home, by the way. Clearly, um, something happened. We can talk about it, or we can stick some shitty TV show on and not talk about it." I present the options to him, imploring the same tactic as my mum does when I have a bad experience.

Eli sighs and leans back, kind of melting into the sofa. "I went to hang out with my friend, Maddie. And Will said he didn't wanna come 'cause he has coursework to do or something." He begins, crossing his arms and then pulling his legs up onto the sofa. "But when we were like an hour in to meeting, her mum phoned her and told her that she had to come home. It was because she'd snuck out and her mum had realised, so obviously she went home."

I can kind of see where this is going, and from the way that his voice shakes a little, it seems like he's getting to the point quite quickly.

"And, you know, I've been staying with Will whilst my parents are at this business conference for the week, so I just went back to his place."

"Oh, god, Eli."

"Yeah, and I have my own key so I just went in. And he wasn't downstairs, so I went to his bedroom, and-" He stutters. I wrap an arm around his shoulder comfortingly. "I guess he thought that I'd be gone the whole day."

"I'm sorry." I tell him.

"It's okay." He replies, almost too quickly. "It's like, it's less that he.. I don't really wanna say it, actually." He trails off, hugging his knees to his chest now. "I guess, to be fair, the other guy is pretty fit. I can get why he'd choose that boy over me, but I wish he had just, I don't know, had the courage to break up with me first." He expresses, and I feel really bad for him. This is one of the few things that makes me glad that I'm aro. With both this and Kylen and Abbie, the whole romantic experience seems very emotionally taxing.

"That's so shit, Eli, I'm sorry."

"Like I said, it's fine. I just, like- I've never had a boyfriend that's lasted more than two months and I'm starting to think that it's just me." He mumbles. "And now I just feel like shit, because all the boys I've ever been with know that they can do better. And then when better comes along, they do."

His words are raw and honest. They leave me feeling bad for him in a way that makes my chest ache, because he doesn't deserve to feel that way.

"Sorry." He apologises. "You don't have to come up with something comforting to say."

I nod, and I'm glad for that, because I don't have anything to say that will help him feel better. I wish I did.

"So, I'm assuming that Will knows that you know?" Is what I do ask him.

"Not yet. His bedroom door was ajar, so he didn't know I was there. Guess he was too busy to hear me open the front door, but I just left as soon as I saw what was going on. I don't know what to do in terms of telling him, but it starts with not staying at his any more."

"Did you wanna stay here?"

"No, it's fine. I have a house key, I can go back home. I just don't really wanna be alone right now. I don't wanna bother you, I would've gone to Shea's or someone else's, but all of my girl-friends are friends with Will too." He says quietly. "And I do need to speak to Kylen, is it gonna be here at any point?"

"He'll be back later I reckon." I tell him, settling into the sofa. I'll let Eli stay here for as long as he needs, and I know that my mum won't mind.

22

Kylo

I've given myself forty-five minutes to do a fifteen minute walk from Everett's house to the park. I just had to get out of the house, he pissed me off. It's okay, though, because I have time to stop at Kev's place first, and then I end up sitting in front of a tree smoking whilst I wait anxiously for Abbie.

She arrives five minutes early, and I only realise because she kicks my shoe. I'm scrolling on my phone and listening to music, so I don't even notice her arrive, but when I feel a force against my right foot, I look up at her, and she gazes down at me with her beautiful brown eyes.

"Fuck, Ky, what happened?" She exclaims, dropping to her knees in front of me. She sort of grabs my face with both hands, eyes filled with concern. Shit. I'd kind of forgotten that I looked all bruised up. "This wasn't Tobias and them lot, was it? I know you said that you annoyed them, but-"

"No, Abs- um," I interrupt her, pleading for a subject change. "It's okay."

"Okay." She nods. "Okay, um, sure. Let's walk and talk." She suggests, clearly sensing my uncomfortableness with the

"You're not– you're not mad?"

"Jesus, Kylen. I'm not mad. Well, I am a little bit, but not about you being trans. I just– I had no idea."

"Yeah, that's kinda the point."

"Did you think that I would stop talking to you over it?"

"Yeah. Why wouldn't you?"

"Because I like you. A lot."

"Oh."

"Christ, you're such an idiot." She chastises. "It's okay. I promise. Oh–" She cuts herself off in surprise when I fling my arms around her shoulders. After actually registering it, she hugs me back, properly. "Hey." She whispers. "Hey, it's okay."

"Well, I just, I've never known how you feel about this kind of thing. I was really scared you would hate me."

"I would never, Ky. I– there's other things that we can do together, and– shit, I feel bad."

"Don't feel bad."

"I kinda made your life hell because I thought you didn't like me."

"I thought you didn't like me." I repeat her sentiment.

"I do." She affirms.

"Yeah, me too." I whisper. Our bodies stay closely intertwined as we speak. "But– our friend groups are really intertwined, and I kinda fucked off all my friends and I don't wanna ruin your reputation or anything."

"It's okay. Your friends are dickheads anyway."

"Yeah, but–"

"Kylen. I don't care about your friends. I care about you."

It's the most amazing thing I've heard in a really long time. All the words that I was going to say, about how I can't hang out with everyone together, and how all her friends hate me, they all die on my tongue. When we're so close together like this, I've never felt more loved.

"Can I kiss you?" I whisper to her. Her pupils expand as we look into each other's eyes.

"Yeah." She says back.

When we kiss this time, it's better than it was in that bedroom during Alfie's party. It's so much better, because I feel like I'm not lying to her whilst I do it. She knows exactly who I am, and she's kissing me like she genuinely likes me. Her touch sends sparks flying down my throat, igniting an unyielding passion.

Abbie shifts herself to move closer to me, and then she's sitting on my lap, giggling as we have to disconnect for her to fully move. And then we go right back to kissing, like nothing bad ever happened between us at all.

We don't care at all about our surroundings, until a dog walker starts strolling down the path in front of our bench.

"Teenagers." He mutters, and Abbie and I have to pull away from each other to burst into laughter. After that, the moment is kind of ruined, but it was really funny, so I decide that it's okay.

"Alright," Abbie says, checking that the dog walker has disappeared. "I feel like you've gotta tell me about why you look like you've been beat up."

Yeah, I suppose I do. It's the least she deserves.

"Um, okay. You know how I got arrested?"

"Yep."

"Well, I was hanging out with Dean at the time, and he kind of did all of the bad stuff and then shoved me to the ground so that the police would catch me and not him. And then I snaked on him to the police to get my charges reduced, so him and his mates beat the shit out of me the other day."

"Oh." Abbie says after a moment of consideration. "That's why the kid that phoned me said that you'd bottled getting the video taken down, like, beyond belief."

"Oh, he said that did he?"

"Yeah. He said that you were having a hard time, and I guess that this," She pauses, gesturing to my injuries. "Is what he was referring to."

And I realise that she's just given me a scapegoat. Everett didn't spill my guts to her, not really. It would be extremely simple for me to just nod and agree.

"Kind of. My parents and stuff, too. And my friends. It's all kind of accumulated into a fucking dumpster fire."

She laughs and wraps an arm around my shoulders. "Maybe we should just run away together." She suggests in obvious jest. "Actually, Ky, I do have a few questions. If it isn't rude."

"Shoot."

"So, um, how long have you been a boy for?"

"Publicly? Like eight years."

"Oh, cool. And, like, okay- stop me if this is rude, okay?"

"I promise."

"How do you look so much like a boy? Not in a weird way, but, like, I wouldn't have even considered it."

I find it really sweet that she seems to care so much about offending me. I'd answer a million questions for her if it meant she could be mine.

"It's a skill." Is the simple answer that I give her. "I take testosterone shots. Like, male hormones, in my thigh. Once a week."

"Ouch, I hate getting needles." She exclaims, drawing in a

breath. "But, like, can I have a go stabbing you with one?"

"Alright, don't get carried away."

Abbie laughs and ruffles her hand through my hair. "And, um, who is that kid that called me?"

This time, it's my turn to laugh. I mean, she did ask. So, I tell her about him. I tell her about how I've been staying at his house a lot. About how he's trans too, and I've been teaching him things, and he's been teaching me things.

She asks me how I met him, and I tell him about the youth club.

"That's cool, actually. Like, you just get to hang out with others."

"It is. It's got quite a good sense of community."

"Can I come? Not forever, but, like, I wanna meet this Everett guy in person, and also maybe get a feel into this side of your life that I didn't know about."

Her words surprise me. I hadn't even considered that she would be okay with me being trans, let alone wanting to come to the club and meet everyone.

"Yeah, um, yeah. That'd be great. It's next on this Thursday."

"I'm sure you'll pick me up." She says. "I can't wait to introduce myself to everyone as your girlfriend."

My head snaps to the side to look at her. She didn't mean that, surely.

"What?"

"I mean, if that's okay. Sorry, I should've asked-"

"No- of course that's okay. You wanna be my girlfriend?"

"Only if you'll be my boyfriend."

"God, Abs, you're amazing." I lower my voice to a whisper, kissing her again. "Yes." I say, and in this moment it's just us. No dog walkers, or Dean fucking Holden, or Shea, or any of my friends. It's just her and I, and it makes everything feel okay.

"I'm really sorry, by the way. That I didn't realise how people were treating you." I say. We have to get everything out in the open if this is gonna work. The worst thing about this is that it was likely some of my friends who were involved in behaving like that.

Abbie nods softly at my words. "Thank you." She whispers, dropping her head onto my shoulder. "Oh, and for what it's worth, too, I'm sorry for letting the whole of the party know I how I felt." She apologises. "We probably should have kept it in the bedroom." She adds, trying not to laugh as we speak.

We both break into laughter at that. "Okay, Abs. From now on, what happens in Leo's parents' bedroom, stays in Leo's parents' bedroom." I tell her, and she giggles whilst leaning into my side.

I'm in a much better mood when I get back to Everett's house than I was when I left. To the point where I feel bad for lashing out at him so much.

There's someone waiting for a parcel when I make it back to Everett's, which allows me to slip into the building without buzzing in. I take the lift up, bouncing on my toes the whole time with excitement.

I have a girlfriend. I have a girlfriend! A girlfriend that knows I'm trans and still wants to be my girlfriend.

I knock against Everett's door at about two o'clock.

He opens the door slowly, and then he looks a bit regretful

when he sees me.

I swamp him in a hug the second that I lay my eyes on him, wrapping him up and kind of lifting him off the ground.

"Woah! Hello." He giggles, being dropped back onto the ground. "Did it go well?"

"I have a girlfriend." I tell him. "I told her that I'm trans and she still wanted to be girlfriend, and I have a girlfriend now."

"That's great!" He yells, hands on my shoulders. "That's so great, congrats, dude."

"Yeah! I'm sorry that I got mad at you earlier."

"It's fine, I'm sorry too. Oh! Um-"

"You and Abbie, huh?" Eli asks after emerging from the living room.

"Oh, Eli. Hi. Yeah." I stutter out, a feeling a little awkward from acting so confident and excitable when Everett wasn't the only person around.

"Well done. Managed to recover from Leo's pretty well." He nods at me. I laugh because it would be majorly awkward if I didn't.

"Eli's just staying here for the day." Everett says. "Will cheated on him so, like, he just needs a bit of company."

"Oh, yikes. I'm sorry." I sympathise. I can't honestly say that I didn't see it coming, though. Either that or a bad breakup, I never liked Will.

"It's fine. He was a bit of a dick anyway." Eli says, crossing his arms in front of his chest. "Actually, Kylen, I need to talk to you about that." He continues, fidgeting with his hands.

"Um, okay." I agree. I can't really think of anything that we would need to talk about. Maybe the relocation of the club? Either way, I do a little point in the direction of the living room, and he nods, taking an exit and then sitting down on the sofa. I sit on the one against the adjacent wall, and Everett sits next to me.

"Basically, so, Will doesn't yet know that I know about his side-thing." He begins. "And, obviously, I wanna tell him that I know, which would undoubtedly end our relationship."

"Oh." I say, beginning to realise where he's going with this.

"Yeah." Eli nods. "But, um, obviously, I won't do it if you don't want me to. If anything got out, I would hate for it to be my fault." He a says, sounding pretty torn up about it.

He's obviously talking about the fact that threatening to end his relationship is the only think that's stopped Will from telling everyone he knows that I'm trans.

But, now with Abbie and everything, I feel like the people that know, know. And the people that don't know, don't need to know. And if they do know, it's not gonna affect me. The people that I need to be okay with it are okay with it.

But, fuck. Everything I've worked for. All the respect that I've spent so long earning to be seen as nothing but a boy. Half the people that I know would never even consider thinking about me as such if they knew I was trans. It's terrifying.

As much as I say that, it's not fair to Eli, or to anyone, even if I haven't known them for years. It's not his fault that his boyfriend (ex-boyfriend-to-be, I guess) is such a douchebag.

"It's okay. It would never be your fault, it would be his. And, you don't need my permission." I say. My tone of voice doesn't exactly sound too convincing, but I do mean it. "You," I instruct, lightly pointing at Eli across the room. "Leave his ass." I finish, and Everett laughs beside me. "And *I* will deal with the fallout on my side."

"Thank you." He says. "I will. In person, though. Maybe

tomorrow." He nods to himself.

"Great, so, we've got time to kill. Why don't we stick that new *Marvel* film on and order some pizza in?" Everett offers. Eli and I both agree, but despite that, I spend the whole of the movie texting Abbie like I'll never get the chance again.

I purposefully tell Everett that I'll meet him at the club on Thursday so that I can swing by and pick Abbie up, just us. The club starts at five-thirty, but I get to hers for just after five so that we can do a nice, leisurely walk there.

She looks as beautiful as always, wearing a pair of white, low-rise cargoes and a dark blue tank top. She has a tote bag slung around her shoulder, and a warm smile on her face.

"Hey." She grins, rising up onto her tip toes to press a kiss to my lips.

"Hi." I giggle back. "Are you excited?"

"Very. I hope your friends at this place like me."

"They will, promise." I whisper, taking her hand. "But they can be quite excitable, so, forgive me if they swarm you with questions."

Abbie and I walk to the club hand in hand after that, and we arrive a couple minutes early. Rowan is sitting at the table that Thalia usually does, spinning a pen between his fingers.

"Kylen, hi." He says with a smile. His eyes glance over to Abbie, but he doesn't say anything other than that.

"Hi, um, this is Abbie. My-" I pause my words, not wanting to make her uncomfortable or anything, because I don't know if she wants to be known that way here.

"His girlfriend." She finishes for me. "I'm just here 'cause

lingering in a conversation that they probably still have to finish by the door for a bit, and Abbie takes a step out of the circle that we've formed to whisper to me.

"Question." She says. "How do I know what to call someone if I can't see their lanyard-card?" She asks me, eyes intent on Mars and Dallas.

"I'll show you a magic trick, Abs." I say to her, and then when Dallas and Mars head over to us, I walk her forwards to meet with them half way. "Hey, guys." I greet the two of them.

"Oh, hi." Mars replies.

"Quick question, what are you guys' pronouns?" I ask them. They both look a little confused for a moment, because they know that I know what their pronouns are. "This is my girlfriend, Abbie. She just asked me how she can tell what someone's pronouns are if she isn't sure. You can just ask them, I promise nobody will get offended by you asking."

"Girlfriend, huh?" Mars asks with a teasing voice. "The same one that you upset at that party?"

"You know it." I reply, deflecting. Abbie and I have spoken about it in a lot of depth since we made up, and we've decided it's probably best to just make a joke out of the situation. We can't explain it to anyone without it outing me, and even though of course Mars and Dallas know that I'm trans, I don't want to break the habit.

"Nice to meet you, Abbie. I'm Dallas, she/they."

"She and they, right, yeah. Are you trans, then?"

"Babe, you can't just ask people if they're trans." I whisper to her.

"Oh, I'm sorry."

Dallas and Mars both find it quite funny. "No worries."

Dallas says. "No, I'm not trans. I'm a cis girl, I just like both she/her and they/them pronouns."

"Right. I didn't know that was a thing."

"Anything can be a thing." Mars answers. "You'll get used to it the more time you spend here. I'm Mars, they/them only."

"That's a cool name." Abbie replies. "After the planet or the Roman god?"

"The planet, but either interpretation is fine." Mars replies with a slight smirk. "It's good to meet you, Abbie."

"Yeah, you too. Is this everyone?"

"Nah." I tell her, patting her on the back. "We're nowhere near done with introductions."

Abbie just smiles at that, leaning into my side. I move my hand to rub up and down her arm comfortingly. I won't tell her until we're alone again later tonight, but I'm beyond proud of her for coming here and doing this for me. For the first time in a while, I feel a sense of hope about the future.

23

Rhett

On Friday morning, Mum drives me to the school so that I can go and pick up my yearbook. Despite the fact that the school year is over, I still have to go in to get it in person.

Kylen has been bouncing between staying with me and staying with Abbie these last few days, and he stayed with her last night, so I didn't have to worry about waking him up when we left really early.

It's also pretty fun that Abbie and I have been texting a lot. We've actually bonded quite strongly over being close to Kylen, and we've both unanimously agreed to accompany him to the children's hospital next week, because he's been telling both of us about how nervous he is to get this blood test. Something I've learnt in the lead up to it that Kylen is pretty nervous of hospital settings, and despite the fact that it's only to check up on his testosterone levels, he's stressing himself out about the appointment.

Thankfully, since he's sixteen, his parents don't need to be there, so Abbie and I decided that we'll walk him down there together. She's a very nice girl, I decided, and I'm glad that

351

she's a part of Kylen's life. He seems a lot happier for it, too.

Either way, his newly found relationship with Abbie Hutchinson has given me considerably more free time. So, it's not like I have anywhere to be, but, when I head into the school, I kind of expect it to be no longer than a ten second interaction.

You know, 'Hi, can I have my yearbook?' followed by 'Sure thing, here it is, bye.'

However, when I do get there, I'm told that I need to pick it up from the year office. So, despite feeling out of place in school in normal clothes and not uniform, I head down the corridor and knock against the door.

"Everett!" Ms Branchford exclaims when she sees me. "How are you?"

"I'm good, yeah. Summer's going well." I let her know. "Just popped by for my yearbook, please."

"Yes, of course. But come sit down - tell me about how it's been." She insists. "I'm swamped in paperwork, I could use the break, honestly."

"Okay." I nod, pulling the chair back and awkwardly perching on the edge of it. "I've been fine."

"Did you want a rich tea, Everett?" She asks, opening her desk drawer and pulling one out from an open packet. I politely accept it from her but end up just holding it because I don't want her to ask me something whilst I'm mid-eating and then have it be awkward because I can't respond. "So, tell me how it's going. Did you go to that youth group after all?"

And, wow, it feels like that was all a very long time ago.

"Yeah. It's been good, actually. It's a nice place to go to."

She smiles broadly at that. "I'm so glad to hear it. Any new friends?"

"A few, actually. There's this one boy that I got quite close to, and then loads of others."

"You seem bubblier." She says. "More upbeat, and you're sitting there pretty confidently." She comments. I hadn't realised that I was, but I guess I've been subconsciously taking Kylen's advice to heart.

"I guess I do feel a lot better."

"That's brilliant, honestly. I'll feel a lot better about sending you off to college now."

College, right. Time has honestly been slipping away from me so quickly that I haven't even thought about it. Just the thought of it send a jolt of panic down my spine. I need to ask some people our age from the club where they're going for college.

"Aha, yeah."

"And, nothing else.. negative has happened since I last saw you?" She asks. I know it's her job to care about our year group and all, but it's a little irritating. I don't want to spill my guts to her, and although nothing has happened, if something had, I wouldn't wanna tell her. All she did last time was tell my mum and make her lose sleep over my well-being, too.

"No." I tell her. "Not like that, anyway."

"Alright. Well, it seems like things are seeming a lot better for you recently."

"Yeah. They are, actually."

"That's amazing. And I'm sure it'll only get better." Ms Branchford smiles, reaching down into a big cardboard box and pulling out a yearbook. On the front, there's a little post-it-note that says '**Everett E'**, which she takes as belonging to me. "Here we are." She says, and then she hands it to me across the desk.

"Thank you."

"Of course." Just then, the landline phone set up on her desk starts to trill. "Ah, okay. I'd better take this. It was really great to catch up, Everett. Good luck with everything."

"Cheers." I say, and she waves me goodbye as she picks up the phone. "Year Eleven office." She answers, and her voice fades out as I shut the door behind me.

I cannot believe that I just thanked someone by saying 'cheers.' Who am I?

I've been spending too much time with a certain boy.

On Saturday night, Kylen shoots me a text asking if he can stay over for the weekend. Of course, I'm more than happy to say yes, and we spend the whole evening catching up about what we've missed since last seeing each other.

I tell him all about seeing Ms Branchford, and then he tells me about getting introduced to Abbie's parents. Apparently they think he's a good guy, which is all he was really hoping for.

And then he asks me something that I wasn't necessarily expecting.

We're sitting, both on my bed. Kylen's phone dangles from his right hand, still open in a TikTok comment section that he's abandoned in lieu of interrogating me.

"Rhett." He says, biting his lip as if considering his next words. "The other day, when I was like, confiding in your mum."

I glance up at him from where my sketchbook rests on my

knees. "Mhm?"

"She said something about you. It was a little cryptic. Kinda implied that you've had some issues with how others have treated you."

I giggle a little and shut my sketchbook whilst I sit up. "What did she say?"

"Just like, that you've given her some insight into modern teenage culture."

"And you took that as 'people have been shit to Everett?'"

"Yeah. It was the context of the situation, I guess. Sorry. Just been playing on my mind."

I look up at him for a second time, with a more weighty expression. To be completely fair to him, he has told me pretty much everything about his past.

"Uh, yeah." I say simply, hands going to find the pencil that I put down on the bed again. "But, nothing as bad as what you've been through."

"Doesn't make it any better for you that someone else has had it worse, you know."

"Yeah." I agree, taking up lightly sketching again so that I don't have to look him in the eyes. "I mean, it's not that interesting. I'll tell you if you wanna know."

"I'm just kinda curious." He says.

"It's just my cousins." I whisper. "When I first came out, a couple years ago, I like, told them and stuff."

Kylen switches his phone off and lets it drop onto the bed. "And it didn't go well?"

"Not really. I guess they were raised differently. They were really mean to me about it, called me delusional and shit. They're only a couple years older than us, but fourteen and sixteen is quite different, as it was at the time." I carry on.

"They're both cis boys, and they just kind of, I don't know. It wasn't a fight, just kinda playful violence that I wasn't reciprocating. And then, um,"

I pause to take a breath and shift so that I'm fully leaning against the headboard of my bed. Kylen blinks at me, almost as if he regrets asking.

"We were in my Auntie and Uncle's back garden. They just kind of cornered me, being mean to me about it, asking me all these invasive questions that were clearly meant to make me feel horrible."

"Yeah. My parents do that too. The questions and stuff." He sympathises.

"Mhm."

"Did anything else happen?"

"Yeah. I don't remember it that well, but I guess I tripped over one of the tiles on the ground trying to get away from them, and then I was concussed and had to get stitches."

"Fuck." Kylen gawps, and I nod a little, pulling the side of my shaggy hair back to show him the scar on the side of my head.

"Fuck, indeed. Um, and obviously the boys were like *'oh, she fell, she fell, we were nowhere near her'*, but despite the concussion, I knew what happened. And I told my mum what happened, and of course, she believed me over them."

"Mhm."

"But my Auntie Kristie believed her sons over me, naturally. She got really annoyed at my mum for insinuating that it was my cousins' fault. Then, they eventually admitted it." I say, and Kylen shuffles a little closer to me for support.

"And my Auntie still took their side. Saying that it wasn't wrong for them to have been worried about me thinking I'm a different gender. Telling my mum that if she's gonna let me mutilate my body, they have every right to ask questions about it."

"Fucking hell, Rhett."

"And, um, my mum and her sister kind of stopped speaking after that. Mum got pushed away by her parents, too. They didn't agree with her letting me socially transition."

"I'm sorry." He says, and I just shrug.

"It's okay. It was just kind of a humbling experience. I've never felt worse for my mum, 'cause she basically had her whole family cut her off for me. And none of it would've happened if I wasn't trans. I know that you don't think I've ever been ashamed of my gender identity, but I was after that. For a long while."

"That's what she meant when she said that it's just been you and her." He realises.

"Probably." I tell him. "I don't know, it's complicated. She still gets most of her family Christmas gifts and stuff, but nothing ever shows up in the post here."

"I feel like I owe you an apology." Kylen says suddenly. "I feel like I assumed that everything with your family was perfect."

"Kinda like how I assumed that everything with your trans-ness was perfect until I actually had the pleasure of getting to know you and the displeasure of meeting your parents." I compare the scenarios. He looks to me with an understanding pair of eyes.

"I guess everything's just a bit more shit than it seems." He mumbles.

"That's not the take-away, man." I correct him. "The take-away is that maybe we shouldn't assume deep things about others from what we see on the surface."

"You ever thought about getting a podcast?" Kylen jokes to me. I dignify him with a laugh before steering our chat back in the more serious direction.

"Speaking of that, have you been back to your parents, yet?" I ask him, and his shoulders start to deflate. Kylen's eyes glaze over his phone as if he wants to escape into it, but then they meet mind.

"No. Not since we snuck out. I know it's really bad. And I know that Alfie is probably worried sick."

"We gave him the phone number, didn't we?"

"Yeah. But he is still quite little. I don't know if he can properly use it without our mum or dad's help. I need to go see him." He laments, fingers dancing against the screen of his phone as he checks his notifications.

"We can go tomorrow, if you want. After the club, maybe. I can come with."

"Yeah. That'd be great."

"And, um, okay. This might not be my place." I start, beginning to voice a thought that I've had for a while. "But, I feel like you can't avoid your parents forever. Maybe we should talk to them about stuff."

"You say that as if I've never tried to have a conversation with them. I have, it's just hard."

"How about, tomorrow morning, we can write down what you wanna say to them. Like, in a letter. That's how I came out to my mum, actually. I wrote her a letter and left it out when I went to school. And, we can do that, and then give it to them. And then go from there. I find that writing your thoughts down helps to articulate them properly, I don't know."

"Yeah." Kylen nods. "I don't know, I guess we can do that.

I just wish we could be on the same page. Like, I don't care if they fuck off from my life the second I'm eighteen, but it's just so hard. With my brother, mainly. I would've moved out and never looked back the second I turned sixteen if it wasn't for him." He sighs, and then he finally picks his phone up and goes back to that comment section, seeking escapism.

"We'll figure it out." I tell him, and I mean it.

True to my word, Kylen and I spend most of Sunday morning drafting the things that he wants to tell his parents into his notes app. He cries twice, and I hug him four times. After an hour, it comes out at about five hundred words, but we whittle it down to four hundred pretty easily.

Following that, Mum shows us where she keeps the nice paper, and he writes what he has to say down on that. He gets his tears on the first page, and then throws it away because he doesn't want his parents to see that writing this upset him. And then, he spells 'genuinely' wrong (g-e-n-u-i-n-e-l-e-y, by the way) on the second attempt, and proceeds to scrunch it up and throw it in the general direction of the bin.

The third time that he tries to copy it out, I get him to pause when tears start to form in his eyes, and we scroll on the hashtag '*#youngroyalsedit*' on TikTok for ten minutes to divert those feelings so that we don't have to sacrifice the paper again.

"Can, um- Can I give you something to do? Whilst I- uh, whilst I do this. I feel kinda awkward that you're just sitting there." He admits between videos. His eyes are red and puffy with tears, and I can't deny him when he's so upset.

"Sure. I can get the colouring book I've been doing. Mindfulness, my mum calls it, but-"

"I have an idea." Kylen cuts me off. His spindly fingers tap against the edge of the table. "I just, if I'm doing something meaningful and shit, then I think you should be to."

"Mindfulness via colouring isn't meaningful to you?" I quirk an eyebrow at him, and he allows a smile to tug at the corner of his mouth.

"Not really." He chastises. "Um, okay. What's on your mind?"

"In general?"

"Like, out of all the things plaguing you, what's occupying the most of your head space right now?" He asks, turning his body to be fully facing mine. It kind of amazes me how quickly he manages to push the evidence of his upset away through body language alone. If there weren't still tear stains on his face, I'd be none the wiser.

"I don't know, uh, college?" I suggest, grasping at straws to give him an answer without dawdling over the thoughts for too long.

"What about it?" He asks back without a beat of hesitation.

And, shit, I guess I actually have to think about it now. I guess the issue is that this is my first chance to properly, fully pass. Being surrounded by people that have never known me before I transitioned. It has to be perfect. I don't know what I'll do if it's not.

"I guess I'm worried." I state plainly. "That nobody is ever gonna see me as anything other than the trans kid. I wanna- I guess, I wanna be more than that to people. You know?"

He nods at me with a hum of agreement, tilting back precariously on his chair and grabbing another sheet of paper.

He places it down in front of me, and then also deposits a pencil on top of it.

"Okay." He says. "So tell me, then. Or, tell yourself. Who are you?"

"What do you mean?"

"I mean, who are you? Without acknowledging your transness at all, who are you? How do you want to be perceived by people?" He asks. I must stare at him in a bit of a stunned silence for too long, because he picks his own pen back up. "Write it down. Whilst I do this, have a think about it, and write it down. It was the first thing that I did when I wanted to go completely stealth, and I stuck it on my mirror to look at every morning." He says, fingers drumming against the table as he looks at me.

Write it down? My eyes dart between him and the paper, and Kylen nods his head as if telling me to get on with it. "I'll do this, and you do that."

Afterwards, he returns to looking at the half-written letter in front of him. It only takes a few seconds for that upset that he was pushing away to creep back onto his face as he reads over the next sentence that he's drafted to write out.

I look away from him and down to the paper in front of me. It was a good question. Without acknowledging my transness, who am I?

My name is Everett. I'm sixteen. I'm a boy.

Good. Simple, even.

I can tell you a lot about different flowers. I like spending time around them, I'd love to spend time around them as a career.

Yeah, okay. Um, what else? I guess I could talk about my hobbies.

I like to draw. Flowers, mostly, but scenery too. I like long walks

361

listening to pop music.

I say that, but I've been neglecting my walks recently. I should get back on that.

I value self-expression a lot. I've had five different hair colours in my life, but the purple has definitely been my favourite so far. I'm a men's size small, but I always buy my clothes in medium because I like them baggy. If there's a TV show that's any good, I've probably watched it. I like films, too. My mum and I have unlimited passes at the cinema. My favourite film is Coraline.

I hardly notice when Kylen throws the sheet that he's writing on away, and pulls a new one out. I'm still trying to figure out what else I have to say. How do I want to be perceived by people?

I want to be thought of as confident. And kind, and approachable.

Yeah. That's right. Who am I? And, I've whittled it down, other than basic facts about myself, to: flowers, drawing, 2000s pop, hair dye, oversized clothing, the media that I consume, and the values that my mum taught me.

I squint at the paper for a second. It's not- It's not finished. It might not be what he said, but I pick the pencil back up and add a little more to the end.

I'm transgender. Also, bi. And also, aro.

After that, I leave the paper alone and watch Kylen as he carries on writing. He doesn't acknowledge that I've finished what I'm doing.

When he signs the end of the note with his name, he pushes it away from him and just drops his head to the table. I read it over for him to make sure that there's no mistakes, because he stressed to me a lot how much he wants it to be perfect.

Once we're both happy with his note, he asks if he can read

over what I wrote.

"Just out of curiosity, I'm not gonna hound you over it." He promises. I hand it to him and he reads it in silence.

"Thought I said without your transness." He smirks as he puts it back onto the table.

"Not gonna hound me, are you?"

"Okay. Fine." He gives up, holding his hands in the air to mimic surrender. He shrugs as he folds the letter he's written up.

"Well," I say, feeling the need to defend myself. "I've realised that it doesn't matter how I want to be seen. I'm trans, and it's a pretty big part of who I am. Just because I want to be seen as a cis boy by cis people doesn't make me any less or more trans."

"This feels like a lesson." Kylen says, eyes narrowed.

"Doesn't have to be. I'm a person that everything I've written down is true about, and I'm sure everything you've written down on your personal fact sheet is true, too."

"Yeah. I just prefer to be known as a boy. A boy who just so happens to be trans. I think maybe you prefer to be known as a trans boy. To yourself, that is. Like, it means a lot to you."

"It does. I don't think the adjective takes away from the noun."

He nods for a moment, and then bites his lip guiltily. "Sorry." He says. "I shouldn't try and disconnect you from your identity."

"Well, to be fair, I have been trying to connect you with yours. It's only just."

"That's actually been helpful, though."

"And you've been helpful to me, too, Kylen. I will genuinely put this on my wall. Maybe by my desk."

"I guess."

"You guess? Dude, if I pass at college it will be because of you. Like, the stuff you taught me about all that." I reassure him. He nods.

"Thanks." Kylen says. He smiles to himself, averting his gaze from mine before he repeats himself. "Thanks."

After that, we relocate to the sofa with our laptops and spend the rest of the morning simultaneously working on our college work with the Spotify mix of both our playlists on through the speaker that I got for Christmas last year.

We get ready to head to the club in good time after that, abandoning our work and making sure to bring the paper note with us, because we're going straight to Kylen's after this.

"Hold on," He says as we pass a corner shop. I wait outside for him, assuming that he's gone in to buy smokes.

He comes out with a bar of chocolate and a little, cheaply made teddy bear instead.

"What?" He asks, stuffing them in his backpack. "Alfie eats this shit up. Literally and metaphorically, I actually think you could consider his bedroom a museum for stuffed animals." He muses.

"That's sweet." I tell him. "Good move on hiding it, 'cause you would get absolutely rinsed at the club if you walked in holding a teddy bear."

"Firstly, you did not just say the words 'absolutely rinsed', you sound too much like me, and secondly, my masculinity is not so fragile that a stuffed bear would infringe upon it." He taunts. "Argh, now I sound like you. What the fuck is going on?" He whispers to himself, laughing, and we take back off down the road with that same energy radiating off of us.

Thalia's back from her holiday when we get to the club, and although we did pitch the idea of the move to Rowan on Thursday, he told us that she was his boss, so we'd best talk to her about it. Which is exactly what we do.

Because the whole of the club is in on it, we don't have to go to her office, since the moment that she comes out for circle, sporting her holiday tan, we basically erupt at her.

It's a jumble of words that are overlapping. Since we've been talking about the move *a lot* on the group chat, everyone is pretty excitable.

Thalia looks a little hopelessly around the circle for a bit, sitting down on her chair.

"Guys, um-" She tries, but is cut off by all of the overlapping words. After a moment, she sighs, and then claps her hands together in the same way that primary school teachers do to control their classes of nine-year-olds.

Everyone goes kind of quiet at that, and she visibly relaxes.

"Right." She says. "One at a time, what's going on?"

All of the eyes in the room naturally drift to me. "Right. While you were away, we did a bit more digging and kinda figured out that we can't make the money that we need." I explain, and Thalia nods in agreement. "So then we thought that we can just find somewhere else to hold the club that we can afford. And Kylen and I met with this lovely lady called Jane and she has a quaint little building that she doesn't use. I'll show you the videos of it, but she agreed to let us have the whole thing to ourselves for only five-hundred."

"Oh, wow, okay." Thalia nods. "I mean- yeah, show me the video of the place. Rowan and I would have to go there ourselves and speak to the owner, too, though. But, um, well done. Seriously."

"Thanks." I smile across the circle.

"Oh my god, also!" Lilia pipes up from two seats down from me. "You totally missed Kylen's girlfriend on Thursday."

Kylen himself groans as he tilts his head back to stare up at the ceiling.

"Yeah! She was actually very nice." Brynn agrees.

"I didn't know you had a girlfriend." Thalia muses with an entertained tone.

"Yeah, her name's Abbie. She might pop in at the general club sometimes."

"Well, I look forward to meeting her when she does." Thalia says, and then she claps her hands in front of her. "Right. So, next week is the last one that we have here. I've been thinking that we could do a little bit of a party to say goodbye to the Aconite Centre, whether we're going somewhere else or not."

The general response from that is that everyone wants a party to happen, myself included. Thalia laughs, nodding. "Okay. Since it'll be a big thing, I'm thinking that we don't run the club this Thursday or Sunday, and we can instead do it on Saturday, the twenty-eighth. It'd be a merge with you lot and the younger group, too."

Saturday twenty-eighth. Why does that sound so familiar to me?

Either way, we all agree that that's what'll happen. Thalia says that her and Rowan will go and check out the Althea site place early next week, and they'll let us know on Saturday.

It's only when I get a moment to speak to Kylen alone at the end of the session that I realise he's a bit on edge. "Everything all good?" I ask him, and he abandons the chair that he's stacking to look over at me.

"I don't- um, I have court on Saturday. But I don't wanna

miss the party, or whatever." He mumbles. Oh. Oh, right. Yeah, that'll be it.

"Maybe, but there's no way in hell you're missing court."

"Yeah, I know." He replies.

"We can ask her to move it."

"We're not asking her to move it because I have court, dude."

"Thalia!" I yell out towards where she's rummaging through some papers.

"Mhm?"

"What time is the party gonna be on Saturday?"

"Well, it'll be longer than a normal session. I was thinking twelve to four."

"Cheers." I say before I turn back to Kylen. "What time do you have to beg for mercy in front of a judge?"

"Nine-thirty." He replies reluctantly.

"Oh, perfect. You'll be done before twelve, no doubt." I reassure him. In reality, I'm about eighty percent sure of that statement. He nods a little vacantly, and I put a hand on his shoulder. "Come on, we can worry about that closer to the time. Let's go give Alfie that bear."

It's only when we get to his house that we realise that Kylen doesn't have a key on him. So, after he stands, fidgeting on the doorstep for a couple minutes, I push past him and press the doorbell.

His mum answers, smile on her face, but it drops when she sees us.

"Oh. I was expecting Alfie home, but it's my other child."

"Hi." Kylen says incredibly awkwardly. "Sorry to disappoint. Where's Alfie?"

"A friend's for tea. He'll be home in the next half an hour. How can I help you?"

"Well, um, I was wondering if we could come in."

His mum looks back down the hallway and then returns her gaze to us. "I don't know," She muses, addressing Kylen by his deadname half way through the sentence. He doesn't visibly react to it. "Not sure what the point of letting you in is if all you're going to do is climb out the window."

There's plenty of things that I know I would confidently say in response to that. But I don't say any of them, because this is Kylen's moment. We're doing this for him.

"I want to talk to you." He says after a moment, squaring his shoulders back. "I want to sit down on the sofa and have a conversation. With you and dad."

"And I want a daughter that knows that's what she is. We don't always get what we want."

"Jen." His dad appears from the stairs. "Let her in." He says softly, and Kylen's mum (Jen?) sighs.

"I suppose your friend wants to come in, too." She mutters.

"Yeah." Kylen says. "He helped me figure out what I need to say to you. Can we talk now, please?"

Jen makes piercing eye contact with me, and then she nods. "Shoes off when you come in, I just cleaned the carpet."

Kylen's shoelaces are already undone, so he has no issue slipping his blue and white Jordan's off his feet. I have to pause a little by the stairs in order to get my Converse off, but I do. And then, we head into the living room.

It's actually my first time being in Kylen's living room. It feel claustrophobic. It's like the opposite of eclectic, and I think that his parents must be big cleaners. The walls are white, and the sofas are made of cream leather. His parents sit on one of the sofas, and Kylen and I take the one opposite.

"If that's what this is about, we're not signing off any surgeries." Kylen's dad opens the conversation with, which feels like a *great* start.

"You're in luck, 'cause that's not what this is about." Kylen replies with a scowl. "I wrote some stuff down. That I want you to read." He explains, pulling the note out of his jacket pocket. It's kind of crumpled up, which only makes it seem more genuine.

Kylen looks away with a roll of his eyes as he hands it to them. Both of his parents look between each other a little curiously, and then his mum unfolds the note and they both start to silently read it.

24

Kylo

Mum + Dad

I know that I'm not the child that you wanted, but I'm still your child. I know that you think a lot of things about me that aren't true, and I need you to know that nothing I've done in these past eight years has just been because I felt like it. Most of this stuff has hurt me a lot more than it has hurt you, and I know you can't even fathom that idea, but I'm hoping that you will one day.

I never wanted to burn bridges between us. I just wanted your support.

Despite that, your upset doesn't change my reality.

My reality is that I'm a boy and I always have been. I'll still be your son whether you disown me or not. I'll still be Alfie's brother whether you stop me from seeing him or not. I know you're disappointed in the way I am, but I'm disappointed in the way you are too.

I don't want to never come home. I don't want to fight with you all the time. In fact, that's genuinely the last thing I want.

I want to live here more than anything. I want to get along with you more than anything. I want to be a proper older brother to

Alfie more than anything. I want you to invite my girlfriend over for dinner, and I want you to hug her and tell her that you can't wait for her to be your daughter-in-law one day. I want you to be proud to take me to family gatherings.

But, just like you both say to me all the time, 'I wants' don't get.

I would tell you how much the things that you do and say hurt me, but you know how much you hurt me. You just don't want to do anything about it. As long as you promise you'd never treat Alfie the way you treat me, I can live with that.

I can also live without you. Physically and mentally. I don't want to. But, I can. I've been doing it for years. I just need you to know that the way you behave won't change a thing about me. If it's what you want, I'll leave and never come back. It'll be the hardest thing I ever do, but I will. You'll have to give me time to get my stuff.

What I'm saying is that I can't do this any more. Even Alfie can understand that more than you. And he's eight.

The last time that I told you that I couldn't do this any more, you told me to suck it up, and then I spent a week in the hospital as a result. This time, I've got people in my life that don't want that to happen again. So, it won't. With or without you, it won't. And that's your decision, whether it'll be with or without you.

I just need to know that we're on the same page. I hope you'll let me know how you feel.

Love, the son that you refuse to accept that you have,
Kylen

The room is silent for a good five minutes whilst they read what I've written for them. And then, the sound of the doorbell slices through the tension. Mum looks up from the note with watery eyes, and then over to the sofa that Everett and I are sitting on.

"Go answer the door." She instructs, flicking her head in the direction of the exit. I nod and stand up, heading down the corridor with Everett following me. The second we leave the room, I hear the whispered and hushed voices of my parents, but I ignore them.

When I open the door, Alfie stands on the doorstep, beaming. Behind him is an adult who I presume is the parent of the kid whose house he was at, probably having dropped him off.

"Kylen!" He exclaims, jumping up off the ground. He's lucky that I catch him in my arms.

"Thank you so much." I tell the parent, and he nods with a smile before walking back to his car up the road. "Hey, Alf."

"What're you doing here? I thought you were gone forever." He pouts, leaning all the way into my chest as I shut the door behind us.

"I'm sorry, teddy bear, I'm here now." I whisper to him, sitting down on the stairs. Everett smiles down at us and then sits on the floor by the door, too.

"Who's this?" Alfie asks.

"That's my friend, Everett." I tell him, and he nods. "Oh! I got you something, Alf."

"A present?"

"Yeah. To say sorry for going away for so long." I explain, and luckily I had left my bag by the door, so it was right there. "Okay, close your eyes and I'll put it in your hands."

"Okay." He giggles, shutting his eyes and holding his hands out towards me. "It's not alive is it?"

"No, it's not alive. It won't bite you." I laugh back, removing the bear from my bag and gently placing it down in his outstretched palms. He gasps at the feel of it, eyes snapping open and grin tripling is size when he sees the stuffed animal. He quickly hugs it to his chest and then keeps it in his right hand as he leaps to give me a hug.

"A bear!" He yells. "I love him."

"What're you gonna call him?" I whisper.

"Mr. Bear-y"

"Wow. Are you sure that's not already taken?"

"There can be more than one 'Mr Bear-y', Ky. There's two Alfies in my year at school."

"Alright, my bad. Mr Bear-y it is." I concede. After that, I give him the chocolate bar, too, which he has a couple squares of immediately, but not without giving one to me and one to Everett, too.

"Teenagers?" My dad then calls from the living room. I give Everett a look before standing up, still holding Alfie in my arms as we head back into the living room.

"Hi, Alfie. How was your friend's?" Mum asks, making arms that suggests she wants to hold him, so I pass him over, despite the fact that he's getting far too old for this.

"It was good!" He exclaims. "Ky got me a teddy bear."

"Wow, we always need more of those, don't we?" She asks, but it's in a jestful slight that doesn't seem genuinely annoyed and more humoured by the ever-growing pile of them in his room. "How about, Alfie, you can find something to watch on the TV upstairs. Maybe, um, Everest, was it?"

"Almost." Everett replies. "Double t, Everett."

"Right, sorry. Maybe Everett can take you upstairs so that dad and I can have a bit of a chat with our eldest."

It upsets me, the lengths that she will go to avoid referring to me in any way. If she fully believed that I was a boy, that sentence would've sounded like: 'Maybe Everett can take you upstairs so that we can have a chat with Kylen', or 'with your brother.'

"Okay." Alfie says, and Everett nods, too.

"Use the TV in my room. Remote should be on the sofa, thanks, Rhett." I tell him.

"Yeah, no worries. Good luck. Come on, Alfie."

They go upstairs, and I'm left standing in the living room awkwardly. Mum sighs loudly, overexaggerated.

"Come and sit down, then." She says gently, shuffling to the edge of the sofa to make room in-between my two parents. I hesitate at the foot of the sofa for a second before slowly sitting down between them.

"Right." Dad says, putting an arm around my shoulder. It's weird. "We know that this is how you feel. But I think you're rushing into things."

"It's been eight years."

"Eight years of you being a child. Your brain hasn't even finished developing, kid." He says lightly. It makes me want to cry.

"I'm gonna tell you the exact same thing that the letter told you. I know who I am. So, I guess either you know who I am, too, or I can leave. And before you fire back, I'm not threatening that because I'm trying to guilt trip you. I'm doing it because the way that you treat me makes me feel worse than anything else in the world."

"You can't just leave." Mum says. "It doesn't work like that, you're a kid."

"I can. I've literally got a whole wash kit at Everett's house, and I'm slowly building one at Abbie's, too."

"We'd call social services. Report you missing."

"No you wouldn't." I reply without a beat of hesitation. "It wouldn't be worth it, I'm a legal adult in a year and a bit anyway."

"I think you forget how much this hurts us," Mum changes the subject, slipping in an endearing nickname version of my deadname. "We've spent the last so many years watching our little girl slip away, and it feels like there's nothing we can do about it."

My eyes find the ridges of the carpet as I slump further back into the sofa. "I know. But, I can't help with that. Of course it's hard, and there's tons of online support groups for parents of kids like me that I'd be more than happy to direct you to if you wanted to try."

"We do try."

"Okay." I grumble with a bit of an eye roll. Mum picks the letter up again and her eyes scan over it.

"Didn't know you had a girlfriend." She mutters.

"Yeah. Abbie. She came here for Alfie's party, remember?"

"I remember her, but I didn't know she was your girl-friend."

"She wasn't at the time, she is now."

"And she thinks you're a boy?" Mum asks, seeming a little bit humoured by it. Dad cringes visibly and interrupts.

"What she means, is, does she know about.. this trans thing? Or is it a lesbian thing?"

"Not a lesbian relationship, no. She's straight. So am I. We're together, she knows I'm trans, and she's still straight."

"But," Mum keeps asking. "She sees you as a boy?"

"I think you might be the only people in my life that don't see me that way." I mumble, and the words weigh heavy on the room like a brick being dropped into a swimming pool.

It's true, though. My friends do. Thalia and Rowan do. My teachers do. Even my eight-year-old brother does. It's just them that don't. "If I grow up, and in two years, I figure out that I was wrong like you're so clearly hoping I do, then there's no harm done either. Not that I will, but you get the point."

"Why don't we agree that we'll work on it?" Mum asks, but it doesn't seem genuine. "We had a chat, and we don't want to lose you. Not after raising you for so long. We can work on it."

"How are you gonna do that?" I ask.

"You're the expert." Dad says, gesturing at me to take centre stage.

"I dunno. Have you ever thought about, like, family counselling or therapy?"

"We've been under the impression that you don't like therapy. I remember that fit you threw about having to see that psychologist whilst all your friends were at the park without you." Dad mutters that last sentence, glancing to my mum, who nods in agreement.

"I would go." I tell them, brushing away the slight. "If it meant that we were gonna work on our relationship, all of us, I would go." I mumble. "I want to go. With you two, and Alfie. Maybe we can figure something out, repair this massive fucking rift in our household."

"This doesn't mean that we're suddenly going to let you get all of your demands." Mum insists.

"It doesn't have to." I tell her. "Maybe it could just give you some peace. Um, both of us, all of us, some peace."

Dad takes a deep breath and then sips his coffee. "I suppose if you can find somewhere."

"Okay." Mum says.

"You'll do it? Go to counselling."

"I suppose so. If it'll make you happy. This doesn't mean anything, though. You understand that, don't you?"

"Yes. Yeah. Thank you." I let out a string of thanks. It feels like a golden ray of sunshine has filtered through the clouds. This is such a big step for me in a way that I will never be able to fathom fully. And for the first time in a very long time, I leave my house with a smile on my face.

"Stop fidgeting with it." Abbie laughs, pulling my hand away from where I'm picking at the adhesive edge of the plaster on my forearm.

"It itches!" I giggle back at her.

"Yeah, if you pull at it, it will itch, dumbass." Everett says from the other side of Abbie.

"I don't know why you two are being so mean, I was really brave just now." I joke with a mock pout.

"Aww, do you want a carton of apple juice and a cookie?" Everett says, patting my back as we walk, leaving the main reception area of the children's hospital.

"Oh, fuck off."

We find ourselves in the middle of town with no other plan of what we're doing, but the entirety of the day at our fingertips.

"Ky, did you figure out what you're wearing on Saturday?"

"Oh, shit. No." I realise. I've been really stressed about this blood test, to the point where the idea that I need to find something nice to wear to court totally slipped my mind.

Abbie huffs, and I see her and Everett look at each other with equally unimpressed glances, as if to say 'this guy, am I right?' in a fed-up manner.

"C'mon. Off we go to the shopping centre." Abbie says, dragging me down the street by my hand.

We take our time shopping, and Abbie gets very meticulous about which colour tie best matches my 'season.' Apparently, I'm a summer, although Everett seems entirely convinced that I'm spring. Much argument about it ends in us just getting a tie in the same colour as my eyes, and also the dyed parts of my hair that Abbie discovered about a week ago when raking her hands through it. She also takes it as a win because the light blue just so happens to be a part of the 'summer' palette, according to *Pinterest*.

In order to try my best not to create an argument about the suit that I'm gonna wear, I take the first one that I see in my size, since I personally could not care less about whether it brings out the cool undertones of my skin colour. It happens to be a mid-grey one, and Abbie makes out with me in the dressing room after I try it on, so it must look at least some degree of good.

"You're gonna be okay." Ashley says to me, brushing a piece of dirt off the front of my suit. We sit together in the cold-toned waiting room of the youth court, having left Everett outside the building. Because I'm only sixteen, the only people allowed in the gallery are my parents, but the purple-haired boy insisted on coming for 'moral support', and his mum insisted on walking me in and giving me a pep talk for the exact same reason.

"What if I'm not?" I ask her helplessly. "What if they make me go to juvie or something?"

"Then you go." Ashley sighs. It's not the response that I wanted to hear. "Just be yourself. Be genuine, but show remorse. It's gonna be fine. No matter what happens, you're still gonna wake up tomorrow morning."

"Okay." I whisper, not entirely convinced. When we finished school, I was under the impression that I would never have to wear my school shoes ever again, but here they are, tapping anxiously against the floor as I sit.

Everything that happens after that is a blur.

Someone who I assume is important because she's wearing a blazer comes in and beckons me using a name that I don't usually answer to. I do today.

The courtroom itself is so much smaller than I was expecting it to be. It makes it a lot easier to feel like the walls are closing in on me. There's no jury or anything, because none of the things I'm being accused of are serious crimes that would warrant it.

The judge, who is a grey-haired, broad-shouldered man with a permanent scowl, spends the whole time addressing me by the first name that he thinks I use. I find out that it's because they prefer to address youth offenders by first name rather than last name to make them feel more at ease. It makes *me* feel a lot less at ease.

The charges against me get read off. I expect the first ones, which are 'vandalism' and 'underage drinking.' I also find out that drunk and disorderly charges only get taken to court if the offender fails to comply or is caught acting drunk and disorderly again soon after, which is a relief to me, because it means one less charge.

The thing that surprises me is that there's no mention of any criminal damage, which the officer at the police station seemed pretty dead-set on charging me with. I don't question it's absence.

The judge (whose name I must have missed whilst zoning out, oops) sighs as he looks down at me, and then over the papers in front of him.

"I don't know a single teenager that's never done something they regret whilst under the influence." He says after a while. "Do you regret it what you did?"

It takes me about two seconds to find my voice with all of the intimidation, and I hope that the judge doesn't mistake it for hesitation.

"Yes." I say, blinking a few times as the words in my brain catch up with my mouth. "Your honour."

"Do you?" He asks, sounding sceptical. Fuck.

"Yeah, I do, I promise. I only did it because-" I start talking frantically, and then have to cut myself off because I realise that, fuck, I should not be saying that. The way that my words trail off and my eyes widen in shock must convey that feeling.

The judge laughs under his breath. "No, carry on. Tell me why you've behaved this way." He insists.

"I- um," I stutter, feeling like a deer in headlights as I look around the room for anyone to tell me whether or not to speak. There's nobody to instruct me, and after I start telling him, the words just fall out of my mouth. "I was trying to impress this boy that I needed a favour from. 'Cause if he gave me the favour, then it would get this girl that I really liked to speak to me." I simplify the scenario. "Your Honour."

Again, the man laughs. "You did it to try and get a girlfriend?"

"Uh, yeah. I guess, Your Honour."

"And, forgive me for asking, did it work out?"

"Not as a result of the crimes." I tell him, and he nods as if he knew I would say that.

"I feel like that's a lesson you probably won't forget," He says, eyes once again hovering over the paper. "That this kind of thing never brings any good."

"Yes, Your Honour."

"Okay." The judge nods. "I'm considering that I could give you a discharge." He states. I have not the slightest clue what that means, and he seems to sense it. "Hypothetically, if I thought that the experience of being arrested and appearing in court is punishment enough, then I can let you go without any other consequences." He explains. "But,"

My heart drops at that. It's always a really good thing, and then, that little three letter word that puts my whole life on the table.

"I worry that if I do that, you might end up thinking that you can do this sort of thing again and get away with it."

"No, your honour, I won't."

"I also notice that you provided the authorities with the name of someone else involved in this incident. And I can imagine that you might have already paid the price for that." He says softly, eyes raking over me, and I imagine he's talking about the evidence of Dean and his friends taking their upset out on me the other day. It's not as prominent as it was this time last week, but the bruises are there still.

"You seem regretful about this." He says. "This is your first offence, and you did plead guilty." He sighs. There's a lot of silence that follows after that. A good three minutes of it. Just as I think I'm about to burst into tears from the pressure, the judge clears his throat.

"Okay. You're going to write a formal apology letter to the owner of the building that you vandalised. You're also going to attend weekly alcohol safety classes for the next month. I hope that I don't need to say it, but if anything like this happens again, it won't be taken as lightly."

"Yes, your honour." I say. "Thank you."

"Okay. Dismissed."

Oh. And that's it, I guess. I can- I can handle that. The judge leaves the room and then I'm taken back into another room where the same woman that guided me in gives me multiple sheets of paper and talks to me about where I have to be and when. I don't focus on it. I'll get an adult that I know to read over it with me properly when I'm not still high on adrenaline.

My parents eventually come into the room as well, and they seem relieved. I am too. We don't say much, but it doesn't matter to me. What they're thinking, I realise, doesn't matter to me.

When I finally do get to leave the courthouse, I'm swamped in a hug that's just a blur of purple before Everett is wrapping his arms around me.

"What did they say?" He asks frantically. His mum also looks very invested in the answer.

"Um, I have go to a class about alcohol safety. And I need to write a letter to the building owner that I spray painted apologising. I was hoping you could help with that."

"*That's it?*" Comes a third voice, and I look down to see Everett's phone in his hand, which is displaying that he's been on a call with Abbie for the last twenty minutes.

"Yeah." I reply. "I know, right?"

"I'm really happy that it's gone okay." Ashley says with a reassuring smile.

Across the car park, another sound rings out. It's the slamming of a door, and I look over just to investigate the noise, enough to see nobody other than Dean Holden, accompanied by a man and a woman who I can only assume are his parents. He cleans up quite nicely, wearing a dark, black suit with a green tie. His eyes latch on to me and they widen.

The sight of him had initially me panicking a little. I mean, after literally beating the shit out of me, it feels only natural. But, the look on my face isn't reciprocated in his.

"Kylen." He whispers, speeding up as he gets closer to us.

"Dean." I reply, surprised.

"Have you already been in?"

"Yep."

"Oh my god, what did you get?" He asks, anxiety thrumming through his voice. I almost have to laugh. I glance over to Everett and then back to Dean.

"Two-hundred of community service. And one of those prison visits where they scare the shit out of us. He said he was feeling generous." I lie easily, and he looks like he's seen a ghost.

"Two-hundred? For you?" He exclaims, going white as a sheet.

"He's a tough guy." I shrug. "I would say good luck but you're a piece of shit." I say to him, and his jaw drops into this angry expression. The sight of it makes me cackle as we walk back to the car park, leaving him to the consequences of his own actions.

I go back home with my parents to change into what I decide to wear to what's now been dubbed our 'end of year' party at the youth club. Alfie helps me pick out a t-shirt, and he decides that it's a red day today, so I wear one of my red *Hoodrich* shirts with dark grey jeans and a black, zip-up hoodie that swamps my shoulders in fabric.

I leave out the front door this time, giving myself twenty minutes to walk down to the Aconite Centre. It's clear that there's a party going on when I'm half way down the street, because the corny 2000's pop music is rhythmically thrumming out of the building.

There's double the people that would usually be in attendance. A lot of the younger kids that we usually wouldn't mix with, and people who I assume are their parents.

The first actual person that I know who I see is Thalia. Considering the events of this morning, I need to speak to her.

She's smiling and chatting away to some parents, so I hover nearby until the conversation ends. When it does, she takes a sip of the squash in her hand.

"Thalia." I say, and she spins around.

"Oh, Kylen. Hi. You look happy."

"Yeah, um, I just wanted to say thanks." I tell her. It comes out a lot more awkwardly than I intended.

"You're welcome, of course. But, can I ask what for?"

"A lot of things." I sigh. "But, mainly paying for the bail and stuff. I'll get the money back to you, but, I thought it was worth letting you know that I had court this morning, and it went well."

Thalia gasps, and then she grins broadly. "I didn't know it was today, you should've told me. I would've been there." She complains lightly. "But, that's amazing. I'm glad."

"They wouldn't have let you in anyway, you're not immediate family." I mumble. There's a lull in our conversation that leaves just enough time for Everett to enter the building, eyes wide with excitement about the whole atmosphere of the place. His eyes lock onto mine and he comes over without hesitation.

"This is so cool, is this what the extra hundred pounds a month is funding?"

Thalia laughs, putting her cup down on a nearby table. "Actually, I need to make an announcement soon, but I'll tell you two boys about it first because you're the most invested." She decides, and Everett nods proudly. "I went to that place you were talking about, and it was pretty perfect actually. We're gonna take a break for the summer and re-start the club over there in September."

A broad grin spreads across my face at her words. It's nothing short of what I expected her to say, but, fuck. The relief is indescribable.

Everett must feel a similar way, because he basically jumps at me in a similar way that Alfie does a lot. If he were any smaller I would have had the leverage to lift him off the ground. His words kind of jumble into one, but from what I can gather, he's very happy. For me, for him, for Thalia and Rowan, for everyone here.

About an hour into the celebration, after Thalia has announced to everyone what's going on, Everett and I end up sneaking off and out of the main hall, just because the noise becomes a little bit too much. We do it under the pretence of getting more chairs for the hoards of parents that have been filtering in and out.

However, when we make it to Hall B, and get into the chair room, we find ourselves lingering. It's essentially a little rectangular space with linoleum floor, and just stacks and stacks of chairs all around. Whenever I would put the chairs from the younger sessions away, I'd always leave a space in the centre of the room. Sometimes when I had a bit of time, I'd just sit in the middle of all the chairs and feel small, like nothing has any consequences.

That was more a thing from when I was a bit younger, but it's the exact place that I sit with Everett to escape all of the music and socialisation.

"Fuck. I can't believe we did it." The boy beside me breathes, sitting down on the floor at the same time that I do.

"I know. We've done a lot." I agree, turning my head to look at him. He smiles.

"Yeah. It's been an eventful few weeks." He says. "I made friends. Actual friends that I feel like I'm gonna keep."

"Well, I lost a few friends. A lot of friends."

"Yeah, but arguably they were bad for you anyway."

"Mhm." I hum. I just don't know what I'm gonna do for college now, 'cause I'm going to the same place as all of them and it'll be hard to avoid a gaggle like that.

Everett clears his throat slightly suddenly. "Um, we don't have to, like, do this any more by the way. The club's alive and well."

"What?"

"That's what we were getting along for, right? To get the club back. We've done it, man. We don't have to get along any more, not if you don't want to."

"Why would I not want to?"

"I don't know. You're a bit cool for me."

"Cool and uncool aren't real things, Rhett. Of course I still wanna be your friend, I wasn't faking it these last weeks."

"You never know, you might've been." He shrugs with a giggle.

"Well, I wasn't. I wouldn't even be able to in good conscience, not after everything you've done for me. Well, you and your mum."

"We just gave you a sofa to sleep on."

"It was more than that and you know it." I say softly. I don't think I'll ever articulate in words how much this last month has changed me. How much this purple-haired, pride-flag-converse-wearing, energetic boy has changed me.

Maybe it was the hair dye. Maybe it's been seeping through my skin and into my brain, making me into a more socially conscious person who actually cares about things. Maybe it's Abbie. Maybe it's been having a maternal figure who actually shows care towards me. Maybe I'm not forcing myself to be something that I'm not. I don't think I'll actually pinpoint the real reason that I've been feeling ten times happier with myself and who I am.

But it has something to do with him.

Even though I feel a lot safer at home recently, and even though I got a girlfriend who makes me more joyful than anything, none of it would've been possible without him. I gave him passing tips and the wisdom of my many years of transness, and he gave me a place to call home. A person to call home.

I don't think I've ever connected with anyone on the level that I have with him. It's a friendship that I don't ever want to risk, and the realisation brings a whole new host of emotions to the forefront of my mind.

"Where are you going to college?" I ask him suddenly.

"South Hill." He answers instantly. "The one up by that massive convention centre."

"Yeah. I know the one, I- um, I'm going to South Hill too." I tell him. I can't believe that I'd never asked him where he was going for school next year. It just didn't come up. I know it's something that he's been really worried about, so at least I know that he'll have me, and I'll have him.

"Oh, shit, that's great." He giggles. "I guess I'll see you there."

"I guess you will." I tell him. I guess that's kind of it. The rest of our future ahead of us, a new start this September. One that I know I need, and one that he probably needs to. It's been an eventful month, but I don't think I've ever been in a better place.

I realise this, and my eyes start to water. Dropping my head back against the chairs that I'm leaning against, I allow myself to sigh as my shoulders sag, and I tilt my gaze over towards the boy beside me with a vulnerable expression, pre-empting the admission that's about to leave my mind.

"Everett?"

"Mhm?"

"I think I might be a crier." I say.

He looks at me with what I can only describe as confusion for a few moments, and then he almost looks prideful. Shuffling to move a little closer to me, Everett wraps his arm around my shoulders and pulls me inwards so that my head rests on his shoulder as I breathe out.

"That's okay." He whispers. "All the best people are."

Epilogue: Everett

September

On the Tuesday before what the group chat has dubbed 'the grand re-opening' of the club, I go back to the Pestler's and pick out my favourite colour Hibiscus plants to give to Thalia so that we can put them outside the cafe-turned-youth-club.

I'm excited to see everyone, especially after such a long summer away.

In the middle of July, my mum and I went away to France, because she realised that it had been almost five years since we'd gone abroad. The two of us had a really good time away, strengthening our bond incredibly. It solidified in my mind that I don't need the rest of my shitty family as long as I have my mum.

We didn't get back home until late August, and at that point it made more sense to wait until the re-opening of the club to see everyone again.

Since I'm already a little familiar with the place from our visit to see Jane back in June, I know exactly where I'm going. Behind the big hall, down the concrete path, past her flower garden.

A wave of tranquillity washes over me when I lay eyes on the new building. It's clear that Thalia and Rowan, or, someone, has been here over the summer doing it up a little. There's a fresh white coat of paint on the outside of the building, and the mangled sign has been restored to just read 'Hibiscus Building.' The only thing missing from it is an array of the flower itself. Good thing that's kinda my field.

When I open the door to go inside, I find out that I'm the first one to arrive. Perfect.

"Everett, hi." Thalia grins from where she's sat on a new-looking chair towards the back of the room. She was previously staring down at a book, but she reinserts her bookmark and places it under the chair upon seeing me. "Good to see you."

"Yeah!" I exclaim, shutting the door and bringing the flowers to her. "I got these. For, like, decoration. They're hibiscus, obviously, but yellow ones, so they represent happiness and good luck and I thought that was quite fitting."

"Aww, that's so considerate. Thank you." She smiles. I had the flowers to her gently and she puts them down on one of the tables to plant later.

"Thalia!" Rowan's voice comes from down the hallway. "Should I put Spice Girls on the playlist or is that before their time?" He asks loudly, coming out of the hallway and into the main space, phone in hand. "Oh. Hi, Everett. Is Spice Girls before your time?"

"You're like, what? Five to ten years older than me?"

"I was born in the 90s, you were born in the 2000s, we are not the same."

"Calling yourself a 90s kid when you were born in '98 is pushing it." Thalia mumbles from where she's standing up to switch on a string of fairy lights. Rowan gasps in fake offence, leaning against the wall. "See, I was actually a 90s kid, like the peak of my childhood was in the 90s."

"I get it, you're both old. Spice Girls is kinda before my time, but everybody knows 'Wannabe.'"

"Firstly, ouch." Rowan says, placing a hand over his heart. "But, point noted." He mumbles, tapping around on his phone. My attention turns back to the door when it swings open once more.

"Are we early or is everyone else late?" Lilia asks with one hand on her hips as she shuts the door behind her.

"We're a couple minutes early." I tell her.

"This place was a pain in the ass to find, by the way. But my dad is really grateful for the car park."

"Language, but, yeah, the car park is great. I don't have to do laps and laps of the avenues around here to find somewhere to park any more." Thalia agrees.

"Oh, hey." I remember, turning to the two adults in the room. "What did you guys do with those back rooms?"

Thalia grins and looks over to Rowan. "Well, we made one of them a shared office."

"Shared office?" Lilia smirks.

"I know, I was just as surprised as you are." Rowan replies, putting on an expression of bafflement.

"And then the other room already had this sofa in it, so we made it into a quiet space. 'Cause something we lacked at the Aconite Centre was a place that people could go to like calm down or chill out. That's kinda what the over-eighteen's lounge became anyway, but this is like an intentional quiet space now. The over-eighteens can deal with sharing a space with fourteen-year-olds and older for a few years."

That actually sounds... really nice. I hope she's put some

plants in there, 'cause those are very calming to most people. LED lights, too, but that might be pushing it.

"Did you keep the TV?" I ask. "I think getting to watch his Netflix shows is important to Kylen."

Having said that, I actually haven't had word from him in a while. Not since I've been off to France, other than the occasional text here and there. Shortly after the club closed for summer, he decided to stop using social media, so the only way I could contact him was through WhatsApp, which I quickly found out that he logs into about once a week.

I did however see him making frequent appearances on Abbie's Instagram story, and when he did get back to me, and I to him, he seemed to be doing pretty well.

"What's important to me?" His voice enters the room, and I turn around to see him hovering in the doorway with a sceptical yet entertained look on his face.

He looks somehow a lot more grown up than he was last time I saw him, despite it only being a couple of months.

His hair has grown out to be a little more shaggy, and it's clear to me, as a veteran of hair dye, that he's let his wash out pretty significantly. The summer has really brought out his freckles, too. There's a smile gracing his features, and a certain light in his eyes that feels new to me.

He's wearing a pair of dark blue, baggy denim jeans that are littered in black scribbles, as well as a white t-shirt with the name of some festival on the front, and a list of artists on the back. His right hand, littered in rings of varying sizes, grasps Abbie's. She has her nails painted in a light coral colour, the same as the dress that she wears. Her hair is shorter than it was before, cut just below her shoulders and wavy. Much like Kylen's silver rings, her necklaces and bracelets are made

393

of the same metal. She waves at me in a little gesture upon entering.

"Oh. Hi." I smile at them, giving Abbie a wave back. "The TV here, for *Criminal Minds.*"

"Oh!" He grins. "You kept it, right?"

"We kept it." Thalia nods, and Kylen laughs, fully stepping into the building. The woman that runs the club beckons him over for a bit of small talk, and as Mars and Brynn enter together and start chatting up a storm with Lilia, I find myself with Abbie, loitering by one of the tables.

"So, give me the gossip that I've missed."

Abbie grins at my words with a slight roll of her eyes, but she fills me in nonetheless. "Well, Shea has been warming up to the idea of Kylen. We started hanging out, like, double dating, I guess? Me and Ky, and Shea and Leo. Went to a festival a couple weeks ago, the four of us."

"Ooh. A festival?"

"Just a little indie one, for the weekend. Had a good time, though." She explains. I'm really glad to hear that he's been hanging out with people - putting himself out there. I'd never admit it to him, but I was worried when I went abroad that he would struggle to socialise with others.

"Oh! Explains the t-shirt."

Abbie looks over to her boyfriend as if she has no idea what I mean, but when she actually locks eyes on where he's showing Thalia something on his phone, realisation washes over her features before translating into amusement.

"Oh, yeah. Could you believe he paid twenty quid for that? I tried to talk him out of it, to no avail."

"You got something against festival t-shirts?"

"Maybe I wouldn't if they'd made the logo a little nicer."

She mutters, only humorous intention behind her comments.

"Don't tell me she's talking bad about my shirt." Kylen whines jokingly, having ended his conversation with Thalia in favour of coming to speak to us.

"Gonna have to stay silent, then." I tell him. Kylen laughs, and then he swings his backpack off his back and into his hands before manhandling the zip.

"You got a haircut." He observes. I actually got it in France (which was a nightmare in terms of communication, by the way) after my hair grew out to the point of unyielding dysphoria and frequent misgendering (en français), fueled by all of their gendered words (oh god, help me).

It's actually not much shorter than it was back in May, and the fact that I've redyed it has made my hair journey appear minimal.

"Keen eye you got there." I tell him, slightly in sardonic jest.

"You know it." He says, voice distracted as he fumbles around in his bag. "Um, I got you a thing, Everett." He explains nervously. Eventually, he ends up pulling a small ring out of a fabric pouch in his bag.

It's a typically more masculine-looking ring, with a golden band that grows into a pink flower. But, it's not any flower. It's a hibiscus plant, and I imagine that he had to go looking specifically for this.

"Oh, fuck. Thank you." I tell him, taking it from his outstretched hand. "This is especially good, 'cause it's pink, and–"

"Yeah, they had them in loads of colours." He cuts me off to dissolve into an anecdote. "But I didn't want accidentally get you one that meant 'eternal sadness' or something, so I actually looked into the meanings and stuff."

I don't have to finish my sentence, because we both know what pink hibiscus represents. Friendship.

"I feel bad. I didn't get you anything." I tell him before accusing him of not warning me about the impromptu gift exchange.

"Trust me, you've given me enough. I promise." He replies smoothly, manually fluffing his hair up. Abbie puts her arm around his shoulders, but she does have to reach up a little to do so. "Oh, and, promise that you won't get jealous. I got your mum something too." He carries on.

"Oh?" I ask, humoured as I cross my arms over my chest and lean against the wall.

Kylen then produces a mini bouquet of tulips from his bag. They're orange and clearly days away from blooming.

"Now, I didn't do any meaning research for these, I just got the nice-looking ones. Don't deep it."

Instead of telling him about the intention behind the flowers, I gasp.

"Getting another woman flowers? When your girlfriend is right there? Tsk, I thought you knew better." I chastise him, and he returns me this unamused, monotone look. Abbie laughs and hits him lightly on the arm.

"Yeah, babe, pretty sure you're meant to wait until your girlfriend leaves the room to do that."

"You're not funny." He deadpans jokingly, still holding out the flowers towards me. I take them from him as my speech continues.

"Did you want me to pass a message along with these? Don't want her to get the wrong idea if I just say 'Kylen got you a bouquet', especially considering the time you called her fit to her face when you were wankered."

Abbie breaks into raucous laughter at that, almost doubling over as Kylen starts to go red with embarrassment. He death glares me for a moment, but I know there's no real upset behind it.

"Just tell her thanks for all the shit she did for me in June. I appreciated it a lot, and now that I can stand on my own two feet again, it feels appropriate. Same goes to you, obviously."

"Okay. Well, um, thank you." I tell him, managing to fit the flowers in my tote bag. The petals peak out of the top, which only serves to add to the aesthetic that I'm going for here. He then tells me very enthusiastic that he paid the club back for his bail last week, because he's recently found employment helping to coach kids at football on Sundays. He seems genuinely happy when he talks about it, and Abbie and I share a impressed smile.

The three of us chat for the next five or so minutes, only halting our discussion when Eli arrives.

Much like the others, in lieu of my trip to France, I haven't seen Eli in a while.

He tells us all about his summer, how he went camping with his family and then swimming in the sea.

"No new romantic adventures, then?" I ask when he finishes his stories. He shakes his head with a smile grazing his lips.

"Not right now." He answers. "I've, um- fuck, this sounds so stupid and corny. I've decided to take some time for myself. Been jumping from boyfriend to boyfriend for years. Honestly I think I just need to step back for a bit." Eli explains, sounding more and more embarrassed about how cheesy it sounds with each word he says.

"Yeah, I think I might start doing that, too." I joke. Eli huffs with his arms crossed. "No, but, seriously. Good for you."

"Thanks." He says, voice dripping with a sarcasm that's typical of him. It's just then that the song currently playing through the speaker fades out, replaced by the opening rhythm of '*Wannabe.*'

"Oh my god, I love the Spice Girls!" Abbie grins widely. Naturally, my eyes wander over to Rowan, who heard that, too. He gives me a look as if to say 'told you so' just as the vocals start. Abbie ends up dragging Eli off because he's the only one that will agree to dance with her.

"So, you, Abbie, Shea and Leo, huh?" I ask after the other two are out of range.

"Yeah, we've been hanging out a bit. Abbie calls it 'double dating' but I feel like that's weird. Like, 'We're double dating Shea and Leo.' Eurgh."

"Does make it sound a bit polyamorous."

"That's what I said."

"So, um, do Shea and Leo know that you're trans?"

Kylen raises and eyebrow at me. "Am I sleeping with Shea and Leo?" He asks, clearly unimpressed with my question. I mediate it by being my usual casually hilarious self.

"Well, I don't know. You are double dating them."

A smile tugs at the corner of Kylen's mouth, but he continues to give me a stern glare. "Okay, okay. No, I assume."

"So they're not entitled to know." He shrugs. "I've thought about it, 'cause coming out to Abbie made me ten times closer to her. But, I feel like that's not the kind of thing that'll bring me closer to those two."

"It's just that Shea is friends with Will, right? I thought he might have told her."

"If he did tell her, she hasn't given me any indication about it. I did, however, find out that they're not, like, homo-trans-phobic or anything. So I don't feel shit hanging out with them." He explains to me. It sounds great for him, this arrangement. Much better than the likes of Tobias and his lot.

"Cool."

"Yeah. You should come hang out some time. Can't promise you won't be third-wheeling, but I think you'd get along." He says. I appreciate the gesture, and I know I'll take him up on his offer, but I'm too distracted to reply.

Kylen, very casually, then pulls out a pastel yellow elf bar, hiding most of it behind his hand as he inhales. I raise my eyebrows and watch as he does a French inhale, probably to hide the smoke, and then slips it back in his pocket.

"Since when do you vape?"

"Since I quit smoking." He answers easily.

"Pretty sure that's still shit for you."

"Vaping is only bad for you if you just start it out of the blue. Technically, if you do it to quit smoking, it's good for you."

"That is not true."

"Give me a bit of credit here, I'm trying."

"I know, sorry." I laugh, just in time for him to take another hit of it. This time, it doesn't go unnoticed.

"Take it outside or put it away." Thalia calls from across the room. Kylen rolls his eyes as he shoves the elf bar in his pocket. "I signed an agreement as part of the lease saying nobody would be smoking or vaping in here, it includes you, too. There's a garden if you need to, but so help me god if you set off the smoke alarm."

Kylen holds his hands up in surrender with a smile as he

399

puts the vape away, and Thalia gives him a thumbs up from the other side of the room.

Something that I failed to notice during our conversation was the steady stream of people that I've never seen before. I guess that with such a long break, some of the younger group's members will have aged up into ours. That doesn't explain the older newcomers, though.

"Right. Circle." Thalia claps her hands in front of her. Rowan lowers the volume of the music into a gentle hum as we all take seats. I sit on Kylen's right and Abbie's left. "Well, everyone. Welcome back, or welcome for the first time!" She greets cheerily once everyone has sat down. "A few new faces today, because we've put a bit more into advertising over the summer, so, we'll start with a name and pronoun circle." She begins. It feels like a triumph to even be sitting here after everything. And now we've got who knows how much more of the club in the future. All these new people, too.

Everyone takes turns introducing themselves, and then Rowan takes control over the circle with a grin.

"Okay. Our icebreaker question for this session is gonna be 'what was the best thing you did this summer?' We'll go clockwise."

What was the best thing I did this summer?

I give myself some time to think about my answer.

I guess I've done a lot of things this summer. Holidaying in France, joining the club, helping to save the club, making a ton of new friends, finishing secondary school, passing in public for the first time, cutting my hair, dyeing my hair.

I'm still thinking about which of those things has been the best when the question loops round to Kylen, who is sat beside me. He's had a busy couple months, too.

"The best thing.." He mutters. "I guess, um," His eyes flicker towards me for a split second. "Finding myself. That was pretty cool." He shrugs, leaning back in his chair and drifting his gaze over to me, signifying that it's my turn to answer the question of the day.

And I know in that moment, just from the smile that naturally sits on his face recently, what the best thing I did this summer was.

Epilogue: Kylen

I'd never been worried about going to Sixth Form until I renounced my whole friend group in June.

I've always had them to protect me, to validate me, and as great as Leo and Shea are, they're not the same. Maybe 'great' is an overstatement, but they're good people. Abbie told me to treat this as a new start. I finished my alcohol safety classes (which were boring as hell and I will never drink in public again, just to avoid the chance of it happening once more).

Dean was there too, but I didn't look in his direction the whole time. I did, however, get the pleasure of hearing him complain about the week that he did in a young offenders prison. I don't know what happened to him other than that, and I don't care, quite franky - he's not in my life and I'm not in his.

Being entirely free of my debts to the criminal justice system, and also the weight of having to act a certain way to fit in with my group of friends, starting college is, as Everett put it over video call last week, my 'chance to re-invent myself.'

I think that's a bit dramatic, but I understand where he's coming from.

"Don't forget your keys." Dad calls from the kitchen. I turn to look over at him just in time to catch a flying keyring. "Good catch." He chuckles.

"Good throw." I reply, stuffing them in the pockets of my

A timetable from a couple of weeks ago tells me exactly which room I need to be in for form this morning. We're a couple minutes before the first bell when we arrive on the school campus, as actual Year Twelves, and so I walk Abbie to her form room.

There's people everywhere – all frantic to find where they have to be, but I'm rather lucky, because this form room happens to be the same one that I had my taster for economics in on the open day in Year Ten.

About half of the class is there when I arrive, mostly unfamiliar faces. The teacher is a kind-looking woman, skin aged and decorated with acne scars. Her smile is inviting as she encourages me to take a seat wherever I want.

I scan the room for options.

The most stressful thing in the room is Tobias Shaw, who I haven't spoken to in months upon months. He doesn't notice me at first, which is a good feeling, because if we made eye contact, I think I'd feel legally obligated to awkwardly stalk over to him.

I evaluate the rest of the people in the form, and it feels like a massive inside joke from the universe when Everett's purple hair catches my eyes.

Even from the distance, I can see that he's sketching some flowers in a notebook. His left leg is bouncing under the table, converse undone to show off his socks with little stars on them.

I glance back to Tobias, and his head is up off the desk and he's staring right at me. He gives me a cocky look, as if he knows that I'm about to sit down next to him and sheepishly apologise for everything.

I don't dignify him with more than three seconds of eye contact before I make a decision – one that I've been working towards all summer.

I don't look back at Tobias as I walk past him and pull out the empty seat next to Everett. He makes a slightly startled noise at another person being in his vicinity, turning his head towards me.

A smile creeps onto his face at the sight of me.

"Kylen Oscar Lysander. Fancy seeing you here." He teases, dropping his pencil to the table in favour of raising his eyebrows at me.

"Yeah. Good to, um, see someone I know and like here."

"Speaking of," Everett says, as if he's been waiting for this moment. "I actually, um- when you were out reconciling with Abbie that time, I drew you a thing. But then I never gave it to you because there was a lot going on." He says, flicking back a significant number of pages in his sketchbook as he speaks. He drew me a thing? Three months ago?

Eventually, he pauses on a certain page, sliding the book towards me to show me the image.

It's the same flower that he'd shown me at that field, with writing surrounding it, each sentence detailing another fact about the plant. He's shaded the edges of the petals in with blue in true minimalistic sketching fashion.

"Oh." I breathe out, kind of surprised by the fact that he would have made this with me in mind. I guess I did get him a present, too, so we're even. "It's cool. Thanks."

He tears the page out of the sketchbook and slides it to me across the table wordlessly. I stick it between two folders in my bag so that it won't get creased or anything during the school day.

By this point, the class has started to populate fully, and the teacher begins doing laps of the classrooms to hand out schedules, making small talk with the students over the natural hubbub of teenage conversation.

"So, um, are you gonna be at the club on Thursday? I've heard rumour that there'll be friendship bracelet making."

"Oh, yeah? Who told you that?"

"I just hear things around." He shrugs with a grin. "Brynn told me that Mars told them that Thalia asked Lilia for help picking out which colours we'd like off the internet."

"Sounds invigorating."

The teacher makes her way to our desk last of all after stepping all around the others, and at this point, she's only holding three timetables - us and presumably someone who hasn't shown up.

"Right." She says, shuffling the papers. "Easy job here. Assuming that neither of you two boys are Louise." The teacher laughs, placing the other two timetables on the desk. "You must be Everett and Kylen?" She says, sliding them between us and urging us to claim the ones with our names at the top. We each take hold of our respective timetables, and she continues to talk as we scan our eyes over them.

"Right, as I've told everyone else, too, these seats are gonna be the seating plan for this year at least. So, why don't you two introduce yourselves and get to know each other a bit?" She suggests, nodding and then retreating back to her desk. *Why don't we introduce ourselves?*

Everett's eyes drift over to mine with a smirk on his face, and the moment that we make eye contact, we both dissolve into laughter against the desk.

409

Also by James P Conway

Updates about all past and upcoming projects can be found both on *www.jamespconway.com* and TikTok *@jamespconway*

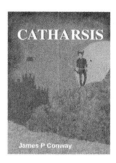

Catharsis
Catharsis is a teenager LGBTQ+ fantasy novel that centres around eighteen-year-old demon Theo Virzor as he navigates inheriting a Kingdom of Hell whilst coming to terms with his sexuality amidst the threat of war and political violence from the Heavens, as well as his father arranging a marriage for him. When he is confronted with the presence of a human in his kingdom, he is forced to take him in and attempt to solve the mystery of how this young man died and why he can't seem to develop a demon form as all other ex-mortals before him. Theo's developing love for this boy proves to be too much of a liability when it ends up costing him more than he bargained for.

Contains explicit language and mature themes of abuse, heavy violence, homophobia, sexual assault, sexual themes, and suicide.